Outstanding praise for Rakesh Satyal and *Blue Boy*

"Rakesh Satyal has managed to write a novel that is as
funny as it is heartbreaking. A brilliant debut!"
—Edmund White

"An involving coming-of-age novel."
—*New York Daily News*

"Compassionate, moving, funny, and wise . . . Rakesh Satyal
exuberantly captures the splendors and dramas of being
twelve, giving us an unforgettable hero who will linger
in the reader's heart."
—David Ebershoff, author of *The Danish Girl*

"*Blue Boy* is an important contribution to its genre."
—*Lambda Literary Review*

"*Blue Boy* proves that if you don't quite fit in, then
you might as well stand out with as much wit, color,
and audacity as you can muster."
—Josh Kilmer-Purcell, author of *I Am Not Myself These Days*

"Lovely . . . Satyal writes with a graceful ease, finding new
humor in common awkward pre-teen moments and giving
readers a delightful and lively young protagonist."
—*Publishers Weekly*

Please turn the page for more outstanding praise!

Blue Boy

RAKESH SATYAL

KENSINGTON BOOKS
http://www.kensingtonbooks.com

KENSINGTON BOOKS are published by

Kensington Publishing Corp.
119 West 40th Street
New York, NY 10018

All Kensington titles, imprints, and distributed lines are available at special quantity discounts for bulk purchases for sales promotion, premiums, fund-raising, educational, or institutional use.

Special book excerpts or customized printings can also be created to fit specific needs. For details, write or phone the office of the Kensington Sales Manager: Kensington Publishing Corp., 119 West 40th Street, New York, NY 10018. Attn. Sales Department. Phone: 1-800-221-2647.

Kensington and the K logo Reg. U.S. Pat. & TM Off.

eISBN-13: 978-0-7582-4576-2
eISBN-10: 0-7582-4576-9

ISBN-13: 978-1-4967-1209-7
ISBN-10: 1-4967-1209-9
First Kensington Trade Paperback Printing: May 2009

10 9 8 7 6 5 4

Printed in the United States of America

In memory of James McMackin

"As fire is shrouded in smoke, a mirror by dust and a child by the womb, so is the universe enveloped in desire."
—Lord Krishna, *The Bhagavad-Gita*

"Without realizing it, the individual composes his life according to the laws of beauty even in times of greatest distress."
—Milan Kundera, *The Unbearable Lightness of Being*

Prologue:
Make-Up-Believe

I'm surprised that my mother still doesn't know.

Surely she must notice her cosmetics diminishing every day. Surely she has noticed that the ends of her lipsticks are rounded, their pointy tips dulled by frequent application to my tiny but full mouth. Surely she has noticed that her eyeshadows have been rubbed to the core, a silver eye looking back at her from the metal bottom of each case. But here she is again, cooking obliviously in the kitchen, adding fire-colored turmeric to the boiling basmati rice and humming in her husky alto.

"I've got homework," I tell her as I pad across the linoleum floor and head for the foyer. I'm in Umbro shorts and a white T-shirt—the standard lazy-boy uniform in these parts—and my legs are tired from running barefoot in our backyard.

"Vatch your feet," she says, pointing a powdered finger at the faint grass streaks my soles are leaving on the floor. I scurry away as I have learned in ballet class, as if grace is an able antidote to dirt.

"Kiran, *beta*! Your dad . . ."

That's all it takes. I stop on the tiled floor of the foyer, open the front door, and step onto the front porch. The smooth cement feels nice under my feet, especially since it is a hot, humid Cincinnati day. I walk the redbrick contour of our house to the nearest spout and struggle to twist the water on. Once I have succeeded, I scrub each sole clean with my hand. As I stand back on the cement, my feet feel icy. In comparison, the rest of my body feels hot and sticky. I wipe my feet on the doormat and go back inside, back into the AC and the sound of my mother's metal ladle stirring lentils.

"Homework," I call out and start up the carpeted stairs. Our staircase splits in two, so that to the left one set of stairs leads to my bedroom and the guest room, and to the right another leads to the master bedroom.

My father is out playing tennis with a family friend. My mother is singing *bhajans* as she stirs *daal*. The master bathroom is all mine. Involuntarily, I sputter the theme from *Mission: Impossible*. But this mission is far from impossible; I have succeeded at it time and again, so that the only impossible mission seems to be not wanting to put on makeup.

The master bathroom is regal in size and stature: a vaulted skylight above, two sparkling brass faucets popping out from the white marble counter. There is whiteness everywhere, shining at me from the tub of the Jacuzzi, from the white tile floor, from the tall white walls. The only conflict of color comes from the bright orange towel that my father keeps near the faucets. He uses it after each time he washes—not to dry his hands but to dry the faucets. "You must alvays vipe them clean or the sink vill be in trouble," he said once, referring to the tarnish that he fears the way a hemophiliac must fear thorns.

Awash in this white, made all the brighter due to the skylight, I set to work. I open my mother's cosmetics drawer and pull out her squat silver makeup case. It makes a high *tink* as I set it on the counter. I roll the drawer shut: it rumbles and thuds. This sound reminds me of my mother's rolling pin pushing balls of dough into *roti*, and I venture a listen against the bathroom door to make sure she is still cooking. There's the ladle once more, tapping against the stainless steel pot.

There are so many lipstick colors to choose from that one would think my mother were a model. The names are almost as exciting as the hues: Fire Engine. Mulberry. Fanfare. I love Fire Engine the most; it looks like the kind of lipstick Cindy Crawford wears in *Sports Illustrated*. And it is a nice complement to my brown skin. But wait—I think I like Mulberry more. It's dark and mysterious, like me. I push it over my lips, over Fire Engine, the two colors mixing into a murky paste. "Oops," I say, the word echoing. I pull a streamer of toilet paper from the dispenser and wipe the goo off, my eyes settling on Fanfare. A fanfare indeed, it is almost orange on my lips. Too orange. More toilet paper.

Magenta.

My mom has a bright magenta *salwaar kameez* that she wears with this lipstick. The front of the *salwaar kameez* is covered in gold embroidery. Once, when my mom was out, I put on this lipstick and then put on that *salwaar kameez* and started crying. I don't know why. Since then, I have not put on Magenta. But something about today—my feet still cold, my torso still hot, the faint strains of my mom trying on some soprano downstairs— makes me want to try on Magenta again. I apply it intently, coloring in my lips as I would a picture, and my mouth transforms into a smudge of passion.

I once asked my mom what they call eyeliner in Hindi. *Kajol*. I don't even call it eyeliner anymore. "Eyeliner" is all well and good—it conjures up Maybelline commercials, girls with lashes as fat as ants—but "*kajol*" is a whole other can of worms. Cleopatra would not have worn eyeliner. Cleopatra would have worn *kajol*. Nefertiti would have worn *kajol*. Even King Tut would have worn it. I am the King of Excess. Here, in my regal bathroom, I put on makeup too thickly, and I like it that way. I like the thickness on my lashes, the lipstick balled in tissue.

I dip my pinky into the tube of mascara and coat it in black. And then I smear it around my eye, consider spreading three long black lines out of it.

But I don't. I don't because I have become entranced by my own eyes in the mirror, how powerful they look when encased in black.

The thud of the ladle once more, punctuated by ardent rolling.

The dusting of durum flour my mother sprinkles on the *roti* must be as delicate as the blush with which I am decorating my cheeks. It is very pink, baby pink. My cheekbones are high, and as I apply the blush, I aim for a sweeping effect, brushing up and over each bone. I flick the brush with melodramatic polish, but in the process I sweep a few choice flecks into my black-bordered eye.

I scream—silently, knowing that even the semblance of a whimper will reach my mother's worrywart ears. I can see it now: me letting out a grace note of pain and the loud rolling pin suddenly stopping, my mother conscious of the sound that flour particles are making as they hit the counter, the flapping of a ladybug's wings, the biorhythm of my father, from miles away, thumping in her ears, and then me—impaled by my pencil as I study! Electrocuted by my calculator! Abducted by local yokels! Even though my mother has come to the Midwest from the most exotic and dangerous of lands, Ohio can scare the hell out of her. India may be full of man-eating tigers, but Ohio is full of Ohioans. One whimper from me is enough to make her die of fright. Or make her come sprinting up the stairs, rolling pin still in hand like she's a Beverly Hillbilly, ready to attack whatever it is that attacks me. Sometimes I shudder thinking just what she would do if she stumbled in, expecting a kidnapping and instead finding me in her best Estée Lauder.

I turn on the faucet and flick a few drops of water in my eye to flush out the rogue rouge. This proves to be a big mistake. My dear *kajol* has followed the blush's lead and heads straight into my eye. My silent scream has turned into a silent caterwaul. I hop around in pain, trying again to use *grands jettés* to alleviate my problems. I go back to the faucet and try to flush the rouge out. This time it seems to work. The pain lessens, and I am left with a half-bloodshot eye, a mess of black and pink oozing from it.

At least my lips still look fabulous. Good ole Magenta.

"Kiran!" my mom calls. "Come help me vith the *roti*!"

I almost respond but realize that my mother expects my voice to come from the other end of the house, not from the master bathroom. She is used to me not coming when she calls the first time anyway, so I continue with the matter at hand. I pick up the bunched tissue again and wipe the mess out from under my eye. I set back to the makeup with more fervor than ever before, making myself a real work of art. I am entranced by the eyes in the mirror once again, entranced by their penetrating stare, how strong yet delicate they look. I choose the bluest eyeshadow that I can find and cover each of my lids in three, four coats. The girl in the mirror has grown so beautiful. She puckers her lips, winks, applies another layer of her Magenta lipstick.

I don't spend much time looking at her; it is the simple fact that she has reached the peak of her beauty that satisfies me, and so after a few turns, a few more balletic moves, free of technique but choreographed instead by my joy, I begin to clean up. My mother may be used to me not coming on the first call, but the second call means business. In a few minutes she will let out that second call and then even the thought of the homework she thinks I've been doing all this time won't compensate for my lack of punctuality. I kiss the Magenta and then sheathe her, place her lovingly in the silver case. Fire Engine and Mulberry are frumpy, as if berating me for having left them in the (pink) dust. "Sorry," I say, stabbing the brush of the *kajol* back in her cap and placing her in the drawer, as well.

I pick up the eyeshadow as if to put it back, but before parting with it I dip my pinky in, turning the tip of my finger blue. An idea, a lightbulb throbs on blue in my head. I smear more blue over my lids and then, doing what I wanted to do before, I begin to make my harlequin lashes, except now they are baby blue. And they are gorgeous.

"Stunning," I whisper to the mirror girl, doing my best Joan Rivers impression. The girl giggles, and when she bats her lashes, they look like enormous blue feathers.

There is something about the contrast of the blue against the Magenta, the way that the brown of my skin disappears under the blue marking, that I find irresistible, that moves my hand as if by magic across the contour of my face, down my thin nose, across my wide, smooth forehead. It makes me wonder why women don't make their faces blue instead of tan or brown or whatever their boring compacts offer them. There is something to be said for creating a natural-looking face, but there is also something to be said for standing out, entrancing, glowing. As my pinky makes its last curve under my chin, I am breathless. Each stroke has moved the energy in the bathroom from this side of the mirror to the other, so that the magenta and black siren over there, bruised blue, seems the only presence in here.

And then—a knock on the door.

"Kiran! Vhat are you doing in there?"

There is powder all over the counter. The tissues are still bunched up in the sink. There is the unmistakable smell of make-up in the air, perfumed and gritty. The sun from the vaulted ceiling falls around me in one focused circle—a spotlight—as if I'm Harrison Ford in *Raiders of the Lost Ark*.

"Kiran, open this door."

"I'm peeing, Mom!" I say, and twist the faucet slightly to mimic the sound of tinkling urine. But in my anxiety I twist a little too hard, and only if my penis were in fact a fjord would it be capable of making the watery racket that ensues.

"Kiran! *Mar kai ga.*" I cringe at this utterance, the precursor to a mother's ginger but firm slap across the face. *You're going to get it.*

I wipe the powder off the counter into my hand, then wash it into the sink. I grab the tissues and throw them into the garbage basket, then realize they are still visible and incriminating, so like a true felon I grab them back and throw them into the toilet. I flush, calling out, "Just a second! Just finished peeing!"

The tissues gone, I feel a wash of relief and I head to the door. I unlock it, but just before opening it I realize: the makeup. It's still on my face. Kiran entered this room and Mirror Girl is leaving it. I grasp to relock the door, but it is already opening, and there's my Beverly Hillbilly mom, rolling pin in her right hand, ladle in her left, and shock on her face.

"*Arre?*" she puffs, that indistinct Indian noise, a mixture of wonder and nonplussed horror.

I have no idea what to say. It is as if I am in my mother's place, watching myself as I have been doing these past few minutes, my blue glow somebody else, a girl in a mirror. But no, there is no mistaking; I am on this side of the doorway, sputtering to provide an explanation. Out of desperation, I look past my mother's shoulder to the small altar of deities she has arranged on the bookshelf near the bed—a bright portrait of Vishnu, gold encircling the tips of His many fingers like rings around a planet; an icon of Lakshmi, red and magenta on Her lush lotus flower; Shiva, eyelids drooping, cobra beaming from His shoulder like Blackbeard's parrot. And then there's Krishna, blue-skinned and smiling secretly into His silver flute, His peacock feather headdress more crown-like than Lakshmi's shining helmet. In this split second, I pray to Him to help me, and then I have a genius idea.

"Kiran, vhat is going on?" my mother says, gesticulating with one hand and sending a poof of flour into the air. With every second that I don't speak, the worry on her face grows. Oddly, she seems younger, not older, as if reduced to a child. After all, confusion is a childish feeling; I know in this moment that, more than anything else, I am confused. Confused enough to say:

"Surprise!"

". . . Vhat?" my mother says.

"Surprise, Mom! Guess who I am!"

It is the perfect thing to say at the moment. Who knows *who* the hell I am?

My mother shakes her head, not sure what to say.

"Mom, I'm Krishna!" I say. "I'm Krishnaji!" I style my hands next to my mouth, miming a flute and trying very hard to smile gracefully.

Relief would be an understatement. My mother drops her rolling pin and ladle on the pink carpet and hugs me tightly, paying no attention to the makeup she is getting all over herself in the process. A string of Hindi prayers issues from her mouth, along with a sigh of pure thankfulness that can only be described as the sound a fire hose makes while swishing out an inferno.

Over my mom's shoulder, Krishna watches, and I swear I see him wink one full lash at me. And then, as my mother begins coughing from my Estée, the blue lightbulb in my head pulses, pulses, a thought exploding it into shards:

"What if I *am* Krishna?"

I.

Kindling

Pageantry

et me tell you something about elementary school: it's full of
Lsly madness. I know most people picture little kids running
around and wreaking havoc, splashing primary-colored paints all
over the walls, liberating slimy class pets like frogs and lizards
and more or less making the river Styx look like Lake Placid.
But it's actually a madhouse in a very different way. It's not just
a madhouse but an *asylum*. In asylums, the harshest, most deranged madnesses are those that are less verbal and more emotional, those that happen internally instead of screamed at the
top of lungs or unleashed by overturning desks. Pushing and
shoving are nothing compared to sly note passing and stares
through slitted eyes. And I'm in the midst of both right now.

A week ago, two Big Events happened. One of the Events was
the announcement of the 1992 Martin Van Buren Elementary
School Fall Talent Show.

"So, class," said Mrs. Nevins, a pencil of a woman—long, thin
body with a perm-topped, eraser-pink face at the tip. "It's not
too early to start thinking about the fall talent show."

Cue the Hallelujah Chorus.

"I know many of you participated last year, and I encourage
all of you to participate again this year. You have a couple of
months to decide on your acts and rehearse them. Then you will
have to fill out this form"—she was handing slips of light blue

paper to each of us—"and describe what your act will be. It can be anything you want—you can dance or sing or play the piano or do a funny skit. Or you could even lip-synch to a song."

She must have been joking because almost everyone lip-synchs to a song. It takes no talent to do this. I'll never forget the disgusting sight that was Kevin Bartlett dressed in a leather jacket and a Beethoven-like wig while he "strummed" a cardboard guitar and "sang" Bon Jovi's "Livin' on a Prayer." Kevin didn't move from his spot. He didn't even really know any of the words besides the chorus, so, minus the music, he was just standing and staring. Everyone was basically listening to the radio for five minutes. But their cheers after he "finished" meant that they loved it. Then there was the "brilliance" that was Cindy Michaels hand-jiving to Madonna's "Papa Don't Preach." Obviously, Cindy's mother, Ms. Lansing, didn't ever stop to listen to the "I got knocked up but I'm going to keep the baby" lyrics, nor the fact that chances were Cindy, who smooched every boy in class, might someday live up to the words. There are countless examples of other lip-synching fiascos that I could mention, but suffice it to say that 99.9 percent of the school is virtually talentless, and there is only that one rare diamond in the rough that shines through the mold.

And I'm a 400-carat stone, baby.

Unfortunately, the announcement of this miraculous annual event coincided with the Other Big Event: Kiran Being Wronged by Two Cold-Hearted Snakes.

Sarah Turner and Melissa Jenkins—elementary school wenches of the worst degree. In the Polaroid of my mind, the three of us sit arranged on the playground swings: Sarah on the left swing, her golden-retriever hair crossed by a purple headband and buoyed at the temples by two elfin ears. Me on the center swing, large brown eyes and mop-top black hair, red sweatsuit sheathing my body, legs crossed as if I'm a hostess. Melissa on the right, a near-clone of Punky Brewster—her hair in brown, almost black, tresses styled on her head (and which used to be in pigtails and fastened with a smiling yellow-sun barrette before she hit sixth grade and thought it too juvenile); freckles sprinkled over her nose; ragtag outfit made of a purple jean jacket and a rainbow of odd accessories—red and green tie-dyed T-shirt, blue Capri pants, orange socks. Amidst the scenery of gray gravel beneath our feet, the swings beneath our bottoms, and the twisted metal shapes of the monkey bars, slides and merry-go-round behind us, we are a brilliant splash of color, and I seem to be the nexus, my dark face and hair forming the stem of my cherry tomato clothing.

But the reality is different.

A week ago, the first day of sixth grade, Sarah and Melissa come up to me just before recess.

"Key-ran," Sarah says, shaking her mane to get it out of her face. "Wanna go swinging today?"

I can't believe my luck; last school year, I used to wander out to the swings all by my lonesome, bucking the Mariah Carey craze and humming Whitney Houston's classic "How Will I Know?" in my puberty-endangered soprano.

"Me?" I say, raising a hand to my chest and widening my eyes as if the girls have just pronounced me Miss America.

"Of course, silly," Melissa says. She tugs at the lapels of her jean jacket and shakes her head from side to side to flaunt her brown 'do.

The two of them lead me out to the swings. As we pass by, our classmates' mouths round into shocked O's. We walk through the gravel, kicking up stones and lifting dust into the air. It is the end of August, still summer, and you can tell that all of the kids feel oddly out of place, stunned to know that the weather can persist even if the vacation cannot. All of us have spent a morning with our summery thirst for diversion pent up, and even though we are in sixth grade now—the highest grade in this school—we cling to recess as much as we ever have, so when Sarah, Melissa, and I reach the swings, we slide into the floppy black seats with a goal to swing until our legs are blue at the knee.

"Let's see who can swing highest," Melissa says, pushing off and demonstrating exemplary technique—a smooth extension of her two gams, pressed together, as she swings forward, then a swift separation as she falls back, bending her knees so that each leg forms a V parallel to the ground. Her lips are pursed in heavy concentration at first, but as she falls into her rhythm, her face becomes supremely serene. I begin to copy, a bouquet of butterflies rising in me—a feeling I mistake at first for fear but later identify, all too sadly, as pride.

I give it everything I have. A breeze forms around me as I swing, the summer day now feeling brisk and cool. I can feel the air blowing through the fabric of my sweatpants, can hear the squeak of the swings' hinges and the breaths of exertion as Sarah and Melissa move higher, can smell faint wisps of their Petit Naté perfume. I push harder, almost coming out of my seat, and I notice that as I swing forward, the girls swing back. This gives me an overwhelming sense of victory, a bragging right of sorts. But I don't dare brag. I want to be humble to my two friends, effervescently graceful, like Whitney.

I swing higher, so out of breath it is like I am in the stratosphere. And then a sound stops my reverie. I look down to see the swings on either side of me dangling, their chains clinking. Just below and in front of me are Sarah and Melissa, their arms folded, mother-like. As I slide past the ground, I jam my feet into the gravel and look up at my new friends.

"We're finished swinging," says Sarah. One shake of her doggy hair. "Let's go on the monkey bars."

I gulp. Monkey barring has never been my best sport. And yes, since I am a bumbling fool when it comes to tennis (which Indians play) and football or basketball (which Americans play), monkey barring is the closest thing to a sport for me.

Sarah and Melissa walk arm in arm to the bars and hoist themselves up. They look down at me, two mermaids sunbathing on a rock.

"Come on, Key-ran," Melissa says. "Are ya scared?"

I am scared, but I grab a bar in each hand and pull.

My body doesn't go any higher. In fact, it goes lower, as my legs swing under me and my sweatpant-covered knees dig into the gravel. I swing forward toughly, yank back, and fall onto my ass, each little jagged pebble like a mini-dagger against my cheeks.

I am lucky Sarah and Melissa don't abandon me on the spot. Others would have: A cluster of buzz-cut third grade boys wearing Transformers T-shirts and playing with the half-car, half-robot toys looks up and grunts. Four girls with big bangs and slap bracelets on their wrists stop their game of four-square, their inflated red rubber ball bouncing away in flimsy flops, then rolling to a stop on the blacktop. At least three games of tag, two between girls, one between a boy and a girl, halt. This is nothing that would be considered huge to a regular person, but when you're the cherry tomato foreign boy ass-down in the gravel, the toy-playing boys transform into the robot men in their hands, smashing and snarling metallically. The stares from the four-square players are so piercing that the girls might as well have chucked the rubber ball at your head, a soft but meaningful thud resounding. And the halted cat-and-mouse games of tag represent this truth: all quarrels, all grievances have stopped, because the attention has turned to you and your worthlessness.

But somehow, through some great stroke of luck, Sarah and Melissa don't look at you that way. They look at each other, trying not to show their laughter so as to avoid hurting your feelings, strengthening you with their compassion. Instead, they dismount, take a hand of yours, and hoist you up. They link their arms in yours and skip you off to The Clearing.

The Clearing is quite a sizeable chunk of land for a school playground. It's several acres big, with patches of seed-shedding dandelions and two rusty goalposts marking a makeshift soccer field in the middle. Along the perimeter of The Clearing runs a series of fitness exercises that the school installed a few years ago as proof that the administrators were capable of making the students healthier. However, once this promise earned more tax money, the fitness course did not receive a proper upkeep, so the wooden structures are pathetic now. There is a warped balance beam that looks like one of those soggy brown runt French fries in a McDonald's Happy Meal. There is a pair of pull-up bars, one short, one tall, that long ago fell over into the uncut grass around them. And there is a set of increasingly tall logs that one is supposed to ascend, the final rough-hewn cylinder the tallest but, of course, the last, so that the only options are to descend the way one came or to jump to one's fate—which many kids have done and, in so doing, have broken their stupid limbs.

It is to the French fry balancing beam that the girls lead me. As we head in that direction, they are more talkative than ever.

"So, Key-ran," Melissa says. "Who's better—Malibu Barbie or Evening Gown Barbie?"

"Evening Gown Barbie," I say. It just comes right out of me, but once I say it, I can't stop. "She is posh and elegant. But my preferred doll is actually Strawberry Shortcake."

Sarah giggles, but Melissa is silent, confused.

"You talk funny," Melissa says.

"It's because he studies extra language arts with Mrs. Goldberg after school," Sarah says. "He's a smarty-pants. You didn't know that, Melissa?"

"Oh, I just forgot. You don't usually talk that much, Key-ran. Otherwise I would know how *smart* you are." She smiles sweetly and winks at Sarah.

I "blush." That's in quotes because the only blush I can get is from the sun's reflection off my red sweatsuit.

"What else do you like about Evening Gown Barbie?" Sarah asks as we near the balance beam.

As unabashedly as before, I tick off my list of Evening Gown Barbie pros:

"Her dress shimmers; her eyeshadow has silver glitter in it, so it gleams extra-specially; her hair is straight, so you can style her golden locks in many different ways; and she comes with a hot pink comb, which you can use to do your own hair when you dress up in the mirror."

This last tidbit is the only thing that seems to impress Sarah and Melissa, who have let go of my arms and flank me—presenting me as a bride to the balance beam.

"Well, don't you like Ken?" Sarah asks, putting one hand on my shoulder, and now something feels a little stranger than usual, especially when I see a small bump form in my sweatpants, like a creature rousing itself to wake.

"Uh, I do like Ken . . ." I say.

"I like Ken, too," Melissa says. There is a devilish glow in her eyes that would never have crossed Punky's.

"But," Sarah says, her face now so close to mine that I can smell her breath—a mixture of candy and warm, almost stinky saliva—"you know Ken is missing something."

Gulp. "Yeah . . ."

"You're gonna show it to us, Key-ran," Melissa says, and I know for certain that Punky never acted like this because Henry Warnemont, her foster parent, would have disowned and re-orphaned her for this kind of slutty behavior. "John Griffin showed us his and we didn't even have to ask. But he bet us five dollars yours is different. He said yours looks like an elephant."

"It does not!" I say, knowing what they mean. I had my traumatic "naked father" moment years ago, at which point I realized there was a certain flesh-related discrepancy between my father's privates and mine. Apparently, the only thing I got as a first-generation Indian was fore*thought*.

I don't think Sarah and Melissa will accept the truth right now, though. Like tourists on a safari, when they want to see an elephant, they want to see an elephant.

As the girls press in, the bulge in my pants gets bigger, and it seems, in that moment, that what makes me plop myself down on the balance beam is that hipward rush of blood instead of trying to dodge Sarah and Melissa's sexual advances. Down I go on the beam, the girls clanking heads as if in a really bad Laurel and Hardy spoof. But soon a more dire collision has occurred.

In the few years since Mr. Hughes, the amply-stomached groundskeeper, stopped looking after the fitness course, it seems the balance beam has formed a porcupine-like covering of thick, sharp splinters. One such splinter punctures through my sweat-pants and an inch into my right cheek.

I want you to remember how I described Sarah and Melissa. Please imagine it. Please imagine the saccharine smiles on their faces. Imagine the countless sleepovers they must have, the boys they discuss with open-jawed squeals, the dress-ups and the dolls and the compacts of makeup, the slam books and kisses against their arms. Imagine the conspiratorial wickedness, the cunning plotting, the yearbook searches, seeking out that perfect victim. Imagine them settling on the foreign kid, the one who wears bright, primary-colored sweatsuits, the one who sings to himself, moves his hips and dances when he thinks no one is looking, who draws intricate pictures of pretty girls, sometimes, even, of these conniving girls. Imagine the "Look at Me, I'm Sandra Dee" scene from *Grease*, that bevy of tough chicks, smoking and boozing and stuffing their bras with quilted Kleenex, then think of what those girls were like in elementary school, what Rizzo did with her biting sarcasm and animalistic instincts before sexing them away in the back of secondhand convertibles.

Got that picture? Can you see those girls? Now imagine what those heartless hussies would do if they saw the foreign kid get a splinter up his ass.

Hear that banshee wail of laughter? Now imagine being the squashed cherry tomato on the beam, realizing you need to modify your moniker for your "best friends": they are not really best friends, but, rather, the best friends *you can get*. The best friends you can get are two girls who laugh at the grimace of pain you make; laugh at the way you wobble your way off the beam—*the splinter coming with you*; laugh as you hop, wincing, across The Clearing, which seems all the more enormous now; laugh at how you have to go up to Mrs. Moehlman, the teacher on duty, and tell her you have to go to the nurse's office for . . .

"For what, honey?"

"For . . . I got a . . . I got a tummyache."

"A *tummy*ache? Honey, then why are you grabbing your behind?"

It really doesn't help that Mrs. Moehlman is wearing sunglasses from which two mini-Kirans look back at you, grimacing and looking mortally constipated.

Over the next few days, the beautiful girls I once deemed my saviors lead the anti-Kiran rally. They're like political muckrakers to the Kiran Sharma campaign, whispering to people about the extraordinary flamboyances of my schoolgoing career. They bring up the time I went to Principal Taylor and asked her if I could go home to see if the cabbage I had planted in the back-yard had grown into a Cabbage Patch Kid yet. They unearth the fact that for three days in third grade, I showed up to class wearing a heavy fog of my mom's Elizabeth Arden Red Door perfume until Mrs. Walters had to pull me aside and tell me it was causing my next-desk neighbor Chris Johnson to break out in hives. Then they uncover the time I had a copy of Judy Blume's *Are You There God? It's Me, Margaret*, that hearty tribute to burgeoning female pubescence, in my desk. I even wanted to do a book report on it, but Mrs. Fisher told me it was too advanced a reading level for second grade, though I suspected this was not the real reason, a) because I was already attempting Sherlock Holmes stories by then, and b) because she asked to borrow the book and never gave it back.

The masses react to these rumors just as fervently as Sarah and Melissa, although the two girls seem to have assumed lordship over them.

We sit in class now, and the giggles happening behind me between the two of them—who, of course, sit side by side—are maddening. This morning, I walked into the classroom, hung up my neon orange coat on my usual hook in the back, and sat down to find my desk plastered with Barbie stickers. Instead of complaining to Mrs. Nevins, and therefore putting a spotlight on the situation, I tried my hardest to scratch them off, but the result was white-paper residue interspersed with a glinting doll eye or a heart-shaped mouth, a white vein of teeth running between its lips. Sarah and Melissa giggle and giggle, and I stare down at the mess and wonder why I can't be happy like Barbie, bearing her Twizzler's-makes-mouths-happy smile.

This is when Mrs. Nevins announces the talent show—the one light at the end of this crumbling-friendship tunnel.

The mere mention of the show has potential acts running through my mind, acts that are several stories and worlds above that talentless circle of lip-synching. I know that my act will involve dancing and singing. Singing for real. I will dance and sing so well that I will forget splinters and swings and gravel and the whispers, whispers, whispers.

"Maybe you can sing us some Whitney Houston at the talent show!" Sarah whispers from behind me as I scrape one more Barbie smile from the desktop.

I think of Whitney and how beautiful she is, how poised, how revered, and I worry that I will never be any of those things. And if Whitney is just a pop star, a mere mortal, then what does it take to be Krishna, the most beautiful of gods? I dig a thumbnail deep into the dirt-collecting stickiness, and I wonder what I can do to ensure that I'm never whispered about again. When even sweet-looking, tiny girls can deceive me, how will I know when I'm ready to reign?

How will I know, Whitney? How will I know?

My Band of One

Iknow only a few phrases in Hindi. So you tell me how the hell I'm supposed to understand Sanskrit.

Sanskrit. That's what the pundit speaks most of the time. My friend Cody, whose parents make him attend church every Sunday, once said to me, "Stop complainin', ya sissy. Our priest says a lot of our prayers in Latin, and ya don't see *me* complainin'. Just take a nap."

But Cody is wrong on two counts. First of all, Sanskrit is nothing like Latin. Latin was spoken by Romans; Sanskrit was spoken by really ancient Indians. After all, even though Ancient Rome was forever ago, do we not remember that before there was a Rome, there had already been an India for a thousand years or more? And at least English shares several words with Latin. Unless you're a yoga instructor, when was the last time you used a Sanskrit word? When was the last time you even used a Hindi word outside of an Indian restaurant?

Second of all, you can't take a nap in temple. It's physically impossible. In church, you have pews, and although there are all these families arranged like Easter Island monoliths on them, smelling of musky perfume and sweat and the woodiness of Bible pages, at least you have those seat backs to support you and your sleep-bobbing head. And when you do have to be awake, at least you get cues, like the first chord of each hymn heaved out of an organ, or a bellowing incantation from the priest.

Not so in temple. I sit on the floor in that manner called Indian-style, men on the left, women on the right, struggling to keep my composure while screaming inside about how God could put me in such an uncomfortable position—made all the more uncomfortable due to the soreness the splinter has left in my cheek. (Nurse Gifford Band-Aided it for me with an unspoken understanding between us that notifying my parents was out of the question.) I know that if I shut my eyes for one instant, I'll pitch backward into the lap of the man behind me. And the pundit continues chanting, his syllables sometimes purring like a tiger, sometimes slippery like *ghee*, the melted butter that coats the scented wood chips he throws into an open flame after each verse.

The one true redemption of temple is that it is full of colors, fragrances, and flames. In short, theater. Which Christians have, yes, with their rosaries and wine and candles and Nativities. But we Indians whip even Catholics in terms of mystery. Their incense is sweet and subtle. Ours is spicier, tangier, like a masala versus a marsala. Their icons are stately, polite, gilding sometimes their only brash embellishment. Our icons are veritable statues, marble, five and a half feet high, wreathed in flashy carnation garlands and smoke.

Okay, so maybe the priests at Cody's church are dressed a little better than our pundit, who wears a too-loose white *kurtha pajama*, the soles of his feet as cracked as dry earth. He has an obsidian comb-over. And he transitions from Hindi to Sanskrit to English so quickly that I often don't know which he is trying to speak. It's Hinglishskrit.

But what Punditji lacks in physical appearance he makes up for in gusto. He smiles cheerily, pulls his cracked feet closer toward him like a little child listening to his own story. And although I can't understand a word of the story, I can understand that the raconteur is jubilant.

Our temple is a pretty ramshackle affair. It is not even a temple, really; it is an old two-story house with gray wood paneling on the outside. It sits on a heavily trafficked road near downtown Cincinnati, squeezed among so many other old, wood-paneled houses that it is almost lost in the shuffle. The main floor of the house is not even used for the temple; it is where the pundit and his wife live, amid numerous framed pictures of Hindu gods, countless incense holders, and so many religious tomes that, aside from one orange couch bursting fluff at the seams and a TV so old it could have contained the first episode of *The Honeymooners* within its walls, the furniture is formed solely out of stacks of books—a Ramayana desk, a Mahabharata coffee table.

But I shouldn't badmouth my temple today. I am having fun. I am sitting just a few paces away from the pundit, who, just before this service, gifted to me a pair of hand cymbals. I eagerly await the end of his speech, when he cues Mrs. Jindal—a squat woman who always wears the same brown *salwaar kameez* and a pair of tinted eyeglasses—to play her harmonium, which she keeps at her side like a pet pooch. Cued, she moves the instrument in front of her and tickles the tiny ivories of her half-accordion, mini-organ of an instrument.

It is to match the verve of the pundit-Jindal duo that, once their musical interlude begins, I start to use those hand cymbals as deftly as I can. The more Mrs. Jindal pumps out breathy chords from the harmonium, the more I *jing jing jing*, the peals bouncing off the peeling paint of the walls and into the ears of the men and women. The blessed thing about temple-going, immigrant Indian adults is that they appreciate the nuances of the ceremony, and it doesn't take much for them to acknowledge the virtuosic nature of my playing. Between slides of my hands, I look up to see smiling affirmation from the men, most of whom are dressed in a white dress shirt buttoned over a V-neck undershirt. Or I look to the ladies' side and see women just as plump as Mrs. Jindal lightly tapping one palm against the other in their laps.

After the musical interlude, it's back to the pundit's droning, back to my confusion. I sit looking at the hand cymbals, enthralled by their gold. I hear a *psssst* from the women's side: it's my mother motioning for me to pay attention. She has perfected the skill of being able to hiss at me across the temple without disturbing anyone else. It is up there with talents like being able to touch her fingers to a hot pan without flinching; being able to tell, by how I say good night, whether or not I've brushed my teeth; and being able to remember random American celebrity names like Mary Stuart Masterson and Tony Goldwyn. In response to my multitalented mother's admonition, I roll my eyes and try to focus on the pundit again. I know that I should be listening to his words, heeding whatever advice I can glean from his garbled Hinglishskrit, but it is not my nature to listen that way. Listening for me concerns very little actual listening and more the attention my eyes can pay. Nothing the pundit says sticks with me more than the trellis made by the cracks on his feet.

A wave of guilt flows through me as I begin to space out again, and in that moment I feel even more Catholic than an altar boy.

Soon it is time for *aarti*, which marks the end of temple. Everyone stands up, eager to sing *"Om Jai Jagdish Hare"*—that is, to stretch their legs. It is time for us all to walk to the altar, take one of the small gold trays that bear candles, and move it in a circle a few times before dropping a dollar bill onto the tray in a dual offering—one to lotus-borne Lakshmi, the goddess of prosperity and wealth, the other to the bevy of plump women who cook the after-temple *prasad*, an assortment of marzipan treats, sweet rice, and oil-glistening *puri*.

Two lines form along the aisle—a plastic throw rug, one that digs into the carpet with myriad pointy teeth. Parents push their children to the front of the lines. I dawdle, trying to avoid being at the front of the line, mainly because I suddenly can't remember which way we are supposed to circle the tray. Clockwise? Counterclockwise? And wait—which way is clockwise anyway? And how many circles to make? Two? Three? Ten?

There is another reason I dawdle. I look up at the ceiling, from which hang, at different corners of the room, steel bells the size of heads. At three of the four bells, the tallest of the Indian men—correction: the anomalous Indian men who happen to be anything over 5'9"—are reaching up and clanging the clappers against the sides of the bell, complementing the pundit, who leads the singing at the front of the room from an old but effective silver microphone. I look up at the bell in my corner, the only one left alone. How I wish I could reach up there and ring the bell, how I wish I could translate my acuity at the hand cymbals to that louder instrument. And just when I am at the height of my wishing, I feel someone rush behind me and grab my legs. I squeal, terrified, but my squeal is unheard due to the peals filling the room. I nearly topple due to the force moving below me, but suddenly I am hoisted within inches of the bell, and when I look down I see my dad's head.

"Ring the bell, Kiran," he encourages, and I am so surprised that I do so right away, as if somewhere among the ringing there will be an explanation of where this burst of affection has come from. Literally bolstered by my father's mirth, I give the other three ringers a run for their gold-tray-borne money. I ring and clang with a virtuosity never before heard in these parts, any of the physical and emotional pain I was feeling beforehand disappearing. The men gathered in our corner look at the tiny totem pole my father and I have made and smile the same serene smiles they aimed toward me during my hand-cymbal performance. From the corner at the other end of the room, Mrs. Jindal looks up from her Elysium Harmonium and acknowledges my music with a grin.

At the end of *aarti*, everyone in the room kneels down and touches his or her forehead—a dot of red powder pushed onto it by the pundit's middle finger—to the orange, frayed, flat carpet in a silent kowtow finale. The ring of the bells, though technically over, is somehow louder during this. The negation of their sound seems to make that sound all the more important, as if for a brief moment I'm a deaf person longing desperately for any mundane noise that used to fall on my ears.

My father is kneeling right next to me. This has never happened before. Usually, he is back with the men while I sit with the children near the front. But now he is arched next to me in the same position as mine, and in this position he doesn't seem all that much bigger than I am. In fact, when I dare a look over, he seems to be scrunching himself as small as he can, his knees almost touching his chin. I come close to laughing—or, I think about what I would look like laughing at him, for I would never have the courage to laugh openly in front of my father. Still, a wave of sadness rushes through me. I am smart enough to realize that this laughter, this perception of his ridiculousness, must be exactly what my father feels every time he looks at me and gives me That Stare—the one that makes me think, immediately, I am wrong. There is something wrong with me.

Just thinking of That Stare makes anything magical that has happened to me in these past several minutes vanish, and the wound from the playground seems to throb again. I am a ball of disappointment, and as everyone stands up and releases the penitence they've mustered for this service, my father is once again tall.

"*Beta*, vhat's wrong," he "asks," although his tone gives no hint of questioning.

"Nothing," I say, stepping back and shrugging.

"*Beta*, vhat is the matter."

"Nothing," I repeat, scurrying away, reminded that there is a language even harder to master than Sanskrit.

*

After we kids eat our *prasad*, teetering as we try to sit cross-legged and balance sectioned foam plates of food on our knees, it is time for us to have our version of Sunday school. Our mothers make us put on our shoes, which everyone has to take off before entering the temple, then push us out of the basement door, which lets onto the parking lot. From there we Hansel-and-Gretel our way along flat, round stepping-stones to the front door of the house, then enter the main floor—taking off our shoes again—and seat ourselves on the spongy brown carpet of the pundit's main sitting room. We use his book-furniture to lean on. The class is taught by the pundit's wife, a woman with an enormous nose that is augmented by her bull-worthy nose ring. She is the only balding woman I have ever seen, a saucer-sized circle of hair missing at the back of her head.

The kids that make up the Sunday school are all celebrities from my childhood. Meaning: they are the core group of Indian friends I have in my life, even if they are more like enemies.

There is Neha Singh, at twelve years old already a great Indian beauty, with eyes as brown as chocolate cake and hair so black you want to fill a Bic pen with it. Too bad those eyes are hidden right now behind enormous, plastic-rimmed glasses. And just two months back, Neha had braces slapped on her perfect teeth, her parents making sure that any potential misalignment was stopped before it began. Still, everyone affords her complete submission, knowing that the moment the glasses and braces come off, the beauty will be back full throttle.

Seated with Neha are the rest of the powerful prepubescent Punjabis:

Shelley Aggarwal, whose real name is Shalini, but her TOEFL-impaired parents are trying hard to make up for their accents by giving her an American nickname. She is a very thin girl with an equally thin, long nose, which is almost hooked at the end. ("Almost hooked" meaning that there is no actual curving under; rather, the point is so fine that it casts a shadow under the tip that gives the illusion of hooking.) She likes to wear saris as much as possible, probably because they make her look older and wiser.

There's Shruti Gupta. Of all the girls, she's the biggest bitch, and if Sarah and Melissa ever wanted to make an Indian friend— not that they ever *would*—Shruti would fit right in with them. She speaks rarely, but when she does, it's usually to show how superior she is. She is in the fifth grade but takes seventh grade math, which she studies at home with her doctor parents. Her parents are so conservative—they conserve so much—that Shruti, though born and raised here, has the same Anglo-accented English they do. The Guptas really do construct the perfect paradox: they practically keep their daughter locked up in a (gold-plated) cage, and yet they both practice very progressive forms of medicine, her father being an internist, her mother a cosmetic surgeon. One day I'll have to solicit both of their services—a cure to prevent me from retching whenever I see Shruti and plastic surgery to get rid of the rock-hard frown she etches onto my face.

Completing Neha's sidekick trio is Neelam Govind. She is a morbidly obese girl with skin so dark she could be Aretha Franklin's twin sister. Her big mouth doesn't just take in food, though; the loudest voice in the world comes out of it frequently.

There are a dozen other Indian girls in the room, ranging from two to twelve, but whether they are older or younger than the quartet, they know they are inferior. There is always one bitch posse in a group, and they reign supreme and alone.

The only people who can match the bitch posse for intimidation are a quartet of boys. Of which, of course, I am not a member.

There is the dreamy Ashok Gupta. He is not related to Shruti; they share the same last name, but "Gupta" is the "Smith" of Indian last names. He is the most adept tennis player of all of the boys and, even at twelve, is a total hunk. The border of his hair, where the women at Supercuts use their clippers to even out the edge, meeting the even brown skin of the back of his neck—it is a perfect thing to me, and I always make it a point to sit behind him, or as close to him as the boys will let me, so that I can stare at his neck and the one tiny beauty mark located over the small bump of his first vertebra.

There is Ajay Govind, Neelam's brother. Though not morbidly obese like Neelam, he still has a paunch like a flesh lifesaver around his waist. He is a study in how nappy Indian hair can get. His hair has gotten long, which is to say that instead of hanging down to his shoulders as would happen to an American boy, it curves around his head into a black cotton candy.

There's Ashish Aggarwal, Shelley's younger-by-one-year brother. He is the closest thing to an Indian Albert Einstein. He has already won the state science fair twice—once in fourth grade and once in fifth grade—both times for finding the freezing point of saltwater. I have no idea what that means, but it earned him a $1,000 savings bond the first year and an invitation to a private grade school the second year (which his parents declined because they, like Shruti's parents, felt that they could teach him better).

And rounding out the quartet—literally—is the male version of Neelam, Arun Gupta. He belongs to Shruti's Guptas, not Ashok's, though he really looks unrelated to either child due to his weight. Every lesson, he is oblivious to the fact that the milk chocolate, chubby inlet of his butt crack is visible to all who sit behind him. This is because he is usually too busy eating his stolen bounty from the *prasad* line—a handful of *jalabi*, a type of neon orange funnel cake so sticky you can see fragments of your reflection when looking at it.

There are a dozen or so other boys, also ranging from two to twelve, but yet again, they all look to this posse.

I've always entertained the idea that both quartets have a hope—which, of course, they would rather die than express—that one day they will pair off as was meant to be, handsome Ashok taking the braces-freed Neha by the thin, gold-bangled wrist; Shelley affectionately burying the mirage hook of her nose into Ajay's thick fro; Ashish and Shruti rapt in ecstasy as they review quadratic equations; and Neelam and Arun devouring a platter of syrupy desserts before devouring each other.

And then there is Kiran.

Here we are, gathered in the only Hindu temple for over a hundred miles—literally, the closest temple is the one in Columbus, a two-hour drive away—leaning against furniture made of paper instead of wood, while our parents pick at the crumbs of their *prasad* downstairs and remember the intricate open-air temples of their youth.

Today, the pundit's wife is wearing an ill-fitting, peach-colored sari, the dough-like protrusion of her bare stomach like a big uncooked cinnamon roll.

"My children, vas today's temple to your likink?" she asks in her thick accent, and I am terrified to hear words of affirmation from the kids around me, as if they actually understood what the pundit was saying this morning.

"Are there any particular qvestions you hef?" she asks, and I feel a little better when no one asks any.

"Come on, children, some qvestions, pleece."

Silence.

Silence is maddening to me. I can't deal with hearing nothing, especially in a classroom setting—and especially in a classroom setting where disembodied Barbie smiles aren't distorting my view. And so, even though I feel a pang of *No, Kiran, you shouldn't talk*, I venture a question.

"Can you tell us about reincarnation?"

I ask this even though I already know what it is. *Reincarnation is when someone has several lives. When they die, they are reborn as another person. And if they did something bad in their past life, they come back as something terrible, like an ant or a retarded person or someone really, really fat. Like Neelam and Arun.* But I ask this particular question because I want her to talk about my new Krishna theory.

"*Beta*, that has nothink to do vith today's temple."

Dammit. I knew she was going to say that.

Thus commences today's derision:

I hear Shruti mutter to Neha, "Neha, what happens when you kill someone?"

Neha says, "I don't know. What?"

"You come back as Kiran in your next life."

Ashish, managing to stop playing games on his Texas Instruments calculator for one second, says to Ajay, "Yo, Ajay, what's the difference between Ganesh and Kiran?"

"I don't know, man. What?"

"Ganeshji has an elephant's head, and Kiran is retarded."

Truly witty repartee, let me tell you, yet biting wit is not necessary to break my heart. My ears burn, and I focus on my sock-clad feet for the next several minutes. I hold back my tears, so instead of the salty stuff dripping out of my eyes, I feel a well of snot build up in my throat. I swallow it in one lump. The only thing that pulls me out of my depression is hearing the word *Krishna.*

"So Krishnaji vas varrior, too, children. Even gods sometimes hef to deal vith var. But notice that Krishnaji does not just at-teck. He says that ve should seek inner peace, and then ve'll make others vant peace. So vhat Punditji is saying is not to be scared about Iraq. Sometimes var is necessary, but from it comes peace."

They are obviously talking about the Persian Gulf, even though the war ended a year ago now. But the neon lime explosions on TV, a stunning shower of green fireballs over nighttime Baghdad, cannot be forgotten. It was all well and good until I realized what I was looking at wasn't a new Nintendo game. Here in the pundit's living room, venturing to look away from my feet, I see that the other kids all have a look of true unrest on their faces, proof that they have the same scary thought I do: bombs were dropped in the world, and people died. Which, when you're a kid, means *Someone is going to drop a bomb on us.*

"Why is Krishnaji blue?" I blurt out. Not entirely relevant, but at least it's on the right subject. The other kids laugh, then stop, wondering, "Wait—why *is* he blue?"

"He vas born blue, *beta*," the pundit's wife says, dismissively. She opens her mouth to speak again, but I'm already shooting more words at her.

"But *why* was he born blue?" I ask.

"Vat do you mean, *beta*? He vas born blue."

"But what does that *mean*?"

"It means he vas born blue. He vas born god. He vas differ-ent."

"But didn't the other kids make fun of him for being blue?"

"Kids making fun of Krishnaji? *Beta*, enough. Nobody made fun of Krishnaji! He vas God!"

"But let's say that, uh, Ashok had blue skin," I say, motioning to Ashok gently and smiling in a friendly way. He sits back in surprise, a grin curling into his mouth. Sweat pricks at my skin; I am not dumb enough to interpret his smile as affirmative. "Even though everyone likes Ashok, he'd still be made fun of if his skin were blue!" The boys chuckle; they wonder what the word "like" means coming from me.

"*Beta*, Ashok is not a god," she says, then adds, "Even though we all love you, Ashok *Beta*." Ashok beams.

"He's also not a fag," Ashish whispers to the boys, putting away his calculator in sudden interest.

I press on now, having nothing to lose.

"I still don't understand why he is blue. And why blue? Why not red or green or orange?" I imagine a red Krishna, his skin the color of roses.

"Vell, *beta*, he just vas. Now, as I vas saying, var . . ."

The only thing that keeps me going as the class ends is the realization that I am even more like Krishna than I thought. He was blue and different but had no real explanation of why. I am so different from everyone, and yet there doesn't seem to be an explanation of my oddity, either. Krishna was different but had the fortune of being a god. He was destined for great things—war-defying, cosmic things.

Again, the thought comes into my head: what if I were simply a reincarnation of Krishna? If so, what those kids don't know—what those derisive posses can't get their thickly black-haired heads around—is that I am destined for great things, too. I am blue, too. You just can't see it yet.

*

After our Sunday School, we kids wend our way back on the stepping-stones and into the bustling hives of our respective parents. Since I am avoiding all contact with my fellow kids after my embarrassment, I observe their parents as I always do, trying to situate my own mom and dad somewhere in the group.

There are five core aunties in our circle of friends. They are as follows:

1) **Nisha Singh, brace-teethed Neha's mother**—a stunning beauty with a collection of saris so blinding in their brightness that her closet must look like a sunrise made of cloth.
2) **Ratika Aggarwal, hook-nosed Shelley's mother**—a business-savvy woman who runs a financial-planning office with her husband. She has bushy eyebrows and a manner of speak-

ing so dry that it seems as if she once knew perfect English but was so insouciant about life that her accent relapsed.

3) **Anita Gupta, brainy Shruti and chubby Arun's mother**—a woman as tiny as my mother but very thin, with a high-pitched voice that sounds like a bird's squawk.

4) **Kavita Gupta, dreamy Ashok's mother**—the most traditional of the Indian women. I have never seen her wide forehead not adorned with a large red bindi. She speaks only Hindi, except when she's feeling especially conservative and speaks Punjabi.

5) **Rashmi Govind, fat Neelam and fro-bearing Ashish's mother**—the really large, jolly one. There's one in every group.

My mother occupies a very interesting place in this bevy. She is, by far, the most Americanized of these mothers. Whereas most of the Indian mothers speak mainly in Hindi, inserting an English word here and there when they can't remember the Hindi word, my mother does the opposite. She speaks in English, and it is only the occasional slang phrase that she says in Hindi. She is always the one who introduces new American fads into the group. It was only a matter of time after my mom got her Gap card that each of these women had one, with the exception of Kavita Gupta.

My mother is a plump woman, but she falls in the middle of the spectrum, somewhere between Anita Gupta's rail of a frame and Rashmi Govind's centripetal force.

Here, then, is the counterpart quintet of husbands:

1) **Harsh Singh, husband of Nisha and father of Neha**—It's really pronounced "Hersh," but, in its English phonetic version, it is the most fitting name I can imagine for him. 5'5", with a fuzzy mustache and a crescent of hair on an otherwise bald head, he is one hundred and fifty pounds of sheer strictness, a heart surgeon who ironically seems to be living without a heart.

2) **Naveen Aggarwal, husband of Ratika and father of Shelley**—

a stuttering, stumbling man who wears oversize glasses that make his eyes look like eight balls. He needs them because he's spent his entire life looking at fine print on all the investment documents he and his dry-humored wife peruse.

3) **Amish Gupta, husband of Anita, father of Shruti and Arun**— He is a pleasant foil to the scratchy-voiced Anita in that he is mild-mannered and soft-spoken. This is probably why he is an internist.

4) **Sachin Gupta, husband of Kavita, father of Ashok**—I have never understood a word this man says. The greatest bafflement is that he's an ear, nose, and throat doctor. How on earth do his patients understand his instructions? Somewhere out there, dozens of men and women with sinus problems are backing up with mucus because of Sachin Gupta's mystery tongue.

5) **Sanjay Govind, husband of Rashmi, father of Neelam and Ashish**—It never fails: the really fat Indian wife will have a really thin husband. Another internist. Now if he could only prevent his wife from filling her innards with more curry.

At parties, my father fits in with this group so well because he is assertive. From the moment he walks into a room, he finishes his movements exactly. He reaches over and shakes everyone's hand, nodding his head slightly each time as if striking a perfect balance between the Indian *Namaste* and the American *How's it goin', pardner*; he sits down on the couch solidly, then lifts his leg to cross it over the other as soon as he is settled. When Harsh Gupta pours him a whiskey, my father takes it with another tough nod of his head, then sits back and listens to the conversation at hand, which is usually about George Bush—and soon, even Bill Clinton—and if he is helping or hurting Indians. The discussion is never about anything that does not relate to Indians. These men miss their homeland terribly. There is a longing, a sadness in their eyes that is difficult to miss.

Perhaps as a result of this homeland-missing wistfulness, my family's drive home from the temple is always quiet, except for the *bhajans* my father plays on the car stereo. While Lata Mangeshkar shivers up scales of notes, my mom, my dad, and I greet our newfound religious loyalty with silence. As I mentioned, silence is my least favorite state of being, and being in a closed space with my father gives me even more jitters than usual. But the one comforting thing is knowing that my mother will be the one to break the silence. She usually does this half an hour into our forty-five-minute return drive. A whole ride home without speaking would be abnormal, but a ride home capped with fifteen minutes of conversation redeems the trip from abnormality. Until my mother speaks, we have before us a drive full of truly Ohioan sights: the compact downtown of Cincinnati, defined by the majestic rind of Riverfront Stadium, where the Reds don their shiny crimson helmets again and again, and the tall mass of the Carew Tower, a lopsided rectangle of tan-colored brick that looks like a half-eaten bar of Kit Kat; past row upon row of maroon-colored apartment buildings, some of their windows smashed, some of their windows open with children peering out; then past nothing but highway, bordered by steakhouses and supermarkets and fast-food restaurants, a billboard here and there advertising the latest Ford pickup on sale at one of the numerous used-car dealerships in these suburbs; past nothing but fields dotted with Queen Anne's lace and weeds bearing pale purple bulbs; then curving off an exit into a compact collage of small office buildings—all earth-toned and evoking the fifties or seventies; past convenience stores, gas stations, and more fast-food restaurants. Finally, as our car rounds past a new Burger King, my mother breaks the silence.

"I talked to Sushil Gupta today." She pulls down the car's sun visor and looks at herself in the mirror. She wipes her eyes, as if to take off the age that has crept over them. She opens them wide, then relaxes, wrinkles seizing them again. "You know, Sushil is still living here, but her husband has his medical practice in Detroit, so she flies there every veekend to see him."

Since my mother has spoken, I can now speak freely. "What? Don't they have a daughter now?"

"Vell, she takes the daughter vith her."

"What kind of arrangement is that? Why doesn't Sushil Auntie just move to Detroit?"

"Vell, all her family is here."

"But her husband is *there!*"

"Vell, he's not going to be there for that long. He vants to take care of his patients instead of just leaving them. So he's getting everything in order before he goes."

"Oh, that makes sense, I guess. When does he plan on moving here?"

"In about two, three years."

Indian logic. It's an oxymoron.

"Wait—if she's here and he's there, how did they meet in the first place?" I ask.

"Her parents put out an ad. In *India Abroad.*"

"That's the most revolting thing I've ever heard." I love saying the word "revolting." Roald Dahl uses it all the time in his books, and it's such a catty, British word. Catty, British words are the best kind of words.

"*Beta*, it's not such a bad idea these days," my mom says. "You know, the more complicated things get over here, the more important it is to find someone vith good Indian morals." She says this with a jab of her finger in the air, and I think back to the master bathroom, when she flailed her flour-dusted arms about. *Arre?*

"Yeah, and I'm sure their lunches in Detroit are some real quality time," I say.

"It's not a bad idea," my father echoes from the wheel, taking a breather from his cat-and-mouse game of weaving through lanes on the highway and tailgating people. "Besides, ve might do that vhen finding your vife!" The silence on my mother's side of the car means she's considered it, too.

I imagine a headline in *India Abroad*, all right:

OHIOAN INDIAN CHILD JUMPS TO DEATH
FROM PARENTS' CAR

Two miles from our house, we stop at a gas station to fill up the car. Stopping at a gas station is an epic event for my father. He watches gas prices as avidly as he watches cricket scores—that is to say, insanely. At any given point in time, he knows every gas price in town to the hundredth of a cent. Ever since the bombs fell in Iraq, the prices have been quavering madly. Which has made my father even more intent in his efforts.

When he gets back into the car from filling the gas, the air is filled with the delicious scent of unleaded. I try hard not to breathe it in; when I was four, I remember him leaning in the front window, pump in hand, and saying, "*Beta*, make sure you never inhale this gas. It vill kill you." Now, several years and countless trips to gas stations later, I sit in the backseat with tension holding my torso hostage, as if invisible marionette strings are attached from my shoulders to the top of my head. As my father starts the car, I think, "This is ridiculous. Breathe, Kiran," and I take one deep breath. But it's useless; the tension returns, stronger than before, and not until we reach home five minutes later and I hop out of the backseat and onto the cement of our serpentine driveway do I breathe freely.

My parents get out of the car, my mother taking a little longer than my father. She has tiny legs and feet and is plump, so every one of her moves has a certain waddle to it. This is particularly endearing when she is shopping; she passes through malls with a waddle-sweep that is both graceful and determined.

There they are, Shashi and Ramesh Sharma: solidly side by side like a salt and pepper shaker set. My mother's hair, which has remained the same length for as long as I can remember, is pulled back in a ponytail and cinched in a white scrunchie to match her white *salwaar kameez*. Her hands are still clasped in front of her, like prayer residue. It resembles the way she stands when greeting guests at our house, just before she tells them to take their shoes off.

My father is wearing his trusty old jacket. It's tan, vinyl, almost Members Only but no cigar. His hair is cut in the most traditional way possible, the way gents have their hair on the Just

For Men boxes that my father stashes below the master bathroom sink. His eyes are very round and have maintained their
intensity after his forty years on Earth. They suddenly disappear
behind a Sony camera. Before I can even register comprehension
on my face, my father has taken a picture of me.

If I gathered every picture he has ever taken of me and stacked
the lot in one pile, I'd have a flipbook of my life. Just thumb
through the stack and see me coming out of the womb, then riding a bigwheel in my OshKosh B'Gosh overalls, then doing ballet in the kitchen. He doesn't need any particular reason to take
a picture. The other day, he took a picture of me spreading peanut
butter on a piece of bread.

My parents head into the house, but I linger outside for a moment. We live in front of Crestview's token park. Like The Clearing, it's an abnormally large piece of land, mainly because it's
really just a forest. But one day someone slapped some tennis
courts, an elaborate swing set, some Druid-like stone shelters, and
a steel gate bearing a PARK CLOSES AT DUSK sign onto the land and
called it a park. Here, at our house, where only the trees—
and not the playground accoutrements—are visible, the park
looks primitive, untouched. As I eye it now, it seems to have lost
none of its mystery after all the times I have stared into it. Sometimes, when I feel grumpy, I try to naysay my entire Ohioan experience and insist that there is no Ohioan beauty that I couldn't
find in New York or Paris or Russia or Madagascar or any of
the other places I gaze at in travel books. But my grumpiness is
futile. There is an implacable intrigue in the gray-brown quilt
that the trees make, and above all, the dark recesses far beyond.
In moments like this one, I realize that what I have been attempting to do with those travel books is re-create the marvels
that have always been in my own backyard.

What is more, in Central Park you might come across dere-
licts playing with Campbell's Soup cans and thinking they're
dogs; you may come across old crones feeding the birds tup-
pence a bag before shoving a fistful of seeds in their own mouths,
crazier birds than the pigeons they feed; you may come across

suicidal lovers or homeless men finding feasts in trash cans; but you most certainly would never find a middle-aged Indian recording crude-oil prices on graph paper as if his life depended on it.

I walk into our house through the side door. Only recently have I been able to detect a slight but ever-present odor of Indian cooking permeating its walls. It gets stronger as I walk into the kitchen. For a long time, I assumed that my house was immune to such an odor. I know that the other Indians in our social circle have always had house odors so stifling that an asthmatic wheeze has attacked me upon entering their foyers from time to time, but I thought my house had always been different, Americanized, as cleanly scented as a Glade air freshener. But a few weeks ago when Cody came over to play, he dropped the bomb on me. "Dude, yer house smells like curry."

"So, vhen do I get to meet *your* future vife?" my dad asks, entering the kitchen with a cat-sized camcorder held out in front of him. He looks at its small fold-out screen, then twists the screen around so that it faces me. I can see the bored yet uncomfortable look in my own eyes.

"Mom, when do we eat?" I ask nervously, trying to ignore the camcorder. We've just eaten *prasad* at temple, but it never satisfies our hunger. *Prasad* feels more like an obligation than a meal.

"*Beta*, it vill be another fifteen minutes. Vhy don't you go change your clothes and then study until it's ready? Here— drink this."

"Okay," I say, downing the murky concoction of vitamins that she gives me in a tall glass. I head for the foyer. My father follows. He has these stages when his affection for family life comes pouring forth. It's nearly impossible to guess when this emotional display will occur, but when it does, it's a full-on wave of giddiness. I can actually converse with him when he's like this, even if it's to berate him:

"Dad, please don't film me while I change!"

"I'll stop filming if you tell me your girlfriend's name." He laughs heartily, flipping the screen back to himself to look at my reaction, as if the screen is a better representation of my feelings than the flesh-and-blood Kiran before him.

"Her name is Stopfilming."

"And her last name?"

"Singh, Dad. Her name is Stopfilming Singh." I dash up the stairs, hearing my father call out, "Vell, at least she's Punjabi . . ."

The Intrigue of a Tit

The next day, I sit down at our kitchen table and try to make a list of facts that I know about Krishna. If I'm going to reclaim Him, if I'm going to assert that the reason I feel so different from everyone is because I am in fact godly, I'm going to have to mold my current life after my past life. I'm going to have to mimic His behavior. Somehow, I know that this has something to do with the talent show, this reorganization of my character. I just don't know exactly how yet.

I know that Krishna is blue-skinned, of course, so on my piece of looseleaf paper, I write

1. Blue skin

I also know that Krishna is one embodiment of Vishnu, the Preserver. You see, there are three main gods on the Hindu roster: Brahma the Creator, who was hatched out of an egg on a never-ending sea; Vishnu the Preserver, many-armed and often so light-skinned that He might just be a luxuriously jaundiced Indian; and Shiva the Destroyer, who sits cross-legged and bears that smiling cobra around His neck. Vishnu has the hardest job, I think. Brahma gets to create and let His creations go, like a doodling toddler. Shiva gets to raze everything, like Cody does while playing *Contra*, a Cold War–inspired Nintendo game that pits a pair of buff muscle men, machine gun bullets crossing their chests, against various enemies that appear on snow skis, on tanks, in underground pipes. But Vishnu has to take care of everything, like Mrs. Garrett took care of her girls on *The Facts of Life*, and this is probably why He has to split himself into so many incarnations. The fact that Krishna is such a recognizable and shining god is all the more impressive; as one of Vishnu's many incarnations, He has to fight against other members of an elite crew, but He emerges as the most extravagant, and therefore most memorable, god.

So I write

2. *Show-off*

I also know that Krishna plays the flute. It is said that when He played His flute in the sylvan Indian pastures, animals would travel from near and far to hear Him play, so beautiful were the melodies He blew out.

"Mom, why are cows so sacred to us?" I once asked, echoing the question that so many of my classmates had asked me before. I had never known how to answer; I just scoffed and acted like it was something everyone should know, or something that was offensive to ask an Indian person.

"*Beta*, vhen you look at the pictures of Krishnaji at the temple, vhat do you see around him?" my mother replied, her fingers smushed into a bowlful of dough.

"Um, a jungle. Lots of plants. Some mountains."

"And cows, *beta*. Cows. Vhen Krishnaji played his flute in the fields, the cows from the farms vould gather around him, and so they are considered holy animals."

I found this explanation somewhat baffling, as I don't recall horses and other stable animals being called holy just because they gathered around Jesus when He was in the manger. But comparing Hinduism and Christianity can be like comparing apples and oranges. Or like comparing a blue-skinned flutist and a long-tressed carpenter, to be more precise.

So Krishna played His flute . . .

3. *Flutist*

. . . and He attracted cows. I put my pen to my lips and think.

I somehow can't see how I might bring cows into my life, especially cows that come across as holy. There are plenty of cows in Ohio, of course, but those cows do not resemble the cows that appear in the paintings at our temple. The cows in the paintings are clean and serene-looking, lulled by Krishna's adept flute-playing. The cows in Ohio look sad, and they are usually covered with smears of mud from the filthy, fenced-off pens that line the road. Their sole purpose is not to be religious icons but to spurt out milk.

Then I remember: Krishna's favorite food is butter. It is His only weakness. In the *Bhagavad-Gita*, which my mother used to read to me, Krishna appears wise and seemingly invincible; He gives advice to the warrior Arjuna in the middle of a battlefield, bookended by the opposing armies of the brothers Duryodhana and Dhritarashtra. Krishna is the fount of wisdom, and He represents everything calm and honest and impenetrable about God and man. And yet butter was His culinary kryptonite, His dairy downfall. When He was a child, the baby-blue Krishna would raid His mother's pantry and steal a pot of butter, which He would set on the ground and wrap His plump little legs around before ingesting all of the creamy smoothness inside. Most portraits of Krishna as a baby show what looks like a little girl, her hair festooned with gold ribbons, a sun or a moon behind her head, and her little, red-palmed hands covered in yellow goo. On her face, there is the pleased look of a child who knows she's done wrong, and yet there is a certain momentum contained within the picture, as if, right when you turn your back on it, the little girl will resume her sloppy eating right away.

I can encapsulate cows and milk at the same time, and so I write

4. Butter eater.

The last thing—which in many ways was the first thing in my mind—is Krishna's status as the ultimate lover. In many pictures, He is pictured with Radha, His consort, a traditionally beautiful Indian girl who wears simple saris but still looks devastatingly beautiful. The two of them are usually sitting on a hillside, with

Radha propped up on one arm and Krishna right behind her, sculpting His frame to fit the curves of her body. It is almost as if Radha is daydreaming but has a luxurious specter whispering things into her ear. Although Krishna wears flashy clothing and has pierced ears and has red lips, there is also something masculine about Him, a tautness in the bulge of His blue biceps and blue chest, a sense of dominance about His posture. He is the lover extraordinaire, aware of the power of his body and his sensuality. I will need to find a girl with whom I can feel entirely comfortable yet whose actions I might be able to control somewhat.

For my last item, I write

5. *Girlfriend*

I look at my list again.

1. *Blue skin*
2. *Show-off*
3. *Flutist*
4. *Butter eater*
5. *Girlfriend*

I have already mastered the art of making myself blue thanks to Estée Lauder, and so I put a check mark next to number one.

I put a check next to number two: I know that I have already succeeded in many ways in making myself extravagant. Still, I will have to find new ways to keep myself continually renowned. This is where the talent show will factor in. I just know it.

Number three. I think for a while, wondering where I may get a flute. I am stumped. Maybe I will steal one from the school. I circle number three.

I come to number four and frown. Butter. Eating butter seems like something inextricable from the persona of Krishna; it is something I will have to do full-force. Being a god is not easy, I tell myself. Gods have to attend to the entire world; they have to listen to everyone's prayers and preserve. I circle number four, knowing that I will have to create a stash of butter to sate my Krishna appetite.

I am just about to consider number five—*Girlfriend*—when

my father comes into the kitchen with a copy of *India Abroad* and seats himself at the table.

"Vhat are you doing, *beta*," he says, smoothing the newspaper in front of him like an archaeologist planning a dig.

"Oh, nothing," I say, folding up my list quickly and clutching it at my side. "Math homework."

"Good," he says, already lost in the newspaper. He acknowledges my mother with a clearing of his throat when she appears, as if by magic, and takes her place at the stove.

*

I am a walking museum of oddities, and the thing I want the most is genuine sympathy from someone. Well, there's Cody, but that's not exactly a strong friendship, either.

Cody Ulrich is a beautiful boy except for one abnormality. He's a pseudo-hunchback. He comes from a line of unflagging chain smokers—his father Earl's license plate reads M EARL BORO— and that included the pregnant Mrs. Ulrich, who decided that lighting a ciggie up after her intrapartum feasts of pickles and strawberry jam would only be fair since she was perpetuating the species and all. The result was a baby born with one dead nerve running along his shoulders, one that pulls them forward.

We met last year in Mrs. Nolan's class. I wish that I could give you some grand reason why we became friends, but the truth is that we were seated next to each other. Cody often forgot to bring a pencil to school, and I was always the person who had to give him one. The second week of class, I lent him one that had red and white stripes on it, like a candy cane, and he looked at me like I had just turned into a unicorn. I expected that he would never talk to me again, but later that day, he wandered over to my empty lunch table, slammed the pencil on the table in front of me, and said, "I guess yer all I got." Thus a friendship was born.

As if to match the elderly slant of his body, Cody has developed the cynical drollness of a Vietnam vet, and I am usually the recipient of this disposition.

"Who gets a splinter in their ass?" he asks over lunch in the cafetorium—which should actually be called a gymnacafetorium, as it is the venue of not just lunch and pageants but games of dodgeball and pep rallies. I am eating my usual sack lunch of Capri-Sun fruit punch, three sticks of celery, a cup of applesauce, and two Ziplocked *roti*, the brown burn spots on them akin to the moles covering Lunchlady Packer's skin. Cody is eating school food: a rectangular piece of pizza so undercooked in the cafeteria kitchen's industrial-sized oven that I think I see ice crystals covering the cheese. "Seriously, Keern. Yer such a sissy."

" 'In *his* ass.' Not 'their.' And I am *not* a sissy," I insist. Cody is the only person to whom I can say anything with any trace of insistence since no matter what he says, he'll always be the token hunchback. "I'm not the one who did something wrong. They pushed me!"

"Well, what were ya thinkin' hangin' out with Sarah and Melissa anyway? They're two of the prettiest girls in school. Why would they be friends with *you*?"

Oftentimes, it seems that Cody is simply a human embodiment of my shame. He always seems to say what my self-esteem has already told me.

"I am floundering," I say, pensively.

"What?"

" 'Flounder.' 'To act clumsily.' It's one of my vocab words for the week. It's also the name of Ariel's sidekick in *The Little Mermaid*, remember?"

He laughs, his hunched shoulder fluttering like the wings of a captured moth. "And ya don't think yer a sissy? Anyway, if yer not too busy watching *The Little Mermaid* for the millionth time, ya wanna come over today after school? My parents are visitin' my grandparents in Louisville today."

I know what this means. It means Cody wants to spend the afternoon looking at *Playboy*.

*

How to explain the universal intrigue of a tit?

There is something ever-calming about the roundness of a tit, its buoyancy, the peacefulness of the concentric circle in its middle, darker. The posturing of a tit can vary so greatly, and yet the allure of it never dissipates. Tilted forward, the iris of the eye looking at the ground, the rest of the flesh fatly stretching. Or facing upward, splayed across a chest, lolling around like a plate of Jell-O, the eye quavering. Or staring straight ahead, serene in its sternness. A tit reminds me of Madonna. It can be brash and wild when it wants to be, and yet there are those "Live to Tell" moments when it's calm and collected.

And there are two of them. So all of this is doubled.

Cody keeps his stack of *Playboy* under the desk in his bedroom. "I figger my parents are goin' to check all of the easy hidin' places," he says. "Under the mattress, in the closet. So why not pick the easiest place of all? They'll never check there."

And it's a miracle they haven't yet. The bounty is easily visible under the desk, but it could be mistaken for a stack of comic books or baseball card catalogs. When we get to Cody's room—me batting away the spaghetti western–style cigarette smoke around us—Cody closes the door, his back extra-hunched with secrecy. He tiptoes over to the stack, his stance becoming more of a wobble, for obvious genital-augmenting reasons. He slides the entire stack out. Not a speck of dust covers the top of it, which makes me immediately aware of just how often Cody looks at smut.

There must be at least twenty issues in the stack, and the two of us devour their contents the way the greedy twits devour candy in *Charlie and the Chocolate Factory*. This action is a mélange of shiny paper and glistening body parts. It is, literally, a dazzling experience. The tits abound like fruits on a tree, connected by a series of sleek, branch-like appendages, the sap-like stretch of a chiseled belly. Cody and I sit on opposite ends of the bed, parallel to the headboard. He lies across the pillows from left to right, while I lie across the foot of the bed from right to left. We are not all that aware of each other; our minds are no longer in Cody's bedroom but, rather, in the flesh before us. The intrigue of a tit is like a miniature fog, a sensual mist, and when there is an innumerable quantity of tit before you, you are lost in the murkiness.

Most of the time, we see only the naked bodies on the page, forgetting all else. But then, as if our bodies have conditioned themselves to have the same sexual rhythm, we rock ourselves back and forth, pushing the weight onto our chests as we make room for our boners.

I have to say this: at this point, I don't really know how sex works. I know that it's the joining of the penis and the vagina (to speak scientifically, which, it seems, is the way to express one's sexual thoughts with the least amount of censure). But I'm not really sure how sex *works*. Sex, for me, is looking at tits and the finely pruned hedges below them. Looking at these magazines, in fact, is as aesthetic a process as anything else in my life. But, all too unfortunately, it is only visual. These women are not in front of me, caressing me or letting me smell their perfume. They are contained to the page, as static as a comic strip. And what is worse: they afford me a look at their bodies but do not engage in action.

I blame this on *Playboy*. If only it gave me some sort of sex visual. It doesn't show people Doing It. This rankles me, and I tell Cody this, snapping him out of his carnal reverie.

"Well, duh. *Playboy* doesn't show people doing it. *Penthouse* does that."

"Why don't you buy *Penthouse*, then?"

"Because my dad doesn't have a subscription to *Penthouse*. Only to *Playboy*. My mom likes the articles in *Playboy*, so she lets him buy it. They've got hund'erds of 'em."

I pick myself up from the bed, disgusted both by my lack of coital knowledge and by the mental picture of Mr. and Mrs. Ulrich "reading" *Playboy* together. Taking into account Mrs. Ulrich's sagging chest, perhaps I should revise my thoughts about tits. Not *all* of them are inviting.

*

Krishna is the god of love. He must know all the ins and outs of lovemaking. Of girlfriends. Of *sex*.

To that end, I have decided to buy a copy of *Penthouse*.

I need to know how people Do It, but I can't ask Cody. The last thing I want to do is give him another opportunity to show me how much I don't know.

I know that I should be working on my act for the talent show, but the tits have grabbed hold of me. I plumb my brain to figure out where I have seen copies of *Penthouse*. I can think of two places—mall bookstores and Dairy Market, the local chain of convenience stores. Dairy Market is out of the question; anytime I'm in there, my parents are with me, my dad buying gas or my mother picking up milk so that she can make homemade yogurt. I decide, then, to start with the mall bookstores, considering that my mother spends at least three nights a week "getting some exercise" at the mall, and I'll be able to move freely while she does so. I have used this method before when buying dolls, which I have purchased in the past by emptying out the contents of my piggy bank. I wanted to ask my mother for the money to buy them, but I knew that even she would not allow me to buy such girly toys. I have been able to hide my purchases from her by making sure she focuses on *her* shopping, *her* shopping bags, and when I get home, I hide my dolls in a toy suitcase beneath my bed. Now, with the magazine, it is time for me to up the ante. And I have my opportunity soon enough.

On Wednesday night, while my father is hard at work in his office, my mom grabs the keys and her purse and takes me to the mall in the minivan.

"*Beta*, vhat has been bothering you?" she asks. I am still healing from the Sarah and Melissa incident—literally—but I don't want to tell my mother what has happened. More embarrassing than making a fool out of yourself in front of your schoolmates is making a fool out of yourself in front of your parents.

"What do you mean?" I say. "Everything's fine."

"*Beta*, I know you better than anyvone. I know something is vrong."

As we drive the rest of the way to the mall, I think about my mother's comment. *I know you better than anyone.* It's probably true; she is my mother, after all. And yet I don't feel that this should be the case. There are so many people my age at school, and I spend so much of my time there, and yet I have not found anyone who truly knows me. And, really, my mother doesn't know me, either. She certainly has no clue that the reason why I hop out of the car with a bouncy step is because I am looking for a more edifying level of smut.

When we get to the mall, I spend a few weary minutes in my mother's company, sighing my boredom as loudly as possible while she sifts through piles of pastel-colored blouses and skirts that are pleated like lampshades. She moves to one of those circular steel clothes racks, the kind with a hollowed-out center that I sometimes like to hide in while my mother shops. My frame is so tiny that I can pretend they are miniature houses, a rainbow of fabric forming their walls.

My mother picks clothes depending on what they cost, not necessarily on what they look like. It's a trick in her mind. She tells herself that if something is on sale, she is saving money—even if she ends up buying ten of the same thing. Like many women, shoes are her favorite purchase, and she will come into the house after a day of shopping with literally ten pairs contained in two white plastic bags, the corners of the shoeboxes pressing against the sides like chicks trying to burst out of their eggs. Today, she has decided she needs a new blouse—or four—to go with the pink pumps she bought last week. As she swishes through the blouses, I envision an entire stack of them on her bed, my mother having snipped off all of their tags and folded them into neat squares that she can put in her closet.

Her arms now full, she looks up, contemplating where a dressing room might be. This is my opportunity to desert her.

"*Beta*, I am going to go try these—"

"Can I go to the bookstore?"

"Of course, *beta*." My mother never objects to my frequent book buying; she figures that I am educating myself and that I could always be wasting my money on rubbish like candy and Hot Wheels toy cars. "Vhat book are you buying?"

"Um, a magazine. A poetry magazine . . ."

"Poetry! My little Zafir," she says, referring to an Urdu poet whom she quotes when sewing extra fabric onto her sari petti-coats to accommodate her older, plumper flesh. "Here's ten dollars," she says, handing me a bill. "Just don't go to the Gap."

My mom has always had a crude vengeance against the Gap— mainly because she loves shopping there and sees it as her greatest weakness. Every time we pass the store in the mall, she gets a glassy look in her eyes. She practically presses her nose to the store's window and breathes a snowflake of condensation onto the glass, like she's a bicultural Little Match Girl. Usually she'll slip me a ten-dollar bill and tell me to go buy something, and by the time she finds me dawdling dangerously near a stack of hot pink Mattel boxes in a toy store, her purse is noticeably larger, a new scarf or mitten set or even a sweater stuffed into it in hasty concealment. Even though she starts wearing the said accou-trements—little threads hanging from where she's ripped off the Gap labels—she continues to use the Gap as her proverbial scapegoat: "Every night, the Doyles' daughter—*vroom* on her car, like she owns the neighborhood, vearing her Gap nonsense."

Tonight in the mall, her fear about the Gap seems like the only worry on her mind. She's totally in the dark as to why I'm leaving her. "Okay, I'll meet you back here in twenty minutes," I say, turning on my right heel and dashing out of the store, an ineffectual admonition of "Don't run!" coming out of my mom's mouth as I round the curve.

The mall is always full of people: the skater posse that hangs out in the food court and drinks Coke after Coke and some-times pours in a capful of their careless parents' Captain Morgan to spice it up; the myriad cliques of Rave-hairsprayed rich chicks giggling over boys who may or may not be at the mall; single mothers carrying their babies along with their canvas tote bags; janitors mopping a patch of floor where a milkshake or an enormous Cinnabon splattered against the checkered marble floor; thirtysomething schoolteachers who turn their gazes to the floor in the hopes of avoiding eye contact with their students. Although there are all these social groups, and as much as they might have in common with each other, as much as they talk about each other and watch each other, they do not coexist boisterously on weeknights. No, on weeknights, the mall is like one big therapist's couch, and the people who frequent it during these evenings are searching for a form of comfort they lack at home. Like tits, for example.

I espy the bookstore across a panorama of gurgling fountains, kiosks selling fanny packs, earrings, and poorly made watches, and a gaggle of black girls playing Skip-It, a game in which they scuttle a plastic ball attached to a plastic string around one foot like a pedestrian form of hula hoop. I walk through this bazaar and am just about to enter the bookstore when I realize something. The store has structured itself so as to deter any smut searchers. The magazines are all at its entrance, arranged like an arsenal on one wall-hugging rack. (No pun intended.) The grandiose presentation, and the proximity to the mall thoroughfare, transform the entrance of this meager chain bookstore into a proscenium and me into the spotlit star of a peep show.

I lean against a pillar, pretending that I'm waiting for someone. Every now and then, I sneak a glance at the rack, trying to locate the *Penthouse* stash. And then I spot it—in the farthest corner, level with the head of the cashier, who stands on a pedestal. One reach of my tiny hand to savor the delectable treats above, and I can see his hand grabbing mine and chopping it off. Or worse, he would tell my mother. He would drag me to the mall security office and tell the police I'm a pervert (or, as I once heard my father calls a sex offender he saw on the news, "a prevert"), then send an intercom announcement all over the mall, the calumny echoing off the marble floors and into every crevice of every dressing room, where my mother, blouse tangled up like a turban around her torso, hears the words, "PAGING MISSUS SHAW . . . SHAW-WHAT? . . . SHAW. WE HAVE YER PERVERT SON . . . WHASSYER NAME AGAIN, SON? KEE- WHAT? KEITH. KEITH SHAW."

Were Krishna's amorous pursuits so depraved? How can I expect to be a paragon of godly behavior when I'm curving around a pillar in the mall to find a bounty of bosoms? Part of me wants to run away from this mall and all the way to our temple, where I can kneel on the floor and curl myself back into a ball, begging God's forgiveness. But another part of me wants to live bravely and learn as much as I can about the body and its pleasures. What to do? I can either slither in there and risk total derision and desolation but have an idea of what happens in flagrante delicto, or I can wait out here, lead a perfectly happy existence and be a kid, putting off sexual complications until later.

I think the choice is clear: Tits tits tits.

I wait until the cashier has left his post and then make my way through mallgoers and a few potted plants to enter the store again. From what I can see, there are only a few people in the store. As I pick up a copy of *Disney Adventures* magazine and pretend to scan its cartoon contents, I realize that the people in here—the guy in the gray blazer reading Robert Fulghum at the front table display, the curly-haired woman cracking the spine of an unbought Danielle Steel paperback, the high schooler flipping through a Superman comic in his puffy Starter jacket—have an air of secrecy, privacy, stealth. Reading, it would seem, is a forbidden act in this town.

I sneak a glance back at the cashier's post and see it is still vacant. I put the *Disney Adventures* down and slide over to the cozy corner of the rack, where the pouting lips, blond hair, and barely clad bust of a minx ooze under the *Penthouse* title. I am just about to reach up and snatch one of the copies away when I hear two deep voices approaching. I turn away and grab up the *Disney Adventures* again.

Two gruff-looking guys walk up to the rack. One of them has a coffee-colored goatee around his mouth and a backward Reds cap on his head; the other has a shaved head and is wearing a plain blue mesh jersey with a long-sleeve white T-shirt under it. The goatee guy reaches up and takes the very copy of *Penthouse* that I wanted. He looks briefly at the front cover, a short but tough grunt escaping him, then tips the cover so that his friend can see it. The friend grunts his assent. A seasoned pro, the goatee guy flips straight to the center, and both men blow air through their nostrils in acknowledgment of the content.

The irony that these guys are looking at a glossy titfest while I'm nose-deep in Mickey Mouse is not lost on me.

From where I stand, I can see bent refractions of tit, but I am not afforded anything more than my usual viewings with Cody. The goateed guy flips through the pages, each time tipping the magazine friendward as if to say it's his handiwork.

"How 'bout that?" Goatee says, and I glimpse four tits rippled on a two-page spread.

"I'm there, I'm there," says the other, sliding one hand up and over his bald head.

They communicate this way for minutes on end, always with these tough-guy expressions, "How 'bout that?" and "I'm there, I'm there," and all I want to scream is "No, you're *not* there! You're *here*, and you're stealing my tits!" I am seething so much at the way they have inserted themselves between me and the magazine that I almost forget my original goal: I am not here to see tits. I am here to see sex. And they seem to be looking only at the former. Blasphemy.

Then I glimpse it: the wax-like chest of a man, two brunettes licking it with bubblegum tongues, and at the base of this shiny flesh, a well-cropped square of pubic hair and the solid cylinder of his penis. I see this for just a moment before the page flips again, and there is the man again, standing behind one of the women, gripping her waist from behind, the other woman licking his ear as if salivating sex into it.

"I'm there, I'm there."

A collage of bodies wafts into my mind. I cannot dismiss the strength of the man's body, the way his head is thrown back, mouth slack-jawed as he pushes himself against the woman in front of him. He seems to be pushing himself against her with every last bit of his strength, and as I look at the two men staring at the magazine, there is a longing in their eyes to do the same thing. Their breathing has become tough, and the grunts come now without their bidding. The more the rumble of their arousal couples with the sexy sheen of the magazine, the harder I become down below and in my mind. The sex—the sheer, mad, throbbing sex of this mundane mall bookstore—fills my head and becomes something huge. My head throbs, and I begin to see spots. *Oh, no.* I have to put out one hand to steady myself.

I drop my magazine.

I kneel down quickly and pick it back up. I look at the men as I rise. They have smirks on their faces, their posture uncomfortable due to their boners and the sight of a clumsy Indian child next to them. They chuckle and stuff the *Penthouse* back into the top of the rack, then swagger out of the store laughing. Their backs now turned to me, I look at them unabashedly, trying to capture every detail of their ragged appearance. My face is throbbing, and I turn back to the rack and look at the issue, which is still crinkling from the hasty way in which Goatee returned it to its smutty place on high. Without thinking twice, I swing up, almost rock climbing, grab the issue, and head for the cash register.

In the back of the store, the cashier is arguing with the lady who had the Danielle Steel book.

"M'am, I'm sorry, but you can't just come in here and read a book like it's your own. Look what you've done to it! You're going to have to buy it."

"I forgot my wallet at home," the lady says unconvincingly, trying to bypass the cashier and make her exit. But he persists, blocking her way and presenting to her the newly enjoyed, green-and-gold paperback.

The more they argue, the more frantic I become. I am standing at the cash register with a dirty magazine that looks like someone just had sex with it instead of a person. I look around me to make sure no one is looking, and the usual white noise of the weeknight mall greets me. I look back again at the quarreling couple and decide that I have no choice. I reach across the desk, grab one of the store's brown paper bags, and rush out, stuffing my bounty into it and never looking back.

Then the fates come into play.

In front of the pillar where I was lingering before, I run into Mrs. Nevins.

"Well, hi, Key-ran," she is in the middle of saying, when she notices the enormous block lettering on the magazine I am shoving into the bag. She blushes, her brows furrowing, and she stutters out something that is half pity, half censure: "Oh, no, Key-ran . . ."

"I—it's not what you think, Mrs.—" I start, and then the unthinkable, yet inevitable, occurs. Behind me, I hear the ardent waddle-step of my mother's Keds against the marble floor and the crunching of her many shopping bags as they slap against her leg.

"Kiran, *beta*," she says as I manage to slip the magazine fully in the bag and clutch it to my stomach. "Who is this?" she asks, concerned, afraid that Mrs. Nevins might be some wacko who's come up to kidnap me.

"I'm Sheila Nevins," she says, extending her hand and continuing to frown. "Mrs. Sharma, I'm sorry to be rude, but I hope you know what your son is holding."

"Rude? Vhy vould that be a rude thing to say? Kiran is a smart child. I am proud of him. He buys magazines like that all the time."

"Excuse me?" Mrs. Nevins says, her eyes widening in shock. She is still wearing what she wore at school today: a green sweatshirt with an appliqué red apple stitched onto its front, a white turtleneck, and very blue jeans. "Mrs. Sharma, apologies again, but you don't take issue with the sort of garbage that your son is carrying?"

"Garbage! Vell, excuse me, but aren't you a teacher? I can't believe you vould object to poetry!"

"Poetry! Is that what you call it? Unbelievable! Good night, Mrs. Sharma. And good night, Key-ran. God help you."

She storms away, giving one disgusted look back. I recognize in her posture the same unease that Mrs. Moehlman exuded as I confessed to her about the splinter.

My mother reacts with a cough-like huff. "Vhat a buffoon,"

she says. "Maybe ve should have you svitch classrooms. Let's go, *beta*."

She slides two bags into my arms and heads for the exit. I follow, nonplussed, a mixture of skin, horror, and guilt weighing me down.

*

My guilt is very strong, but my lust overrides my guilt.

When my mother and I get home, I push away the encounter with Mrs. Nevins as I have learned to push away all of my other school-related humiliations. I focus on the task at hand. As my mother gets a quick talk from my father in his study ("Vhy do you need ten blouses at once? For each of your incarnations?"), I run upstairs with my magazine, go into my room, shut the door, and lock it. It is exhilarating to have a new thrill, a new pursuit. Yes, the makeup and dolls have yielded fun and fulfilling experiences, but the carnal delight of what I hold in my hands, the limbs that are wedged into the binding of this slippery magazine, carry more promise than anything I have undertaken before—as the pressure in my groin attests.

I unwrap the magazine from the brown paper bag and flip to its center again. The dueling tits greet me once more, but it is the man's body that I can't shake out of my head. I turn the page to see it again. This man's penis does not seem consistent with the rest of his body. It seems like it belongs to someone or something else; it has a life of its own. I am at attention like this man; like his, my dick seems to be stretching into some other space. I grip my dick, and the heartbeat I can feel through it seems separate from my own, like the time I held a chinchilla in science class and felt the rough beat of her tiny heart against her rib cage. Until now, I have thought of my privates as a part of my body, as simply an extension of myself. But the throbbing I feel, coupled with the way in which this man swaggers around, despite being frozen in pictures—the way he holds his dick up to the full, sticky, Fire Engine lips of one of the women, the way he pushes it into her, the way he places one hand on his hip as he stands over the other woman, who lies sprawled on a table, and lets it work its magic—makes me realize that my desires are a bubble around me, my body encased in another throbbing heart. Somehow, in the pages of this dirty magazine, I have discovered that we do not hold our sexuality but that our sexuality holds us.

Over the next week, every time I pull out the magazine, which grows dog-eared, the ink on the cover smudged with my fingerprints—as if I am making as big of an impression on the magazine as it is making on me—the women's bodies change. I can see not just their sexiness but the *beauty* of them. There is less of a desire to fondle the tits, to call them "tits" at all. As Cody continues to unload numerous epithets for the pendulous balls of flesh, I simply look at them as a lovely appetizer before turning the page and marveling at the ripe, searching penis of the latest charlatan that has swaggered onto the scene, and the ways in which he satisfies his girls.

The man's body, the ripples of his chest, remind me of something. The weight of these women's breasts—*that's what they are,* breasts! *Not tits*—remind me of something: their limbs glow. I stash the magazine, dash from my room, make sure both of my parents are downstairs—the sounds of a midday tea being made, my mother taking out the cups, my father grunting as he places the kettle on the stove—and go into the master bedroom.

There it is again—the mini-temple, the shrine on top of the bookcase. In each painting, the gods glow; each limb is like a shaft of light, each body like a quietly fiery star. There is Krishna again, made up and smiling and ostentatiously blue, a star of the stage that is this bookcase top. For a solid ten minutes, until my mother calls me down to have some tea, I braid my physical desires with this vision of godlike beauty. My fascination is becoming a real quest: a quest to find and live up to my lost Krishna self. This way—and this way alone—I can achieve the sort of nirvana that I've heard the pundit speak of. The religious paintings are ordaining me to be this glowing man of lust. Perhaps, I think, it is not a question of getting affection from other people, being desired, but understanding the pull of your own desires that should fuel us. I have spent too much time trying to earn the respect of others when I should be focusing on my own potential.

A path of smut has led me to a higher level of edification than I could have ever imagined. From this moment onward, I will not discount lust as an extraordinary force. I will let it grip my body and lead me the rest of the way.

*

This is all an elegant way of saying that I start jerking off like it's my job.

Radhas to My Left,
Ragamuffins to My Right

For several years, I have been in love with Strawberry Short-cake.

Whoever created that ragamuffin princess knew exactly what they were doing. Most toys rely simply on beauty and pastels to make them desirable. Barbie—glamorous, pink. My Little Pony—foal-cute, pink. Jem—rockstarry, glittery pink. But Strawberry Shortcake has the extra advantage of sweets. Not just candy, but sweets. Not just Skittles and Starbursts and Milky Ways but luscious cakes and pastries and fruits. Incidentally, "sweets" is the word that my parents use to describe desserts. It's one of the few Anglo-Indian verbal tics of theirs that says exactly what I want it to say.

But back to SS, as I like to call her. I like everything about her. Her wacky sense of style, those green-and-white-striped leggings that fit snugly around her toes and all the way up around her tiny waist. The red-and-white apron-cum-dress she wears, which conveys culinary adeptness and chic leisure at the same time. The enormous puffy pink hat with a strawberry decal on the front of it, so big that SS could easily pull it down over herself and disappear into a world sunlit pink. This is what I do many weekend afternoons in my bed: pull my pink blanket all around myself and look at the light pastel tent it makes around me, all the while munching on a little treat I've brought to enjoy—a handful of Cocoa Puffs, a few Fig Newtons, or a piece of leftover bakery cake from the Indian wedding, graduation, or engagement parties we attend frequently. I lie in my bed with SS on one side and my sweet treat on the other, and I think about marriage.

This morning, my mother sat me down and gave me her monthly marriage talk. She crossed her hands on the table as if she were both a presiding judge and a plaintiff bringing a case against me.

"*Beta*, this is tough time for you. Not only do you have to look out for the American girls anymore. Now you have to vatch the Indian ones. It used to be just the American girls who vanted a little hanky-panky, but now the Indian girls vant to hank and pank, too. And then there are these Indian girls who marry Indian men just to get their visas. And then vonce they're over here, they start going to the Gap and run off vith all of your money."

Now she was blaming the Gap for the downfall of the good Indian wife.

"Still, I vill find you a good girl," she continued. I opened my mouth to complain. "Quiet, *beta*. Indians don't just meet each other and have everything go all hanky-panky and start dancing to loud music. Girls are trouble. Your dad and I vill keep you out of trouble."

"But Mom," I ask, "weren't you once a girl?"

"Homevork time."

I lie in bed now with SS at my side and wonder why I can't find a girl like her to be my girlfriend. I think about my mom's rules:

"First, she must be good to me. Indian girls must always respect Indian mothers. Second, she must be able to cook. Not these instant foods—*idli* powder and *dosai* mix and that nonsense. I mean *real* food vith *real* ingredients. Third, she must be pretty. Those are the only requirements. And of course, she should be vell-educated and Punjabi and have parents ve know and like."

Vell, SS has got most of these things down. She's well-dressed and she's a good cook, and she must be well-educated because her strawberries are always fresh: Tanya Gibbons, a girl in my class whose parents are corn farmers, boasts that being a good farmer is a lot harder than people think because it takes a lot of planning and hard work.

SS always fends off the Purple Pieman, so she clearly has street smarts, too. And even though she doesn't have any family, per se, she does have all of her fruit friends, which I also own—Blueberry Muffin, Apricot, Apple Dumplin', Huckleberry—and they are all nice and could get along with anybody, even my parents. And she could clearly be a good mother because she always takes care of her cat, Custard, who is also pink and fruit-scented. Being a good mother isn't even directly in my mom's requests, so it's like extra credit for SS.

But there's the problem of her not being Indian. Even though I know SS is perfect in almost every other way, I know this is a big flaw of hers.

Of course I know that SS is only a doll. And I know that I shouldn't even be playing with dolls in the first place—not just because I'm a boy but because I'm probably getting too old to play with dolls anyway. But this is my fantasy, and I wrap myself up in it like I do my pink blanket, leaving reality and maturity behind. My fantasy may have big flaws, but lots of relationships have big flaws. Mr. and Mrs. Doyle, our neighbors, always yell at each other, and I once heard Mr. Doyle say to Mrs. Doyle, "A million cars park in your garage!" At the time, I didn't know what he meant, thinking, "A million cars? They only have one old Impala."

*

Take my parents, for instance. They're both Indian, yet they have their share of problems. When I was really little, the fights would occur right in front of me. I will never forget the first time I walked in on my parents arguing in the living room. This was in our old place, the one we lived in until I was seven, a tiny split-level house. The inside of the house was stiflingly tight, ten stairs shared among three floors. It was when I was four years old, in a room with dirty white carpet and one of those walls that's one big mirror, that I saw my father throw a cushion at my mom, who was sobbing on the sofa. Who knows what they were arguing about—it could have been my mom's shopping sprees—but the point wasn't what they were arguing about so much as the fact that they were arguing. The rounded hunch of my father's pose, the mixture of sternness and fire in his eyes, his irises surrounded by white all around, like a cartoon villain. The small figure of my mother, in her pink floral nightgown, and the way the tears on her face transformed her pale brown face into a beet. The way she clutched the cushion he had thrown at her, which didn't hit her and bounce off but was caught in her pleading hands, her fingers pushing grooves into its red velvet. I stumbled in, descending from my room to the TV room downstairs; the cushion was thrown; I took the mental snapshot; and then averting my eyes from my father, who turned to look at me, I caught the reflection of all three of us in the mirror wall—my father's hefty stance, made all the larger since he was closer to the mirror, my mother half-obscured by the potted plant that stood in the corner, and me in between them, dressed in shorts and a T-shirt, nonplussed and frightened and so small that I looked like a clay doll.

Four years later, we moved into a newly built house, the one where we live now, a resplendent, grand affair. My tight-fisted Certified Public Accountant father's penny-pinching had paid off, and instead of ten steps, our house had stairways everywhere: that split staircase in the foyer that leads "up-a-stair," as my father calls it; a triple-decker, carpeted staircase leading into our finished basement, which holds a Ping-Pong table—a staple of any Indian household even if its one kid doesn't play Ping-Pong—and another large-screen TV. Gone is the mirror wall; now there are gold-framed mirrors everywhere, along with a motley crew of furniture. Indians are never able to throw anything away, and so my mother and father have insisted on using as much of their old furniture as possible. Therefore, though our sitting room has cathedral ceilings and tan plush carpeting, in it sits, almost boastingly, the blue couch from our old house, the back of it faded and sunburned from where it used to sit against the window; two rocking chairs that are straight out of an old Mother Goose picture book; and one "new" peach couch that still has the plastic wrapped on it a year after purchase. The walls are decorated with various photos that my dad has taken, with an occasional peacock feather tacked to the wall for no ostensible purpose. It is in this living room that I sit these days, doodling a picture of SS with Crayola markers, and hear the echoes of shouts from the master bedroom. It is worse this way, I think—with them out of sight. Who knows what is going on up there? What strange things are thrown . . . ? I imagine my mother sitting on the bed, weeping, and my father grabbing things from her dresser—a bottle of lotion, a powder puff, a hand mirror—and chucking them into my mother's strong-reflexed hands, which spring up and catch them as they once caught that blood-red pillow.

Only after the fights have subsided for the morning does my mother reappear, positioning herself in front of the stove and cooking with a newly sharpened vengeance, her fingers pecking into dough. If I interrupt this state, she responds with something bitter like

"I'll show him who makes this house run."

or

"I didn't come to this country for this."

or even, one time, startling me so much I was convinced for a week that my mother had been possessed,

"Oh, go to Hell,"

which, not being able to enter the gates of Hades so easily, I took as meaning "go to your room" and locked myself away with SS on one side and a big bag full of depression on the other.

*

The day after my mom's lecture, I am in the kitchen with her, helping to make dinner. I sit at the kitchen table with a big tub full of boiled potatoes that I peel happily, the softened whiteness sticking under my fingernails. At first the potatoes are so hot that the steam starts to numb my palms, but after a few minutes the burning turns to warmth and I am soothed.

"Mom," I say. "Tell me about Krishna and Radha."

My mother, in the process of throwing cumin seeds into popping oil, mimics the effervescent sizzle upon hearing this request.

"*Bahut acha, beta*"—*very good*—"Okay. Radha vas Krishna's great love. Now *there's* a good Indian girl. She vas a daughter of a yogi in Krishna's town. She vas very beautiful—"

"Yes, with long black hair, and *kajol* around her eyes," I chime in.

"*Acha, beta*! You remember the meaning of *kajol*."

She opens the cupboard and pulls out an Old El Paso salsa bottle whose contents she has replaced with masala. She opens the bottle and dumps some of the masala into the seeds and oil, a soft searing sound issuing forth.

"Yes, she vore *kajol*, and everyday Krishna vould try to voo her by playing his silver flute. Every day he vould play and try to make her come hear him, and then vone day she came and fell under the spell of his playing."

"He had her in a spell? Isn't that cheating?"

"No, *beta*. She vas moved by the powver of the Almighty. Together, Krishna and Radha became the highest example of love."

As she talks about the Krishna-Radha paragon of romance, she pours a few cups of water into the seed-oil-masala mixture, and a deep rumble accompanied by a cloud of steam arises from the pot. I pull out another potato and peel a sliver around its contour, the newly sliced skin curling around my finger. A small stream of steam, like a forked tongue, escapes.

And then, as she adds fistfuls of rice to her pot, my mother says, "In Hindi the vord for 'lover' and 'Krishna' is often the same. And I've alvays thought that your name sounds like Krishna's. I think maybe that's vhy I named you Kiran."

Sometimes I feel like my mind works like a Bollywood movie: I see the world as a fast sequence of colorful and even disturbing images. In my mind, I imagine an army of me fanning out across a dirty Bombay street, each Kiran dressed in a different pastel color but all of them united in their blue skin. Then I see those tiny Kirans running into forests and lying under bamboo trees, lotus flowers like pillows under their heads, reclining with beautiful Indian women with huge breasts, bigger breasts than the women in *Penthouse.* And I imagine every tiny Krishna Kiran romancing these women, gods and lovers united.

Here at the kitchen table, I swear that a pink bubble erupts through me, and I imagine my blue feet, my blue legs, my blue waist, my blue torso and arms and neck and face turning lavender as the pink bubble passes through them. And then, in a gush, the blue returns, brighter than ever, as if having swallowed the pink bubble. Blue splotches appear like sapphires in my vision, and suddenly the potatoes are sliding all over the floor, wobbling and naked without their brown coats. The floor is wet with the still-warm water, and I am looking up at the ceiling. Rather, I *would* be looking at the ceiling, if I could see anything. I have gone blind. The blue has turned black.

"*Arre!*" my mom exclaims, then kneels down. Her hands are still covered in the scent of spices, but she helps me to sit upright anyway. She leans me against the island in the kitchen, then takes a towel from the cupboard, soaks it in cold water, and puts it on my forehead.

My father appears from his office, his face wrinkled in worry.

"Vhat is going on," he asks, and the fire in his eyes from the fight earlier in the day dissipates, replaced with genuine concern. Upon seeing me, he realizes it's another one of my migraines and comes to my mother's side, helping me into a chair and saying soothing words, his voice calm and comforting. "It's okay, *beta,* just drink some vater—here." He hands me a glass of water my mother has presented to him.

I heave out a few sighs. The only thing I can feel is the water down my throat—and the prick of plastic limbs from SS, who is stuffed in my sweatpants pocket. I think of her, of us lounging in a patch of strawberries like we're Krishna and Radha, and something about this brings me back. My vision blurs back in, like the opening of an old black-and-white Indian movie star-

ring Raj Kapoor, and the image of my father and mother becomes half clear.

"Kiran *Beta*, are you okay?" my father asks. He puts one
hand on my shoulder.

A mixture of smoke and steam rises from the burning rice behind him.

A Dairy Downfall

Krishna's great weakness was butter. Mine is headaches.

A few years ago, I started having migraines. Every once in a while, something sends my head into throbbing pain, and it isn't predictable as to what that catalyst will be. I feel a flash of heat inside of me, and then my vision becomes crowded with light.

People who've had near-death experiences describe a warm, white light creeping into their vision. This is sort of what I see when I have a migraine, except I see light in splashes of different colors. Each headache, then, is like a little death.

I tell my mother this after I come to and am lying in bed, but she shakes her head no. "*Arre, beta*, don't be so dramatic. Just keep the towvel on your forehead. You don't want to miss school tomorrow."

But I *do* want to miss school tomorrow. I still have to contend with Sarah, Melissa, and Co. every day, and I'd much rather stay home and spend the day rummaging through Estée and looking at porn. And there's the terrifying thought of having my migraine return at school. Luckily, to this day, I've never had one there, although I've felt them creeping up on me before. Once, when John Griffin put a worm on my chair after recess, I felt my face getting hot and quickly rushed to the bathroom, where I hid in a stall and took deep breaths until I felt a normal body temperature again.

Luckily, I have a mother who insists on feeding me body-building vitamins. She has put me in the habit of taking a Centrum tablet every day, like I'm seventy instead of twelve. She also insists that I take gingko biloba and echinacea pills, and three times a week, she mixes me a glass of a supplement called colloidal silver, which an American friend of hers has taken for years and which is apparently amazing for your immune system. My mother makes this concoction as methodically as she makes everything else on her stove; she uses the same wide stainless steel pot in which she makes *daal*. I have yet to see her various remedies make a huge difference in my health, but I appreciate her diligence all the same.

I wish there were some medicine that could make my headaches productive, perhaps giving me a huge burst of intelligence every time I have one. Some way to transform my headaches from debilitating to empowering. Until then, I focus on Krishna's downfall instead.

I, like Krishna, have always loved butter. But I usually like it *in* things, not just by itself. I like when my mom makes *roti* because she uses a long, thin brush to spread a warm layer of Land O' Lakes on the circular bread, the stuff softening the dough. I like butter pecan ice cream, mostly for its peaceful color. I love Butterfinger candy bars, the shock of orange they send through me. I love butternut squash, which my mom likes to mash into a paste, mixing in masala, salt, pepper, and butter. I scoop it up in one oily, buttery, soft *roti*.

But it's an altogether different thing to eat butter by itself.

It's 1992, and people these days have become obsessed with butter and its various forms—and, specifically, the cholesterol they all carry. This is the most sumptuous of times for people who have warring, sadomasochistic personalities, the type of people who love depriving themselves of creaminess. A chief member of this group—a doggedly dedicated member—is my father. His two halves—the nutritionist sadist and the starved masochist—are a match made in Heaven.

As we sit at lunch, my father extols the benefits of playing the butter assassin.

"Vhat you eat now vill affect your whole life," he says, tearing a dry *roti* and popping a paperlike sliver into his mouth. "All these people think, 'Oh, I am young and strong. Nothing can hurt me.' But they are all idiots. You guys have to cut out all of this rubbish." He gestures at our oily *roti*, the small, stainless steel dishes full of plain yogurt, the tall glasses of buttermilk infused with pepper and lemon juice that we concoct to simulate *lassi*. "Or you vill be noplace."

But he doesn't take all of our oily food away. Despite his personal nutritional battle, I think he sees the food before me and my mom as a necessary part of our Indianness, as if somewhere amidst the sour dairy swirls there is a secret potion that keeps us as Eastern as possible. All the same, he keeps tabs on whatever we eat, switching our boxes of Corn Pops and Apple Jacks with Shredded Wheat and Fiber One—unaware that he's merely exchanging loads of crap with cereals that make your crap plentiful. He banished the cookie jar he got for my mother one Valentine's Day—one of those mail-order affairs where you can choose what is written on the side of the jar. The ad displayed a sample jar whose side read "Mary's Homemade Cookies," but my father changed it to "Shashi's Homemade Chum Chum," overlooking the fact that *chum chum* (aka Indian desserts) have to be kept in the refrigerator—or as my parents call it, "REFrigerator"—or they'll be as crumbly as a mummy. Now, via a stepstool, my father has consigned the jar to the highest shelf in the pantry, along with a candy dish of rainbow-colored, sugar-coated fennel seeds.

But I will not be deterred, despite my fright. The Sunday after my fainting spell, I go grocery shopping with my mother. I wait until she is busy selecting the perfect bouquet of coriander before I disappear into the refrigerated strip of dairy goods. Skipping the small armada of blue-, red-, and purple-capped milk cartons, I survey the vast stacks of butter products: the tubs of margarine; the little brick boxes of butter, each containing four wax-papered bars; the new, circus-like product exclaiming its incredulity that the substance inside is really butter. I grab the biggest contestant, a tub of Country Crock, and head for the cashiers. I plan to pay this time. I don't want to risk shoplifting again, considering the bad karma that happened with Mrs. Nevins right after I stole that magazine. I must make a truly weird sight: a small Indian boy hoisting a tub of processed butter product onto the checkout line, puffing my exertion into the heavily rouged face of THELMA, as her matte black name tag announces. I pay in change, the guts of my piggy bank clattering a chorus as I dump them onto the steel counter, like they did when I bought my SS dolls. Thelma groans, then counts the coins one by one, holding them in one hand and sliding them into the other as she registers the amount in her head. It is a process not unlike the way my mother screens uncooked lentil seeds when cooking, dropping deformed shapes into the receptacle of her left palm. Once I've purchased the product, I wrap the plastic bag tightly around the butter and retreat back into the store. Thelma sends another puzzled groan my way.

I find my mother nose-deep in produce. I slide my load of Crock onto the little shelf under the shopping cart, a place my mother would never think to look, no matter how low to the ground her five-foot-tall body is. I'm the one who pushes the cart anyway, an activity I do with gusto, adding a few pas de bourrée as I move along.

When we check out, Thelma thankfully does not say anything about the butter because she is too nonplussed by the mammoth cornucopia my mother has set on the conveyer belt: an Amazon of greenery: coriander, lettuce, green beans, lentils, peppers; three large cartons of plain yogurt, proof that my mother is single-handedly keeping Dannon in business; bottles of Wesson cooking oil standing as rigidly and gravely as bishops; cylinders of Morton salt, bottles of crushed black and red pepper, bags of sugar the size of infants. And this is only the American stop; after this, we have to take a twenty-minute drive to Asian Bazaar, a small store that feels like a speakeasy, where smelly Indian men, their mustaches like ink blots, sell my mother enormous bags of durum flour, corn flour, masala, and turmeric. Sam Walton would shit his linen pants if he knew that two tiny Punjabi men had innovated bulk food purchases this adeptly.

Come to think of it, I guess I could have just asked my mother to buy the Country Crock, but I am so used to sneaking around these days that such a thought never even crosses my mind until this instant.

When we get home from Asian Bazaar—my body aching from carrying everything into the house and my mother's hands covered in coupon paper cuts—I tuck the Country Crock under my arm and dash to my room. I yell "Homework!", shut and lock the door, and sit on the floor in hasty tribute to my blue-skinned past incarnation.

At first, when I open the lid and peel back the wrapper, the butter, swirled so that one point sticks straight up in the center, intimidates me. But there it is again—that disarming, light yellow, the type of color that mothers paint nurseries when they are trying to be different from the usual blue and pink. I scoop a fingerful of butter out and roll it into the skin of my fingers, then smear a smidge into my cheek to see if it makes an adequate moisturizer. Oily, but it seems to do the trick.

I'm stalling. I know that it's going to be gross, but I have to do it. It's in my blood. Actually, it's in my soul. I take a deep breath and then gobble up a teaspoon's worth.

Surprise of surprises—well, I guess the surprise of surprises would be if my current behavior were considered sane—but surprise of surprises, it tastes good. It tastes mildly sweet; I feel like I've discovered an albino fudge. As I scoop more and more butter into my mouth, I come to a fuller realization of just what is happening here: I am a genius rediscovering the roots of his genius. It's like picking up a piece of writing that you wrote years ago; you have forgotten everything you wrote down—be it a book report from school or those first song lyrics you composed at the age of eight—because you were in that moment and the art was merely using you as a vessel, passing through you and leaving little of itself on your memory. You feel the tiniest stab of recollection when you rediscover it, but mostly you are in awe of how it was *you* who wrote down these words and felt something so creative in that moment. Or it's like picking up an old, lost photo and remembering faintly the joy or apprehension you felt at that moment, but also remarking that this was you, this was a person, this was someone doing something and it escaped you. This butter, though processed and preserved and probably not even yellow until a high-tech food coloring is thrown into its folds, joins my present self to my past self. As I cap the butter and put it back in the plastic bag, as I tiptoe downstairs to the basement, to the old fridge whose freezer my mom stuffs full of tomato puree she's made in our blender, as I open the "Crisp" drawer and stash the tub, as I rush back up the stairs and pant heavily in the kitchen, I feel like a crown of peacock feathers has grown from my temples, which are again, after centuries, as blue as vein.

I must wear this crown tentatively, though. My father has set himself the task of eradicating all butter from his diet, while I have set myself the task of slurping fistfuls of Country Crock. This is a problem.

Somehow I think he knows what I am up to. I worry that he can smell the butter on my breath. My lips start to chap because I instinctively wipe my mouth again and again to make sure there is no more greasy shine left. Krishna certainly never had chapped lips. In every picture I've seen of Him, His lips are plump, as well as shiny with lipstick. So I start to take extra-special care of my lips, pilfering one of my mother's many tubes of Chap-Stick and using it often.

Once I have managed to eat the butter without any detection from my father, I feel like I have triumphed over him in the same way that I have over my mother. Just as I have managed to put on her makeup, I have managed to eat my father's nutritional enemy. Something I have never felt before becomes clear to me: I am taking a sort of hurtful pride in being devious to them. I am transforming my weaknesses into ruses, and in doing so, I am becoming surer of myself. I am the calm in the middle of the battle.

*

On Saturday, I practice my ballet exercises in the kitchen. I am listening to a tape of ballet commands that Marcy, my

teacher, gave each of us students. The instructions are enunci-
ated by a nasal-voiced man who sounds like Richard Simmons.
I assent, gripping the counter with my left hand and moving my
right arm according to the position I am in. In third position, I
curve it in front of me as if I'm Snow White catching a dove on
her forearm. In fifth position, I curve it over my head and feel
taller. I do every step perfectly until my father walks into the
kitchen—dripping with sweat and smelling of grass. He has just
mowed the lawn. The remnants of grass give off a pungent
smell, but at least it's not the type of grass that Tiffany Myers
smells like when she comes to school. Her father works in "produce," but his best goods are not on display under a miniature
sprinkler system.

"Press, point, toe-ball-heel," says the faux Richard, and I press
my foot into the floor, lift it, and melt it back onto the ground,
staring over my father's head.

"*Beta*, could you stop for von minute." My father reaches
down and takes off his sneakers, and I'm surprised not to see a
cloud of odor rising from them.

"I can't stop," I say quickly, afraid that I'll miss one of faux
Richard's words, which I take as Gospel. My biggest goal in life
right now is to dance my God-driven way across the school
stage in November, so my practice time is precious. Only two
months left.

"*Beta*, please stop, we have to talk."

This is a first. My father never asks to talk to me. Sure, we
have our brief, in-passing chats—he once stopped to tell me to
make sure I use shampoo only three times a week or I'll end up
as bald as Gandhi—but he's never asked me to sit down. Especially after lawn mowing, which he usually follows up with a
hot cup of tea and the Indian news that comes to our TV cour-
tesy of a dish satellite, an alien insect crawling up our house.

I cease posing and flick faux Richard off, stopping him in the
middle of a "*Relevé!*" I walk over to the kitchen table, pull out
a chair, and sit on it attentively, nervously, digging my toes into
the ground and causing a muffled, tough sound of leather against
linoleum.

"*Arre*, don't do that, *beta*! You'll ruin the ground!" my father says. He takes off his baseball cap and reveals a mess of sweat-drenched hair that looks like a pile of steamed spinach.

"Sorry," I say, and I resume my attempt at stock-still composure. I am certain he can see the buttery sheen on my lips again, and I lick them to remove it, feeling chapped crackles under the buds of my tongue.

"*Beta*, something has been bothering me."

I almost pee myself. I mean that, literally, a drop or two of urine slithers out of me and into my shorts. It's not the fact that my father has figured out that I'm eating butter—as terrifying a thought as that may be—it's that he's figured out I've been hiding something from him. I know from the way his mouth purses into a wrinkle when my mother shows up with a cluster of shopping bags—and the inevitable muffled "discussion" that ensues from the master bedroom—that hiding things from him is not the way to go.

"Now, vhere is your hiding place?" he says.

Oh, no—the Country Crock.

The strange thing is how calm his face seems but how tough the reprobation in his eyes is. I think back to two minutes ago—how happy I was dancing away without a care in the world, hearing the *chuck* of his lawn mower—and now I'm sitting at a table, terrified. This house is full of such surprises. No zone is safe—none—and no matter how secretive my binges have been in my bedroom all this time, he will find out what I've been up to. There is no getting anything past my father.

"Vhere is your hiding place?" he asks again, and I know he knows I'm scared. This is his technique, to question me until I crack. And why question such a technique when it makes me confess? A confession that goes something like this:

"In the refrigerator downstairs. And I know it's wrong! I know I shouldn't be eating it but it tastes really good and I'm in good shape—I'm doing really well in ballet class—and I'm not fat or anything so I think it's fine! I mean you only started cutting butter out of your diet now and you're so much older than

I am. So I don't understand why I can't have some from time to time—"

"Vait a second, vait a second," my father says, shaking his head from side to side and rubbing his forehead as if to rouse his mind to wake. "Vhat are you talking about? Vhat's in the refrigerator downstairs?"

I don't know how to respond. I am baffled. My father slides out from the table, opens the basement door that leads into our kitchen, and descends swiftly, his now-bare feet plopping with purpose, his fingers pulling on the string attached to a bulb that lights the cellar netherworld, his fingers now encircling the downstairs refrigerator's door, the sound of the padded door unsmushing, and then the fumbling, fumbling, fumbling, opening the "Crisp" drawer, the tough exhalation of recognition. He emerges with a gaping mouth that mimics the black hole of the basement doorway. The tub of Country Crock sits on his palm like a caricature of itself, overly yellow and swollen.

"Is this vhat you're talking about?" He seethes. He examines the surface of the margarine closer, then tilts it toward me so that I can see the deep grooves my fingers have cut into the goo.

I've lost so much at this point that I might as well just retort back. "Well, what were *you* talking about?"

"Vhat am *I* talking about? Vhat am *I* talking about? I'm talking about vhat I found on the lawn!" And somehow, from his back pocket, even though the back pocket belongs to his pair of too-tight sky blue lawn-mowing shorts, he produces Blueberry Muffin—SS's best friend and confidante. Her painted eyes seem to be pleading with me, and they are all the more affecting due to their smallness—tiny pinpoints of worry. Her blue rubber hat is askew, and on its summit are the initials KS, which I scrawled upon it with a black felt tip marker.

This is going to be so much worse than him finding out that I am eating butter. Why did I think that eating butter, of all my actions, would be the worst one for him to discover? I have been too, too frivolous. In my attempt to hide things from him, I've forgotten just how many deviant behaviors I'm engaged in. A pang hits me as I think of the makeup, the porn, the butter, the dolls. Which is the most incriminating? Which one would I want *least* for him to find?

"Kiran *Beta*, vhy vould you have a doll like this? I know that you are getting older and that you are getting interested in girls, but this is not the time for hanky-panky. You must focus on your studies and that is it. There vill be time for girls later."

Somehow, it seems that my father has been able to pick up on my other closed-door behavior, too. I shudder thinking how he might have espied me taking off Blueberry's clothing one day so that I could see what she looked like underneath—a shiny body of peach plastic, with a cinched chest and wider waist, the opposite of Barbie's top-heavy physique. I would never have done such a thing to SS; I turned her away from us, hid her head in my comforter while I examined Blueberry. I even felt a blush of shame when I buttoned Blueberry's clothes back on. Here, in the kitchen, I feel truly violated that my father has deduced this behavior, that he has breached the sacredness of the subtle furrow in Blueberry's peach plastic back, the thin tenderness of her peach plastic legs, the vacant, smooth peach plastic nothing of her sex.

But I say nothing more. I look straight into my father's angry eyes.

"Kiran." He adopts an ever harsher tone of warning. "*Beta*, do you know vhen I vas growing up in India, my dad used to slap me if I looked right into his eyes? Here they tell you, 'Look at me vhen I'm talking to you,' but there you keep your eyes down."

I obey, looking at the shiny wood of the kitchen table.

"*Beta*, you have to stop doing things like this. Do you know vhat people vill think? Vhy vould you ruin your life by doing all of this nonsense? You are a strange boy, Kiran, and you need to change your habits or you are going to be noplace."

He walks out of the kitchen and into the laundry room with Blueberry and the Country Crock in his hands, and then I hear the door to the garage open. There is another series of sounds, and this time it is more tear-inducing than fear-inducing: the flapping of his bare soles against the smooth, oil-stained cement floor, the opening of the big black plastic trash can, and then the solid thud of Blueberry's own plastic hitting the bottom. The solidness of the thud means there is no Glad bag, no other trash aside from the accumulated sludge at the bottom. Then there is a larger sound: the Country Crock, devastatingly heavy, hitting with a ferocious crush, a splash of butter escaping from its cracked-open lid. When my father comes back in, I avoid his eyes. I wait until he has gone upstairs before I walk over to the counter, shaking, and flick the portable stereo back on.

"*-levé!*" faux Richard bellows, and I stand on tiptoe. It is when I think of Blueberry's azure tresses stained through with greasy grime, her beautiful body slathered in butter, that I feel the heat inside of me, turn off the stereo, go to my room, and release another potential headache by way of tears. At one point, I think to hold SS near me but fear that I might see in her eyes what I have just seen in my father's.

You'll Go Down
in Hi-sto-ry (Like Lincoln!)

The talent show is a big deal. An enormous deal. And not just because it allows me the opportunity to show my worth to the rest of the school. It also allows me the opportunity to erase all of my past wrongs.

I am the reigning king of the fall talent show, having successfully executed three routines, in third, fourth, and fifth grades. None from kindergarten through second grade, because the teachers think those grades are too early to perform anything of real worth, although let me remind you of Kevin Bartlett's Bon Jovi performance to underline that age is not an indication of having any artistic relevance. My past routines, in chronological order, were as follows:

1) **Third grade**—a rousing rendition of "Do Your Ears Hang Low?," that old classic, which I sang in three variations: regular, staccato, and adagio.
2) **Fourth grade**—a rousing rendition of Dionne Warwick's "I'll Never Love This Way Again," a touching ballad;
3) **Fifth grade**—

You know, fifth grade is too epic for me to tack onto a numbered list. Fifth grade was monumental, a defining artistic experience, the moment I really came into myself as an artist and realized my true creative potential. I decided that I would present a rousing rendition of "Kiss the Girl" from *The Little Mermaid*. Unless you're totally mental and don't know, "Kiss the Girl" is a really pivotal scene in the movie, in which Ariel, the mermaid who has been transformed into a human by the evil sea witch Ursula, and who has only three days to get Prince Eric to smooch her, has seduced the prince into a boat ride through a blue lagoon. During this, she is serenaded by her trusty sidekick Sebastian the Crab. In his song, Sebastian urges Eric to kiss his red-haired boat companion, thereby breaking the sea witch's spell and letting everyone live happily ever after.

For my theatrical rendering, I enlisted the help of two students in the class who shared my less-than-ideal oddball status. Despite all of my obvious social faults, I had one thing going for me: I was thin. My Eric and Ariel, on the other hand, were Eric Banner and Lindsay Bailey, the two fattest kids in our class. Round and bumbling, they were boobs in both senses of the word. Eric, a wisp of a mullet curling off the nape of his neck, was dressed in his cartoon namesake's token white shirt, and he sweated so badly that twin circles of perspiration tainted the fabric under his arms. This sight was deflected somewhat by Lindsay's getup: since she didn't own a red wig, she took a fringed cheerleading skirt—an oddity, since I don't think Lindsay ever cheered in her life due to cellulite reasons—and put it on her nappy, dirty-blond tangles. Instead of Ariel's stately navy blue dress, Lindsay put on what looked like a cassock, obviously a hand-me-down from her Frigidaire of a mother, who helped us out on classroom party days and whose actual gender was up for debate. Still, the way I placed Eric and Lindsay center stage, each perched on one knee, and told them to stare at each other unmoving and unflinching, was as masterly a situation as could be staged.

As for me, in order to look like the crab-crimson Sebastian, I donned the best and smoothest of my red sweatsuits. But the kicker was the enormous red beanbag I used for a crab shell. As Eric and Lindsay took their places centerstage, I set up shop upstage right, prostrating myself stomach-down on the dusty floor, flipping the beanbag onto my back, and then taking up the microphone. Unfortunately, the stage had no curtain, so we had to do all of this while completely visible to the audience. There was no accompaniment—how else could the audience really hear me?—but this made for a dramatic effect, and the stunned looks on the parents' faces after I finished singing told me—at least at the time—that they had just witnessed a piece of theater better and more moving than anything they had ever seen.

Like all great artists, however, my genius was not justly greeted by my peers. The day after I urged Eric to kiss Lindsay, my classmates didn't react with the adulation I had expected. John Griffin still sent spitballs my way when I walked down the hall, and just when I finished wiping them off my shiny black hair, Jeff Rollins and his goons crab-walked past me, then got up and started doing wayward arabesques, calling out, "I'm Key-ran!" I shrugged them off as best as I could and told myself that an even more rousing performance the next year—this year—would redeem me.

All the same, I took another step backward later that year, when, in March, my school had History Day. All of us were supposed to dress up as an important historical figure and give a presentation two minutes long—an eternity to a little child, or even an adult. For some reason, my father's rabid Indian patriotism failed to penetrate my young mind, and so instead of going as Gandhi, donning fake wire spectacles and one of those bald head rubber caps and extolling the virtues of nonviolence, or going as Nehru, sporting a collarless suit, I aimed for that most Indian of historical figures, a true paragon of Hinduism:

Abraham Lincoln.

Except I didn't go as the Honest Abe you would naturally conjure up—tall stovetop hat, bushy muttonchops, long, black waistcoat. Instead, I chose to model myself after a picture of Abe I saw in a picture book in the school library, a slender little volume with crude illustrations that looked like paint-by-number drawings. In the picture I chose as my model, Abe was all of twelve years old, playing outside his family's cabin in a yellow T-shirt and brown pants. And so that's exactly what I wore—a yellow polo shirt and brown pants. I was a small Indian boy wearing a yellow shirt and brown pants and claiming to be Abraham Lincoln. It's a miracle the teacher didn't commit me to a loony bin on the spot.

For my presentation, I told people about how Abraham Lincoln was called Honest Abe and how he was shot, at a theater, by a man named *John Wilkes Booth*—a real tongue-twister for a second grader, and it took me about five whole seconds to pronounce the name, so intent was I on capturing every last melodramatic inflection and insisted that everyone repeat after me, even insisting they replicate the slippery sibilance at the end of my "Wilkes." I really wanted them all to have that name ingrained in their minds and in their pronunciation, and I'm sure I made many a mother's eyebrow rise that evening when she witnessed her son or daughter roaming the house reciting a presidential assassin's name in trance-like concentration.

After making sure everyone knew that tidbit, I told a joke. A side-splitting joke, one that I hoped would make every kid in the class forget I had shown up for the first day of school with a bundle of pink things—a pink Trapper Keeper, a pink pencil, a pink ruler, a pink notebook, and pink sunglasses that I wore perched on top of my head like I was Poochie, that popular eighties cartoon dog who had hot-pink hair.

In this presentation joke, a teacher is telling her classroom of young children about Abraham Lincoln's arduous journey to and from school as a child.

> *"Class," she says, "Abraham Lincoln had to walk seven miles to and from school every day when he was little."*
> *To which everyone in the class responds with utter disbelief and a nonplussed silence. Everyone, that is, except tiny Timmy in the back, who raises his hand.*
> *"Yes, Timmy?" says the teacher.*
> *"Why couldn't he catch the bus like everyone else?"*

Ha ha, hee hee, it's not like this joke is vintage Johnny Carson or David Letterman, it's not like it's so funny that people will die of laughter-induced convulsions. But to a roomful of elementary-schoolers, it was hysterical. It was so funny to Mrs. Nolan's class that more than one classmate snarfed—that is, nose-vomited—the Mott's Apple Juice that Joey Harmon had passed out as part of his Johnny Appleseed presentation. It was so funny that for a second, though dressed in my yellow and brown cryptic garments, I felt as important and righteous as the real, grave-faced Abe.

Everyone finished their presentations, the class full on Stephanie Ralston's Clara Barton cupcakes (white frosting with a red cross squeezed on) and Steven Young's Daniel Boone donuts (a cop-out, first, because they were just regular Dunkin' Donuts and second, because Daniel Boone *never ate donuts in his life*)—and then a life-changing event occurred: The local news showed up.

The local news broadcasts reign supreme in Cincinnati, so much so that their set pieces seem to change every day. On Monday the whole color scheme might be blue and on Tuesday it could be red, a whole new lighting system rigged to better present the reporters, who sit behind their desks so uprightly that they are like gods pronouncing judgments from on high. More important than the regular reporters, though, are the weather people, for people in this town cannot live without knowing what the weather is going to be like this evening, in half an hour, or just seconds from now. Every week brings another satellite or radar, a different style to the weather graphics: sunglasses added to the orange-rimmed yellow suns or multicolored sparkling raindrops glowing underneath the storm clouds or a little booth set up for the weatherman away from all the other reporters, as if he is too gifted with foresight to be bothered by the physical proximity of anyone who might disrupt his prognostication. So focused are these Cincinnatians on the weather ahead that they never seem to notice that the weather at present is nothing like the noble weatherman predicted.

On History Day, the most important of Channel 7's reporters came to our school—Melinda Maines. She was the ultimate combo: a weatherwoman who covered special interest stories, as well. She could be hiding under a tarp while tracking a tornado one day, then offering crap-colored food pellets to lambs at a petting zoo the next. Blond bouffant, power-suited, earrings complementing whatever bright color of suit she chose to wear, she had electric blue eyes, as if just by staring at someone she could cause them to make their stories more interesting. After all, her interviewees knew that Melinda could always be on the other side of town interviewing a war veteran or examining caterpillar fur to see how rough the winter would be.

The moment everyone heard Melinda Maines was in the building, we all went into a gleeful panic. Mrs. Nolan made us clean up the crumbs all over our desks and went hopping around the room fixing people's costumes—Gretchen Lee's Sacajawea feather headdress, Chris Henry's pomegranate of a Pete Rose baseball helmet. Then she lined us all up like we were the von Trapp children, ready to serenade the news crew with "The Sound of Music." I tried to stand confidently, as if unfazed by their arrival, but inside I was a human thunderstorm, raging more fervently than any monster nimbus that Melinda had confronted in the past. When you are young and you see that metal and plastic box come carried on a thick man's shoulder, its lens shining like a deity, you feel a heightening of everything that is you, a literal exaltation that makes your eyebrows lift along with your rib cage.

When Melinda Maines and her chrome-wielding entourage entered our classroom, it seemed like a movie set. And the way Melinda's hips swung into the room, swaddled in green polyester, the way her Wind Song perfume wafted through like an Ohio Valley cold front, stiffened my spine and made me beam on the classroom's fraying red carpet.

Fate intervened in its most graceful, gracious way, and Mrs. Nolan, still playing Captain von Trapp, announced cheerfully, "I have just the person for your broadcast!" and was suddenly behind me, pushing me toward Melinda. Before I knew it, I was standing in the hallway, lit by more lights than Michelangelo's David and telling my joke to the crew.

After I recited the joke with more enunciation than my John Wilkes Booth essay, Melinda leaned down to me and said, "Now, make sure you tell your mom and dad that you're going to be on the six o'clock news tonight." The time was very important; there was the four o'clock news, the five o'clock news, the six o'clock news, the seven o'clock news. It was like Cincinnati had set up its own CNN Headline News channel, made complete by a token measly interview with a brown person.

I ran the mile and a half home from school—Abe would've been proud—and gushed the news to my parents. We turned the TV on in anticipation. My dad set the VCR to recording, then set up his camcorder in front of the den's TV to film the filming. When six o'clock finally rolled around, we all watched with bated breath, or breath occasionally interrupted by the dried masala peas my mom gave each of us in small stainless steel bowls. News story after news story—a fire in Hyde Park, triplets born in Bellevue, the unveiling of the fifth Doppler radar in Cincinnati—and then finally, there was Melinda, dressed in a new blue suit, her neon eyes sparkling.

"Today was History Day at Crestview's Martin Van Buren Elementary School. Ellen Nolan's fifth grade class dressed up as historical figures from all walks of life . . ."

That was a lie, actually. Even though there was no specification that History Day was American History Day, none of us dressed as anyone foreign—no Winston Churchills or Golda Meirs or, of course, Mahatma Gandhis.

Melinda's crew did panoramic shots of the classroom, and then showed little novelties like the salt-and-peppered hair of David Brewer's Ronald Reagan and the fishbowl of a helmet that Christa Monroe wore as Christa McAuliffe. Where was I? Where could I be? Where was the cheerful pejorative aura I exuded? We all sat, rolling peas in our hands, and then—

"But some kids were a little confused . . ." Melinda said.

Immediately, there was a close-up of little Kiran, yellow shirt aglow, asking—almost pleading—"Why couldn't he catch the bus like everyone else?"

It turned out that Melinda Maines *was* diabolical. In one cleverly rendered sound bite, I had fallen farther down than I already was. She had some nerve, Judas-kissing Honest Abe with a bald-faced lie.

Needless to say, History Day was transformed into a day of social crumbling. Every time I got on the bus to go to school, snickers would erupt like a chorus of cicadas, and any time Abe Lincoln came up in our social studies—you can't believe the number of times he does—someone would inevitably deliver that line, "Why couldn't he just catch the bus like everyone else?"

This fall's talent show is one big bus of acceptance, a bus that all the other kids are riding. Despite whatever successes I've had in the past, the last "performance" I've given is marred with shame, and the only solution is to do the best act of my career this year. Maybe, just maybe, if I perform my routine flawlessly, as electric blue as Melinda's satanic eyes, I'll finally be able to catch that bus of acceptance. Just like everyone else.

Hold Me Closer,
Tiny *Danseur*

"Do ya have Ballerina Barbie, Keern? Because you could always wear her tutu."

Sarah and Melissa's badgering of me has permeated not only my daily doings at school but one of my true safe havens: ballet class. Our school offers an hour-long class on Wednesday afternoons that makes this "hump" day the highlight of my week, and I usually rely on the swift movements of my body for a weekly burst of happiness. But as I slide my leg in a *rond de jambe*, I feel like I'm back at my desk in the classroom, peeling off more Barbie smiles.

Our ballet class is not in a fancy dance studio. It takes place in the school's multipurpose room, a smallish rectangle with mirrors on one side of it and a floor made of large, white tiles with black specks in them. A makeshift barre has been affixed to the mirrored wall with small, clear reinforcements that look like quartz. We stand at the barre, reflections of ourselves in our periphery. But since the girls are behind me, they can look at my reflection without me being able to look at theirs. Still, I know what they see: everyone else wearing leotards, a couple of the extra-chic girls like Sarah and Melissa wearing leg warmers, while I wear a black T-shirt, black tights, black slippers. Black hair, brown skin.

Marcy, who gave me the Richard Simmons-esque practice tape,

is our teacher—and a high schooler. She has become obsessed
with Kenny G, so much so that she has plastered at least a quar-
ter of the wall opposite the barre with magazine pictures of him.
Right now, the stereo is switching from one glossy jazz tune to
the next. Marcy has a mass of permed hair. The grape-like smell
of her hairspray pervades the entire "studio," and it is as if we
kids are put under its spell as she instructs us. We oblige, entirely silent and expressionless. Well, aside from Sarah and
Melissa, who continue to hiss at me when Marcy is busy instructing someone else.

"Key-ran, is that a splinter sticking out of yer ass?" Melissa
says. Sarah giggles, then reaches forward and pinches my butt
cheek.

I squeal. "Marcy! Sarah is touching me!"

Marcy rolls her eyes and says, "Sarah, stop," but her warning
is so limp that I can tell she doesn't believe me. This is probably
why she gave me the lamest award at last year's end-of-the-year
ceremony. Instead of "Best Arabesque," which I was *dying* to
receive, she gave me "Best Attendance." Attendance isn't even a
ballet technique.

"What are ya doin' for the talent show?" Sarah continues.
"Dressin' like Madonna?" I can hear her shaggy hair flopping
as she shakes her head in mockery.

I stay silent.

"*We're* doin' a dance to Janet Jackson," Melissa brags. "To
'Rhythm Nation.'"

"I can't wait to see that," I say, "since you two have the worst
rhythm in our entire class."

"Kye-run!" Marcy yells. "Please stop talking!"

I frown and growl quietly. I wish I could give Marcy an award
for "Best Awful Dance Teacher."

"Yeah, stop talking, Key-ran," Sarah taunts. "Just keep doing
yer *ballet.*"

As I slide my left foot in another circle, I feel that it is making
the retort I want to make. What those girls don't understand is
that dancing and talking are one and the same for me. If I were
Kenny G, dancing would be my saxophone.

I get my penchant for dancing from my mother. She once showed me an old photo album filled with black-and-white pictures of her as a little girl performing *khatak*, a form of classical Indian dance, a mixture of foot patterns and mysterious hand gestures—and ankle bells, always ankle bells—that conveys stories from the Ramayana and other Indian texts. Every good Indian girl studies dance, and my mother was no different: in each photo, she wore an intricate sari with shiny frazzles forming its hem; garlands of carnations crossed her torso; gold jewelry encircled her wrists, ankles, half her nose. All the while, my mother was dutifully fulfilling her role as an Indian girl, carrying on her face a look of enjoyment coupled with obligation. (Incidentally, her expression was the same in a separate album— a barely opened, dust-encased brick labeled "Wedding" that I excavated from the bottom of my father's bookcase.) My mother became quite a success, charming onlookers all over Delhi with her foot-pounding and sharp features—the slightly hooked nose, the hairpin-wide gap between her straight front teeth, the almond-shaped eyes locked in *kajol*, the delicate hands painted with *mendhi*. When flipping through the plastic-covered pages of that photo album with me, a different smile crept across her face, the sort of distanced reaction that occurs when you look at photos of other people's adorable offspring. It was as if my mother were admiring someone else's child. Or someone else's childhood.

My mother's *khatak* past instilled in her the desire to make dance a part of my life. Of course, I had a natural ability for artistic movement. When I was four, summer afternoons often found me clad in my Fruit of the Loom underpants and a Mickey Mouse T-shirt striking poses on top of the black Toyota Corolla that we had before my father could afford to buy us a beige Mercedes. Its hood, a shiny mirror, afforded me a flattering view of myself. I had a white, Duracell-operated Casio radio that I would plop down next to the car and use as a vessel to ferry Cyndi Lauper's voice all over the cul-de-sac. While Cyndi hiccupped her way through songs, I would put my arms over my head and mimic Farrah Fawcett in her *Charlie's Angels* pose, or

alternate with kicks à la those by Lynda Carter in *Wonder Woman*.
I did this whenever my father said he needed to wash the car. He
would never have let me dance on top of it, but he had a tendency to announce his household chores a few days before he
did them, as if the sheer announcement would will him into
doing his part. Whenever I heard him utter, between bites of *roti*
and curried cauliflower at dinner, "*Arre*, I need to vash that stupid car," I knew the next day would be my time to shine. As
soon as my father left the house, I would head to the car with
the radio in one hand and a pair of plastic sunglasses in the other.
My mother encouraged me. She would often sit on the driveway, a cup of tea in her hands, and watch me perform. A few
days later, my father would set to work on the car, baffled as to
how such a smudged mess could have ended up on the hood. He
would sigh deeply, then wash the car in his penny-pinching way:
concerned about saving on our water bill, he would spray the
Corolla in one swift motion from one bumper to the other—just
once—before shutting off the nozzle and then scrubbing the car
with a big, soapy sponge, which he would dip into a small bucket
of water between waxes. He would counteract his entire cleaning process once he took the bucket of soiled water and—to
avoid the horror of having to hose the car down again and
"waste" more water—poured it over the car to wash away the
soap before toweling down the metal. Staggering into the kitchen
from the heat outside, his years-old polo shirt a mess of suds and
sweat, he would grunt, "You von't belief those bloody birds.
Not only do they do caca all over the car, but they smear up the
hood, too. Eh, *bhagwan* [aka God], I need some food!"

My mother would oblige, whipping up a small stack of *roti*
and a hodgepodge of curried vegetables. As she set them down
in front of my father, she would sneak a glance at me and shake
her head almost imperceptibly from side to side, as good *khatak*
girls can do. I would acknowledge her gesture with a flourish of
my still-sunglassed face like I was Gloria Swanson in *Sunset
Boulevard*.

My mother supposed I would take after her and study *khatak*.
She certainly did her darnedest for this to be the case. Once, she

dragged me to a performance in Indianapolis by a barrel-chested dancer who called himself Hanuman, after the Hindu monkey god. The resemblance, terrifyingly enough, was uncanny. The man's upper lip was convex and snout-like, and his long limbs and hairy torso put me in mind of King Louie from *The Jungle Book*. Reportedly, he held the Guinness world record for the longest dance ever performed, a sweat-drenched *khatak* performance in Jalandhar that lasted three days and that must have put dents in the Punjabi dirt. Learning of this achievement was not exactly comforting for me. As my mother and I pushed ourselves into the narrow wooden seats of that Indiana auditorium, amidst a crowd of Indians gushing their anticipation to each other in Hindi, I doubted that the meager buffet table of food in the lobby would be enough to feed us all for three days. The performance was listed in the program as lasting "only" three hours, and in my mind, I imagined this three-hour tour veering as horribly off course as Gilligan's cruise. When Hanuman finished his ecstatic dance not three but *five* hours later, my mother was on her feet applauding while I was plotting the quickest ways for us to get to the professional curry before everyone else.

Then there was the time that she tried to set up private dance lessons with a pockmarked woman named Hema who wore her hair in a carnation-laden ponytail. Hema must have been so busy studying dance that she forgot to change the carnations regularly, and so her hair often became a sharp-smelling mess of crinkled brown petals and split ends.

At first, my mother made me think she had simply found a friend in this woman. She would invite Hema Auntie over for tea and have me serve tiny butter cookies—or "biscuits," to be Anglo-observant. While I served, my mother and Hema would discuss dancing.

"I used to love dancing vhen I vas young," my mother said, sipping her tea in a half-slurp that to Indians conveys an enjoyment of food but to Americans is the most annoying sound on Earth. "The first time I met Ramesh, it was vhen ve vere little and I had just finished dancing at a *sangeet* for my cousin Geeta. She was getting married to a boy from Kerala with skin like tamarind chutney." But then she went into Hindi, and I was lost. If it weren't for Hema, I would have tugged at my mother's clothing and begged her to tell me in English the story of how she met my father. But instead, I went to the counter and loaded our stainless steel serving tray with more biscuits.

"How did you start dancing, Hema?" my mother asked.

"Ess soon ess I came out of my mother! But that is nut important, Shashi," Hema replied in her weighty accent, her teacup in one hand and a strand of oily hair twirled in the other. "Vhat is important is how Kiran vill larn, ha? Kiran *Beta*, ev'ry child should larn haw to dence *khatak*. *Beta*, I show you."

Then she got up and led me to the open expanse of the family room, with its big Persian rug (or "Indian rug," as my father would call it), and demonstrated certain key steps for me. The next time she came to visit, she even tried to teach me the famous pose of the Durga, the many-limbed goddess who has one leg raised and her front set of hands clasped in a bloom at her side. This, she told me, was one of the fundamental poses of Indian dance but also a rather impossible pose to strike. Indeed it was, as I wobbled for a second before losing my balance and landing facedown on the carpet.

I was always so busy trying to do what Hema told me that I didn't notice how the tea and biscuits stopped being a part of her visits as the weeks went on. It was only a month later when I saw my mother handing Hema a check at the end of her visit— with not a drop of tea in either of their bellies—that I realized what was going on.

"Mom!" I cried after the front door closed and Hema was gone. "I didn't ask for Hema Auntie to teach me!"

"Oh, Kiran *Beta*, it is good for you. I didn't vant to study *khatak* when I first started, either, but then I grew to love it. This is vhy American children are alvays so naughty. Their parents send them clothes from the Gap instead of teaching them things. Not everything is easy, *beta*. You have to vork hard, and then you get God's blessings later."

"I don't think these are God's blessings," I said, pulling up my shirt and showing her the collage of bruises covering my torso. Finally, the sight of my battered body made my mother desist. Even now, I wouldn't incur bruises to turn myself Krishna blue. At least I don't think I would.

All the same, my mother would drop in other asides about *khatak* the same way she would drop blobs of corn batter into a pot of hot oil when making *pakora*.

"You know, *beta*, good health is all in your posture. You know how I learned good posture? *Khatak*." Plop.

Or, one particularly odd time, when heading out the front door to go shopping, she said, "I never vore such beautiful saris as I did vhen I danced." It was as if she knew the promise of luxurious fabric would perk my ears up. But I was too deep in concentration to think about her words carefully; I was waiting for her to go shopping so that I could play with her makeup again.

*

In the end, it was inevitable that I would choose ballet.

It was in third grade that they began to offer the ballet class at my school. Mrs. Fisher gave us all a sheet that specified the after-school programs available to us. There were karate, basketball, ceramics, Tee Ball, and ballet. Most of the boys went for the basketball class, which made no sense—most of them played basketball after school on the blacktop anyway, even when it was chilly outside, so why they chose an indoor league was beyond me. To the girls, ballet was the best option, of course. And I wanted to be near the girls. I wanted to be in the world of tights and pastels and fleet feet.

I was the only boy. Even when I turned in my sign-up sheet—which had been encouragingly signed by my mother, who thought ballet "a graceful dance that can prepare you for *khatak*"—Mrs. Fisher, her forehead crinkling under a poof of Clairol-hued bangs, asked if I was sure.

"Keern, honey, I think you checked the wrong box." She leaned over her desk, covering the tests she was grading as if afraid my balletic cooties would get all over them. "Why don't you join the basketball league, honey?" she whispered. "Or at least ceramics. You could make a nice pot."

"But I like ballet!" I said—too loudly, it turned out, because the boys in the classroom started calling me "Ballerina."

Shuddering off the name-calling, I went with my mother that afternoon to buy the supplies listed on a sheet that Mrs. Fisher finally handed over to me. The store of choice was a tiny place called Pansy's, a small wooden box—knobby hardwood floors, wood-paneled walls speckled with the silver heads of tiny nails, wood benches and wooden cubbies full of salmon-colored boxes that contained different styles and sizes of ballet slippers. The owner, Pansy, was an overweight woman in her mid-forties who wore zebra-print spandex pants and a faded black KISS T-shirt that could have clothed all four members of that band. Her hair looked like orange yarn, and she took a hit of a Virginia Slim every ten seconds.

"This is a ballet store, hon," she puffed at my mother, who was an odd blast of color in the middle of the store—she was wearing a pool-bottom-blue *salwaar kameez* topped with her white cardigan, and her hair fell in one fat black braid, cinched by a silver scrunchie.

"Oh, this is a *ballet store*? Oh, dear, forgive me, ma'am. I thought it vas a bar," said my mother, in one of those wacky moments when I looked up at her and wondered who she really was. "My son is starting ballet class and needs to buy a pair of shoes."

"Yer *son*?"

"Yes, my son," my mother said, cradling my head in her hand instead of pushing me forward. Her hand felt cold but comforting, the nails long and manicured and scraping softly against my cheek. "Can you help us?"

"Well, of course I can help ya, honey," Pansy said. She took a deep hit from her cigarette, dropped it onto the dusty wooden floor, and put it out with her shoe, which was a cross between a bathroom slipper and a ballet slipper. "Come over here, kid." She gave an exasperated glance at the cashier, who looked like a less-pretty Geena Davis and whose register looked like it had come out of Frosty's, the closed-down '50s diner on Route 4. My mother must have noticed the glance between the two ladies, but she had apparently decided to ignore it. She crossed her hands in front of her—her gold bangles jingled—and I sat down on a bench as Pansy motioned for me to do.

"What size shoe are ya, hon?" Pansy asked, her arms akimbo on fleshy hips.

"He's a size five," my mother said.

"Wow—tiny little guy. Okay, hon, take off your shoes and socks so we can try these babies on. I gotta go into the back room for those teensy-weensy feet."

I unstuck the two Velcro strips holding each sneaker together and slid the shoes onto the floor. I had to wear the Velcro kind because I still wasn't particularly good at tying my shoes; it should have been easy enough for a smart kid like me, but I had just never gotten the rhythm of it down right. I always ended up tying a huge, garbled knot that would take me twenty minutes to untie or that would lead me to slide the constricted shoes off my feet with a grimace on my face. One time, I had to throw out a pair of sneakers because I had knotted them so tightly that not even my father could untie them, try as he may have to undo the knot with a Phillips screwdriver. Whose handle, now that I think of my eating fad, looked like butterscotch.

Pansy emerged from behind a black velvet curtain. She had a stack of slim boxes in her hands, and although it didn't look like her load was particularly heavy, she was grunting as if she were carrying an elephant.

"It's been ages since I had a boy in here," she said, attempting to set the entire stack onto the bench but dropping the top three boxes. "Had to blow dust off these black slippers."

"*Black* slippers?" I said.

"Yeah, black slippers, toots. Unless ya wanted pink ones like the girls!" She laughed an emphysemic laugh, happy enough to make me want to slug her.

"Well, I . . ."

"Oh, ya want the pink ones, hon?" She laughed again, and the movement of the snot in her throat sounded like a car wash.

"No," I said quickly, and I looked behind me to see my mom's reaction to this exchange. Not surprisingly, she was too busy examining a tableful of fancy, satin-covered shoes, tongue pinched between her lips.

My heart did a bungee jump in my torso, plummeting almost through my butt, then retracted, ending up somewhere just below where it had been previously. To think that I would not be able to wear pink slippers! The cheekiness in Pansy's stare, the smirk in her fat lips, told me that choosing pink was forbidden, an instant path to ridicule. And so, although sad I couldn't get the type of pink slippers that would match SS's hat, I said nothing as Pansy opened one of the boxes on the bench and pulled out a pair of nice-smelling black slippers that were crinkled at the toe, a tiny bow protruding from the crinkle. She slid the slipper onto my right foot. A thin elastic black band crossed over the delicate bones of my foot. The leather was cold and comforting, but it was also the charred version of my pink dreams.

All the same, it seemed like kismet when Pansy told me, in a bedtime story tone, that the first pair I tried on was *juuuuust riiiiight*. My mother looked on with a cheerful expression. I hopped over to her and placed my arms around her waist, then buried my head just a bit into her stomach. She cradled me, and we stood like this as Ugly Geena Davis rang up our order.

"You have a pretty boy," Pansy said to my mother as we turned to leave the store.

"Thank you, Ms. Pansy," my mother said, pulling me closer to her side as we left. It was only just before the door to the store squeezed shut and I heard Pansy and Ugly Geena Davis cackling that I realized "Ms. Pansy" was being ironic.

*

When I arrived at the first ballet class, the girls all giggled. I was too busy being excited to pay much attention to their reactions. (Had I paid attention, I might have seen a younger Sarah and Melissa making fun of me, which would have precluded the splinter situation from ever happening.) I was now in love with my slippers, regardless of their color; I had held them in my hands before going to bed every night, and when I finally had occasion to put them on in class, I felt like a legitimate dancer. I wanted to run up and down the room, wanted to tumble, wanted to flail my arms about and leap. I had once caught a quick glimpse of *Flashdance* (before my mother walked into the room and turned the TV off), and I wanted to be like Jennifer Beals, dancing like a maniac up and down shiny hardwood.

I thought we would be wild in action from the get-go, but everything was so slow, so measured. Learn this position, start from the toes up, position your leg this way, bend your wrist like this, focus on your hips, align your body like building blocks. We practiced the five fundamental ballet positions so many times that I thought my body would forget how to perform any other action. The more that Marcy walked past, correcting our poses, the woozier I became from the grape fog of her lacquered hair; there were several times when I thought I might pass out. The only thing that prevented me from doing so was knowing that I would never hear the end of it.

But I slowly came to understand the graceful wisdom of Marcy's teachings. I worked hard in her class, and it seemed like ballet was the first physical activity that used my energy effectively. Once I learned arabesques, *jettés, attitudes,* and pirouettes, I felt that I had a physical vocabulary for myself. There were, of course, increased jeers when the school found out that I was a *danseur*—or a "ballerina," they still called me, not knowing the proper term for a male ballet dancer—but for the first time, I felt that I had the upper hand. When Timmy Justice asked me for the millionth time why I hadn't worn my tutu to math class, I about-faced from him with the grace of a piqué turn. When Gary Martin leaped past me flapping his hands like wings while I tried to read on the playground, I jettéd away and finished with a pirouette on another bench. My backtalk became more physical than verbal. It was as if I could stop the nervous stammers when I spoke by finding another form of communication. Through dance, I could craft sentences that didn't falter, ideas that moved swiftly instead of bumping into the rickety machine of my mouth. And over time, I felt that when I did have to speak, my dancing informed my speech. In time, I learned to make words dance.

I want you to see the world the way that I see it. I want you to feel the lift of my body when I see the beauty of a pirouette or the ecstatic fact of a swishing sari. I want you to see the beauty in locking your face in colorful makeup and the beauty in twirling around and puckering your lips. I want you to know the meaning of dance, the things you do when no one is home, when you grab your ballet slippers and slap them on your feet and fly around the house, leaping over footrests and spinning around the island in the kitchen. I want you to understand the joy of pulling out several sheets from a paper towel roll and running around the empty house with it trailing behind you, then letting it go, letting yourself fall to the ground, and then letting the white streamer float onto you. I want you to understand how fluent my feet are, how they kiss the linoleum, the carpet, the kitchen table, armchairs, desks, beds. I want you to understand that this is the world, this is the acceptance, this is the big bear hug and the gold-star sticker. There is such beauty in the world, despite all of the harsh realities about it, and they are contained here for me. They are contained in a *plié*, in a *rond de jambe*. I have my own language. I *am* my own language.

In crafting my talent show act, I need to be as fluent as possible in Dance, and so I ignore Sarah and Melissa for the rest of today's lesson and focus on the picture of a graceful Krishna that I have in my mind. I imagine Him drawing His blue left foot through the dust of a sylvan pathway, and I know that I need to create an act that melds His mind and His body with my mind and my body. With that goal at the forefront of my thoughts, I decide to learn as much as I can about my past incarnation and fashion a ballet based on Him.

Choosing My Religion

I think the reason I've always read at a higher level is because I recognized my true friends from the get-go. Subconsciously, I always knew that I belonged with Frances Hodgson Burnett more than I belonged with pigtailed harlots. Therefore, just as my bed and the dance studio became sanctuaries, the local library became a safe haven.

It's an austere building to most people. It is as if the city officials want to scare the citizens into illiteracy (a tactic that seems to have worked, considering the number of kids in my school who have trouble reading). It is composed of three domed, brown brick edifices of different heights that have mildewy stripes of green growth wedged into the seams, and although the library was never a church, its windows are stained glass. Inside, stacks of books lie covered in dust and rainbow patches that the sunlight throws through the colored panes. The floor is wooden, knotted, and the sounds of feet, coughs, and turning pages echo easily. The librarians are so stereotypically librarian that they may have singlehandedly given rise to the stereotype: they are all female; they wear cardigans in earth tones; they wear spectacles; their hair is curly and gray; their long fingers are entwined in pulsing veins as they grasp a black stamp and press the due date in the back of the books.

The library is drafty, and when you pull a book from a shelf, an exhalation of wind greets you. There is a children's section located on the second floor, in a small corner in which the librarians have plastered various READ posters that feature random celebrities—Tom Selleck, Oprah Winfrey, LeVar Burton—but there are never any children there. In fact, the only people under eighteen who seem to enter this library are high school students. And me.

The fact that other children my age do not come here is comforting. The library is the only place in this city where I feel completely free from the usual classroom calumny. Books are much better companions to me than people. A book's content never changes, and yet it is always intriguing; something you read can mean something completely different to you at a different time. This is not the case with my classmates. If I've learned anything, it's that people can be devastating at any moment.

The Eastern Religions section of the library is, not surprisingly, rather small, and it is tucked away in one of the dankest corners of the building, right next to a forbidding stone doorway that leads to the bathrooms (which emit a mixed odor of must, urinal cakes, and soap). Doreen, one of the librarians, walks me to the section with extra-defiant, annoyed steps. Her beige pantyhose wrinkles at the ankles, and her olive, schoolmarmish skirt is loud in its polyester swishing. Doreen motions to the three shelves that house the "extensive" collection and turns on her cushioned heel without a word.

The books, unlike those in most other sections of the library, are not categorized alphabetically or even by subject, although most of them seem to be about Buddhism. I flip through books by Thich Naht Hahn, the Dalai Lama, and, terrifyingly enough, that guy from *Highlander*. On the bottom shelf, squeezed between *The Tao of Pooh* and *The Te of Piglet*, I find three fat books on Hinduism that, contrary to their A. A. Milne knockoff counterparts, are in pristine condition. I pull this trio of books off the shelf and tote the small stack to the nearest table, which is round and wide and looks like it might have come from the court of King Arthur. I open the first one, *A Journey Through Hinduism*, which is about five hundred pages long and bears a picture of the "Om symbol"—in essence, the number 30 with a swish over it. I flip to the index and look up "Krishna." There are several entries. I hum excitedly and flip to the section that seems the longest. A beautiful portrait of Krishna playing the flute greets me. Instinctively, my hand reaches up to my hair to fix it, as if this picture is the master bathroom mirror. The image on the page may not mimic my movement, but all the same, I sense a slight wink of a blue-lidded eye as I begin to pore over the information inside.

*

As I amass more and more information from the library, the desk in my bedroom becomes a maelstrom of papers. I have taken to drawing pictures of myself, which acts as an ample substitute for putting on makeup when I can't sneak into the master bathroom. I have spent so much time looking at my face in the mirror that I have learned every last detail: The roundness of my eyes, the whites so visible all around that the only reason one can tell I have eyelids at all is because my lashes are so long. My cute button of a nose, the tip of it rounded in a very un-Indian way. My high cheekbones. Every time I start a new drawing, I place my face on the page first, then use my markers to create a new outfit for myself. In one picture, I wear nothing but a headdress and a gown made of peacock feathers. In another, I wear a garment made out of sari-like material—bright red and magenta with frayed gold embroidery—but make certain that it does not look like a sari; as lost as I am in my art, I do not forget the fact that my parents might see my handiwork. In yet another picture, I am naked, although I stop the drawing at my waist, giving the impression that I am merely bare-chested.

In this picture, as in all the others, my skin is blue. My blue Crayola marker runs out of ink because I use it so much. After a while, instead of starting my drawings in black marker, using that dark color as the outline—a *kajol* of the body—I use only dark blue to do the outlines. I have an epiphany and excavate my pastel markers from the bottom of my large crafts bin. I pull out the sky blue marker and from then on use this marker to shade my skin. I do the outlines in dark blue, then fill in the curve of a shoulder or the shield of a pectoral with the lighter, peaceful blue. In one hasty move, I tear up the drawings I have done before, for the earlier blue seems too blunt. I am blue, but I am not a tough, hard, dark, frightening blue. My blueness is melodic.

Only after I have created a thick stack of drawings do I realize what I have been doing. I lift my pen off of the page, sit back in my chair, and realize that all along I have been designing my costume for the talent show ballet. I haven't started choreographing. I haven't even thought of the plot. But here I am, drawing intricate costumes for myself.

I put my pen down. *You should move in order*, I tell myself. I should be thinking of what the story is going to be, which particular episode or episodes of my past life I want to reenact, not crafting clothes for scenes I haven't even conceived. But no sooner have I put down my pen than I find myself drawing again, crafting my face, then surrounding it in a swath of orange flames. Never mind that I don't know how to rig a flaming costume. Never mind that I don't even know if this picture is supposed to be a costume. I draw what I feel.

I begin to tape my pictures on the wall in front of my desk. The prime spot is a few inches above the desk, center, and I have a featured drawing there every day. Meanwhile, I have the books I've checked out from the library stacked on one end of the desk, various pages sticking out where I have made Xeroxes and bookmarked their original pages with the copies.

My drawing habit follows me out of my bedroom into the classroom, as I find myself doodling all of the time. When we do problems in math class, I print my name and Mrs. Nevins's name neatly in the top right corner as instructed, then, once she begins talking into the blackboard, I lose myself. My thoughts become so ornate that even my numbers have curlicues. The curlicues evolve into peacock feathers, jars of butter, and when I am writing a "6" as part of a math problem, it will become one of my round eyes, wrapped in lashes. An equation is a body, the equal sign the stretch of its tummy.

One day, Mrs. Nevins teaches us a very grown-up word, especially for sixth graders; she learned the word, she says, from reading her "favorite book ever," *Jurassic Park*. The word is "iteration"—when something mutates into something else but retains something of its original form. In the same vein—in the same *blue* vein—my world becomes a series of iterated bodies. Or, to be more exact, one body. Mine is one body, iterated, like a god's.

*

From my studies, I discover that Vishnu has ten incarnations—from a bull to a tortoise to a lion to even a powerful midget. But it is Krishna who is the most memorable of these figures, even more memorable than Rama, the hero of the *Ramayana*. Krishna beats Rama because of all of his talents—his flute-playing, his ability to charm cowherdesses, and of course his skin. The most important thing I discover is that Krishna has an incarnation that has yet to appear. The tenth one is still waiting to happen. *Not anymore*, I think. *I* am the tenth incarnation.

I read about myself in the *Mahabharata*. As Doreen walks by my table in the library, she gives a worried glance at the huge tome before me, and I huddle over it and give her a dirty look. Her shoes scuffle away, and as I lean over the table again, I feel like they are the musical overture to the story happening on the pages before me, like the lion roaring before a Metro-Goldwyn-Mayer movie. I pull out a Butterfinger from my bookbag and unwrap it quietly, seeing as eating is not allowed in here. I nibble it in secretive bites as I lean back over the book.

Continuing the ages-long battle between good and evil, the demons of the world chose to infiltrate the ancient kingdoms of India by disguising themselves as rulers of the land. The most evil of these rulers, Kamsa, heard tell of a young woman named Devaki who, a sage foretold, would give birth to eight sons. The eighth, the sage said, would rise against Kamsa and kill him. Ruthlessly, the king had Devaki imprisoned and killed her first six children. Her last two sons, however, were switched with children from another town. One of the children who was switched to safety was Krishna, who was really Vishnu descended to Earth as a human child. Eventually, Krishna was taken to Gokula, where he was able to grow up without being hunted. All the same, he encountered trouble around every corner—often because he went looking for it. In fact, he seemed to invite it wherever he went, fighting with serpents and angry animals and killing demons along the way.

I tell Cody the findings of my studies during lunch, but as usual he's full of criticism.

"Keern, yer rippin' that story off of the Bible." He's eating cafeteria food again, a hamburger with orange cheese oozing from under the bun, which looks like a baseball mitt.

"I am not ripping anything off. The stories are there, in the Upanishads."

"I'm punishing you?"

"The *Upanishads*. The ancient Indian texts. The Indian Bible, basically."

"See—there! Ya just admitted it. *The Indian Bible.*"

"No, I mean—how else am I supposed to explain things to you? I have to use the words of your religion to explain mine to you."

"Why do ya have to explain it to me in the first place?"

"Will you just listen to me? It's a cool story. He escaped the hand of a king who wanted to kill him. The child could do anything."

"But that's the story of Moses."

"Well, I don't remember the story of Moses, but I know this isn't made up."

Cody proceeds to tell me the story of Moses, how he survived the wrath of Ramses, how he was sent out from Israel to escape the Pharaoh's blood-seeking soldiers. I smile during the whole story.

"What are you smilin' about?" Cody asks.

"Cody, Hinduism is much older than Christianity. We got there first. It's the Bible that ripped off the Hindus."

"It was not! Ya don' know what yer talkin' about. And listen to what yer sayin'. Snakes? Demons? Weirdos with blue skin? It sounds like a cartoon."

"Oh, but a man who walks on water—before turning it into *wine*—and heals the blind and dies only to come back to life is believable? It sounds more like an episode of Captain Planet."

With this, Cody picks up his tray, slides out of the cafeteria table bench, and harrumphs away, my fingers still frozen in the act of counting Jesus' achievements. He almost bumps into Sarah and Melissa, who giggle meanly at him as he lurches away.

For the rest of the day, I regret what I have said to Cody. I don't have anything against Jesus. In fact, Jesus is cool, as so many bumper stickers in this town would attest. He is a loving figure, a man of billowing white robes and white skin. In my studies, I have discovered that certain warriors, like Bharat, Rama's brother, had very white skin, a sign of purity and loyalty. So Jesus is pure and loyal. What is more, the feats that I numbered off to Cody are more Hindu than anything else; what could be more Hindu than controlling the elements, performing magical actions, transforming a normal human setting into a carnival of wonder and awe? Hinduism did come before Christianity, but why separate the two, anyway? In terms of vitality and spirit, isn't Hinduism Christianity and Christianity Hinduism? Our houses of worship may be vastly different, but there is a shared movement toward life, light, jubilance.

This is religion for me: jubilance. And so I go, again and again, into my sanctuaries, my bedroom, a blank page, and the library, where jubilant light from the stained glass oversees my new faith.

The Early Bird
Catches the Squirm

A fledgling god has to be fluent not only in dance and mirth
but in speech. Eloquence and godliness go hand in hand.
Or, more precisely, hand in *hands*. So it's no small benefit that
one person who is entirely supportive of my act is Mrs. Goldberg, the teacher with whom I study language arts after school
every Tuesday and Thursday.

Mrs. Goldberg is about as normal-looking a woman as you
could ever see. She is not too thin or too fat; her skin is not too
fair or too red; her brown hair is shoulder-length and partly
curly, caught between short and long. The only makeup she ever
wears is a muted shade of maroon lipstick. Her outfits consist of
cotton skirt-and-sweater sets and a modestly placed gold brooch
at her right breast. Her gray eyes are kind, with a middling number of wrinkles surrounding them, and she smells of nice perfume.

I started studying with Mrs. Goldberg because other teachers
didn't have the time to teach me. At least that is the reason I was
given. In truth, I think it's because they just don't know enough
to be able to teach me advanced language arts. One day, when
we were all going to read Roald Dahl's *Matilda* together in class,
Mrs. Nevins told us, "Class, we don't have a large *amount* of
books, so we'll have to share," and it took every last fiber of my

being not to slug her over the head for saying "amount" instead of "number." Oftentimes, with Mrs. Nevins, I feel like Roald Dahl's leading lady; Matilda was too brilliant a talent for the rest of her school, too, and had to best a hefty behemoth of a principal to find happiness. But she had Miss Honey, her demure and pretty schoolteacher, to help her. That is how I see Mrs. Goldberg, who always greets me by looking up from the papers she's grading, then gets up and pulls a chair close to her desk so we can study together.

"Hi, Kiran," she says when I enter her classroom today. She is the only person in this school who says my name properly. She even puts a small roll of the tongue at the "r," sounding altogether Indian when she does so. She pulls a chair next to hers and motions for me to sit down.

"How is everything going?" she asks, picking up her stack of graded papers and tapping it against the table to straighten it.

"Everything's great," I say, not wanting to share how unbearable the past few weeks have been.

"Kiran, I know that everything isn't great. Is there anything you want to talk about? Any, um, *splintery* situations?"

"Mrs. Goldberg!" I say. "How did you find out?"

"Oh, Kiran, word gets around. Believe me, no place is home to more rumors than the teachers' lounge. So what really happened?"

I proceed to tell Mrs. Goldberg everything, how Sarah and Melissa lured me to the fitness course, how they pushed me down and told me they wanted to see me naked, how I had to make up different stories to cover up the real reason I had a splinter in my butt. The whole time, Mrs. Goldberg listens quietly, nodding her head, the slight curls of her brown hair drooping as if expressing pity.

After I finish my story, Mrs. Goldberg sighs heavily and sits back in her chair. "Well, Kiran, the girls' behavior is totally unacceptable. I will be certain to speak with Principal Taylor about this. These girls must receive some form of punishment."

"No!" I say. "No, Mrs. Goldberg, please. Don't punish Sarah

and Melissa. You don't understand: if you punish them, they'll only hate me more. They'll only find other ways to make fun of me and hurt me. Please don't punish them."

"Kiran, running from the problem is no solution. You have to take a stand for yourself and prevent such things from happening again. If you run from Sarah and Melissa now, they won't only feel like they can make fun of you again—they'll feel it is *right* to make fun of other kids. And *that* is just not right! This is the opportunity to do something meaningful, Kiran."

"Mrs. Goldberg," I say, clasping my hands on the table and assuming my own teacher-like pose. "Let *me* teach *you* something now. If you tell Principal Taylor about what these girls did and Principal Taylor punishes them, then I look like a tattletale. And being a tattletale is the worst thing you can be."

I am speaking the truth. In the past, I thought that by telling on my classmates, I would put an end to the name-calling and the pranks. Once, when John Griffin, whose fists are like small hams, made me give him my lunch (a feast of *daal* and rice that he looked at with horror before throwing it in a huge Hefty trash can), I marched right into Mrs. Hatton's room nearby and told her what he had done. I added graphic detail, saying John unlocked the Ziploc of sweaty basmati rice and threw its contents at me. I said he forcefed me the *daal* like I was an infant and he was an insanity-ridden salesman from Gerber Baby Foods. Mrs. Hatton's red face cringed with anger and disgust, and she marched right out from behind her desk and went on the prowl for John Griffin. She found him playing with a couple of his friends out on the playground and immediately started yelling at him. I stood in the doorway from the school to the playground and watched her berate him.

Then Mrs. Hatton did the worst thing she could have done: she pointed back at me, who was cowering in the doorway. I know that she meant well, meant to show John Griffin how much he had hurt me by presenting me as a tortured victim. But even from my cowardly position, I could see the glint in John Griffin's eye. What Mrs. Hatton did not understand was that kids like John Griffin thrive on having such an effect. They enjoy seeing people cower. And even though the first solution you might proffer, then, is to react with courage instead of cowardice, it is not such an easy proposition. Because when John Griffin and his goons corner you in the same hallway the next day and slug you with their porcine fists, when they call you a *feggit*, when you feel the actual pain of it all—not some theoretical fear that has taught you that, *ouch, a fist in the gut must hurt*, but the real, real pain of a tightly clenched ball of fingers and fire pushing too far into your groin—then you know courage is simply an imaginary construct that people have made to disguise their inferiority.

"Mrs. Goldberg," I say. "Please don't make me a tattletale. Please. I beseech you."

I picked this handy phrase up from *Romeo and Juliet* and have been using it like it's going out of style. Whenever I say it, I imagine that I'm long- and raven-locked, with white cleavage stayed by a red velvet dress.

"I beseech you, Mrs. Goldberg. I can't deal with the extra pressure. I just can't." Even though I am not crying, I imagine that I am, one fat tear rolling off my chin and plopping onto the fake wooden top of her desk.

Mrs. Goldberg watches me without judgment. Her eyes don't criticize, but they also don't encourage. She reaches one hand forward and puts it on mine, her palm cold but soothing, like a poultice. (Another word from *Romeo and Juliet*; I said it the other day when my dad used Ben-Gay after his tennis match with Sanjay Uncle. My dad didn't seem to understand the word; he asked why I was talking about turkey.) Mrs. Goldberg's nods her head and relents, picking up her copy of *Warriner's English Grammar* and asking that I turn to page 132 in my copy.

I am learning how to diagram sentences. It's a pretty fascinating activity, one that unifies two of my greatest loves—drawing and language. Mrs. Goldberg teaches me how to find the subject and predicate of sentences, how to draw a spade-shaped diagram and place the subject on the handle and the predicate in the scoop like a piece of earth. The more intricate the sentences we choose, the more intricate the diagrams become, and I find today that there is little difference between the many-limbed bodies I draw in my blue reverie and the spindly drawings that are our grammatical fare. It doesn't take me long to voice this perceived similarity to Mrs. Goldberg, albeit accidentally.

"Drawing these diagrams is just as fun as drawing everything else," I say, finishing the last one with a final flourish of my pen.

"Really? And what, pray tell, have you been drawing?" Mrs. Goldberg says while taking a sip from her white coffee mug. The mug has a picture of a very red apple printed on it, the emerald sprig of a leaf curling off its top.

My first impulse is to tell her that I've been drawing pictures of myself from a past life, but something stops me. It feels weird even to me as I say it in my head, and I decide to proceed with more restraint.

"I've been drawing pictures of the Hindu god Krishna."

"Which god is that?" she asks, not in an ignorant way but in a genuinely concerned way.

"He's the blue-skinned god. The god of love."

"The god of love, huh? A regular Casanova, that one."

I let slide the fact that Mrs. Goldberg has just compared a pillar of my religion with a lecherous gigolo simply because she at least knows who Casanova was.

"So, what sort of pictures have you been drawing, Kiran?" Mrs. Goldberg asks, and once again, she mimics with ease the rolled "r" in the name.

I unzip my bright pink Jordache backpack and take out a stack of drawings that, with its bright hues of marker, looks sort of like the marked-up spelling tests on her desk. I straighten the stack like Mrs. Goldberg has done with those tests, and then I hand her the drawings. A bubble rises through me as I realize that she may not share my enthusiasm for this art, may think it odd, may think me a lunatic. As she flips through the drawings, I notice just how many peacock feathers I've drawn, just how garish some of the hues appear, and I have half a mind to grab the stack right back, smile awkwardly, and run out the door yelling, "See you on Thursday, Mrs. Goldberg!" But instead, I shift my focus from the drawings to Mrs. Goldberg's face, which is static. Each time she looks at another drawing, her face seems calmer and more unmoving; the drawings are terrifying her into paralysis. When she has finally turned the last page—a rainbow of color, with a sky-blue Krishna surrounded by magenta veils and glowing golden stars—she looks at me with a face that seems years younger, smooth.

In a few seconds I will find out that Mrs. Goldberg loves the drawings. Her face will break into a proud smile and she will embrace me, her body a cloud of Folgers and that nice perfume (I'm pretty sure it's Elizabeth Taylor's White Diamonds). She will flip through the pages one at a time, showing me what she likes about each one, telling me how creative they are and how sophisticated the artistry is even though I am so young. ("So young!" she exclaims over and over, as if proclaiming herself equally young with each squeal.) She will hug me again, then tell me that she is going to go to Mrs. Buchanan, the art teacher, first thing in the morning and tell her to put these drawings in our lobby's display case. She will make me feel wonderful, accepted, and she will make me return to my talent show with a renewed sense of purpose and artistic zeal.

But let us go back to that moment of not knowing. Let us go back to the blank expression on Mrs. Goldberg's face. For after the initial joy I feel at her acceptance, I realize that my first impulse was to expect the worst. I have been conditioned to feel ashamed. By my classmates. By the other Indian kids. By my father.

When someone motions to strike you, when someone throws something at you, you flinch or wince. But I have *always* felt that something is being hurled at me, so I guess I could say that I have lived my life in a perpetual flinch. Even though I draw my drawings in a sort of ecstatic flush, somewhere in my mind lurks a constant desire to prove people wrong, to best people by showing them how free my mind can be. It saddens me in this moment that I expect shame instead of the enthusiasm that Mrs. Goldberg so readily gives me. When, I wonder to myself, will my default emotion be confident, shameless optimism?

"Kiran, I can't wait to speak to Mrs. Buchanan about displaying these," Mrs. Goldberg says, taking a light pink Post-it note and writing on it with a black felt tip marker, "See Barbara." As in Barbara Buchanan. "Why don't you come to my office tomorrow during lunchtime and we'll speak to Mrs. Buchanan together?"

*

The next day during lunchtime, I meet Mrs. Goldberg in her office. She smiles when I enter the room, and I can't tell at first if it's because she's excited about my art or if it's because I decided to use some of my mom's Caress soap to shampoo my hair this morning and the stuff wouldn't wash out completely and now I have a shiny, sticky pompadour. I should have learned the last time when I tried this—it was the Oil of Olay that my mother uses on her face—and though it didn't transform my hair into the thick disaster it is right now, it made my hair shine really, really brightly.

Mrs. Goldberg doesn't dwell too much on this, although she does do a doubletake once I come closer. "Let's get a move on!" she says brightly, and I stride alongside her through the school corridors, feeling somewhat excited to be walking with a teacher I respect so much, and to be away from all the other kids, who are either finishing up their lunches or playing on the blacktop. I feel a twinge of guilt when I remember that I forgot to tell Cody I'd be missing lunch, and I imagine him hunched all by himself at the lunch table, munching on cold pizza or cold fries or warm ice cream. Although given our recent fight, he may not mind my absence after all.

Mrs. Buchanan's "classroom" is actually a big, unfinished space with cold, dusty cement floors, high ceilings striped with exposed, half-rusted I-beams, hanging lightbulbs that look like fiery tears, and long, wide tables covered in acrylic paint and modeling clay smudges and papier mâché. Mrs. Buchanan stands

in the middle of this avant-garde scene and is as unlikely an occupant as you could possibly imagine. She wears dark brown
leggings and a woolly cardigan. She has cropped gray hair and
thick glasses and enormous breasts that stick out like torpedoes.
She stands with her hands clasped against the soft hump of her
pelvis, as if she's been expecting us all morning. It's really a terrifying sight. Doesn't this woman have anything better to do
with her time than stand in the middle of a crazily constructed
room and wait for people to walk in the door?

It's a rather lonely profession, teaching. I guess Mrs. Buchanan
has to spend most hours of the day, most days of the week, in
this maddening room. Away from Mr. Buchanan, who must be
a heavy oaf of a man who loves beer and football and who wears
plaid flannel shirts and a John Deere trucker hat. Or maybe he's
a thin, mousy man whose eyes are level with his wife's ample
bosom and who works as a clerk in some depressing office. Or
maybe he's dead, resurrected for this odd woman in the projects
her students create—she sees his eyes reflected in a pair of blue
beads glued to a sock puppet's face or thinks of his warm breath
when she lifts the lid off the kiln and heated air wafts out.

"Hi, Linda," Mrs. Buchanan says to Mrs. Goldberg, and I
laugh internally at this salutation. It's crazy to think that teachers
have real first names, real lives, and I never think of Mrs. Goldberg as Linda. "Mrs. Goldberg" indicates a caring, encouraging
lady, but "Linda" conjures up a free-spirited woman who wears
long, flannel jumpers in the fall, the collars turned up like they
are in L.L.Bean catalogs, and who has a golden retriever and a
sandy-haired, rosy-cheeked husband.

"Hi, Mrs. Buchanan," Mrs. Goldberg says, putting her hands
on my shoulders and pushing me forward. "You know Kiran,
don't you?"

Boy, does she. There's one thing that I forgot to tell you about
Mrs. Buchanan. In addition to being my art teacher, she once
yelled at me really loudly.

It was when I was doing my own papier mâché head for her
class. In case you don't know how to make a papier mâché
head, it involves taking a balloon and blowing it up, then cover-

ing it with newspaper strips that are coated in a paste of flour and water and glue, then letting them dry and harden, then taking a pin and popping the balloon inside, and then painting this oval-shaped mass so that it looks like a head. I thought long and hard about what to do for mine—we only got one chance at it, and every fourth grade class had its papier mâché heads displayed prominently in Mrs. Buchanan's studio before a select few were hung out in the lobby. Since every other grade had Mrs. Buchanan for art class, it was always a big deal to have a nice papier mâché head displayed in her room because it was a sort of instant celebrity. Likewise, people who made terrible papier mâché heads became instant pariahs; Marcy Smith made a Madonna head that looked like someone had thrown acid in the Material Girl's face and teased her hair out into a wispy mess, and it was only a couple of days after it was displayed that people started transforming "Like a Virgin" into "Like a Monster" and serenading Marcy with it everywhere she went. So I thought long and hard about what I could do, knowing that I would have to execute the creation of this project deftly so as to avoid ridicule. Naturally, the first image that came to mind was Strawberry Shortcake, but I eventually decided against this because, in the freak instance that I made a terrible head, I couldn't bear the thought of it defiling SS's beautiful visage. Sculpting her strawberry hat alone would require some marvelously intricate papier mâché-ing, and I just couldn't risk it. SS must be perfect, and papier mâché is an imperfect art.

It was when I had my chin resting on my hand, daydreaming about the project, staring at the wall of the classroom and the paintings some other students had done, that I discovered my muse. One of the kids had painted a portrait of Early Bird, the bright yellow-and-pink mascot from McDonald's. Early Bird basically looks like Daisy Duck, except with yellow feathers and long brownish orange braids and an aviator cap and pink clothes. So I guess she looks nothing like Daisy Duck. (I just like the name "Daisy Duck.") Anyway, I was really inspired by her. Every kid would know who she was because we all live for McDonald's, and all of us, at some point in time, had had a birthday party

there, with stacks of puffy hamburgers and greasy golden fries
and soft-serve cones and a birthday cake with sugary red, blue,
and yellow balloons on its top.

Since she was accessible to boys and girls alike, Early Bird
didn't make for too girly a sight; I could get away with making
a feminine character because she represented something so exciting and delicious to all of us. And she presented a creative
challenge without being all that hard to conjure up. For starters,
Early Bird's head is bottom-heavy, not top-heavy like most heads,
and so I would have the chance to do something different: I
would flip my balloon upside down and use the narrow end of
the balloon as the summit of Early Bird's head, while the wider,
rounder end would form her plump chin. Painting her actual
face would not be too hard, and I could even place my old swim-
ming goggles on top of her head and paint their border pink.

The more I worked on the head, the more ingenious my ideas
became. I managed to sculpt Early Bird's beak out of leftover
papier mâché. The kids around me began to notice the exciting
genesis of this birdy creation over the next few weeks, and soon
their own projects began to suffer because they were too busy
watching me—how I painted Early Bird's bright eyes, placing
one tiny dot of white paint in each large black pupil to show the
light reflecting off it, and how I braided orange yarn to make
her hair. Each time Mrs. Buchanan walked by my table, I would
cover my head playfully and wag my finger at her, promising her
she would be impressed with the results.

Finally, we all had to present our projects to the rest of the
class. By this point, I had crafted a throw cloth out of Brawny
paper towels to prevent others from seeing Early Bird. When it
was my turn to present, I carried the Brawny-plastered orb to
the front of the room like Salome carrying the head of John the
Baptist. I pulled off the sheets in one swift move, and the classroom ooh'd and aah'd at what I'd done.

I expected Mrs. Buchanan to echo their awe, but instead, she
crossed her arms and frowned.

"Key-ran! How could you?"

As this was the last thing I expected to hear, I reacted with a mixture of sadness and confusion. Interestingly enough, so did the rest of the students in the class.

"Key-ran, what made you think of doing this bird as your head?"

"I like Early Bird," I said. "And so does everyone else."

"Is that all?"

"Yes!"

"Is that so?" Mrs. Buchanan got up from her desk and swayed her skirted self over to the wall opposite my chair. She put one thick index finger to the picture of Early Bird that had sparked my epiphany. She raised an eyebrow at me, an eyebrow knitted with consternation and exasperation. She looked like the ever-disappointed Bea Arthur in *Golden Girls*. "What about this?" she said.

I shuddered. "What about it?"

"Key-ran! How can you be so careless about copying!"

"Copying!" I said. "I didn't copy! I took inspiration from it!"

" 'Inspiration'! Oh, come on, Key-ran. That's a big word to use, even for you. I know the difference between inspiration and copying when I see it!"

"Just think of this as a form of flattery!" I said, almost screaming with purpose. "I am not copying. I am using Early Bird as an icon."

Mrs. Buchanan harrumphed loudly, in that way that conveys ignorance instead of informed anger.

At this point, Cody, bless his soul, piped up. "Mrs. Buchanan, I think it's really cool." To my surprise, the class agreed, a few similar supporting comments spewing forth. But Mrs. Buchanan would not hear of it.

"Class, I want you to learn something from this. There is a difference between inspiration and copying, and this is *copying*." With that, she walked over to me and tried to take the head from my hands. I held on to it for a second but had to let go; the force of her hefty pull was about to rip the damn thing in two. As Mrs. Buchanan headed back to her desk, the head swinging in her hand, I imagined Early Bird's face contorting into a pained scream. (Although I guess I can't say "scream," since Mrs. Buchanan would probably say I was ripping off Edvard Munch. Not that the ignorant cow would know who Edvard Munch is.)

Mrs. Buchanan made me stay after class that day and went on for almost ten minutes about how plagiarism—*plagiarism*, she called it!—was the most reprehensible of crimes and how I needed to learn that now before my lying got me into more trouble. Throughout the speech, she held Early Bird's head up as if it were a stinking thing. During the speech, Mrs. Buchanan kept saying, "Look at me," so I had to hold my head erect and look into her stern face. Inside, I was crushed, but the more Mrs. Buchanan spoke, the more I stuck out my chin. At one point, Mrs. Buchanan reproached me for not looking repentant. I assured her that I was, and yet something curled inside of me—a desire to be defiant.

"I don't know what it is with you people," she finally said, almost under her breath. At the time, I thought "you people" meant "smart people," and this became yet another reason for me to stick out my chin. "Listen, Key-ran," she said. "I have to go out of town tomorrow, so I don't have the time to give this the attention it deserves. But I hope you've learned your lessons here today. If I ever hear of you copying again, I will tell Principal Taylor, ya hear me?"

I nodded.

"*Ya hear me?*" she repeated more loudly, as if my nod had never happened.

"Yes!" I said.

"Good," she said. "Now you may go."

The next week, when I went back to art class (art class, after all, like gym and computer class, happened only once a week), I noticed a marked difference in Mrs. Buchanan's behavior. She treated me like a felon, frowning every time she passed me and showing extra caution when I asked to use the restroom. It was the first time I had ever felt that an adult hated me. Sure, I often got the feeling that I was annoying to my father or to certain teachers, but there was such coldness in this woman's reactions to me that I didn't know how to respond to her. Who, I thought, could so thoroughly detest a child? Especially someone who spent all of her time around children!

The artistic expertise behind my project could not be denied, but I still got a grade of Unsatisfactory on it. Obviously, Mrs. Buchanan's fury had overlooked my brilliance.

My mother was not pleased when she got my midterm report card and saw that I had an "average" grade in art class. Luckily, my earlier art projects—an etching of Mickey Mouse, a pink-glazed flowerpot, and a mobile made of strawberry images—had leveled out the overall grade, but I had never gotten just "average" reviews about my art. My mother raised an eyebrow at me over the kitchen table.

"I can explain," I said.

"Vell, you better, *beta*," she said.

"I—I didn't do so well on my last project," I said. My mother didn't know I had been crafting an Early Bird head; usually, I would tell her what exciting new projects I had under wraps, but I had kept this one a surprise so that she could be stunned at the finished product. That plan had obviously misfired. "It's the only time I've ever had something go wrong. I promise it won't happen again."

My mother clicked her tongue, a snappy sound of disappointment, and then got up to watch the news. Thankfully, she did not share my report card with my dad, who never asked to see my grades but simply asked my mother what she thought. For some reason, he always trusts her judgment in academic matters. I guess he sees it as a part of mothering.

That incident with Mrs. Buchanan cost me so many things. It made me lose a little bit of respect in my mother's eyes. It made me lose my perfect grade, since I ended up with a Satisfactory at the end of the term instead of my usual Excellent. It made me lose a coveted spot on the art classroom wall, and for a whole month I was forced to stare at the mediocre faces that the other students created. (Tracy Nichols was stupid enough to make her own Madonna to erase the memory of Marcy Smith's version.

Tracy's ended up just as deformed, with wiry yarn hair that skewed in several directions like a bundle of garden snakes, and the demonic masses that had composed "Like a Monster" brought out the ditty again.) But what the incident with Mrs. Buchanan did not make me lose was my artistic drive. I knew 100 percent that my head had been perfection. I carried this knowledge with me like it was a grenade.

As I stand before Mrs. Buchanan with Mrs. Goldberg now, I can feel that grenade inside me as surely as the rolling pump of my heart . . . and yet I know that it can disintegrate into a mess of cinders with a barb or something as simple as an arched, maligning eyebrow.

"Hi, Mrs. Buchanan," Mrs. Goldberg says as I half-hide behind her. Mrs. Buchanan wears a bemused smile so subtle that Mrs. Goldberg probably can't even see it.

"Well, hello, Mrs. Goldberg," my enemy says. "What is so urgent that it couldn't wait until after school?" She says this with a laugh as horrid as her scraped-up Payless flats.

"This is Kiran," Mrs. Goldberg says. "He's a star student of mine and—well, I would assume that you've met Kiran already, Mrs. Buchanan, since he must have been in your art class. Surely you must realize that he is a very talented artist."

Mrs. Buchanan smiles that same bemused smile and looks down at me for a second. Or pretends to look at me. She looks instead at the patch of cement floor to my right, then looks back up at Mrs. Goldberg. "Yes, I seem to recall having this young fellow in my class. A good artist, but he could use some more discipline."

Mrs. Goldberg is unfazed by this criticism. "Well, it seems that Kiran benefits most from his own study," she says. "He recently showed me some drawings that he did, and I think they are spectacular. So spectacular, in fact, that I think they deserve to be displayed in the lobby."

Here is where Mrs. Buchanan flinches a little bit, but she is saved: a group of students scurries by the doorway, and she uses the distraction of their passing as a way to conceal her distaste.

She rallies, however. "Well, Mrs. Goldberg," she chimes, "how lovely! And what exciting project does this young fellow have in store for us?"

Stop calling me "this young fellow," you ignorant excuse for a teacher.

Mrs. Goldberg insists that we take my stack of drawings to Mrs. Buchanan's desk. Mrs. Goldberg points out the things that she likes, remarking how she loves the peacock feathers in particular. I stand by, flattered at how much Mrs. Goldberg is gushing. It is such a vindication to see someone so enthusiastic about my work at the very desk where Mrs. Buchanan gave me such a stern talking-to. In the middle of another of Mrs. Goldberg's effusive statements, I look to the wall where my Early Bird might have once hung. Right now, Mrs. Buchanan has displayed the crayon drawings of rainbows that her first graders have done. My first grade rainbow had been the most brilliant and eye-catching, folding over itself into a bow tie shape.

There is a slight shift of Mrs. Buchanan's shoulders that gives away her rejection before it even occurs. She says, "I'm sorry, Linda, but I can't put these drawings out there."

"And why not?" Mrs. Goldberg says, truly surprised. She crosses her arms in front of her. "They're spectacular drawings, Barbara."

Whoa—now Linda's pulling out the first name!

Mrs. Buchanan stands up and crosses her arms, too. "I'm sorry, Linda, but these are religious drawings. I have an order from Glenda specifically saying that we cannot assign or display religious drawings. I'm sorry, but that's my final word."

Glenda is Principal Taylor. It's over.

Mrs. Goldberg and I head back to her classroom, leaving a smug Mrs. Buchanan in her classroom exactly the way she was when we entered—arms crossed in the middle of the room. Mrs. Goldberg is visibly upset when we get to her desk, but her students are starting to filter in, so she cannot keep the conversation going too long.

"I'm so sorry, Kiran," she says. "If I had known she was

going to be such a—such a stickler, I would never have tried anything. I just thought this might be a nice change for you, given the whole . . . splinter thing. Mrs. Buchanan does have a point, though. These are religious drawings, and that's not a point you want to press." Then she says, under her breath, "*Believe me.*"

I ask her what she means.

"Oh, well, let's just say that it's not always the easiest thing being 'Mrs. Goldberg' around here. . . ."

I don't know what she's talking about. I mull it over all day, as well as the next morning. As usual, it is Cody who puts two and two together for me at lunch.

"She's Jewish," he says. Today, he's eating a delicacy that the cafeteria calls "hot turkey on bun." It looks like woodchips sautéed in mayonnaise and squeezed between two waffles. "Goldberg is a Jewish last name."

"How do you know that?"

"How *don't* you know that?" Cody says. He chomps through the off-white slime in his sandwich.

I don't want to upset Cody again, but I'm too intrigued by Mrs. Goldberg to stop. "No one knows that," I say. "There aren't even any Jewish people in this school."

"Sure, there are. I think there are nine. Rachel Goldstein, Hannah Schwartz, Beth Meister." He thinks for a second. "I know there are more."

"But how do you know they're Jewish?"

"Their last names. They have Jewish last names."

Cody goes on to explain to me how this works, how people with "stein" or "berg" at the end of their names are Jewish and how there are other, more subtle names that you can peg as Jewish if you think about it. It's the first time I've ever heard of such a thing. I've always felt that I'm the only person who has a different-sounding name, but it turns out that these other kids know what it's like to feel out of place, too.

So Mrs. Goldberg's Jewish! It endears her to me more than ever before because it means she knows where I'm coming from.

I have a thought: if Mrs. Goldberg knows what it feels like to be an outcast, then she would truly appreciate my talent show act. It's my duty to show Mrs. Goldberg, and everyone else, that you can stand up for yourself in subtle but meaningful ways. Like papier mâché, we might be fragile, but we can also be things of beauty.

Singh Singh

Krishna is gregarious. He is full of merriment and goodwill, and he is the center of attention. In folktales, he assumes a Scheherazade-like status, beguiling people with his charm and sending both yogis and milkmaids running his way in party-hearty delight.

To that end, neo-Krishna is headed tonight to a good ole-fashioned hub of Indian chicanery.

Every weekend, our circle of Indian families has a party. It never fails—every Saturday night, there will be one, and no one ever makes plans for Saturday night because it is just a given that you will have to load up the family in the Mercedes, drive twenty miles to the house of choice—the mother of the family carrying a potluck dish—and mingle from 7 p.m. to 1 a.m. with the Indian subset in your region. Very rarely do different Indian social circles mix and mingle with each other outside of the temple. At parties, North Indians mix with North Indians; South Indians mix with South Indians. On the rare occasion when the two subsets coincide, it is in small doses: one South Indian family, a little darker-skinned, will be in the midst of a room of caramel-skinned Punjabis, like a chewy chocolate center. Or a North Indian family, used to lighter, more delicate food, will stand in the corner and gorge itself on decadent South Indian treats like *dosai*. But for the most part, the various groups stay split, and sometimes I amuse myself by imagining how many different types of Indians are moving like so many marbles on hardwood to their respective fetes. I imagine a wide-pan shot like they do in the movies sometimes, like in *Rain Man*—part of which was shot in this Cincinnati paradise—when Tom Cruise is living up to his surname and cruising down the highway, and the camera, like a robin, glides down from the sky, lowers itself to the car, and zooms into the plush vehicular upholstery to reveal the actions inside. Instead of Tom, there is my dad, one hand on the wheel, my mother, a tangy-smelling fireball of curry in her lap, and I, staring out the window above the red and white lights on the highway and imagining cameras zooming into carfuls of Indians.

Tonight, the Family Sharma is heading to a "get-together" at the house of Neha Singh, the young beauty who has temporarily fallen prey to her braces. Her mother, Nisha, is a slender beauty, save for the enormous bags she has under her eyes from serving her husband day and night. The Singhs run a very tight ship: their house is absolutely spotless, with marble floors and plastic over everything that can have it: the sofas, the remote controls (of which there are many—TV, VCR, stereo, satellite), even some of the brass door handles. Nisha Auntie reuses Ziploc bags. Harsh Uncle is known for conserving electricity, and he'll turn off the lights in empty rooms and yell, "Vhat is this—*Diwali*?!" referring to the annual Hindu festival of light. There are entire sections of the Singhs' house that are never open to guests and are barely open to the Singhs themselves—Harsh Uncle's study, one of the house's parlors (which is "just for show," they say), the master bedroom, the laundry room adjacent to the garage. Considering the abbreviated space that remains after this No Trespassing mentality, it is a marvel that the Singhs can keep their house so neat and clean, especially considering that Neha has a ten-year-old sister, Kirti, who spends most of her time in her room reading but who turns into a whirling dervish when she's not studying. When their parents are in sight, these children are two of the most obedient people you could ever imagine. When the parents disappear, the children become just plain rude. They never learned proper manners from their parents, only forced reticence, and there is no more surefire way to engender impoliteness in children than this method.

The Harshness, then, is one of the reasons why I am not looking forward to this evening. The other, though, is the armada of kids from the temple Sunday school.

One blessing that I have in my life is that none of the other kids from our set goes to my school. We kids are split among four or five different school districts, our parents living in different suburbs of Cincinnati. Therefore, the only Indian kids with whom I interact on a normal basis are the Punjabi kids at these parties.

"Normal" is a troubling word, though. I have never been able to decide which life of mine is normal, my school-bound American one or my party-bound Indian one. On the whole, I seem to think of my school life as my real life. I spend five days out of the week at school, and the people there, since they are part of my everyday life and part of my hometown and people that I see at the supermarket or at local restaurants (on the rare occasions when we eat out), are the ones that matter on a regular basis. I do not, on the contrary, think of Indian kids as my reality. I just don't see them all that often, so I feel like I always have to learn them again. When you are used to seeing a lunch line at the cafeteria that ends with trays loaded with pizza, milk, and sandwiches, it is hard to think of a dinner line of rice, curry, and yogurt as "regular." When you are used to expending most of your energy on living with the difference of your skin, it is hard to think of people whose skin is the same as yours as "regular."

Whenever our families get together, they render suburban streets virtually unusable. The cars line both ends of the street, sometimes not even facing the direction in which cars are supposed to move. After all, people drive on the left in India, and since we are here, walking into the Singhs' behemoth of a house with a desire to be wholly Indian all evening, it is only fitting that we should drive as they drive. When in Delhi, do as the Delhians do.

When Nisha Singh opens the door, she is wearing a stunning orange-yellow sari, a group of gold bangles encircling each of her forearms. The bags under her eyes are grayer than ever, but she has pulled her hair back into a bun and fastened it with a lovely gold barrette. When Nisha Singh opens the door, what she sees in the doorway is an odd trio. Under his beige windbreaker, which he wears open, my father is wearing a frayed, maroon sweater with the collar of a white dress shirt popping out limply at the neckline. Even though he has tried to comb his hair and part it firmly to one side, it is a storm, tangled and tousled, attempting perfection but missing its target. My mother is wearing a pistachio-colored *salwaar kameez* with her white cardigan over it, and her hair is in a ponytail, streaks of gray at her temples, over the crest of her head, in the knot of her pink scrunchie, and down her back. I am dressed in a Cincinnati Reds sweatshirt that my dad got for free at the supermarket during a special promotion, and I am wearing a pair of baggy Skidz jeans, a luxury for which I begged my mother in an attempt to be cool like the other kids in my class.

"*Namaste*, Shashi," Nisha says, putting her palms together and bowing her head slightly.

"*Namaste*," my mom says, stepping through the doorway and bowing with her dish of curry held in front of her, as if Nisha Auntie is a bouncer and this dish our ticket to enter the house.

"*Namaste, ji*," Nisha Auntie says to my father, who returns her nod a little too enthusiastically—as all men in our circle do, so taken are they with Nisha Auntie's looks.

She closes the door, and the three of us Sharmas proceed to take our shoes off and leave them by the doorway with a battalion of other shoes. It looks like we're all French children leaving our shoes out for Father Christmas. The three of us walk through a small hallway into the Singhs' kitchen, which is grand. In the center of it is an island that could be a sacrificial table in biblical times. Around the island, all of the aunties are arranging their potluck dishes, a chorus of crinkling foil resounding. Every dish is in a stainless steel container, and the arrangement of the containers looks like a futuristic city. In one squat pan is a steaming pile of rice, dyed yellow with turmeric. In another is a stack of oily *roti*, insulated with a layer of soft paper towels. Dishes of curried peas, potatoes, okra, cauliflower. Bowls of yogurt, butter, and chutney (tamarind, mint, coconut). In a discreet corner of the kitchen counter sits a large tin of assam tea leaves and a full tea serving set; Indians need their tea, or at least the promise of it, as soon as they finish eating.

"*Arre*, Kiran *Beta*, *kya hall hai?*" asks the heavy Rashmi Govind when I walk in. She bounds toward me, and before I can turn my head, she has pulled me into her cleavage.

"Hello, Neha," says my mother in addressing the little princess, who has entered in a demure beige *salwaar kameez* and who takes my father's jacket and my mother's cardigan with a garbled "*Na-mush-te*," the result of her metal mouth. Her hair is clasped behind her head in the same style as her mother's. As always, despite her tooth gear, she is lovely. The way she slings the jacket and the cardigan over her arm, the way she scurries out of the kitchen and into the foyer, up the stairs to her room, where she will put the outerwear with the rest of the visitors' coats and things on her bed—it is graceful, ladylike. The bitchy ones always seem to master this grace so well.

I say hello to all of the aunties, my palms together, my head bowing dutifully. My mother once told me that the Indian child who always says hello to every elder in the room will forever be well-loved, and so far as I can see, her advice was sound. The aunties always greet me enthusiastically because I know how to observe decorum. Anita Gupta screeches laryngitically when I ask if she has brought her spicy *channa* again. Ratika Auntie dryly offers some murky Hindi as I say hello, and Kavita Auntie expounds on it with more Hindi. Here, in the crucial opening moments of this get-together, my eye for ostentation serves me well.

Next, I head into the den, where the men are comfy on sofas. Each of them sits with one leg crossed over the other, ankle resting on knee. As in temple, most of them wear a white dress shirt, the fabric thin as a shroud, the outline of a white V-neck T-shirt visible from underneath. Some of them, like my father, augment this look with a sweater or a blazer from the seventies—not to make a retro statement but to make a vocational one. These are men who do not usually change before they come to parties; they like working, they like looking like they work, and they like looking like they just came from work. When I say hello to them, they eye me with caution, as if they can see me becoming more American, and less Indian, each moment. Naveen Uncle's stutters upon seeing me pretty much sum up all of these men's unsure feelings about my presence here.

The mothers hang out in the kitchen. The fathers hang out in the den. The kids hang out in the basement.

Indian kids very rarely hang out in each other's bedrooms. Hanging out in bedrooms means that we are having sex, so we are relegated to the basement. This is somewhat true of American families, but on the Indian end, everything is done ten times more vehemently. Every Indian house that we go to has a well-finished basement—a huge investment, in the sense that it basically means paying for a third level of the house. But if tons of money—extra rolls of plush carpet, wide, white drywall, and shiny brass fixtures—can ensure that the kids will avoid a bed, Indian parents are more than glad to cough up the dollars. Indeed, during this early '90s boom, most Indian families, like mine, have graduated from their first, split-level, '70s-style homes and have built their own homes. Not with their own two hands, of course, but they have provided the sturdy, glint-eyed, firm-handshaked American men in this area with homes to build and money for those homes. And so, in this stage of the Indian domestic evolution, the finished basement has become as standard an amenity as a study where the Man of the House can take calls from frantic patients/review investment accounts/worry about the next twenty years/avoid his wife.

As I walk to the basement door, I can hear the sounds of the other kids playing. The loudest noise is that of a Ping-Pong ball being slammed against rubber-sheathed paddles. The boys love Ping-Pong so much that it is hard for me to picture any of them without seeing a wide, green table in front of him. The smack of the ball resonates throughout the basement and into the air ducts that cross the basement ceiling. The echoes are *so loud*, and I think the only reason why they don't drive the parents crazy is because the mothers have the hum of the stove fan and the fathers have their laughter and booze to drown them out.

In addition to the ball, I can hear squeals, the boys' and girls' almost indistinguishable from each other. As I open the basement door, I find myself wishing the room were full of only girls. Even though I have endured some difficult situations with females recently, I identify better with the way they express themselves. The girls talk of things that interest me, things like *Saved by the Bell* and *Full House* and Barbie. To me, they are more than just girls. They are a manner of speaking, peppered with slang and cast in a joyous lilt. But the boys talk of cars, of video games, of sports. I don't like those things. Or, on the rare instances when I do, it's for other reasons. I like cars when I can dance on them. I like video games when I get to save the damsel in distress, like hopping to the rescue of Princess Toadstool in *Super Mario Brothers*. And I like sports when—

Never mind, I never like sports.

I descend the stairs and see a familiar scene. Handsome Ashok is playing Ping-Pong with nappy-haired Ajay. Ashok moves the paddle effortlessly; instead of standing up to the table and pecking at the ball, he stands a foot behind the table and when the ball comes toward him, he holds out his paddle and catches the ball on it, as if nestling it, then swerves his arm up and across, releasing the ball to the other end of the table, where Ajay lunges forward to hit it and loses it in the net. While Ajay reaches his paddle across the table to scrape the ball back to him, I look to the other end of the room, where Shruti the Big Bitch is sitting on a white wicker bench. Fat Neelam is sitting on the stone frame

of the fireplace, her plump arms plopped on her knees. She is listening attentively to what Shruti is saying, as is Shelley, who is
trying to compensate for the sharp almost-hook of her nose
with an enormous gold nose ring looped through it. In the corner
behind the girls, Ashish and Arun are playing Egyptian Ratscrew.

At first, I'm not sure how to enter the daunting hubbub of the
basement, but then I remember that there's a TV under the slant
of the staircase, so I whip around when I get to the bottom of
the stairs and plop myself on the couch opposite the tube. I flick
through channels until I come to *Antiques Roadshow*. On the
screen, a spaghetti noodle of a woman with huge plastic glasses
affixed to her face and a wispy mess of mousy hair that looks
like she just put her hands on one of those lightning balls they
have in children's museums is having an ornate mantle clock ap-
praised by a silver-haired man. She looks so uncomfortable and
can't seem to figure out what to do with her hands. She clasps
them in front of her, then puts one on her hip and the other on
the table, as if attempting to do her best *Price Is Right* Girl impression. Then she puts both hands behind her back, like a little
child being complimented in public by a doting parent. It doesn't
even seem like she is paying attention to what the man is telling
her, despite the stream of exciting words that is pouring from his
mouth. At one point, the rhythm of his speech slackens, and a
quizzical tone creeps into it. Suddenly, I become very concerned
about this poor woman. She grows ever more visibly addled as
the appraisal progresses, and the more she fidgets (her arms are
now behind her head), the higher the potential heartbreak becomes. I well up inside. Nothing gets me like this moment before the blow—the moment of hope overtaken by fear—and
even though this woman and I have nothing in common, I think
her to be a part of me.

"Buella," the silvery man says, "You brought in this antique
mantle clock that has been in your family for three generations.
Now, you had an appraisal done about eleven years ago?"

"That's correct!" Buella says, with a fan of one hand accen-
tuating the GRITTY EXCITEMENT of her situation.

"And at that time, the curator told you that the clock was worth roughly a thousand dollars?"

"That's correct!" Buella repeats, fanning her hand again.

"Well, Buella, I must tell you that, after my assessment today, even taking into consideration the gold plating around the edge and the topaz-encrusted crest here, this clock is worth *only*"— there is a glint of melodrama in his voice, tinged with a bit of sarcasm, as if he is just pulling our legs, so that Buella and I both lean forward, our hands flailing around us, ready to hear the grand figure Mr. Silver is about to dispense to us, which is— drumrollllllllllllll—

"This show sucks," Arun says, plopping his fat butt down on the couch and flipping channels away from Buella and her Moment of Truth. We are flipping away, away, through reruns of *M*A*S*H* and a grave-faced Peter Arnett on CNN and a Saturday night showing of *Pretty in Pink* to ESPN, which Arun settles on with a grin and a hefty lean against the back of the couch, remote propped on his knee. I want to turn around and scream at him, pummel him, grab the remote back and see if I can catch Buella while she's either leaping for joy or sobbing. But instead I lean forward and dip a Dorito into a small dish of salsa that Nisha Auntie has put out for us.

"So, Kiran, what's new?" Arun asks, taking my cue and grabbing a handful of Doritos at once, the orange dust on them covering his hands like the turmeric that stains my mother's hands when she cooks.

"Umm, nothing too new," I say, surprised that Arun is speaking to me in so normal a manner. "School."

"Besides school."

"Well, we have the fall talent show coming up."

"Talent show? Talent shows are for dorks."

Even though Arun looks ridiculous right now, Dorito crumbs all over his shirt front, chubby cheeks rising and falling as he chews, he has a certain authority in calling me a dork for a reason I can't quite put my finger on. Or I guess I can put *a* finger on it, as I stand up and flick him off gracefully, then turn on one heel and stomp off. I give a quick glance back to see his non-plussed reaction, but he is entirely engrossed in his ESPN, not having even seen my effrontery.

I walk over to the girls. I sit down on the floor next to Neelam.

"Zack is totally hotter than Slater," she is saying. It seems that the girls have this conversation during every single party—that is, who the hottest guy on *Saved by the Bell* is. "Zack has nice hair and nice arms."

"Please," says Shelley, putting one hand up in protest. "Slater is totally hotter. You think Zack has nice arms? Slater has huge *muscles*. That shot of him lifting weights during the theme song? He's got a perfect body."

Neelam rolls her eyes. I can see her large frame stiffen a little bit when Shelley speaks the words "perfect body."

"Hi, Kiran," Shruti says. "Who do you think is hotter, Kiran—Zack or Slater?" She stares at me for a second, then laughs, the other girls joining in. I laugh, too, making a melodramatic sourpuss face as if to say, *Oh, Shruti, you're such a card!*

"Here's a good question," Shelley says. "Who do you like better—Kelly, Jesse, or Lisa?"

" 'Whom do you like best?' " I say.

"What?" Shelley says, confused.

" 'Whom do you like best?' " I repeat.

"Wait—I just asked you guys that," Shelley says, still confused.

"No, no," I say. "I'm not asking you. What you said was grammatically incorrect. It should be 'Whom do you like best?' Not 'Who do you like better?' See, 'who' becomes an objective case because it is the object of the sentence. As for 'better,' there are more than two possible options given, so you can't say which one of the three is better because it's not a one-on-one comparison. You have to choose which is best of the three. You see what I mean?"

She looks at me as if I just smacked her mother across the face. "You're such a show-off, Kiran."

Show-off.

"I just thought you might want to know what was right!" I say.

"Well, when I want your opinion, I'll ask you for it."

"Well, in that case, my opinion is that I like Lisa best."

She crosses her arms and pouts, then rolls her eyes to the other girls, who laugh and proceed to ignore me as they discuss other TV shows—*Full House* (of course), *Growing Pains* (Neelam decides that Kirk Cameron is the hottest guy on TV, an opinion with which Shruti agrees), and *Beverly Hills 90210*, which warrants a half-hour discussion that touches on everything from Shannen Doherty's lopsided face to Jenny Garth's good skin to Luke Perry's forehead to Jason Priestly's hair and, since it's the same style, whether his hair or Zack "Saved by the Bell" Morris's hair is better.

"I like Zack's hair best," Shelley says, shooting me a sharp glare. Annoyed at her literal and grammatical ignorance, I cough out, "Better."

Then Shelley pulls the trump card out. She starts speaking in Hindi. Right away, my thorough comprehension of all things *Saved by the Bell* deteriorates into a heady mix of intricate, nasal Hindi sounds peppered with the same character names. Shelley gives one last dismissive look at me before smiling slightly and continuing her conversation. She knows I'm the only one whose Hindi is terrible at best.

Why is this? I often ask myself. Have I been lazy? There were times when my mother tried to sit me down at the kitchen table and teach me the alphabet or a few choice words, but I eventually pushed away the books that she gave me, opting instead to sing to myself in my room or dance in the backyard or have another tryst with Estée. Or were my parents too focused on learning English to devote enough time to my Hindi? I still remember the two of them listening to this set of white cassette tapes that had a man not unlike my Richard Simmons ballet coach indicating the proper ways to pronounce certain English words. They would sit on the couch—the same one my mom sat on crying that day when my father threw the pillow at her—repeating the sounds on the tape like zombies as they stared blankly at the tea in the their cups. Or were they just busy? Was my mom too industrious frying *puri* in a dark well of vegetable oil to beg me back to the kitchen table to study? Was my father too busy calculating figures in his head, his face greenlit by the accountant's lamp on his desk? Whatever the reason, I am walking away from Shelley now.

I don't even dare join the Ping-Pong, although I do give a quick look at the game and try to imagine myself playing Ashok and hitting the ball like he does. Then I realize that it's not as Ashok's *opponent* I'm imagining myself but as Ashok himself.

I venture upstairs and pass the kitchenful of aunties again. My mother is sitting at the kitchen table eating a handful of dried chickpeas. Ratika Aggarwal is droning in that same dry tone next to her and my mother is nodding her head. To anyone else she would seem attentive and engrossed, but to me she is simply considerate. She is not really paying attention to Ratika Auntie's monologue about the prices of Indian groceries these days. My mother is too big a spendthrift to listen to Ratika's monetary talk; she hears my father talking about these things enough already. For my mother, thinking of money probably conjures up the same vision that I have: my father hunched over stacks of bills and spreadsheets and indigo-inked receipts. Instead, the glaze over my mother's eyes tells me she is thinking of sliding her foot into a new pump, its tan belly rounding under the pressure. I catch my mother's attention for a second. She smiles and shakes her head from side to side in that *khatak* way, then lifts her chin and raises her eyebrows in question, as if worried that I am in trouble. I shake my head "no" and point toward the bathroom that is tucked around the corner in a dark cove, indicating that I have to use it, even though I don't. As I duck into it, my mother relaxes and returns to Ratika Auntie's conversation.

I flick on the light and the fan and shut the door. The Singhs' house is decorated very much like ours, which is to say that it's pretty bare. It is all white, only the pearly pink of the bottled hand soap and the peach flip of the hand towel adding color to the surroundings. Even the trash can is the same off-white as the floor, as if it's an animal blending in with its surroundings. I put down the lid of the toilet and sit on top of it, resting my elbows on my knees.

By this point, you must think I'm kidding. No one spends parties like this—in the bathroom, staring at a plain white wall, tracing his finger along its blank surface, standing in front of the bathroom mirror and imagining another crest of peacock feathers creeping over his head. No one takes the hand soap bottle and uses it as a microphone and mimes singing "One Moment in Time." No one turns on the hot water and puts his hands under the running water and just stands there, *just stands there for five minutes*, clearing his mind. But why shouldn't I do this? It's called a restroom, after all. I am just trying to get some rest.

I stay in here for about twenty minutes until the locked doorknob has been jiggled for the third time by someone waiting. When I emerge, I expect the person to accost me, but it seems that he or she has gone to use another restroom. I consider going downstairs and wresting the remote control from Arun to return to *Antiques Roadshow*, but I chicken out. I can't go into the den and join the men because kids never hang around such conversations. I consider joining my mother and the aunties in the kitchen, but then I will have to suffer Rashmi Auntie's flesh again. And so it is upstairs I go, my socked feet light on the cool marble. I make sure to keep an eye out for Neha, who seems to have disappeared but as the eldest child of the party-giving family must perform various errands throughout the house.

The coolest part about the Singhs' house is the prayer room they have upstairs. It is no bigger than a closet—in truth, I'm sure the contractor who built this house thought that's what it was going to be before the Singhs requested him to slap marble tiles all over its walls, its floor, even its ceiling—but the Singhs have crammed all of their shiny Hindu icons into it. For each god, there is a painting depicting Him or Her and then a miniature gold statuette of the same god below the framed picture. A sturdy, bright pink Hanuman lifts a pile of emerald land into the air above Him while His metal remora lifts a smaller patch below. A fat Ganesh, His elephant head brilliant white, smiles over a similarly gleaming round chunk beneath Him. I spot myself in the corner—in the corner!—playing my silver flute sweetly while I play a gold flute below myself. But overtaking all other gods in the Singhs' shrine is Lakshmi, the beautiful goddess of wealth and prosperity. Copiously and beautifully armed, She drops shiny gold coins, strung on wires, into the water around Her while Her mini-self mimics the same movement. Hers is the only statue that is not gold metal; instead, it is porcelain, accented in bright hues, the skin white but Her crown orange, sari magenta, lotus flower pink. If unobstructed by my body, Her eyes, rimmed in a thick coat of *kajol*, would stare out of the painting, through the doorway, and down the long hallway to the high arch of the master bedroom, which is guarded by two large, sliding pine doors.

I don't know what possesses me, but I take the picture of Lakshmi off its pedestal, kiss it, then switch it with the portrait of me. Then I switch the corresponding statues, kissing the porcelain Lakshmi, so small that I basically engulf Her crowned head. I make sure my portrait is centered, my statue as well, then flick off the light and continue my wandering.

As I expected, Neha's sister, Kirti, is in her room reading. She has spread herself widthwise across the bed with a book in her hands. I wander in, half-expecting Kirti to throw a fit, but she hardly makes a noise when I enter. She's one of those whiny brats who goes through manic-depressive nadirs when she has so fully exhausted herself that she no longer possesses the strength to be the bitch she is meant to be.

Kirti is a tiny girl, with a narrow face and thick eyebrows that could stand a tweezing or two. She could go either way when she grows up—she could develop into a presentable Indian girl or an ugly hag. (My mother has four terms to describe the looks of young Indian girls: "ugly," "passable," "presentable," and

"That is the type of girl you vant to marry, Kiran.") I look at the pastel green cover of Kirti's book and see that it's a Baby-sitters Club book. I have read my share of those books—a short rainbow of them takes up half a shelf on one of the bookcases in my bedroom—so I begin to talk to Kirti about the characters. I talk about Kristy and Dawn and how much I love the name Stacey. The book slowly droops down as Kirti listens more intently to me, surprised that I know as much about these girls as she does. Girls always seem so surprised about how much I know about things like this, and yet I don't see anything all that crazy about it. These are great books, and there's no shame in knowing a lot about them. Just because they're about girls doesn't mean they're only for girls. How do boys expect to understand girls unless they learn their manners? The best way to get to know a girl is to read her books, play with her toys, like her TV shows—that way, you link your interests to hers. And you prime yourself to find a girlfriend.

Kirti changes during our conversation. This is the girl who once cut off another girl's hair with a butter knife at a wedding because the girl said her sari was wrapped wrong. But Kirti engages in our discussion with great gusto. As the conversation progresses, she starts calling me Kiran Sahib, *sahib* being a term that Indian kids use to address an elder. I feel proud to have touched someone like this; it's the first time in a long while that I feel heartened by someone at one of these parties, and for a second it actually makes me feel guilty for having tampered with the Singhs' icons. At one point, Kirti lifts herself up and hugs me, burying her head in my chest, and I feel for a second that she loves me. I feel for a second that . . . she is my Radha. *Girlfriend*. Pride sifts into my chest as Kirti continues to hug me. The peacock feathers at my crown multiply.

Finally, I pull away and take my leave, waving heartily to Kirti. I do not want to tread too heavily on such a delicate courtship. She smiles, then returns to her book with more energy than before, a Cheshire cat grin on her thin face.

From downstairs, I can hear Rashmi Auntie calling, "Dinner!

Dinner's ready, everyvone!" her voice trembling with excitement. She sounds as if she's a citizen of a water-starved town in a Texas gulch and the first raindrop in a month has just plopped onto the powdery dirt of Main Street. I can hear the scrape of a metal ladle against a stainless-steel pot—most likely Nisha Auntie stirring her famed *pakora kurdi*, a yellow stew of spices and dumplings garnished with cilantro, ginger, and onions. I can hear the pouring of water into stainless-steel cups, which makes tinkles along the marble countertop as the line of eaters forms around the island in the kitchen. I can even hear Neha giggling. She is probably standing obediently aside, letting the guests take their share first before loading her plate up. But above this, I hear the collective rumble of Indians babbling and laughing, their gregariousness heightened by the steaming, redolent promise of food in front of them.

I am starving, yet I can't bear the thought of going down there right now. After the small treat of having Kirti fawn over me, I don't want to return to the social trauma of being amidst the other Indians. So while they enjoy their food downstairs, I walk to the massive master bedroom doors and try to slide one open. I am prepared for it to be locked, but it slides open unhindered. I enter the darkness of the Singhs' bedroom, then slide the door closed behind me.

The Singhs' bedroom smells strange. There is the stale scent of past spice mixed with the smell of laundered bedding and a faint wisp of perfume, rose water, and dress socks. When I find the light switch and flick it on, I see that the bedroom is almost empty except for a few things: a shiny wooden dresser, a heavy-looking mirror arching above it; the neat slab of the master bed, an end table on each side of it bearing a fat, rust-colored lamp; and an ironing board, the iron still perched on top of it like a metal penguin. In the far left corner of the bedroom is the cave of a walk-in closet. In the far right corner of the bedroom is the darkened master bathroom.

I walk to the bathroom doorway and flick on the master bathroom light. The bathroom is a lot larger than ours at home.

It is another shrine of marble and porcelain, but there are about ten yards between its pair of sinks and a closed door that presumably hides the toilet and shower area. The mirror above the sinks glimmers and sparkles with light, and when I look at myself in it, I seem prettier than I ever have been. Before I can register what I am doing, I have locked the bathroom door, and my wrists are being caressed by the cool plastic of Nisha Auntie's makeup compacts, lipsticks, and mascaras.

Nisha Auntie's cosmetics look eerily like my mother's; even though the two woman could not look more different in person, it seems that the instruments of their decoration are exactly the same. Nisha Auntie even has the same Mulberry lipstick that my mom has, and when I put it on, I feel relieved, like I've discovered an old friend. I discover yet another friend when I see the lovely girl in the mirror, her face halfway covered in blue eyeshadow, her index finger rounding over her still-brown left cheek and drawing a stripe of blue across it. She jumps gaily from foot to foot, hums gently, and it is only when she hears a sound across the room that she stops, her blue face falling.

The door to the toilet has opened, and from its darkness emerge Neha and Ashok, their faces just as nervous and worried as mine. Ashok's dress shirt is untucked, and Neha's hair is tousled and wispy. I have never seen either of them look so disheveled. Then I realize that no matter how odd they look to me, I look odder than anything they could have ever imagined.

"Kiran?" Neha says, still managing to giggle as she comes forward, Ashok trailing behind. "Kiran, what are you doing? That'sh my mom'sh makeup! What in the world—?" Her words are still smushy from her braces, but they are nevertheless strong.

"I don't know," I say. There is a pause. "I'm dressing up as Krishnaji." This time when I say it, it does not at all seem convincing. In my head, an image of Cody appears, his head capped in a wig of long, brown hair. He looks at me and says, "I'm dressing up as Jesus!"

"What are *you* doing?" I ask, bending over the sink and

splashing my face with cold water to remove my incomplete job. I turn back to Neha and Ashok, who look at each other, non-plussed.

"Um," Ashok says. "Neha was just showing me where the bathroom was because, um, the other ones were full." He looks at me timidly, flustered. Oddly enough, he is more handsome to me like this, the pleading in his eyes making them rounder, more pronounced, more piercing. Even Neha looks prettier, despite her messy appearance. I know why. Disarmed and reduced to this state of quiet begging, they are—for the first time—on my plane.

Aware of this, I stick my chest out and say, "If Neha was showing you where the bathroom was, why is it dark in there? Why did she have to go in with you? And why are your clothes messed up?" I feel strong and magnificent; the girl in the mirror is living in me, haughty and hot.

Neha counters with a heft in her step and one strong index finger pointed at me. "Look, Kiran, thish ish a tricky shituation for all of ush." She licks her braces softly. Her agitation is making her salivate in an animalistic way. "How about we jusht call it a draw? We won't tell if you won't tell."

I consider, for a second, the pleasure of running downstairs and announcing my discovery to the rest of the household, Neha and Ashok clutching each other on the stairwell like a panic-stricken Romeo and Juliet. I consider the pleasure of seeing Neha shamed in front of everyone, the clacking of her braces, the loosening of Nisha Auntie's face as she is saddled with a wanton hussy for a daughter. *I could be so cruel*, I think, standing here and sizing up this panting duo. Cruelty sends a shiver up my spine and steels me.

I am just about to naysay their suggestion when I think of them countering my announcement with handfuls of cosmetics. It's true—Neha's is the best solution. If one side of this argument is ridiculed, the other half has to come with it. There is no emotion stronger in this marble and porcelain corridor than shared vengeance.

"Fine," I say, stepping back. "But you two better watch out.

I'll be watching." Quickly, I return the cosmetics to the drawer and leave the bathroom, giving one last look at Neha and Ashok. When I turn away, they sigh.

Parties are about linking with others socially, but they are also about evolution—the evolution of relationships. Tonight my experimentation has evolved into blackmail, culpability, complicity. And more than anything, the structure of these parties has evolved: the basement can no longer contain the rising lust of us Indian kids.

Chai for Two
(and Two for *Chai*)

My parents spend their time at home as if they can't stand
each other's presence but as if long ago, during their wedding, right after they tied their sashes together and walked around
a fire, they signed a pact that physically bound them to each
other. While I sit on the couch in the shorts and T-shirt I used as
pajamas last night, eating masala-spiced Chex Mix and watching CNN on our monstrous TV, I notice that they move in a
give-and-take manner that contrasts with their verbal spats. My
mother will get up from the loveseat to make some *chai*, and
when she does so, my father will get up from the kitchen table,
where he's peeled a grapefruit and left a pile of citrus skin, and
push back in the recliner. After making the tea, my mother
pours three cups—very little milk and no sugar for herself, very
little milk and two sugars for my father, and a lot of milk and a
lot of sugar for me—gives me mine first and then offers a cup to
my sprawled father, who takes the small china cylinder without
looking at her. The zaniness of it is the silence, the pure silence,
the unmeeting of eyes, the carelessness of the heat that passes
between them.

In the Urdu *quewwali* songs that my father likes to play on
our stereo, Nusrat Fateh Ali Khan sing-shouts stories about
women with hands as hot as fire, women whose softest touch

can render a man aflame. Although my mother is the one who translates these songs for me, there seems to be no such fire left in her hands. Even in restaurants, waiters say something when they serve you, you acknowledge their presence with a polite, if barely audible, thank you. They don't just present you with something amid a cloud of impenetrable nothingness, you don't just take their food and turn away, without a word. Yet the decorum here seems delicately calibrated, the way in which she comes up from the basement while he steps outside with a glass of *lassi*, in which he goes upstairs for a nap and she comes downstairs for a snack, in which he settles into his office and rustles papers while she unwraps the ball of curdled, milky sourness that will be tomorrow's *paneer*. This all seems fragile yet impressive, the result of years of normal Indian being. When, I wonder, did my mother stop being my father's Radha?

As I've mentioned, silence has never been my bag. As smooth as my parents' cool interaction may be, the silence of it gives me only one option: to think of a companion who would not allow such a silence. I sit on the couch and watch Wolf Blitzer and wonder what it would be like to live with a man like him. Wolf: his eloquence, his style, his wit—they are so undeniably un-Ohioan, and these qualities—the lilt of Wolf's voice, the poetic phrases he forms with this voice, using words like "essentially," "Shi'ite," "*jihad*"—they are powerful in this noiseless land of moping parents, crabapples, and hometown chili contests.

It is a lazy Sunday. The delicate rhythm of my parents' movement downstairs is the perfect soundtrack. With each new hour, a certain tension grows, marked periodically by another plate of steaming, cotton-fluffy rice or another cup of *chai* or *another cup of chai* or another block of *Headline News* or a long nap, interrupted once in a while by the telephone ringing. I go upstairs, roll over in bed, and look longingly at SS, who stares up at the ceiling, arms splayed, feet pointing straight upward. Today, she seems unmoving, inanimate, the un-alive self that most people think she is. Today is a sterile day. I don't feel like drawing or dancing or singing or tiptoeing to the master bedroom. I simply listen to my parents' plodding choregraphy downstairs, hide SS from view, and jerk off, Ashok's face in the bathroom assaulting me. Then I roll back over into a tea- and boredom-drunk sleep.

*

When I get up from my latest nap, the house is awash in dusk and there is the faint smell of incense burning downstairs. My heartbeat freezes. My mother usually burns incense at five o'clock every morning, right after she has showered and her hair hangs black and wet in tangles to her shoulders; I once got up too early for school and walked in on her bowed in prayer over the kitchen sink, the incense curling up over her head, my mother inhaling as if to breathe it in. I was only seven, but when my mother turned around and I saw her completely disarmed, her face fresh and pale from shower moisture, it was the first time I realized that she was something besides a mother and a wife—she was her own person, who could get up and do whatever she wanted before my father and I fumbled awake and needed scrambled eggs, tea, a drive to school. This usually happens in the morning, however. The only time my mother ever burns incense in the evening is when there has been a fight.

I steel myself as I descend the steps. There is not a single light switch flicked on, but when I tiptoe into the kitchen, there stands my mother in a lavender nightgown, her back to me but her hunched posture suggesting that she is praying over the sink. A putter of Sanskrit escapes from her mouth. Smoke from the thin stick of incense seems to fill the entire kitchen.

I watch her for a few minutes, and it is more because I am choked up than because I revere her religious rites that I keep from speaking. I wait to say anything until she turns around. I offer an ineloquent "Hi."

"Hi, *beta*," my mother says, stepping forward to give me a hug. I just now notice that her hair is wet: a nighttime shower. "Are you hungry?"

"No," I say. My mother turns to wash the few dishes that are in the sink. She uses one flat palm under the stream of water to massage the crumbs and streaks of grease from the plates, then places them gently in the blue skeleton of the dishwasher rack. I seat myself at the kitchen table, unsure how to broach the topic.

"Mom, is everything okay?"

"Everything is fine, *beta*." She turns around and looks at me with what she thinks is genuine surprise on her face.

"Mom, your mouth is quivering. Something is up."

"*Beta*, it's nothing to vorry about. You know how these things are."

"No, Mom, I don't," I say softly. "What's going on?"

She turns off the sink and walks over to the table, clasping the back of one of the chairs with her tiny, pink-bellied fingers. "It's just the same thing as alvays, Kiran. Nothing changes here."

I stare.

She sits. "It's nothing to vorry about. You know, sometimes things just don't vork out." She rubs the pads of her thumbs and forefingers together, and I see that she is rolling a small piece of dough between them. Dough is like an Indian mom's stress ball. *Squeeze, squeeze, roll, roll.* She pushes the two rounded pieces together and then flattens the big ball against the table into a flat disk.

"Mom, what are you doing?" I laugh. This is why I love my mother—these altogether random but endearing childish habits of hers. Here I am, trying my best to remedy her ennui, and all she is doing is carving an "Om" into a doughy circle with one long fingernail. She returns my laugh, and we sit here for the next five minutes just laughing, trading the dough back and forth. I make a miniature version of her, which is basically one fat doughy ball. She slaps my arm in amused offense, then crafts a whip by rubbing the stuff into one long, spaghetti-like cord.

There is a lull after this diverting distraction, but my mother breaks the silence gently.

"Everything is fine, *beta*. Your dad just does some things from time to time that bother me."

"What—the gas station notebook?"

Another round of laughter ensues. She mentions the way he saves UPC symbols from all of the food they eat, as if someday Nabisco will announce to the public that bringing in an enormous trash bag full of Cheez-It barcodes will guarantee a $100,000 prize. I mention the way he keeps a record of all the letters he's mailed, as if years from now we'll all just need to know when he mailed in that $1 rebate to Crest on May 10, 1985.

Talking about my father causes me a lot of worry. He is obviously not at home, otherwise my mom would not be speaking so freely and loudly, but the act of making fun of him feels criminal, especially when I can imagine him sitting at the kitchen table with us, his brow furrowed with consternation and hurt. As I imagine him, the tension in my body feels like a row of insistent worker ants is marching its way up my spine, up and down each vertebra.

"I just vant you to be happy, Kiran."

It is a sort of odd thing for her to say, but I say, "I just want you to be happy, too, Mom."

"I am happy," she says.

"Me, too," I say.

"Now take your medicine."

Just as the dusk dissipates, so does our time here. My father comes back just as the two of us have sat down to watch another block of CNN, another series of bombings reported across seas. He has a bag of groceries whose contents he empties into the appropriate places in the refrigerator and the pantry, then sits down to join us. My mother gets up to make some tea. I slide away to my room, still unable to look at my father without seeing Blueberry Muffin clutched in his hand.

When I am at last asleep, I dream in *quewwali*, with high-pitched, strained vocals cascading through my mind as severed hands *enflambé* encircle me. From this emerges a mess of all the incense-igniting matches my mother has used over the years—cold, coallike lumps of burnt cardboard and tiny anthills of gray ash.

II.

Brushfire

Hunks of Junk

When my mother is not able to make an escape to the mall, she takes me to garage sales. As long as the weather is not life-threatening, there is at least one sale in our neighborhood each weekend, a fact that is so reliable that the same six or seven lampposts in our neighborhood are perpetually adorned with flyers of differing colors but similar words. Usually, the hosts offer some sort of treat—brownies, lemonade, sometimes beer; one year, the Davies, a quintet of corpulent eccentrics who looked like a set of matryoshka dolls, actually roasted a pig outside on their lawn, not realizing that its meaty smoke was permeating the rugs and dresses they had for sale. The roasting met with various reactions. In one corner, there were the seasoned neighbors who had long ago accepted their one-floor, redbrick boxes and who saw a barbecue of this ilk as grand and delectable. In the other corner, there were the folks who had only recently become neighbors and who did not live in brick boxes but in the houses they had built, in the many-floored, shiny wood-banistered, drywall-enclosed edifices popular at the time. My family theoretically fit into this latter group, but my mother was the secret bridge between the two groups, part of the nouveau riche but not progressive enough to pass up a good sale.

My mom takes me to a garage sale held by the unfortunately named Hilda Hinderlong, a fiftysomething who lives in a clunky house with smudged white paneling and a porch roof held up by pillars that look like Styrofoam. Her garage and its wares are both so cluttered that it is hard to tell where the mess ends and the sale begins. It also makes me wonder if Hilda Hinderlong keeps any of her belongings in her house. It certainly does not seem so when I sneak a peek through her front screen door; since there is a similar door at the back of the house, when you look directly at the building, you see a wind tunnel cutting through it. The image looks as if a battalion has just launched a cannonball through Hilda Hinderlong's residence.

Paintings of various sea scenes, of waves sweeping and frothing, lie askew throughout the sale, some of them depicting beach-strewn wreckage that is in better condition than the furniture on display. A trio of dining room chairs, missing a fourth sibling, mope on legs that look like they are about to disintegrate in termite dust. A lamp bumpy with cracks looks to have been shattered and then reassembled with the aid of a glue gun. An old light fixture, once a stunning assortment of crystals and bulbs, now retains so few of its original adornments that it looks like a crab that tried to dress in drag. (Not to be confused with an Indian who tried to dress like a crab.) Hilda Hinderlong sits amid the refuse in a plastic lawn chair, her wide legs hugged by sky blue slacks and, as I can see at their bases, webs of purple varicose veins. She is drinking a glass of Crystal Light Pink Lemonade, the identity of which is obvious because both the pitcher of additional rose-colored liquid and the tin of powder sit next to her on a rickety end table. As if both the table and the instant mix are for sale.

People in this neighborhood have a tendency to move things around more than they actually purchase anything. Mr. Young, whose name is misleading because he is upward of ninety, picks up a fork coated in the rainbow fog of tarnish and stares at it for a solid minute, then spots a small statue of a dolphin from Busch Gardens on the other side of the driveway, walks to it, and sets the fork down on top of a clock. Dinner plates, all broken in different ways, dot the refuse like buoys. The seascape paintings are picked up and observed, then laid down as people imagine them actually hanging in their living rooms. All the same, these same people feel no shame in picking up equally bizarre objects and buying them. Within fifteen minutes of being there, my mom and I have witnessed the acquisition of a set of kitchen knives, half of whose handles are splintered; a porcelain statue of Captain Hook; a footstool with a huge shamrock embroidered on its top; a hand mirror with ceramic roses crowning it (I scowl inside seeing it whisked away by a young girl and her mother who do not seem part of our neighborhood); and a pair of dumbbells coated in teal rubber that Hilda Hinderlong must have used in a Jazzercise class years ago.

My mother approaches this sale as she would any store: she loads herself up with anything that strikes her as must-have. Which, as already noted, is not a scant number of objects. She shows her usual determination, as if on an Easter egg hunt. She slings a pink cardigan sweater over one shoulder, a gaudy sapphire sequin purse over the other, and places a baseball cap from Shell gas station on her head. At one point, she picks up a hula hoop and I cringe thinking that she is going to try to loop it around herself for safekeeping. Luckily, she sets it down, probably realizing that she would never use a hula hoop. At one point, she leafs through a *Life* magazine with a picture of Michael Jackson on the cover and begins reading it avidly. She tucks it under her arm and carries it around before seeing the Busch Gardens statue and placing the magazine on top of Mr. Young's discarded fork.

While my mother shops away, I scan the lot for a stash of toys. Unfortunately, since Hilda Hinderlong is a spinster, there doesn't seem to be anything that tickles my fancy. There is one doll, but it is scary, made of wood and with painted eyes that look demonic. The stand on which she perches looks like a vise that some mad scientist constructed. I spot a faded blue velvet chair—really, is Hilda Hinderlong keeping *anything*?—and plop down on it, flipping through a deck of cards from a place called Ritz! and trying to find all the queens. The queen of diamonds is missing.

It's when I set the cards down with a sigh that I spot the flute. It sits in a box with a golf putter, a red thermos, and a series of pickle jars. It is not, in fact a flute; it is more aptly called a recorder, one of those fat rods that has two bulbous ends and openings that look like the work of a hole punch. This one is brown, and whoever once played it—could it have been Hilda herself?—must have once had a name tag on it because there is gobbed-over sticky residue along its side where a label once clung. Aside from this, however, it looks almost pristine, probably taken up as a hobby that was never fully realized. I walk over to the box and pick up the recorder, eyeing it and gripping it in my hand tightly. I've seen girls in my school carrying these around, usually taking the place of a pom-pom or cheerleading baton in their hands. I am instantly aware that I haven't seen any boys carrying them around. But like many other things in my life, this enables instead of deters me.

A recorder is a flute. In my head, I cross number 3—"*Flute*"—off my list of Krishna goals.

While my mom heads over to Hilda Hinderlong to barter, I dawdle behind her with my newfound instrument the way underage riders dawdle in line for a big kids' roller coaster at the amusement park. I watch as my mother coolly negotiates Hilda down to five dollars on the cardigan and ten on the sequined purse. She also buys the baseball cap, which is for my father, I'm sure. Normally, he greets anything she buys for him with a confused annoyance; since he never buys anything new for himself, he doesn't understand what could compel someone to do it for him. But since my mother is able to get the hat for a mere pittance (two dollars, it turns out), she knows that my father's reaction will melt into pride—pride that he owns something for so cheap a price. He will say, "Veeeery good," and then put it on his head. My mother is also, unfortunately, buying the dolphin, which she had better show to my father before the cap. He will know, as I do, why she has bought it—she has added it to her store of random gifts that she can give people. Instead of buying people specific gifts for particular occasions, my mother builds up a stash of stock gifts that she can dole out when necessary. It acts as part of her therapy shopping; if she's buying things for others, then she is not feeding her addiction, *obviously*. My father will rub his forehead, trying to decide whether this current purchase warrants a scolding, then will probably discard his anger when he sees the cap. That's the way it works.

After my mother buys the cap, I chime in. "Mom, can I get this?" I hold out the recorder, which looks very large in my small hand. Her face crinkles at first, but when she realizes what it is, she motions with her head to Hilda, encouraging me to present it for purchase. I give it to Hilda, who smiles.

"Ah, I had totally forgotten about this thing," she said. She holds it up and eyes it tenderly. "It belonged to my niece."

"What happened to her?" I ask.

"Oh, she got tired of it really quickly. It was like so many other things she bought. You know how kids are," she says, looking at my mother for approval. My mom nods and smiles. "They pick something up every day, acting as if it's the only thing in the world that they want, and then drop it when they spot something else. In her case, it was Hank Himmelfarb." She grunts. "So listen to me, pumpkin: stick with it. Give it a chance. Oh, now, you've gone and forgotten the manual."

She rises from the chair—a painful process to watch, during which her legs look ready to pop—and goes over to the box in which I found the flute. She rummages through the pickle jars, which tinkle sadly in response, and extracts a yellowed song-book. She hands it to me with the flute, as if insisting they belong together. I flip through the manual; scales are printed on its pages in brown ink indicating various runs and songs. "Row, Row, Row Your Boat" is the first selection, followed by "Amazing Grace," "America the Beautiful," and "When the Saints Go Marching In." Holding the recorder and the book in my hands automatically makes me feel stronger, and I thank Hilda Hinderlong gratefully.

"No prob, pumpkin. And remember what I said: stick with it."

As we walk home, my mother hands me the dolphin statue and the cardigan. She unzips her big white purse and places the sequined purse inside. Then, she takes the cardigan from me and pulls it over her *salwaar kameez*. It's almost as if she planned the outfit, the pink cardigan complementing the light blue of her pajama. When we get home, she shows my father the statue, which elicits the frown I expected. Then, like a magician, she pulls out the baseball cap.

I run the path to my bedroom so often these days that I now imagine it lined with roses and palm trees—the entrance to a tropical paradise. Or sometimes I imagine that a royal red carpet lines it, flashbulbs capturing my spritely figure as it rushes past. I enter my bedroom—or studio, as it is now, with my drawings growing in number—and attack the songbook.

I practice as much as possible, carrying the flute and book in my backpack to school and using my recess time to go through the songs. There is a precision to the fingering that suits me. In a certain way, it surprises me that the instructions the book provides actually cause the correct music to spring forth. Making music on the recorder is not some mysterious, elusive process but something that occurs naturally if you learn the right sequence of movements.

*

I find that the only place where no one will bother me on the playground is The Clearing. I haven't been back here since the Sarah and Melissa incident, and I am not stupid enough to make my journey here conspicuous. If anyone were to see my return, they would regurgitate the stories of my embarrassment with renewed, evil glee. There should be a term for evil glee—glevil. Those bullies are one big Republic of Glevil, and I am exiled out of their country to this hideaway of gorse and broom. I stay clear of the balance beam that ravaged my tender butt-flesh and opt instead for the grass itself, which, though it is deep into autumn and the ground is somewhat chill, feels comfortable.

I find after a few days of practicing that I no longer need the book to guide me. I can play all four tunes with equal grace, and I see a direct link between the way I memorize dances and how my fingers remember the notes.

In the pauses between songs, I think how lucky I am to have found such a haven. Sure, I have to face the direction of the playground to make sure no one is sneaking up on me, and the impending end of recess weighs on me all the same, but here, where the giggling screams of heartless girls are staccato on the wind instead of pointed at my face—that wind blowing through the maple trees lightly—I feel more comfortable than usual. It pops into my head how little I've talked to Cody since our argument; I've seen him in class and briefly at lunch, but I haven't hung out with him in days. Usually, this might bother me—especially because he has all that porn—but right now it makes me feel relieved. I have no one to answer to out here but myself and this flute.

After practicing "America the Beautiful" for a third time, I set my flute down and take a minute to look at my school. It bears the slightly tacky façade of a building built in the sixties or seventies, with orange brick and windows framed in brown paneling. I think about how much time I spend in that place and how weird it is that so much drama should be contained in one edifice. Mrs. Buchanan is in there right now, probably sitting at her desk with a spell book that she hides in a drawer and uses to perform voodoo charms on me from afar. My anger has not abated whatsoever in the week since she rejected my drawings. Now that I think about it, even Mrs. Goldberg has kept her distance since that meeting. I imagine her in her room right now, holding the drawing she asked if she could keep when returning the stack to me (it is one with Krishna swaddled in orange robes). Just thinking of her and Mrs. Buchanan and Principal Taylor and that whole drama makes me want to stay out here forever. Sometimes, I think, my biggest wish on the face of the planet is to have no friends at all. I'd rather burrow into this grass and stay here for the next few months and hibernate like a bear, forgetting everything, even forget the talent show.

No, wait—as soon as I have this thought, I snap out of my daze and return to the flute more determined than before. It may do to shun friends, to shun the school, to find refuge in myself, but I must never lose sight of my artistic goals. My plan, my happiness, depends on this performance.

When I hear Mrs. Moehlman calling all the kids back into the school at the end of recess, I start to walk back from The Clearing like Dickon in *The Secret Garden*, although hugging the perimeter. But maybe it's the image of Dickon, pan pipe in hand, that propels me forward; maybe it's the revelation I've had about keeping to myself; but whatever it is, when I hit the blacktop, I keep on going. I go back into the school and walk down the hallway, lost in the throng of children. And, so easily that I am shocked when I reflect on it later, I pass out of the front of the building and keep on walking, leaving school and its people behind.

*

It is noon on a Wednesday and the sun is out.

Martin Van Buren Elementary School is situated in a residential neighborhood full of ranch-style homes in varying shades of brick. It is fall, and the leaves are beautiful on the trees and gathered in crispy piles on the ground. Dressed in my navy blue sweatpants and a brown flannel pullover, I feel equipped for the weather. I stroll down the sidewalk, not wanting to stare directly into people's front windows but turning my head slowly as I walk past, getting as big an eyeful of the lives contained inside without drawing too much attention to myself. About half of the houses are empty, but the other half usually displays a turned-on TV and the darkened figure of an adult moving inside. It strikes me as some great secret—while we're cooped up trying to learn fractions and endure the social jungle that is school, these adults are watching TV and eating popcorn and cookies and watching soap operas. The day I stayed home from school sick (only once in all these years, last winter, and that was because I had a 103-degree temperature), I got to watch *Days of Our Lives* and thought it was the most transcendent show I'd ever seen, although there wasn't nearly enough romance in it as I imagined, just a lot of people talking to themselves and this slick Mafioso-looking slab of a villain named Stefano. That the women in the houses I pass get to sit home and watch these shows during the day makes me fume with jealousy, although after the third lawn strewn with a variety of toys, I remember that there are real nightmares to deal with, after all.

When I get to one of the main roads of the town, Yates Avenue, I panic for the first time since my departure. It hits me that right now, Mrs. Nevins is urging everyone to open their teal vocab books, which is usually when I get to read by myself at the back of the classroom, since I study with Mrs. Goldberg, and now is the most noticeable moment for me to be absent, since everyone in the class is always acutely aware of my special treatment. As cars pass me on Yates, it seems that the passengers in them are looking at me and criticizing me for my midday escape. I make a particularly strange sight, I'm sure, a lone child standing on a street corner caught between the residential and commercial areas of town and holding a recorder. If I put out my thumb to hitchhike, the probability of someone actually stopping to help me would be even lower than usual. Even a kidnapper would drive past the sight of me and accelerate.

When the crosswalk lights up for me to pass, I cross the street swiftly. I have passed by this intersection so many times with my family (it is, in fact, one of the intersections we pass in silence on our way home from temple), but it looks so vastly different when experienced this way. Whereas the pavement usually appears as just a blur of gray, I can see from up close the individual pebbles flattened in its surface. Black holes of expectorated gum dot the surface, along with one particularly pronounced scuff of car wheels. When I get to the other side of the road, I look back just to make sure that no one is following me. I can see the top floor of the school through the trees and the top stripes of the American flag outside it billowing in the wind.

I now enter a residential neighborhood adjacent to my own. Even though I am relatively close to my house, this area feels strange and new. The only time I ever come here is to visit our town's biggest public park, and the moment I think of the park, I know that it is my destination. Despite the relative lack of natural charm in my hometown, this patch of land, Gerber Park, is quite impressive, two square miles of hilly lawns, tiny, open-air wooden lodges for holding barbecues and birthday parties, swing sets, and hiking trails. It is situated at the end of the road that I'm now traversing, and the closer its entrance becomes, the faster I walk. Two cream-colored butterflies flutter across my line of sight, and I liken them to the way my stomach feels. There is something springlike about them, which puzzles me on this autumn day, but I imagine that they stayed in the cold for the sole purpose of making this beautiful sight for me.

The Parks and Recreation Department has not done a particularly good job of tending to the grounds, and a thick carpet of crinkled brown leaves covers the grass. This is paradise for me, and I stomp through the leaves, sending puffs of leaf and earth dust into the air. The wind blows, pricking my skin through my sweatpants, and the carpet shifts in turn. I scan the panorama of the park and don't see a soul. This is, then, my new playground. Let the other kids infest the school blacktop, let them banish me to the edge of The Clearing; I now have a playground that puts theirs to shame, and for the next fifteen minutes, I roll around in the leaves, play "America the Beautiful" on my recorder and sing to myself. I come to a small birch tree, one branch of which has grown out parallel to the ground. I grab the penitent branch and treat it like a barre, practicing *ronds de jambe* that rake through leaves. At one point, a robin bobs in front of me, inquisitive as the drivers on the road, and another shudder passes through me as I imagine Mrs. Nevins walking to Principal Taylor's office to tell her I'm missing; Mrs. Goldberg hearing the news in passing and looking up and down the hallways for me; Mrs. Buchanan cackling and pouring herself a large brandy from a snifter she hides in her kiln. And then, zap, I am back here in the park, and it's so quiet, except for the wind and the leaves and the chirp the robin gives before flying off and leaving me to my own devices.

Speaking of devices, I hear the faint grumble of a car, and then the grumble gets louder. I hide behind the tree, which, being a birch, is too thin to fully conceal me, and I curse the fact that I didn't find a maple tree to hang around. The car emerges, and it's a blue pickup truck, its grille slightly askew and its tires wobbly. Despite its delicate frame, it charges ahead with purpose. It drives down the main park road, which weaves around trees and lodges, and because the park is a pretty open space, I can see it drive to the summit of the park, a roundabout where another huge American flag towers over a small stone wall. From there, you can see the entire city of Crestview, and most kids' favorite thing to do is to pick out their own house from this lookout point. Mine always looks sorely out of place, bigger and newer than the other houses around it.

My parents.

What on Earth will they do when they find out I've done this?

I begin to walk back to the entrance of the park, terrified. I can't believe how foolish I've been. My dad will lose his mind when he finds out that this has happened, and my mother will end up giving me a huge speech in which she likens my absence from school to the first cigarette that someone smokes: *"Just as one puff leads to cancer, so one missed assignment leads to not becoming a doctor, beta."* Even though I am petrified to endure these reactions, I know that the longer I stay out here, the more intense the anger will be, so now I start running back.

And it's Wednesday! I have ballet class on Wednesdays! Now I am sprinting back as fast as I can.

Then something stops me. Maybe it's the wind heaving extra hard for one second, but something turns my head in the direction of the pickup truck. Instantly, I must know who is in that truck. It's the middle of the day on a Wednesday, now around one o'clock. Mothers are watching soap operas in the dim daytime comfort of their homes, but what is happening in the park?

Just as I have walked the perimeter of The Clearing, I now walk the perimeter of the park, along a wall of interwoven maples and pines and birches. Whereas the leaves on the ground were a thing of enjoyment before, they are now a hindrance, the crinkling under my feet a way for the occupant of that truck to find me out. Of course, only if that person had sonic hearing would they hear me, but I am extra paranoid because I am extra intrigued.

I get to a good vantage point at one of the lodges, where I can crouch behind a large green trash can and see straight to the truck. It is about thirty yards away. From here, I can make out the silhouettes of three people piled into the two seats of the truck. There is a flurry of movement, as if they are laughing hard, and then the front doors open and three high school–age people file out. There are two guys and a girl. One guy has his hair cropped short and dyed platinum blond. He is wearing a Michael Jordan Chicago Bulls jersey over a white T-shirt and long jeans, and despite his baggy clothing, I can make out the strong heft of his body. Even from where I am, I can see the shiny rings of gold piercing his ears. The other guy is skinnier, shorter, with spiked brown hair and gold rings in his ears, too. He is wearing a bright blue hooded sweatshirt and equally baggy, but black, jeans.

The girl looks out of place with these guys. Whereas the guys are joking wholeheartedly and look very sure of themselves, the girl laughs almost like an afterthought. She is wearing a puffy, black Pittsburgh Steelers Starter jacket. Her hair is dyed platinum blond, as well, and is long and curly. Her eyes are very pronounced, encased in mascara (it is most surely not *kajol*; I don't think mascara can be called *kajol* when there is a Starter jacket involved), and her mouth is a bright red oval of lipstick. Her skin, like theirs, is very pale, and when she laughs her teeth look yellowed in comparison.

They are all smoking in different rhythms and resemble, at one point, as they file away from the truck, a human calliope. They kick through the leaves as if they have done this many times before, and I recognize that they are "those kids" that my parents warn me about—the ones who "play hooky." It's not just some joke that my parents make; there really are people who blow off their studies and do nothing all day. Another twinge of fear pierces me (Mrs. Moehlman is being berated now by Principal Taylor for not keeping better charge of the students; Mrs. Goldberg is walking around the playground wondering if I'm at the swings; Mrs. Buchanan is drunk off her ass), but I follow behind these kids all the same, too obsessed with them to pay much heed to my fear.

They head toward one of the hiking trails, a snakelike stripe of dirt that disappears into a canopy of tall, colorful trees. The boy in the jersey leads, with the other boy following behind and the girl last. Once they disappear, I contemplate how to go about following them without their knowing I'm there. I decide that I'm just going to have to make my way through the trees and bushes without taking the trail. I start, then, through the bushes, which are not as tangled as I might have feared. I slip through them quite easily, in fact, and although the occasional twig scratches me through my sweatpants, I am able to use my recorder as a machete to whack through the underbrush. "When the Saints Go Marching In" pops into my head with a pang of irony.

After about five minutes, I come to a big tree whose thick trunk hides me completely from view. The trio has stopped at a tiny brook littered with small white stones. It is at the bottom of a dusty halfpipe of earth, tree roots, and weeds. My tree overlooks this and thankfully puts me out of the line of sight of these people. The spiky-haired boy and the girl flick their cigarettes away, but the blond boy keeps puffing on his.

"Give me a hit of that shit," says the spiky-haired boy, who sweeps his hand in a mock move of stealing the blond boy's cigarette. The blond boy ejects a quick chuckle and says, "Fuck you, dude." He sucks on the cigarette very deeply, then exhales a blue, almost purple cloud of smoke. The spiky-haired boy leans forward and pretends to chomp at the smoke. The girl laughs a deep laugh, and says, "You're fucking crazy, dude." Hearing her curse instantly transforms her for me into a femme fatale, albeit an ungraceful one. She is, I think, even more masculine than these boys, her clothes more male than androgynous, her bearing and laugh more adult. I can't tell, however, if she is more or less wizened than the boys.

"Shut up," the spiky-haired boy says, this time successfully taking the cigarette from his friend and puffing deeply on it.

"Whyn't you make me?" the girl says. It is not so much a threat as a weak rejoinder.

"I'll make you," the blond boy says. He moves toward the girl, who stuffs her hands deeply into her back jean pockets, juts her chin into the air, and grins. Then the blond boy leans in and kisses her. As they kiss, the girl keeps her hands in her back pockets, simply receiving more than giving back. It's not the way I've ever seen people kiss in the movies. I always envision kissing to be a passionate embrace in which two people clutch each other tightly and work together to create a balance of tongues and lips. But this type of kissing seems perfunctory. All the same, I begin to rise in my sweatpants, and my heart beats so hard that I can barely hear the wind anymore.

I know what is about to happen but cannot quite believe that I am here to witness it. The blond boy and the girl sprawl themselves out on one of the large rocks and pull each other's pants down. Their private parts look so different from the ones I've seen in my magazine. Whereas in the magazine, private parts are groomed and compact, statuesque to some degree, the parts I see now are a blur of pink and hair. The girl leans over and gives the boy a blow job. He holds her head like it's a cleaning machine buffing his penis. Meanwhile, the spiky-haired boy has thrown the cigarette into the water and taken himself out. He plays with himself and watches with a stare that is so intense it seems murderous. Then, he proceeds to walk to the girl and enters her.

The boys take turns with her, and she acquiesces to whatever their bodies suggest. Sometimes the boys direct each other in such a utilitarian manner that it's as if they are working on some project together. I notice more than anything how these guys are careful not to touch each other. Their eyes never meet, nor do they ever meet the girl's gaze. She seems to expect this, and her eyes are either closed or downcast for the goings-on. She is eerily silent most of the time, but there is the occasional squeal from her, and then, gradually, a pant tinged with laughter. The boys, meanwhile, grunt toughly and continually. They are now completely naked, as is the girl, the tips of her hair partially wet and darkened brown with water. The blond boy's body is strong and toned, and I am fascinated by how he is muscled like the men I've seen in movies and in *Penthouse* but also real, normal. The leaner boy's body is crude but intriguing at the same time; although he does not possess the physical sculpture of the other boy, his sexual urge is even greater, and he savors the entire process, handling the girl's body as if it's a pet. The girl's body acts as a vessel for its lovers; her breasts, though large, seems superfluous, despite how many cursory caresses the boys may give them.

They finish with the blond boy on top of her, the spiky-haired boy in her mouth. When the boys come, they do it all over her, and my stomach does not know what to with itself. It turns and swells at the same time; it is as if the butterflies from before are engaging in a furious wrestle. I do not know if I am disgusted or impressed. What I do know is that what I have just witnessed has rendered *Penthouse* entirely futile. Seeing this up close, seeing the actual performance of these acts, has become such an entirely different sexual activity that I feel my obsession augmented from a visual experience to a pressing need to *feel* these bodies, to know what those hands and parts would feel like on me.

Before I can have another thought, I feel a hand on my back. I jump and turn, almost falling off the lip of the embankment, and the recorder slips from my hands and falls with a clunk on the pebbles below. There in front of me stands a park ranger, his eyes hidden behind a pair of sunglasses so black that I can't tell if he's looking at me or at the kids, whose excited squeals die as they scramble away.

*

The ranger, who, according to his gold name tag is named Rodney, takes me to the jeep he has parked at the trail's entrance. He makes me walk in front of him, and I feel his eyes all over me. I still haven't seen those eyes, but from his heavy steps on the ground, crushing the leaves, I can tell that he is both angry and confused about what to make of me. I can't believe that he has just let those kids go and has targeted me, but I guess a tiny and stunned kid is a much easier target than three sexual deviants.

His car is a white Cherokee with CRESTVIEW PARKS AND RECREATION decal'd on the side. He doesn't open the door for me but stands beside the car, arms akimbo, until I reluctantly pull the handle and get inside. There is a plush squirrel hanging from the rearview mirror, and a bit of tension drains out of me at the sight of it. Rodney walks to his side of the car, cracks open his door, and plops himself onto the front seat. He is wearing a white dress shirt, black slacks, a black tie, and Timberland boots. He is just a little overweight and is flushed from our trip. He breathes heavily onto the dashboard, and it ricochets back into my face. His breath is pleasant, minty. I see the reason why when I look below the stereo and see a bunch of red and white peppermint candies, the kind you get at restaurants, stuffed into the open glove compartment. At my feet, five or six discarded wrappers lie on the black floor mat.

He starts the engine and pulls away. A wedding ring so big that it looks like the spoils of some jousting tournament lights up his left hand. The ring immediately conjures up a family life, and I imagine that he has two or three children, maybe class-mates of mine, and a warm, pretty wife who takes care of them. Maybe she's at home watching Stefano plot the deaths of several swanlike prima donnas.

We drive in silence through the park. It is still empty. I spot the birch tree where I did my ballet exercises and think about how distant that moment seems now. The sideways branch makes me think of something else, too, and I shake my head to get rid of the memory of those two boys' bodies. Rodney notices my twitch and looks over at me. I look down at my feet, afraid to meet his gaze.

"What were ya doin' out there, boy?" he says. His voice is very deep.

I don't know what to say, so I don't say anything at all. I just keep staring at my feet.

"I guess that's a pretty stupid question," he says. "Look, boy, I don't know whatcha were doin' out here and don' really care. Thing is, I know, well, um, whatcha might have seen might make ya wonder about some stuff, but—"

He stops himself. It dawns on me that he finds this situation as difficult to process as I do. He grips the steering wheel tightly, and I can see his palms sliding as he does so, a thin film of sweat coating the leather. Suddenly, his right arm reaches out, and I wince, thinking he's going to hit me. Instead, he reaches into the glove compartment and extracts a mint, which he pops out of its wrapper with just his right hand. He puts it into his mouth and crunches on it, crinkles the wrapper nervously in his hand, then tosses the wrapper lightly at my feet.

"Where am I takin' ya, boy?" he says. I look over and see tiny shards of candy stuck to his bottom lip.

"I don't know," I say.

"You don't know?"

"Well, I don't know where I should go. I was at school."

"Which school—Van Buren?"

"Yes."

"Well," he says, flicking his left wrist and revealing a thick black watch with about twenty buttons on it. The time is displayed in bright green numbers: 1:47. "It's ten till, now. You've still got another two or so hours of school left, boy."

He drives me back to the school, which looks exactly the way I left it. Rodney parks the car in the lot—a couple of rows of teachers' cars, mainly tiny compact ones with Jesus fish attached to their rear bumpers. Then says, "Alrighty, let's go."

We get out of the car, and again, he waits for me to walk ahead. I feel naked, as I normally walk into this entrance with a backpack strapped on. Rodney escorts me into the main lobby, which is as empty as the park.

"Well, boy, here ya go," he says. He is still red, still nervous. He looks like a frightened child compared to the sex-crazed boys—no, *men*—from earlier. But there is something endearing about Rodney. Somewhere deep down, he understands the awkwardness of my situation and doesn't seem to pass all that much judgment on me. It's maybe the nicest a stranger has ever been to me. Then he is gone.

I walk down the hallway toward Mrs. Nevins's room. I pass the art display where Mrs. Goldberg wanted to hang my drawings. A collection of jungles made from multicolored construction paper are in the center spot right now. One child has made palm trees out of blue and orange construction paper. Although I guess I take the same freewheeling approach to color in my drawings, I still recognize a higher level of inspiration and execution in my work. The choice of color here seems arbitrary, as if the so-called "artist" merely ran out of the "right" colors of green and brown.

Our school is so unpatrolled. I've heard of hall monitors before, but it's not until now that I realize our school doesn't have them. Therefore, I reach Mrs. Nevins's door without being spotted by anyone important, save the students who are gazing, dreamlike, out the doors of their classrooms. I can hear Mrs. Nevins talking to the class about the latest reading comprehension section we were assigned—an abridged version of *Dr. Jekyll and Mr. Hyde*. Right now she is at the blackboard, which faces the door, and she will see me enter. But if I wait until she finishes speaking and goes to her desk, which is on the opposite side of the room, she may not see me but will probably hear me enter anyway. I decide that I have a better chance with the second option; at least in that case, there is a possibility she won't hear, or see, me. I wait until I hear her high heels click over to her desk. Then I take a deep breath and enter.

She doesn't notice me at first, and I am almost to my desk when Sarah says, "Mrs. Nevins, why is Key-ran out of his seat?"

Mrs. Nevins looks up and says. "What? Key-ran, why are you out of your seat?" She gives me the same disappointed look she gave me at the mall, except now, in light of that unfortunate run-in, it seems more intense.

"I was in the restroom," I lie quickly. It just pours straight out of me. I think of the dirty yellow tile of our school bathroom, then see it replaced by the sylvan calm of the park. The park seems like another planet to me now.

"Key-ran, you are supposed to ask to use the restroom." She walks to the blackboard, where she writes my name in neat cursive. She has never so gracefully or properly spoken my name the way she spells it on the board now.

Normally, having my name on the blackboard would break

my heart, but here, narrowly saved from my big disappearance, I see it as a blessing.

"But Mrs. Nevins—" Sarah tries to add. Mrs. Nevins gives her a firm "Shh, Sarah, let's finish our exercise." I take this rare moment to turn around and smirk at Sarah, who makes a sourpuss face and returns to her work.

I can't believe my luck. They didn't even notice I was gone! What luck!

It doesn't hit me until ten minutes later that this is not a good thing. No one here even noticed I was missing. The moment from earlier, when I lay on The Clearing with the recorder as my sole companion, comes flooding back to me, and my eyes well up as I picture the way the flute looked when dropped on those pebbles. I may have lost Blueberry Muffin in a tumble, but I will get that flute back the next chance I get. Part of me hopes that those high schoolers won't be there, but a bigger, fiercer part of me hopes that they are.

Creepover

Trying to forget what I have seen in the park, I try to shift all of my focus to the talent show act. I have decided against including anyone else in the act; after the disaster of using Lindsay and Eric as Ariel and Eric, I know that keeping things to myself is the way to go. I have devised a collage of various performative elements: I will sing, dance, play the flute, and act. The song I have chosen, quite logically, is "How Will I Know?" It's one of the few songs I have on cassette, and the tune has begun to represent the particular nature of my situation: I live in a world of so many emotions, many of them whimsical and happy but many of them uncertain and frightening, and Whitney's music captures all of them in one glossy nugget of a song. It conjures up a feeling of bright colors and bright feelings, tinged with the darkness of not knowing how things will turn out. Most of all, it longs for a love who will understand my confusion. Whether I am a god or a mortal, I need that listening ear. Krishna pined for Radha. I long for the same sort of consort, and I proceed in merry bewilderment.

The piece will begin with me upstage right, kneeling down, head bowed. I will then freestyle dance to the song and act out certain Krishna-related activities: I'll mime a butter pot that I will dip one hand into and then pretend to slurp imaginary butter off my fingers; I will pick up my recorder and play the chorus of the song into the microphone, which will be on a stand at the center of the stage. I will sing along when not playing the flute. Throughout the song, I will pretend that there is an imaginary lover of mine onstage, and I will sing to her. At certain intervals I will dance with her, one arm held up as if around her waist, the other outstretched the way ballroom dancers do. The key is to move like a ballroom dancer but to have my feet evoke *khatak* dancing, so that, again, there is an homage to my Indian self while still paying tribute to my current existence. I simply want the piece to evoke a certain romance mixed with the grandeur of Krishna's spirit, all the while showing the audience why I deserve both.

I've had a secret dream to make my Indian and American worlds collide. Even though it's nice that the Indian kids I know don't go to my school (and therefore they are not there to double my usual ridicule), sometimes I think that the other kids in my school would respect me more if they knew I had another life. Sort of the way that Sarah and Melissa interacted one time recently when talking about their weekend plans.

"Mel-belle, wanna come over tomorrow afternoon?" Sarah said, putting her reading textbook into her backpack at the end of a Friday.

Melissa said, "I don't know. I have to check with my mom." She, too, was packing up her things, putting her number two pencils into a shiny plastic pencil case with hearts printed on it.

Sarah shook her head slightly and shrugged. "Okay, don't worry about it. I think Amber Johnson might come over, too, so if you can't make it, don't worry." She pulled her backpack on and stood up, waiting for the bell to ring.

Melissa's face immediately fell. Jealousy and surprise occupied it in equal parts. It was startling to me that someone whose emotions I tracked so closely should be so poor at concealing them. As the wheels of her jealous and bruised mind turned, her face contorted back into a bright smile. "I'll be there," she replied eventually. "And I'll bring Girl Talk," this board game in which girls use a fake phone to feign gossip.

("Hey, Key-ran, wanna come play, too?" Melissa added, conscious that I had been listening to their conversation so intently. I ignored her and resumed sketching a picture of SS on a piece of looseleaf.)

Just like Melissa was dumbstruck by Sarah's sudden loyalty to another party, so I imagine my American cohorts would be if they understood the nuances of my Indian life. What these American kids don't know is that we Indians have an annual talent show, too, even if it's not called such. In our Indian world, we have an evening of song and dance to celebrate Holi, the holiday that marks the beginning of spring. Every year, countless girls dance mindlessly to Indian songs much in the way that American kids lip-synch. The girls dress in saris, baring their midriffs, and although these girls' fathers would never let them show the equivalent amount of skin in American dress, it seems A-OK to let it happen when petticoats and wraps are involved. Some girls lip-synch to the music, showing that they have both a command of what the lyrics are saying and Hindi itself; other girls do not move their mouths but look altogether terrified to be performing in public. Whether they like it or not, it is expected of good Indian girls to do so.

Two years ago, the Indian mothers in our clan insisted on organizing a group dance among all of us kids. It was a type of dance called *fogana* in which you hold a painted wooden stick in each hand and click your sticks against everyone else's in a certain pattern. Oftentimes, there will two concentric circles of children rotating in opposite directions, the kids in the inner circle clicking sticks with the kids in the outer circle. Then the group will split into pairs that continue to click their sticks together.

Most of the girls were particularly good at *fogana*, having danced to Indian music their whole lives. Even Neelam, whose sari looked quite unflattering, knew all the right steps and looked positively radiant. The boys, on the other hand, were not very good—aside from me, who, from my scant lessons with the carnation-ponytailed Hema and my ballet training, could remember the routine quite well. I refrained from instructing the other boys in how to dance; I knew that they didn't want to hear it from me, and there was more than one occasion in which they voiced their resentment and said my dedication to dancing solidified my status as a pansy. Still, they had to look like pansies whether they wanted to or not: the day of the performance, Nisha Auntie went around and put eyeliner on the boys and girls alike, along with a thin coat of pink lipstick on our mouths to make them pop from the audience. (Ashok in particular looked pretty with makeup on. Ajay, on the other hand, looked like a clown.) It felt so strange to me to have someone else apply my makeup; I worried that Nisha Auntie would see the fear on my face as she applied mine and realize that I was already an experienced professional in such matters. But when she put the makeup on me, she did it in as perfunctory a manner as when she did it to Neha, who looked resplendent in a red sari with gold trim and ten gold bangles on each wrist. Little did Nisha Auntie know that only two years later, I'd be putting *her* lipstick on my face.

As we stood in the wings of the high school auditorium used for the event, I wondered what the students of this school would do if they came in on this Sunday afternoon and saw us. Where cheerleaders may have stood with their pom-poms fluttering; where choir members may have sung in a concert; where basketball players may have high-fived each other before taking the stage for a rousing pep rally in their honor, we Indian kids stood dressed in *kurtha pajama* and saris, holding wooden sticks and wiping sweat off our made-up, brown faces. Each of us boys had a magenta sash tied around our head, the knot on the side in the style some sort of fortune-telling gypsy might wear. This was so removed from the Midwestern machismo of the residents of this city, and somewhere deep down, I wanted those people to see this lifestyle because it carried with it an exoticism that they didn't know.

Even now, I envision what it would be like for people like Sarah and Melissa and John Griffin and Cody to see me dancing *fogana*. I wonder what it would be like for them to see me in an entirely different element, among people of a different heritage, *my* heritage, joyous instead of ridiculed. I wonder what I would be to them, dressed in a gleaming white *kurtha* and vibrant red sash. If transformed into a resplendent *fogana* aficionado, perhaps I might just win the respect of my very American, very unIndian classmates.

I know the reason why I didn't get as excited about that Indian talent show as I did about my school's talent show was because, in the end, there was no American audience in that venue. Now that I am bringing that Indian spirit to these Americans, however, the real anticipation begins. I have an occasion to show them the romanticized Indian spirit I have always wanted to have.

*

Sometime over the last week, Cody has managed to make a good friend out of Donny Howard, a blue-eyed, freckled ostrich of a boy with thin, long legs and a slumping posture that practically mimics Cody's own hunch. I notice the two of them hanging out during recess when they play basketball on the blacktop. I've never even known Cody to attempt something as physically strenuous as basketball, what with his mild deformity, but he moves with a stealth that is as smooth as it is surprising. Donny is made for basketball due to his height, but Cody gives him a run for his money, engaging in court-long skirmishes again and again.

When I come back from The Clearing after my daily exile there, I see this sweaty duo patting each other on the back. They start exchanging comments and glances in class the way Sarah and Melissa do, and I can't help but feel snubbed by Cody. Cody may not be a flawless friend, but he is still the closest thing that I have ever had to one, and seeing him move on to Donny makes my stomach feel like Jell-O. Doesn't he realize that, at the very least, if I had never lent him pencils, he would have flunked out of school by now? Why, without me, he might not even be a student here anymore! The nerve of him!

Friday, when our school has its annual Halloween party, Cody and Donny come dressed as pirates, with long black wigs stuffed under bandanas and plastic swords with large gold handles. I dress in a demure orange sweatshirt and black sweatpants; I learned last year, after wearing an assortment of rainbow-colored clothing and saying that I was Rainbow Brite's boyfriend, that keeping my Halloween costume conservative is the way to go. So I am extra sad at seeing these two boys dress to their hearts' desires, and I imagine that they will wear these same costumes this Saturday, the actual day of Halloween, while I will be sitting with my mother on our front porch and helping her pass out candy. (Not surprisingly, my mother is too paranoid to let me go trick-or-treating in this town.)

For the first time today, while all of us kids fill the cafeteria with our costumed selves, the lunch table includes Cody, me, and Donny. I am eating my *roti* like it's a burrito, having rolled it up and consuming the end of it in tiny bites. Donny does not seem to have much to eat in the way of lunch. He eyes my lunch more keenly than most students, out of both puzzlement and hunger, but when I offer him a bite, he recoils. Instead, he starts in on some Cheetos and a can of Coke. He picks one Cheeto at a time out of the yellow-and-red foil bag, dandruffy crumbs falling on the table with each motion. I don't know where he finds the energy to play basketball as fervently as he does if that is the sort of diet he follows. Cody, meanwhile, is eating a sweaty hot dog squeezed into a near-burnt bun, and the locks of his wig keep falling into its ketchup and mustard.

"My mom said you guys can stay over tonight if ya want," Cody says. It comes out of left field; Donny looks at Cody dumbfounded, then looks over at me. I am instantly aware that I am the third wheel here. This has been obvious during the short duration of this slipshod trio anyway, but the prospect of the three of us involved in a sleepover takes this to knew heights—or, depths. Donny's body language clearly shows that he finds this proposition awkward. Cody, on other hand, continues to eat his hot dog nonchalantly.

"Cool," I say, stuffing my unfinished *roti* into my lunch bag to make Donny somewhat less uncomfortable. Then I lean over to him and whisper, "We get to look at titties."

Donny greets this with the initial confusion that you might

expect, not seeing the direct link between a sleepover and smut. But as the connection slowly dawns upon him, he straightens up.

"So what? My dad's got tons of mags I can bring," Donny says. "He's got fuckin' *Hustler*."

"What's *Fuckin' Hustler*?" I ask, saying the F-word quietly.

"It's the best fuckin' thing ever," Donny says. "You'll see."

When we get back to the classroom after lunch, Cody complains about his wig being too hot and takes it off. He tosses it into the coat closet with his things. I don't miss a beat, and by the end of the day, Cody is rummaging through the closet and cursing the wig's disappearance while I sling my newly-fat backpack on with a secretive grin and say, "See you tonight."

*

My mother is excited about the sleepover, probably because it's the first one I've ever attended. Well, there was the one time our Indian group partied way too long into the evening at Ratika Aggarwal's house and we all made makeshift beds out of the many couches and plush carpet floors, each family in a different area. Mine was in the den, my mother insisting on the floor because she said it was better for her back, leaving me and my dad squashed onto a loveseat. But that was not a real sleepover, and nothing was more awkward than seeing various Indian women emerge from sleep looking like morning-after prom dates and pouring themselves tea from the same ravaged pot.

No, this sleepover is the legitimate kind, and in the car ride to Cody's house with my mother, my sleeping bag rolled into a bun on my lap and my backpack full of toiletries, pajamas, and a change of clothes at my feet, I conjure up visions of the pillow fights the girls in the Baby-sitters Club books have. Then I snap out of my reverie and remember that no such scenario will happen this evening. I am with Donny and Cody, not Stacey and Krissy, and I cannot expect Donny and Cody to have read those books—and, what is more, to understand why pillow fights and painting one's nails would be so much fun. The image of Donny and Cody playing basketball pops into my head, and I try to

imagine myself there, dribbling with ease, flicking the ball toward the hoop with a deft movement of my wrist and the ball
collapsing into the hoop with a light swish of the net. That is
what I need to imagine for tonight. No girls, no girly things, no
mirror girl. Just Kiran, a boy.

My mom stops the car when we pull up in front of the Ulrichs' house. At first, I assume she is about to give me a lecture-
cum-pep talk, but then she pulls the key from the ignition and
gets out of the car. I sit in my seat, puzzled, wondering why she
steps up onto the curb and puts a foot onto the Ulrichs' driveway. Then she turns around, equally puzzled and says, the words
muffled through the car window's glass, "Are you coming?" I
cringe as I realize that my mother wants to walk me to the front
door.

I get out of the car with my sleepover goodies in tow. My
mother walks back to the car and shuts the door behind me.
"Mom, you don't have to walk me to the house. I've got it."

"*Beta*, I vant at least a qvick word with Beverly if my son is
going to be in her home all night."

"Mom, please. Please. I don't want to look like a loser."

"You're embarrassed of me?" she asks. There is a smirk on
her face that is in direct opposition to the gravity of this situation.

"YES," I reply.

Her face crumples in mock hurt, and then she laughs and
heads up the driveway. I love her to pieces, but in this instant, I
want to beat her over the head with my backpack.

I experience the entrance to Cody's house as if I've never seen
it before. The front doorway is a picture frame of white metal
peppered with rusty slivers. In a brick corner next to it, a potted
plant lies in cold ruins. A welcome mat that has apparently survived an elephant stampede bears "The Ulrichs." My mother
rings the bell, a firefly stuck in a small white box to the left of
the doorway, and I can hear the shuffle of feet as someone walks
to the door. The lock is turned, and the door opens with a quick
crack. There stands Beverly, a cigarette in one hand as usual.
She is about six inches taller than my mom, her bushy brown

hair adding even more height, and raised one step up from the porch, she looks like an Amazon. The smoke emanating from her cigarette rises slowly next to her. She is wearing faded blue jeans and an oversize T-shirt that has a gaggle of beagles and hearts covering its front. This is a particularly strange image given that the Ulrichs don't have a dog.

"Well, hi, there, Shashi," she chimes. She pronounces my mother's name wrong, making the first syllable rhyme with "rash" instead of "rush."

"Hello, Beverly," my mother says. "Thanks so much for hosting Kiran tonight. Please be advised that sometimes he gets headaches, but he has his medicine, so I'm just letting you know."

My mother has a phobia of other people administering medicine. One time, at Neha Singh's house, I had a fever and wanted some Tylenol, but she advised me not to accept any from the Singhs because she said if something went wrong, the Singhs could get in big trouble if the medicine didn't agree with me and I died on the premises. This was frightening enough because of the legal ramifications that she described, but it was all the more terrifying because it implied that I was going to expire.

"I'm sure he'll be just fine," Beverly says. She takes a drag from her cigarette.

A thumping of feet comes from the staircase, and Cody and Donny emerge. I wince: this is exactly the type of sight I wanted to avoid, me standing on the porch with my mother next to me while my two potential buddies look down upon us. I can already detect an air of judgment from Donny and Cody, who stop in their tracks once they see my mother. Spurred by their stares, I say, "Bye, Mom," then step through the doorway, not looking back.

"Bye, *beta*," she says. "Give me a call in the morning. Thank you, Beverly." The jingle of her bangles tells me that she has just put her hands together in a *Namaste*. Then she leaves, the keys jingling in her hand before Beverly shuts the door.

"All right, boys," she says. "I'm gonna watch my soaps, so try to keep it down." Beverly tapes her soap operas every day since she works as a receptionist at a dentist's office. She then settles down in front of the TV at night with a can of Diet Coke and a pack of cigarettes to catch up on her viewing. One time when Cody and I had finished looking at magazines upstairs, I went downstairs to get a glass of water and saw her sitting in the adjoining living room with her back turned to me. The lights were all turned off and the smoke was encircling her head in the TV-glowing room. She was sniffling, and at first my heart sank in seeing this woman weep at the sight of the beautiful men and women before her, but then she coughed so hard that I could hear the phlegm in her throat and realized her sniffles were not the result of crying but of her habit.

"Come on, Keern," Cody says to me, turning back up the stairs. Then he whispers, "Donny brought the goods."

I make as if to follow Cody, but Donny stays still, perplexed.

"What does 'beta' mean?" he asks.

"It's Hindi," I say.

He looks at me blankly.

"I mean, it's Indian. It means . . . Well, it basically means 'child.'"

There is a pause, and then he says, "Huh. Cool."

He follows Cody, and I feel a small rush of Indian pride just hearing him voice this unexpected affirmation. Then I follow him to the porn.

*

Hustler puts *Penthouse* to shame.

Donny fans out the magazines on Cody's bed, then holds up one with the cover of a blond, orange-skinned woman in white lingerie sucking on one of her fingers. "This one is fuckin' awesome," he says. The magazines give Donny a confidence that he has not otherwise exhibited, save for the way he smoothly lays a basketball into a hoop. He flicks the issue in his hand to Cody, who catches it and opens it up hungrily, sprawling himself out on the bed. Donny sits down in the chair in front of Cody's never-used desk, picks up another issue, and chucks it at me. I fumble it, and the magazine lands on the carpet. It has opened up to a spread of another blond vixen, this one perched at the tip of a large penis. There is no professional artistry or glossiness in the photograph, the way there might be in a *Penthouse* shot. The photo seems as if some amateur took it with a second-rate camera in his home. The woman looks very cheap, and a thin film of chalky makeup half covers the few bumpy zits that cross her forehead and chin. I kneel down to the magazine instead of picking it up and then curl myself on the floor with it, turning the pages and revealing more and more images of naked blondes, all of them blondes, half of them smiling and the other half crumpled in frozen screams of ecstasy. In most of the pictures, the men appear not as men but as parts. In one shot, the same blonde from the issue that Donny held up and gave to Cody is sucking on her finger again, with a man's hairy and thick hand cupping one of her breasts. In another shot, a woman is astride a man, with only the shaft of his penis inside her visible. In one way, it's as if the men are being objectified more than the women. They are only their penises, their arms, the flexed, tough shanks of their legs bearing the weight of the women on top of them.

But then there are the ads in back of the magazine. Unlike the ads in *Penthouse*, these ads show both men and women fully naked, playing with themselves. I don't know if I'm supposed to look at these. I glance over at Cody and Donny, and they are flipping through the main sections of the magazine. I quickly flip back to the front of my issue, trying to conceal the naked men that I've been examining. If Cody and Donny caught me looking at naked men . . . I cannot even think about such a thing. The entire school would find out, and I would never, ever be able to show my face at school again. Nothing is more terrifying than knowing that one glance out of place could destroy my entire existence.

"Look at this," Donny says. Cody and I both look over at him. He holds an issue in both hands, spread like it's an accordion. There, in plain view, is one woman on her back, with one man inside her and another in her mouth.

"Awesome," says Cody. His hunch makes him not unlike some delightfully perverted Igor.

Until now, I have not felt the urge to tell Donny and Cody about the scene I witnessed in the park. It's partially because voicing my delinquency from school frightens me. But I think it's also because what happened there was so personal, so unique, that I don't want to share it with anyone. However, I see from the way these boys look at those pictures that it is in my best interests to tell them what I've seen. It is a route to instant respect. And, I realize, this is my chance to go back and get my beloved recorder.

"I've seen people do that before," I say, trying my hardest not to quiver.

"No shit," says Cody. "I've seen it a million times before."

"No," I reply. "I mean that I've seen people do that in person."

Donny and Cody laugh. I look down at the floor. They notice this and stop, realizing that I am being serious.

"Wait—you're fuckin' with us," Cody says. "When did you see that?"

"Last week." I look over to Donny, whose mouth is open, not in disbelief, but in awe.

I tell them everything about my escape to the park—well, except for the ballet exercises—and try to convey every last detail about the threesome. I offer the words "tits" and "ass" and "dick" timidly at first, then can feel my speech strengthening as I continue, turning myself on as much as I am turning Donny and Cody on. They are clearly trying to conceal their boners, covering their crotches with the magazines as if their hands just happened to fall into their laps that way. When I tell them about the boys covering the girl in their cum, Donny and Cody both smile eerily, and now I start to feel a little ashamed for having told them these details, while at the same time I am bristling with excitement.

"I don't believe ya," Cody says after I finish, but I can tell he doesn't mean it. He knows that my delivery has been too thorough and heartfelt for the story to be untrue.

"No," Donny says. "I've heard stuff like that happens all the time in the park, 'specially at night. Jared Morgan says his brother goes there all the time to make out with girls."

"Wait," Cody says. "Keern, ya said ya went there during school. What about if we go at night?"

We fall silent.

*

Thankfully, Cody and Donny are not foolish enough to attempt sneaking out of the house without a word to Beverly. That never works in the movies. The parent, after a cursory good night, always has some reason to come check on the kids more thoroughly and finds the pillows that they've rigged under their blankets to act as makeshift bodies. Then police and dogs and all that crap ensues, waking up neighbors and leaving someone like Beverly Ulrich smoking like a fiend on her front porch and amassing cigarette butts around herself like fallen tears. No, it is better for us to take a different approach and get ourselves out of the house with her consent.

We go downstairs quietly. Donny and I wait in the kitchen while Cody walks up to his mother, who is still watching her soaps. On the screen, a woman with dark brown hair pulled into a ponytail and a pearl choker around her neck is talking to herself. From this angle, with Beverly sitting in her plush throne, smoking a cigarette and nodding slightly, the woman on the screen looks like a henchwoman from some James Bond movie reporting to her mastermind boss. Cody looks like the doomed messenger who has to tell the boss that Bond, James Bond, just exploded her heat-seeking missile or made away with her five-hundred-carat ruby.

"Mom, can we go to 7-Eleven?" Cody asks. "We wanna get slurpies." The 7-Eleven is a mere ten-minute walk from the Ulrichs' house, sitting right outside their subdivision like an old-time general store.

I hear Beverly sigh as she picks up the remote. A big green PAUSE appears on the screen.

"Whaddya want slurpies at eleven o'clock for? We've got Puddin' Pops in the freezer."

You do? I think. I love Pudding Pops.

"I don't want Puddin' Pops," Cody says. "I told Donny and

Keern about this really good flavor of slurpie and now they're gonna be mad if we don't get to try it."

It sounds like the stupidest reason ever.

"Well, babe, yer just gonna have to have it later because it's too late."

"Mom! Come on. I'll do the dishes for a week."

"Whoa!" Beverly says, turning to face Cody for the first time. "Ya really want those slurpies, huh?"

I'm not sure why Beverly thinks this is such a feat, considering that the Ulrichs eat pizza almost every day of the week and use paper plates each time. But Donny and I stir with anticipation anyway, sensing that the tide may be turning our way.

"Please, Mom! Pleeeeease!" Cody falls to his knees in mock-desperation, wailing like a little girl and making Beverly lough (laugh + cough).

"Okay, okay," she says, picking up the remote again. "Go, but you better be back in a half hour. Now git; I'm missing my soaps."

Cody leaps up and comes back to us. We all run back up the stairs, stumbling over them in the process. Donny slaps me on the back at one point, but instead of hurting, it makes me smile even more. Once again, he has acknowledged my particular genius.

Cody pulls a jean jacket out of his closet while Donny and I both put on our own jackets. Donny's is a big, black nylon jacket with a hood and a thin, linty white flannel lining. Mine is the usual neon madness.

"Okay, we got four bikes. Donny, you can take my dad's, but ya have to careful. He'll be pissed if anything happens to it. Keern, ya can take my mom's bike."

"I have to take a girly bike?" I ask. I feign frustration but deep down am excited because I've always wanted a bike with a basket and pom-poms on its handlebars. My own bike at home, which I rarely use, is a red Schwinn with handles like bare bones.

"No, my mom's is just a regular blue bike. I don't even know why she has one. She hasn't ridden it in years."

When we get to the garage, though, it turns out that Beverly's bike has pretty much disintegrated from neglect. The frame is rusty and the tires flat. So I "have" to take Becca's bike. Becca is Cody's older sister, who is at her own sleepover tonight. Although her bike does not have a basket or pom-poms, it is pink, and though I whine and frown dramatically, I feel like I have just won a raffle.

The garage door opens with a creaky trumpeting, and the three of us push down the driveway. Donny and Cody take the lead side by side while I follow behind. And then, emboldened by the thought of the recorder being back at my lips, I push between them and say, "Last one there's a rotten egg."

*

The park is definitely a different place at night. It's startling how dark it is. Where the trees were individual skeletons in the daylight, they now coalesce into one impenetrable fortress, the tips of their branches like spikes atop a castle rampart. The moon hides behind thick clouds, and the sparse light does little to light our way. I am no longer in the lead, my tiny legs nothing compared to Donny and Cody's sturdy, basketball-honed limbs.

"We have to look out for park rangers," I say, thinking back to Rodney—although I realize that he would have to have the most unforgiving boss ever to have a shift that lasts the whole school day into the night. Still, there must be someone on duty right now, especially given the situation that Donny has told us about. "We should leave our bikes over here and stick to the perimeter of the trees."

"What's the 'perimeter'?" Donny asks. I explain what it is to him, baffled at how he could already have forgotten what it is, when we learned about perimeters last year. Once I've explained it to him, we proceed to creep around it, getting pricked here and there by an errant branch or a waist-high crackle of under-brush. At one point, Cody warns us to look out for poison ivy, prompting us all to realize that it's way too dark for us to differ-entiate it from any other plant in this darkness. I already begin to itch, remembering the time that my dad got it and spent a week grunting on the couch with his legs looking like something a Doberman pinscher had gnawed on. Cody notices me scratching and begins to mutter "sissy" under his breath like a spiteful mantra.

I take the lead soon enough, trying to find the trail that leads to the creek of sin. After a ten-minute period of walking back and forth and getting annoyed sighs from both Cody and Donny, I finally find it. Just before we try to follow it, however, we hear the distant roar of an engine and snap our heads to the front entrance, where, across the expanse of a field, we can see a park ranger's white jeep approaching. I dart onto the trail, looking behind me to make sure Donny and Cody are following, but they stay where they are, gesticulating toward each other nervously. I stop and whisper to them as loudly as I can to come along. They finally get a move on, running up to me. Like I did on my last trip here, I abandon the path and push my way into the tall grass and gnarled branches lining it. The other two follow, practically stomping me into the ground in their haste.

Slowly, our pace lets up and we stop in a huddled triangle. The jeep is distant again, and its beams barely light up our sneakers now.

"That was close," Cody says.

"You guys almost trampled me," I say. "Let's not forget whose idea this was in the first place."

"Well, excuuuse me," Cody says. "We haven't even seen nothin' yet. Where are all the people, Keern?"

I open my mouth to remind Cody that Donny was the one who told us about coming here in the night in the first place, but then I think better of it. I don't want to say anything negative about Donny.

"Come this way," I say. I proceed farther through the brambles, smacking away branches strongly like the boys did before, now propelled forward by the fear that I've led the boys astray. It hadn't really occurred to me that I could fail. True, Donny was the one who told us that people come here at night, but it was my original story about the woods that brought us to that subject in the first place. If I don't show them something truly sex-ridden tonight, they will not only neglect me the way they did before but will discredit my story about the woods entirely. As my sneakers thresh further through the tangled mess, I have the terrifying fear that these boys will spurn me as publicly as Sarah and Melissa did. And it will be worse in this case because I will have been spurned by my own kind. Just as these thin switches of wood are smacking me in the face now, even more sissy comments than usual will be hurled at me.

Then, about ten feet in front of me, I see the deep ridge where I spied on the threesome. I hear the small tinkle of the creek, which sounds so creepy in this darkness that it makes me shake a little. But there is the promise of someone being down there, so I turn around and put my finger to my lips. "Shhhh. This is where I saw them."

The guys tiptoe behind me as I move toward the edge. It's still so dark, but I can slowly make out the water below. I guess all those carrots that my mother has always made me eat have helped my eyes because I can even make out the tiny pebbles at the bottom of the creek. Unfortunately, I can't make out any canoodling teenagers. Because there aren't any canoodling teenagers.

I can feel Donny and Cody's disappointment, and I swear that I can even see with eyes in the back of my head the look of collective exasperation that they give each other. I am about to push past them back into the underbrush, but then we all hear it: the far-off sound of older voices moving somewhere nearby.

Instinctively, the three of us kneel down on the ground, no longer caring about poison ivy but caring only for what we might witness. The voices we hear are mixed, some deep, some girly, and I know that all three of us are fantasizing about a wild orgy.

After about a minute of the three of us trying to breathe as lightly as we can, we see the people pass by. They are walking parallel to the creek, not toward it, and they are on our side, so that for a second I think they may find us. But their conversation is more brazen than ours; they do not whisper but chat as if they are moving down a high school hallway, laughing here and there with raspy voices. Their voices are probably like that due to the cigarettes they are smoking. The tiny fires of the cigarettes look spectral, like some devious fairies moving through the trees. The smoke surrounds them like the small clouds of their breath in the night chill. As they pass where we are kneeling, I can see that there are three guys and two girls. All of them have long hair. Even the guys have earrings, and I can make out a mustache on one of them. I can't hear what they're saying, even though one of them, the shortest guy, seems to be making quite a ruckus, jumping up and down in his jean jacket.

The group starts to move toward the creek, although they have now passed out of our range of hearing. They start down a decline toward the creek that I hadn't noticed even in the daylight, and for a second, they disappear from view. Once Donny, Cody, and I have all turned ourselves back in the direction of the creek, I can make them out. One of the guys throws his cigarette into the water, then begins kneeling down and arranging something. I hear the things he is setting up making a tiny clinking noise.

"What is he doing?" I whisper.

Then I hear glass shattering. I almost scream out, and I hear Donny and Cody startle, as well. The group of kids is laughing harder now, harder as each shattering sound happens. They have set up bottles of some sort to use as target practice, but the way they are cackling does not make it sound like child's play. Somehow, they seem even more sinister than the other group of kids, their cackles and the destruction of the glass almost demonic.

"Let's get out of here," says Cody, turning to leave. Donny follows him stealthily.

But: my recorder.

I hate to think of it surrounded by all this destruction. Worse, I imagine that one of these cretins will find it, pick it up, and wreak havoc on it with his devil-mouth. I shudder, thinking that with all the glass that has shattered everywhere, it's quite possible that a few shards have already scratched its surface.

"Keern, what are you doin'?" Cody asks in the loudest whisper-yell mix that he can muster against the carousing below us. "Let's go!" I see him dart off through the underbrush, hunched over even more than he normally is. He resembles a frightened mole scurrying through the brush. Donny, ever the contrast, lumbers behind him, a jungle-lost giraffe. But I do not follow their lead. An overwhelming sense of futility has come over me. Sure, I did provide these guys with quite a sight, but it was far from the one that I had seen or that, more important, I wanted them to see. And then I realize that what's weighing me down is the disappointment of not having seen that exhilarating tangle of bodies again. Already in my mind, I've envisioned the rugged yet sturdy bodies of these misfits painted in the chameleon glow of the burning fire below. I've recast the earlier images from the daytime threesome into a nighttime wrestle of pasty white limbs burned orange-yellow against a stark blackness. But as in so many other instances in life, the dream is greater than the reality, and now I am left with nothing but a loud, unruly, and unkempt bunch of hooligans who don't even have the decency to fuck each other in front of me.

I sit down on my haunches, resting my arms on my knees, and continue to watch them. From this angle, they look like some sort of tribal party. It is one of the more exotic sights I've seen in this city. Really, I wonder if this is the sort of activity that kept people like Krishna's fellow villagers happy ages ago. Perhaps they, too, took clay pots that they had fashioned with their hands and stacked them in a pyramid, like the staggered temples lining the Ganges that I've seen in picture books on our coffee table. Perhaps Krishna started off their party by taking a slingshot and a tiny rock—or, on grander nights, a shining golden arrow from the golden holster on his back—and dashing the first pots apart with a flick of his fingers against string. Perhaps the villagers would drink their salty tea or sugary milk or grainy, dark wine and laugh and dance and practice their yogi positions, then punch each other in the shoulders until the skin looked as blue as Krishna's. What do people really do, anyway, when there is nothing to do? The bowery of a thick Indian forest, the dirty basin of a common Ohioan park—how different are they, really? They both act as de facto playgrounds for local people, all of them looking for a way to escape the mundane together.

But unlike these people, unlike that forest full of yogis, I ex-

perience these forests alone. My companions—the modern equiv-
alents of Krishna's loyal brother, Balarama—have deserted me.
I, like Krishna, must see the world alone and process its beauty
by myself.

My recorder. Still knelt over, I scan the dirt down there for it
but again do not see it. I remember that Cody and Donny are
somewhere behind me, but I am pretty sure that they did not
hesitate all that much to hoist themselves up on their bikes and
take off (Cody cursing me because his sister's bike had to be left
behind). I guess I wouldn't be so happy if I were those guys right
now, either. I know that if someone had promised me what I
promised them and then came up empty-handed, I would not
only desert him but push him off the cliff.

At least if I got pushed off the cliff I'd die with my recorder,
though.

The kids run around in the mess they've created and the
sound of glass tinkling against the dirt continues for so long that
one would think they had bought all of the beer in the world to
blow up. And still no sex of any kind. Maybe they are so drunk
that they can't even attempt it. Their grunts would indicate as
much.

I hear noises to my left, a flick of sticks and leaves that hint at
the presence of another person here. The hairs on my neck stand
up as I remember the way that Rodney crept up on me, but the
sounds are thankfully too far away to be centered on me. Again,
the flicking continues, and for a second I panic, thinking that
what I'm hearing might be some sort of wild animal. Are there
coyotes in Ohio? I can't remember. Maybe it's a deer.

As I have found myself doing more and more these days, I
sate my curiosity by deciding to sneak toward the source of that
sound. Once more, the fear of wolves comes over me, but then I
hear the sound again and realize that it's more deliberate, more
human. Someone else has decided to view these proceedings.
Every time I hear another flick, I creep forward a little more.
The kids below the ridge are so loud and ridiculous that one's
attention almost certainly has to go to them before it comes to me.

The flicking sound leads me to a section of the woods with

more open-air lodges where people can cook out during warm weather. During the day, it is a rustic venue with a pleasant setting of stone pillars and wooden roofs edged by plump evergreen bushes and stately trees. In the night, the lodges are like tombs, the trees and bushes like watchful undertakers. A big knot wells up in my throat just from my being here, and coupled with the cold, which only now gets to me, I have a hard time stifling the occasional hiccup that my mouth ejects. In the dark, it is hard for me to make out where the instigator of my pursuit has gone, but then I hear a cough that—for as little as I've known him—I immediately recognize as belonging to Rodney.

I freeze. What if Rodney catches me? The repercussions of that are way too scary for me to bear, considering that he has no school to take me back to but, rather, someone's home. Good God, I think, what if Cody and Donny are already back home, telling Cody's mom? But no, if anything, they have snuck back into the house as slyly as they left it, shrugging off my absence and thinking I'll have to answer for myself when the time comes. Meanwhile, what they don't know is that I am trapped here now.

The night starts to turn darker, and I blink several times to clear my vision. Just barely, I can make out the tip of Rodney's ranger hat and the faint gleam of the golden star on his breast. Then I realize what he is doing: he is watching these kids. Not in a critical, law-abiding way, but in a creepy surveillance sort of way. I immediately identify his secretive, hunched posture as the same one I was in while I watched the threesome unfolding below me. Rodney—sweet Rodney—is as much a voyeur as I am.

But my voyeur status suddenly fails as the night becomes darker and thicker around me. It is not until I hear the sound of my own moan that I realize I am having a migraine. It is not until I feel the scratch of the thistles against my cheek that I know that I've have fallen. And it's not until I see Rodney hovering above me that I black out entirely.

Krishna Ambushed

Rashmi Govind's eyes glow at the sight of all the food at her party.

Even though she has the biggest kitchen out of any of the families—a huge island sits like a glacier in the middle—there is hardly enough room for all the potluck treats that people bring. Our gatherings look like they are sponsored by Reynolds Wrap. Foiled dishes cover the counter, spelunk in the sink, rest on top of the toaster oven, cram into the regular oven. The women all chatter except for my mother, who helps Rashmi Auntie go from dish to dish and unfoil. The kids have banded together and demanded that pizza be ordered. The parents often cave to this desire of ours; they know that this leaves more Indian food for them (Rashmi Auntie in particular leads that charge) and that for the mere price of ten dollars a couple, the children can shut the hell up instead of begging nonstop for the pizza. So half of the kitchen is dominated by oversized cardboard rectangle boxes from Little Caesars, each wrapped in paper and bearing the company's logo (a mess of squiggles that depict a bedraggled Roman spearing a pizza). As my mother tears through more Reynolds Wrap, the kids tear open each box and unleash the greasy smell of the pizza, which just barely outshines the smell from the various curries.

The Govinds are having not just our usual type of party but a

Diwali party. While the American kids in this town were galli-vanting around for Halloween, we Indian kids were enduring a slipshod *puja* in their den. The pundit and his wife came to pre-side over this religious ceremony. They seemed strange to me when out of their temple element. Seated between Amit Aggarwal's enormous eight-ball eyes and Amish Gupta's limp, demure frame, the pundit looked like a counselor trying to bring two dejected men to an agreement.

Now, the kids take the pizza and head to the basement. The Govinds' basement is only partially finished. Half of it is extrav-agantly furnished, and the other half, beyond a demi-wall of vertical wooden beams, acts as a dark concrete home for the furnace. The whole thing looks like the set of a sitcom.

Shruti is holding court again in the middle of the furnished section, and the girls are once again arranged around her like ladies-in-waiting. Just looking at Shruti makes me sad. She has everything. She is wearing a lovely magenta *salwaar kameez* and large gold earrings. Her hair is long and black, and it falls un-fettered along her shoulders, one strand resting between the bumps of her fledgling bosom. Even her hooked nose looks pretty tonight, lending to her the sort of exotic gravity that Lakshmi exudes in the religious portraits I've been studying. I am in a cor-ner on the other side of the room, a few feet away from where Ajay, Ashish, and Arun are switching off at playing air hockey on a sturdy, expensive table that the Govinds bought from Sam's Warehouse. I am sitting on a hassock upholstered in Indian pais-ley cloth. I hold a slice of pepperoni pizza in one hand and ca-ress grooves in the paisley fabric with the other. No one is talking to me, and I am talking to no one. I have learned my lesson.

It is not until after I've finished my pizza that I realize that Neha and Ashok are nowhere in sight: Shruti looks particularly regal because Neha is not there to steal her thunder; Ajay, Ashish, and Arun have a similar air about them with Ashok out of the picture. Even Ashish, playing games as usual on his calculator, seems stouter without Ashok here.

Why do I go looking for Ashok and Neha? I have already been put in a very awkward situation by catching them in the act and them seeing me in my most extravagant makeup creation. You would think such an embarrassment would be enough to quell my curiosity and make me stay rooted to this hassock, gazing at Shruti and her coterie. But then I envision Ashok and Neha touching each other: I envision her hand around Ashok's beauty-marked neck, and I need to see it. I have learned my lesson not to speak to the other kids. Why can't I learn my lesson not to seek out such things? I think it is because I don't want to learn that lesson. I don't want to heed the unspoken advice that the world is giving me, in the incident with Sarah and Melissa, in the experience in the park, in the sleepover. Sex *must* be solace.

I leave the basement and go upstairs. All of the aunties are still in the kitchen. My mother and Rashmi Auntie are wrapping up all of the food that took them several minutes to unwrap. It is startling how quickly Indian people eat and how quickly a kitchen goes from expectant and mouth-watering to messy. I endure the usual cheek squeezing from Rashmi Auntie (who apparently has the short-term memory of a goldfish because she did this just an hour ago), as well as an awkward conversation with Anita Auntie, whose squawk is extra high tonight and almost annihilates my eardrums. My mother gives me her usual nod, and I return it provisionally. The anticipation of catching Ashok and Neha in the act wells up in me. I go into the Govinds' foyer, which is a bit smaller than the Singhs'. Everyone's shoes are spread out on the marble floor, like baby turtles emerging from the sea. Then I notice two larger patches of marble, where two pairs of shoes must once have lain. And in that moment, I know where to find the lovers.

*

As I near the Govinds' poolhouse, I wonder if this is the way that Krishna once approached the *gopi* that He would romance in the forests near Gokula. Did He feel the same flutter up His throat that I feel? Did His stomach feel full of lead, His heart like something struggling to hatch? I imagine Him sweeping through tall green grass, His blue body glowing and imparting to the foliage an eerie but sensual coloring. The *gopi* would see

Him the way you see a lightning bug slowly flickering itself closer to you, before you catch it in your hands and watch it glow all over them: Krishna's tapered, glistening limbs would mist into view before the *gopi*'s red-painted nails and henna-scrawled palms caressed Him. Though a god, the most powerful of beings, He must have still felt somewhat vulnerable amidst a bevy of *kajol*-encased eyes and sensuous whispers. Despite whatever great physical feats He may have performed, despite sending demons screaming back to their fiery hell and vanquishing giant snakes with a patter of His little dancing feet, He must have seen a greater physical challenge in trying to satisfy these women and then picking Radha out of all of them, playing the lover extraordinaire to her.

Not that I am so naïve as to think that romance is the reason Neha and Ashok have snuck out to the poolhouse. I still remember the mischief behind their stunned eyes in that bathroom: their unconvincing acting about what they were up to showed me all the more clearly just how carnal their desires were. I feel all the more regal knowing that I'm about to catch them in another vulnerable state.

Yet all the while, there is the tension, the fluttering in my chest.

The poolhouse is not particularly big, but the embellishments on it are ornate nevertheless. It has a clay tile roof and white stucco walls, evoking a mini-Mexico in the middle of this neighborhood. Its windows are shiny panels of glass intersected into four small squares, and in warm weather there would be an elegant creeping of vines up its side. In the fall, however, the vines are thin brown spines. I creep along the walls lightly, the grass crunching softly under my sneakers. From here, my back against the wall, I can see the back of Rashmi Auntie's house. All of the windows are lit except for one small square in the top left where the master bathroom is. If this were Harsh Singh's house and he yelled his usual "What is this—Diwali?!" you could tell him it actually was.

For a second, I wonder if there are other kids fooling around in there. For all I know, given the way things—and people—have been going down these days, Arun and Neelam have begun acting out their freak-child fantasies in the recesses of that porcelain paradise. Below that possible rendezvous, in the bright, large window that crosses the entire kitchen, the aunties are laughing, their *salwaar kameezes* an array of bright blues, reds, and yellows. In the bottom right corner, I can make out the white shirts and crossed legs of the uncles conversing in the sitting room. It will be an hour or two before they break out the cards and the aunties filter into that room to play or encourage.

I could just run back into the house right now. I could leave Neha and Ashok to their dealings and learn from my mistakes. *I could learn from the sleepover.* But I can't. Or don't want to. I don't know which reason is the real one. And not knowing makes me flutter more. I turn around and kneel down, then slowly rise and peer into one of the windows.

Despite whatever scandalous scenes I've envisioned, it still surprises me to see Neha and Ashok doing pretty much what I expected. Somewhere deep inside, I think I expected to be disappointed, to have attributed to them a raucous sexuality they didn't really possess. But even in the dark of the poolhouse, I can still make out the tangle of their bodies. They are full-on making out, with Ashok's shirt so unbuttoned and opened that it's pretty much off and the front of Neha's *salwaar kameez* also unbuttoned, the sliver of her training bra showing through. The thing that stuns me is how passionate their embrace is. There is no air of experimentation, the sort of detached, mechanical movement that I saw with the kids in the park. Even though Neha and Ashok are not moving nearly as fast as those kids, there is still something important in what they are doing. There is something emotional about it, as if they have been longing for each other since last weekend's party. Their embrace is—dare I say it?—*loving.*

A potent feeling of jealousy comes over me. My eyes practically burn looking at these two. The flutter in my chest transforms into a hard pounding. Why do these two get to be the ones who have all the fun? Why does Ashok get to hold Neha and embrace her? And why does he also get to do so passionately? Why does Neha, who has no regard for anyone but herself, who struts around like a queen and gets whatever she wants, get Ashok, too? They don't have to put up with people like Sarah and Melissa and John Griffin. They don't have to sit in the middle of a field and call it solace. They don't have to sneak around their own houses to do the things that make them happy. They don't have to address their fathers with heads downcast, afraid to be themselves.

Looking at Neha and Ashok, I feel, for the first time in my life, absolutely ashamed of who I am. In the past, when I've made myself up, dressed up, and played with my dolls and danced, I've always felt happier, freer. I've felt like I was really myself. But in this moment, I truly realize how different, how *weird* those things are. It is as if I am a fly on the tall white walls of my parents' bathroom: I see this little boy smothering his face with sticky pastes and prancing around, and the view disgusts me. How does a boy like that ever get to be a boy like Ashok? He doesn't. There is no intersection. Ashok gets to be Ashok and gets romance and sex. Kiran gets to be Kiran and gets nothing but Kiran. Kiran doesn't even get to be the girl in the mirror. *Neha* gets to be the girl in the mirror.

But perhaps Kiran can be a tattletale.

*

My march back to the house is as fast and ferocious as my trip to the poolhouse was slow and luxurious. I enter the front door and almost forget to take off my sneakers. The house is full of laughing. The men are howling, talking over each other, each uncle trying to add to the hilarity by telling another zinger. The women are howling, too, each auntie slapping one hand against the other every time they double over with laughter. The sounds of Ajay and Arun's air hockey paddles on the metal table waft up through the vents and provide counterpoint tinkles to the women's high-pitched wailing. In short, everyone seems comfortable. But I am determined to upend that comfort. It's time for me to be the one laughing.

Nisha Singh is sitting at the kitchen table sipping from a delicate porcelain cup, holding the saucer under it with one of her

perfectly manicured hands. She is wearing a beautiful passion-
fruit-colored sari, and two large, sunlike gold earrings hang from
her ears. Her eyes are calm with snobbery. My resolve strength-
ens just looking at her. Neha gets everything she wants because
Nisha gets everything she wants. This is another one of those
pivotal moments, like the one when Mrs. Goldberg prepared to
give me her verdict on my drawings. There is so much contained
in this moment, so many possible outcomes, and like Mrs. Goldberg with me in that instant, I have the power to make or break
Neha and Nisha Singh.

"Kiran *Beta*, what is it?"

I am so focused on Nisha Auntie that I almost forget that my
own mother is also sitting at the kitchen table. Her lavender *salwaar kameez* looks very plain compared to Nisha Auntie's bright
sari, and her teacup sits empty on the table, a crinkled napkin
bearing crumbs from various desserts next to it. The puzzlement
in her face tells me how unconcealed my own face is. I have not
disguised my devilish intent.

"Nisha Auntie," I say, ignoring my mother. "I have something
to tell you."

"Kiran, vhat is it?" my mother repeats. She can sense that
something is up. Nisha Auntie looks at me with the same calm
expression, lowering her cup and saucer as if they're getting in
the way of our interaction.

"Auntie, I saw Neha and Ashok doing something in the poolhouse. Something . . . bad."

Nisha Auntie's expression takes a few seconds to crack, but
gradually, the meaning of what I'm saying sinks in and the cocktail of shock, anger, and disgust in her eyes is my first prize. The
second is the way she almost throws the cup and saucer onto the
table, so firmly do they leave her hands, so firmly does she stand
up and march out of the kitchen, almost tripping over her sari.
"Neha!" she is calling out repeatedly.

"Kiran!" my own mother is calling out. I look over at her. Her
glare is not so much a cocktail as a shot of anger on icy rocks.
She has stood up, too, and Ratika and Kavita Aunties, also seated
at the table, form a tribunal that is castigating me with its eyes

instead of words. I return their looks with a haughty disdain. I do not care what these ladies think. More than usual, I feel somewhere deep down that they don't "count." They have nothing to do with the kids I see at school, the place where I am five days a week, the place where I have to watch my every last move. I see these ladies once, sometimes twice, a week, and we exchange quick salutations or good-byes before I go slump in a basement, stare at myself in a bathroom, or get back into my parents' car to go home. I owe them nothing, and they can give nothing to me but a reason to feel less Indian, less like the rest of their privileged kids. Less like Neha and Ashok—who must be cowering as they are found out in the poolhouse. I can't wait to see them brought into this kitchen, their ears pinched by their mothers' firm grips, shoved before the tribunal, the judgment directed at them instead of me. Me, who never hurt a fly because I never realized that I *was* that annoying fly all along.

Then, like a slideshow of terror, I see it all fall apart. Neha is in the kitchen with her mother, all buttoned up and prim, her eyes stunned to everyone else but vengeful to me, who has seen that look too often on the faces of little girls to mistake it for confusion. Then Ashok is there, hockey paddle in hand, equally collected, concealing his eyes even better than Neha; manliness, however fledgling, is his veil. Neha and Ashok must have spotted me spying, and they stealthily returned to their respective circles. Anita Auntie has now joined the tribunal, and soon a few of the uncles have appeared, too. Somewhere behind the gathering crowd, I can sense my father. I cannot see him, but I can sense him fiercely. And then, perhaps worst of all, the pundit appears, clearly unable to register what is going on.

Everyone's focus is on me. I am again a clay doll, tiny, unimportant. Then Neha speaks.

"Kiran likesh to play with makeup," she says. Out it comes—no warning or buildup. Heard by itself, this statement actually doesn't make any sense. Nisha Auntie's face scrunches up in confusion, and she turns to Neha and asks, "Vhat?"

"Kiran likesh to put on makeup, Mom," Neha repeats. "I

caught him putting it on in your bedroom a couple of weeksh ago. He was jusht ushing all of your makeup without ashking. Not that he should be ushing it anyway because only *girlsh* ush makeup!" Neha is grinning evilly, and she gives me a sharp, haughty jab of her eyes.

"*Arre?* I don't understand," Rashmi Auntie says, stepping forward with a Styrofoam plate full of *saag paneer*. The fingers of her right hand are stained with the spinach goo and hover over it to pinch up another bite. She looks at my mother.

While Neha explains more thoroughly, I look at my mother, too. Immediately, her face gives her away. She is looking down, not at me, her eyes zapped with recognition and guilt. In that instant, I see that she has known all along what I've been up to with her makeup. It was as I always feared: she has seen the powder disappearing little by little, has caught the tiny flecks of color that must have been left on her counter. She must have realized after hearing my Krishna confession that I was stalling, covering up my deviant deed as frivolously as I covered my face in blue. My bathroom self has never been alone. My mother has always been in there, too.

The Indian parents are all in the kitchen now. The uncles, as one might expect, are at a complete loss as to how to handle a situation like this. They cup their tumblers lined with Johnny Walker Black Label with one hand and stare into the murky orange liquid. A couple of them saunter away, picking up their conversation. A few of them—Harsh Uncle in particular—stare at me as intently as Nisha Auntie is now staring at me. And my father . . . my father. He does not hold a tumbler. His hands, instead, are clasped in front of him, and he is staring at the floor. He does not look up, and yet I can feel his stare. It practically ricochets off the shiny linoleum of this kitchen floor and stabs into my eyes, which are welling up with tears.

"But Neha and Ashok . . ." I quaver. "I saw them . . . they're the bad ones. They have been fooling around with each other."

Instantaneously, all of the aunties step forward, gasping. Nisha Auntie yells, "You shut up! *Tum karab larka ho.*" *You are a bad boy*. She looks up at my mother, a quick castigation of my mother's parenting. "Shashi, *kya hogiya?*" *What is happening?*

"Kiran tried to lie and shay that I wash doing shomething bad sho that you wouldn't find out," Neha continues. Behind her, I spot Kirti, another Baby-sitters Club book in her hand. She is wide-eyed, taking in the entire situation. Any familiarity she may have seen in me has dissipated and I am back to what I always was, an object of laughter to her. I am Kiran Bhaiyya no more. She is my Radha no more.

Now it is my time to lunge. I see my right hand claw at the air, just missing Neha's face as she screams and steps back. I feel a couple of hands pull me back and am so furious that I don't even notice that I'm being turned around or that a hand is swinging through the air to slap me. It stings badly, and I scream out "Fuck!" This obviously solicits another round of gasps from the aunties, and when thinking about this later, I think how glorious it would have been to keep on cursing until Rashmi Auntie fainted into her *saag*. In the moment, though, all I can think of is how weak I feel under Nisha Auntie's wrath, under the forceful slap that her hand has made against my cheek. I've seen that same gold-bangled hand slap against its twin at many a wedding, when Nisha Auntie joins her bevy for a dance of *garba*, a circular assortment of women twirling and clapping and laughing.

But it's not Nisha Auntie's hand. It's a hand that I've seen dusted in flour more times than I can count, that I've seen clutching the papered twine of shopping bags after being manicured in shiny red. It is my mother's hand, and it is my mother's face that now hovers over me, tears in her eyes.

The party does not end after this episode—at least, for everyone else. As for us Sharmas, the rest of our time in the Govinds' house is a carefully staged slinking away. After my mother strikes me, she leads me away to the foyer, where she instructs me to run upstairs and retrieve our three coats from the coat room. As I mentioned before, the coat room in an Indian house is not an actual vestibule but rather a designated bedroom on the top floor where one of the household's kids is expected to take everyone's poofy fall or winter layers. Soon enough, a tall, wide pile of faux fur, faux wool, and nylon appears, and somehow, everyone's scarves and gloves and mittens and those stitched, long, serpentine belts that circumnavigate women's coats via a series of thick loops become all tangled and head-scratchingly lost. Lost like That Sock in a laundry machine. It takes me a good five to ten minutes to recover all of the components of our coats. I find my brilliant neon one easily enough and put it on, but I underestimate the time it takes to get the other things—the belt to my mother's gray coat, the two matching black gloves that have fallen out from being tucked into my father's sleeves. By the time I find them, I have sweated rather profusely because of the heat of having my coat on and the stress of my search. I realize as I stagger out of the bedroom with our collective family mess that my eyes are still wet with tears.

As I descend the stairs in the large foyer, I am struck by the consternation in my mother's face. She is not making any effort to talk to any of the aunties before we leave. Perhaps even odder, they aren't attempting to communicate with her, either. Somehow, in an unspoken way, it seems that everyone has agreed that the only possible solution is for the three of us to simply take our leave, extricate ourselves. My mother gives my father his coat, which he takes silently. She wraps her own coat around herself and doesn't even try to thread the belt back through its loops. She holds the belt in her hand instead, not even coiling it, so that it dangles limply. She opens the door and doesn't move. I realize that I am expected to leave first. It is fall, almost winter—it is cold outside. I cannot feel the heat of my flame right now. I can feel only the frigid night air and the coldness of my parents, who sit in silence with me as we drive back to the house. This time, there is no breaking of the silence as there is on our way back from temple. There is only the sound of the engine, my father's deft hands against the steering wheel, the faint sound of air blowing through my mother's nostrils.

It is the last party that the three of us attend for two months.

*

When we get home, my parents walk straight to the kitchen, *our* tribunal room. As we walk into it, I imagine all of the aunties gathered here. They have refilled their teacups and hover expectantly over the curls of steam like excited moviegoers over popcorn. But no one else is in here, just my parents. My mother takes the teakettle and goes to the sink to fill it up. She sets it on the stove and flicks on the switch. She takes down two mugs, not three. She reaches for the tea bags, which she keeps in a tiny tin jar next to the stove.

Without even a hint of warning, my father grabs one of the mugs and throws it across the room. I don't even have time to think of ducking before it hits the opposite wall. One might have expected it to smash against the wall, porcelain shards flying through the air, hailing over the linoleum, but that is not what happens. Instead, the sheer force of the mug punches a foot-wide hole into the wall, and the mug falls into the narrow passage between that wall and the one behind it. My father gasps and runs to the hole, peering into it and clutching his chest as if he's having a heart attack. He keeps gasping for air, each gasp seeming as if to say, in a crescendo, *This is going to cost a fortune!* I want to burst out laughing and run away at the same time, and when I look at my mom, I assume that she'll have the same conflicted expression on her face that I do. She has her head in her hands, and I assume that she is trying to stifle her laughter.

That's not the case. When she removes her hands, her consternation persists, and if anything, it hardens when I look at her. I search her face, hoping to find the old mom who would have conspired with me, held me close and patted my head. That Mom is gone now. That Mom barely flinches as my father yells and screams in Hindi, stomping on the ground, pointing a finger at me while he yells at my mom what I can only assume to be a renunciation of my "weirdness." He continues for several minutes, only once in a while looking at me. I gladly avoid his stare. Only a couple of times does my mother respond to my father, but each time she does, he cuts her off and continues screaming. His voice becomes hoarse.

This is a delinquent outburst that has been simmering for the past week since Rodney brought me back home in the middle of the night. The next thing I remembered after passing out in the park was being back in his jeep, coming to and hearing my recently awakened feet crunching candy wrappers beneath them. Somehow, while emerging from the blackness, I answered Rodney's inquiry about where I lived by telling him my actual address instead of Cody's, and so he showed up at my house almost tugging me by the back of my coat. He did me at least the favor of saying he found me in the park, not telling them what I was observing, although he clearly couldn't tell them what that was for his own personal reasons. My mother greeted him with the expected confusion, and when she questioned me about why I was there, I simply told her that I went there with Cody and Donny to play.

"But vhy?" she asked. "Vhat vas in the park?"

"We just thought it would be cool."

"But there is nothing in the park at night! And vhere vere Cody and Donny, anyway?"

"They . . . they were there."

"The ranger said he found you alone."

"Well, they were there. They must have run away when they saw the cop. Why are you even questioning me about this? I did a bad thing, and I'm sorry. But at least I'm okay!"

"You are not okay, Kiran," my mother said, getting up from the kitchen table. She went to the oven and cracked it open. Inside was a porcelain casserole full of milk; she was making a batch of yogurt. For years, she has used the same culture to make her yogurt. One tiny teaspoon of culture has lived throughout the years, giving birth to creamy dish after creamy dish. Perhaps that culture existed before I was even born, just like Indian culture.

What I did not tell her about—what I can hardly tell myself about even now—is how, just before he took me into the house, Rodney smiled at me, more with his eyes than with his mouth, and put his hand on my stomach. He let it stay there briefly, his face a smiling knot of concentration, then suddenly came to, pulled his hand away, and looked at me with a frightened clarity. The rousing of my groin, as in the past, told me that something sexual had just eluded me. But then we were outside, then he was tugging me, and it was over.

My father keeps on yelling, scolding my mother about me—not just with regard to tonight's spectacle but with regard to my detour from last weekend, I'd wager. And it occurs to me that for some cruel reason, my migraine problem does not resurface now. Sure, it can happen at the least convenient times, like in the park, but now, when I would much rather pass out and earn at least a little sympathy from my parents, it's nowhere to be seen. My body has opted for the cruelest possible attack on my mind; it forces my mind to endure every possible pain.

Finally, just when it seems that my father is going to lose his voice entirely, he storms upstairs, and I hear the master bedroom door slam.

My mother, after a few silent moments during which I continue to look at the floor, makes the tea. She takes the one remaining mug and goes to the sitting room, leaving the teakettle cooling on the stove. I take her cue and go upstairs, which should feel like a relief but, because of my mother's cold behavior, feels like a silent exile. Whatever the reason, once I reach my bedroom, I collapse on my bed, expecting tears but instead falling straight to sleep.

*

That night, Rodney appears to me in a dream. Instead of being alone in the park, he is accompanied by a man who wears a white sweatshirt and a baseball cap. They kiss.

The kiss is more comical than shocking at first because of the tussle between their hats. The wide brim of Rodney's ranger hat dwarfs the smaller one of his companion's baseball cap, and when they kiss, both of the hats slink backward from touching each other, edging off their owners' heads. I can't even make out the two men's mouths; instead, it is the steady movement of their heads that gives them away. As my eyes adjust more and more to the nocturnal park, I can see their arms around each

other. Once in a while, one or both of them will take a breath of
air and a small wind of condensation will once again rise from
them. Then it is back to their embrace.

WHAT IN GOD'S SAKE IS GOING ON IN THIS PARK? I
scream to myself in my head. For the love of all that is holy,
when did Crestview become such a den of sin?! I am raging
now, almost doubled over from my anger. Where have I been all
this time? How long has this debauchery been happening? I give
a quick look around me to see if I can sense anyone else moving
through the underbrush, if there are any other visitors to the
Crestview Fuck Park this evening. No, it doesn't seem so, although for all I know, the massive swing set at the other end of
the park is being used as a sexual jungle gym, a bunch of drunken
people bouncing around on the seats before bouncing around
on each other. Such a thing could have been happening all these
years while I lay in my bed at home, trying to sleep, pining for
something greater than myself.

That is, until Rodney and his companion start to take off
their clothes. Now, in a delayed reaction, I realize when I see the
masculine heft of their bodies that I am not looking at a man
and a woman, as I have in the past. I realize that this is the first
time I have ever seen two men kissing. My stomach does not
prove a very reliable barometer of my feelings about this; simultaneously, it recoils with distaste and expands with eagerness.
But there is the movement of these men's bodies to guide me.
There is the way that they embrace each other, as if attacking
each other. Their clothes are mere casualties in the line of battle;
slowly, they fall to the ground. All the while, the hats keep spar-
ring until they, too, fall. When I see Rodney push the man away
from him, almost slamming him against one of the stone pillars,
I feel that something even more drastic is about to happen. Sure
enough, Rodney turns the other man around and begins to do
to him what I saw those boys doing to that girl.

Only now am I able to fully understand what being called gay
means. It does not just mean that you play with dolls. It does
not just mean that you can't play basketball. It does not just
mean that you hang out with girls instead of boys because you

feel more comfortable that way. It does not just mean that you take ballet. It does not just mean that you think over and over again about the mole on a boy's neck, and it does not just mean that you feel a flutter in your stomach when a boy compliments you.

It means that you are wired for a different life entirely. It means that your body, your feelings, your responses toward all other people are different. You do not look at men the same; you do not make love to them the same way. Your sex will be more rugged, rawer. Rodney, once soft-spoken and endearing, approaches this other man with a violent pleasure that I would never have expected of him. His wife must have no knowledge of this whatsoever. He must exist away from her. He must feel the way I feel when I walk through the hallways at my school or when I walk through the cavernous, curry-smelling houses of our Indian friends. Being gay is a self-contained, alternate world.

All the same, I feel an undeniable distaste about Rodney and his companion. Their physical act is too new to me to register as normal or natural. Instead, I feel myself repulsed just as much as I can't look away. Is that what I am expected to do with my body? No, no, it can't be. I am not made for that. I want to be normal. I need to be more like my friends, not less like them.

But if I make myself too normal, I lose my godlike presence. If I renounce my individuality, I make myself as vulnerable as all those other babies were to King Kamsa. If I renounce my singular power, I am no longer that one blue boy protected by his own powers. Which will I choose—conformity or delectable deformity?

I wake up in a fit.

What sort of dream, what sort of mirage is this? Don't mirages show us what we *desire* to see? Isn't a mirage the pool of water in a desert? But in my dream, I felt as repulsed as I was intrigued. What if I had not just let Rodney's hand rest on my stomach but had touched his hand in turn? Would I be the man in the baseball cap?

I don't know how I got to this place. How, in just a few weeks, has my lust been cracked open like this? I feel absolutely different. Sometimes I feel like I am so sexually charged that I might blaze myself up, that this blue flame is burning so intensely that I will explode. I spend too many nights not being able to sleep, jerking off or tangled in my comforter, its pink fabric like a sheet of scratchy insulation, the cotton candy-like type that I could see when my father's mug punched that hole in the wall.

I need to be Krishna. I just *need* to be. That can be the only possible explanation for this madness. Yes, I know that Krishna is simply one avatar of Vishnu and that, by asking for reincarnation, what I'm really asking for is to be Vishnu. But that's not it; every time I see a picture of Krishna, I cannot help but see myself. I cannot help but recognize something glowing—hurt, but glowing—in His beautiful, made-up eyes and in His brilliant skin. The way my body burns with longing can only be the work of some Greater Force—a divine force. I recall Cody saying that "smite" is his pastor's favorite word. Perhaps I am being *smitten* with a celestial wind of lust. Buffeted by *bhagwan*.

All the while, Neha and Ashok are continuing their normalcy, their steady romance. I had no part of their romance before, and I certainly have no part of it now. The same can be said of my supposed friendship with Cody and Donny. The other children I know are living their lives, growing up while I grow apart. I remain the lone warrior, staring out my window at the sky, which turns blue as the sun comes up. What is the sky, I think, but the blue, bruised skin of the Earth?

Then I fall back asleep.

Deus Ex Melanin

I wake up gradually the next morning. Once in a while, I hear the sound of a kitchen cabinet thudding shut or a large spoon hitting the side of a stainless steel pot or the padding of my mother's feet against the linoleum. Or I hear the powerful heave of my father sneezing in the cool morning air or the sound of his accountant's calculator printing numbers onto thin scrolls of paper with a screeching zap. These plain, regular sounds comfort me; they show me that there is a way for things to go back to the way they were.

I go downstairs carefully, checking to make sure that my dad is still in his study and my mother still in the kitchen. It is a question of whom I should address first, since each of them can hear me talking to the other. My father would probably appreciate getting the first hello, but with his outburst last night, perhaps it is wiser for me to say hello to my mother and get her on my side before approaching him. But would my mom even be on my side? Her behavior last night would indicate no. I end up making it halfway down the stairs before deciding to turn around and go back to my room. I shut the door, deciding to hide out in here for a little while longer before facing those two.

I take out my markers and paper and start drawing again. In all the hubbub of the past week, I have really neglected the planning particulars of my talent show act. I have yet to pare down the details and decide what this show is going to *be*. Sure, it can be a really beautiful montage of interpretive dance and song, but I can't just get up on a stage and expect a miracle to happen. I'm no Hanuman, that dancer we saw so many years back. I can't just get up on a stage and improvise for hours on end. Well, I *could*, but I don't think it would do as much justice to my great Krishna revelation to wing it. I need to decide on what my outfits are going to be, where I'm going to stand and what steps I am actually going to do. With less than two weeks to go until the show, I am going to have to make some real decisions.

I start with a blank sheet of paper, as I have so many times before. I draw a blue body with my marker. I pause for a few seconds, trying to decide which color I should make my costume. I can't wear a dozen different costumes; I must pick the color that best captures what I want to convey in the piece. When I realize what it should be, I let out a small sigh of relief, and soon I am drawing beautiful, flowing magenta pants as the bottom of the outfit. The other details come soon thereafter. I ridge the pants in flecks of yellow and orange to evoke gold. I draw a half dozen shining bangles on each wrist and then craft the well-made face of the drawing—full, red lips, dark eyes rimmed in *kajol*. It seems so right, after everything that's happened in these past few days, to have stripped away all the different visions I've had and settle on this one simple yet graceful image of myself.

I know just how to make this costume, too. My mother has an old magenta sari that she keeps tucked away far in her closet, behind several other saris—many of them magenta yet new—and I can use that for the pants. She also has so many sets of bangles that I could take a few and escape her observation. I shudder, remembering that I thought the same thing about the makeup, only to find out that my mother knew all along about that, as well.

The door to my bedroom opens and my mother walks in. She looks very tired and is still in her nightgown. Her eyes are puffy. Usually, this shows me that she's been crying, but that doesn't seem like the reason right now. I think they are puffy because she's been standing at the stove all morning.

"Vhat are you doing," she asks, although now I hear it: she has phrased the question in that terse manner that my dad uses, when his questions are not questions but statements.

"Drawing," I say softly.

"Drawing vhat?"

"Just drawing. Trying to work on my talent show act."

She bows her head and touches it with one hand. Her fingers still have flour on them, and her nails are full of dough.

"Kiran, I don't vant you to do the talent show anymore," she says. "I need you to focus on your schoolvork and try to put things back together."

I am completely speechless. This is the first time in my entire life that my mother has not supported me outright. Where is the woman who stood up to Pansy, making sure I got my ballet slippers without a real fight? Where is the woman who still smiled when I decided not to take *khatak* but chose ballet instead? Most of all, where is the woman who sat across from me at that kitchen table and laughed and bonded with me? I do not see her in this woman. I do not see her in this woman's puffy eyes or in her harsh words.

"But Mom, I have to do the show."

"No, you don't. You've done it enough. You need to focus."

I fight back a knot in my throat and persist, extemporizing a lie. "But I already gave Mrs. Nevins my permission slip and they've already made the programs and set the order, so I can't quit now." This could very well be true, but I don't know for sure. All I know is that I have to do the show. There is no question. Surely my mother can understand that.

"Listen, Kiran." She closes my bedroom door. "I am tired of this. I am tired of your behavior. You don't think I see vhat you do, these dolls you play with, this makeup problem? I am your mother. I see these things. I have tried to ask what is going on vith you, but you never give me a straight answer, and I am tired of trying to figure you out. Vhat am I supposed to say to your dad vhen he asks me about you? He is alvays asking vhy you are so different, vhy you act so strangely, and I can't give him any excuses anymore. You need to show me that you can behave and focus on vhat is important."

She leaves immediately, opening the door and walking out. I hear her steps along the stairs, the sliding of her hand along the banister. My father is still tallying figures, and his calculator is still spitting up paper.

I look down at my drawing, where a couple of tears have dropped and smudged the marker. One has landed just to the right of my face, so that the right eye bleeds black into the rest of the face. I rip it up, wanting to scream but even in this emotional storm knowing that I can't. I don't want my parents to hear me scream. So I just keep ripping. I look around my room and rip all the other pictures to shreds. I stuff them into my trash can, punch the pile deep into it.

Sitting on the floor and panting, I already regret what I've done. All of those hours of creation gone to waste. I have to get out of this room, which I do, walking down the stairs and opening the front door and stepping outside. It is no longer hot but cold, our lawn shellacked with frost, the idea of fog suggested in the street.

My gaze is pulled somewhere else, though. On the porch, rimmed in dirt and scratched—but there all the same—is my recorder.

*

Two days later, on Tuesday, Mrs. Goldberg can sense my addled state. The sentences I have diagrammed for homework are all jumbled up, subjects and predicates switched so that the sentences, when reconstructed, read things like "I my homework to do like" or "With the boy his dog running went." What is more, there is no doodling in the margins as I normally do. After going through a few spelling flash cards—including the words "magnanimous," "incongruent," and "mellifluous"—Mrs. Goldberg puts a hand on my shoulder and squeezes it gently.

"Kiran, are you all right? You seem a little down."

"Do I?" I say. "I'm totally fine. I did have a little bit of a fever this weekend."

She puts the back of her hand against my forehead. Her hand is cool and fragrant, a touch of lilac in it. "Really? You feel all right to me."

"Yeah, well, I still feel a little under the weather."

She examines me with her eyes for a second, the way one might do to an apple before taking a bite of it. "Now that you mention it, you do look a little zapped. But are you sure there is nothing else?"

"I'm sure."

"Okay. By the way, my husband saw the drawing you gave me and said he thought it was really beautiful. You really have quite a gift, Kiran."

I try to smile, but I can tell how fake it looks when I do so. Mrs. Goldberg's face falls, and I realize that I have to tell her what has happened with the talent show.

"Mrs. Goldberg, can I ask you a serious question?"

"Sure, Kiran."

"Have you ever felt . . . different from everyone else? Like you didn't belong anywhere?"

She sighs. "Kiran, I think everyone feels that way from time to time. And especially at your age. It's not easy being twelve."

"Yes, but it's even harder being *me* at twelve. I don't feel like any of the other kids understand me."

"But you seem to have a few good friends. I've seen you hanging out with Cody Ulrich and Donny Howard lately. They are nice boys."

I cringe, inside at least. Yesterday, when I ran into them on the playground, they didn't act the way I expected them to. I expected an outright badgering, with Cody telling me how I ruined the sleepover and Donny saying that it was my fault that they didn't see anything good. Instead, they looked at me quizzically, like an exotic bird they'd never seen in these parts—a peacock on the blacktop. When I mustered up the courage to ask them what happened at the rest of the sleepover, Cody scoffed.

"We had a great time, thank ya very much. My mom wouldn't've even known ya were gone if yer stupid mom would have kept her mouth shut and not called 'er."

I wanted to shout at him to leave my mother out of this, but I was too embarrassed that she had thought to call Beverly in the first place. My mother was too smart to think that my escape was all Beverly's fault, but she had wanted to embarrass me by scolding her; she had further sealed the punishment by depriving me of the talent show. My mother was smart.

"Cody and Donny are not really my friends," I tell Mrs. Goldberg. "Nobody is. I don't have any real friends. All I really have is you, Mrs. Goldberg."

"That's sweet, Kiran, but it's not true. You have your family, you have your faith. And you have your intelligence. You are the brightest student I've had in fifteen years of teaching. That is something to be proud of, and people will see that. Maybe they don't right now, but they will."

"Do you feel like you're sort of an outsider because you're Jewish, Mrs. Goldberg?"

She is speechless at first. Eventually, she goes with, "I'd rather not get too caught up in the religion question in light of what happened the other day with Mrs. Buchanan—she was right, you know, in keeping school and religion separate. But yes, I guess I've felt like an outsider sometimes, having been in a minority."

Something about the word "minority" stops the conversation for me. "Thanks for the talk, Mrs. Goldberg. I appreciate it." I say this weakly, and I can tell that Mrs. Goldberg is not all that satisfied with our conversation from the way she sighs, then takes a sip of her coffee. Fifteen years of teaching. She has been at this for a little while. Perhaps she does know more than I think. Perhaps her advice is sound.

But as I wait outside the school for my mom to come pick me up, I think again about the word "minority." Being a minority implies being part of a group. But to what group do I belong? Yes, I am Indian, but my recent experiences have only reiterated that I am not really a part of that group. There are so many unique qualities about me that I can't be put into one category. It reminds of Venn diagrams, which Mrs. Nevins taught us about—those intersecting circles that represent different groups; when they overlap, the area that they both contain is something that they have in common. What happens when you are represented by so many circles that the area you take up is so miniscule no one else could possibly fit into it?

When my mother arrives, I get into the car in silence. She looks a little better, her eyes not puffy, but I can tell that she is still upset with me. It is not until we turn onto our street that she looks over at me to say something. Then I hear her make a disapproving click with her tongue.

"*Beta*, are you feeling all right? You look a little strange."

"I do?"

"You look very tired."

"Well, I haven't been sleeping well."

Her tongue clicks again, but this time I can tell that it is not a click of disapproval but of compassion. She cannot stop from sympathizing with her son, and I loosen up a little bit knowing that the old version of my mom hasn't left entirely.

When we get home, my father is still not back from work. We pass through the kitchen as we normally do, except now there is that unsightly hole in the wall. My father called a contractor to come and fill it as soon as possible, but the contractor took one look at it, whistled softly, and said he hadn't brought the right tools to take care of a project that serious. The contractor came across as a no-muss, no-fuss guy. He stood there in his plaid flannel shirt and dirty jeans, his hair in tangled, dishwater curls, chewing gum and breathing heavily through his nostrils. He was an ugly man, and that had perhaps hardened him against people like my father, who shook his head at the contractor's inability to take care of the mess. I was stunned to hear this man reply, in turn, "Sir, don't shake yer head at me. This here's a big ole hole and you shoulda been more specific on the phone when ya called me." It was the first time I had ever heard someone talk to my father like that, and even he seemed taken aback by this snippy remark. The contractor left soon afterward, and my father was in an even worse mood because of the quick but effective dressing-down he'd received in front of my mother and me. I heard him saying various curses under his breath while he was in his study, and even though my mother and I didn't look at each other conspiratorially as we would have in the past, I could feel us both dying to do so.

As we pass through the kitchen this afternoon, my mother tells me to go take a nap. I gladly comply, knowing that every minute I spend sleeping is a minute I don't have to spend around that gaping hole in the wall.

When I get to my bedroom, I do something that I haven't done in days: I reach under my bed and pull out SS. Her bonnet is covered in a couple of dust bunnies, and I wipe them off lovingly. As sometimes happens with the icons in the master bedroom, I feel like her expression has changed a little bit. I am almost positive of it—the curl of her smile has drooped slightly, not as joyous or as cheeky as it once was. SS is aging just like me. She is becoming aware of the harsher realities of life. I think of all the other SS dolls in the world. There must be thousands, maybe hundreds of thousands. How in the world did this particular one end up with me? Does this SS ever wonder what life would have been like to end up with someone like Sarah or Melissa, *girls* for whom she was really made who would brush her hair and keep her on a shelf, not under a bed? Does this SS feel abused, neglected, depressed? For certain, Sarah and Melissa's dads wouldn't have taken their daughters' best friend in the world and thrown her into a trash bin.

When I wake up from my nap, it is dark outside, the sun having made its early fall descent. Through the curtains, I can make out the deep purple of the sky, a tangle of black branches silhouetted against it. Something about this time of the day makes me feel queasy, and when I sit up, I realize that I have an awful headache. SS has fallen off the bed, landing on her head, even more proof that I am as dangerous an owner as she could ever have had. I slide off my bed and head to the bathroom. My bathroom is not as grand as my parents'—it is barely big enough to fit the shower, the sink, the toilet, and a hamper—but it does have a bright pink bathmat, which I begged my mother for when I saw it at the mall.

After relieving myself, I wash my hands and splash water on my face. The cold water against my hot face doesn't feel good;

instead, it makes me feel depressed. It is a Tuesday evening in a dusky house in Ohio. My mother is cooking and my father is probably down in his study. The only thing that this cold water does is bring me back to this evening—this unexciting, boring evening. I look up at the mirror and pat my face with a small white hand towel.

I drop the towel into the sink. I touch my face, then shake my head, blink, and look again to make sure what I've seen is real. Sure enough, when I look back, I see it again. My skin—very faintly but undeniably—has turned blue.

*

Even after looking at myself for a solid half hour in the mirror, ignoring my mother's first call to dinner as I have done in the past when making myself up, even after sitting on my bed for another five minutes, almost cackling with laughter because of my ecstasy, I still cannot quite wrap my head around what has happened. The blue pallor of my face is so subtle, so much so that I don't even know if I would detect it if I didn't stare at myself in mirrors all of the time—but I am certain of what I have seen. My skin looks the same shade it does after I've wiped the eyeshadow from my face, a few miniscule particles of blue still wedged into the curve of my nose or a corner of my eye.

My heart is beating so hard against my ribs that it feels like a cardinal is trapped inside of me, fighting to get out. The little hairs inside my ears pulse with its energy. I have knotted my toes into the carpet at my feet. My hands clutch the side of my bed and squeeze it tightly. What was earlier an uncomfortable blush on my face is now an exhilarating warmth. How did this happen? A giggle escapes me when I realize that the only possible explanation is that God has proven to me that I am His reincarnation. This is why I have had to suffer so much. Sitting here, giddy with this knowledge, I know that it has all been worth it.

"Kiran!" my mother calls again. I panic, wondering how I can hide such a thing from her and my father. But then I remember how neither my mother nor Mrs. Goldberg said anything. They just said I looked different, but they didn't say my face had turned blue. Perhaps my parents won't even notice.

I go downstairs and expect my parents to be seated at the kitchen table, where we normally eat dinner. They are in the dining room instead. Obviously. My father would rather eat dirt than sit next to that monstrosity in the kitchen wall. The dining room is a much brighter room than our kitchen, with a huge crystal light fixture that tosses rainbow prisms and solid white beams all over the walls. I walk straight to my seat, sit down, and bow my head in prayer to detract from any attention that might otherwise be brought to my face.

"Are you feeling better, Kiran?" my mother asks as she sets my father's food in front of him. She has made *rajma*—curried red beans—along with soft basmati rice and fried okra. In the center of the table she places the casserole dish full of yogurt that she had in the oven the other night. When she opens the dish, I can see that two big spoonfuls have been scooped out, probably by my mother herself, who loves to snack on yogurt sprinkled with sugar when she watches the evening news on the couch.

"I feel much better," I respond. My mother nods approvingly as she goes back into the kitchen to get my food. My dad is silent at his end of the table, tearing off a bite of his *roti*, wrapping some of the *rajma* in it, and popping it in his mouth. He frowns, and I know it's because he doesn't think there's enough salt in it. Despite his recent efforts to eat healthier, my father cannot live without flavor, and so I say, "I'll get the salt," walk to the kitchen, and take it to him. I place it right beside his plate and go back to my seat. He says, "Thanks, *beta*," quietly, politely, and I feel much better hearing some kindness come from him.

He opens up a little bit. "How was school, *beta*?" As my mom comes back into the dining room, I notice for the first time how quiet it is. Normally when we eat dinner, we sit in the kitchen and watch news on the neighboring living room's television. Tonight, we have our conversation to get us by.

"School is fine. I got an A on my math test." This is a lie. I actually got an A-, but I feel the obligation to kick the grade up a notch to stay in my father's good graces.

"*Good* job, *beta*," he says. Math is his profession, after all, and it's the subject that he thinks is the most important for me to learn. One time, he asked me why I couldn't study math after school instead of language arts. I told him that math was a universal language whereas English was a specific one, so I obviously needed to focus on that specific language more. He didn't really understand that explanation and, frankly, neither did I. I was only extemporizing because I hate math and would have rather eaten cyanide than study it more.

"I thought . . ." I stop myself, afraid.

"You thought vhat?" my mother asks, taking a sip of water.

"I thought that . . . maybe because I did so well on my test . . . I could still do the talent show." It's my new skin talking. My recent discovery has emboldened me, and I say these words without thinking.

"Kiran. Ve already talked about this."

"But Mom! I've been working so hard—"

"Kiran."

I glance over at my dad and catch him making angry eyes at my mother. He tries to avert his stare once I look over, but I catch it just in time. I was wrong to think that he had loosened up. Of course—there is still several hundred dollars' worth of damage in the kitchen. I should have waited for the wall to heal, if not the emotional scars, before pressing my luck.

We finish the rest of dinner in relative silence. My mother can never sit down for long during dinner; she is always bringing us more *roti* or water, and so she contributes little to the conversation on most nights anyway. I begin to miss Peter Jennings so much; if he were on right now, he would make this whole situation much less awkward. Instead, I have only my father's eating to keep me company.

After dinner, I go to the bathroom and stare at my face again. It's not surprising that they should have missed the change; when I look at it again up here, I almost can't see it. For a second, I think that I made the whole thing up in my head and it never happened. I press my face close to the glass and examine my pores, trying to see the sparkling blue but seeing only brown. Then, when I step back, it pops out again. It's strange, but from certain angles, it appears bluer than it does in others. It's chameleonic.

I don't sleep a wink that night. When I catch the bus the next day, sitting in the front seat like I normally do to avoid the other kids, I am simultaneously so tired and excited that I want to fall asleep and dance at the same time. All throughout the school day, I keep thinking that someone will notice how different I look, but if my own parents weren't able to see the difference, these people certainly will not. By the end of the day, I am so tired that I forget I have ballet rehearsal in the multipurpose room. I am five minutes late, and Marcy has an annoyed face when I show up.

I don't care, though. Marcy teaches us a complicated sequence of pas de bourrée, pas de chat, and a *jetté*, and I perform it flawlessly, landing after the *jetté* in a soundless pounce. As I hit the ground, I decide not to listen to my mother's admonition. I am doing the talent show whether she likes it or not. Behold the stealthy blue god.

Like Father,
Like Someone Else

The next day, Thursday morning, I ask my mother if she can take me to the library after I'm finished studying with Mrs. Goldberg. I tell her that I have to do a book report on *Bridge to Terabithia* for Mrs. Nevins's class by Monday and that I need to use three resources from the library in the course of writing the paper. She is watching a rerun of *Rhoda* on TV and nods approvingly over her cup of tea. She doesn't suspect what I am going to be up to there—sewing my costume for the show. Last night, while she and my father were watching CNN *Headline News*, I crept upstairs, went straight to her closet, and fished out that old magenta sari and an old gold *dupatta*, or sash, then rummaged through the bottom of the closet to extract two spools of yellow thread and a needle from the sewing notions she keeps down there.

One thing I didn't expect to find at the bottom of mother's closet was a pair of ankle bells—tiny, tarnished metal bells strung together on red velvet ribbon. They were the bells she was wearing in that photo album. They tinkled as I pulled them out, and I had to steady them as I ran back to my room so that they didn't give me away.

After my mother gives me her head nod this morning, I leave the house with the fruits of my reaping tucked into my backpack (save the ankle bells, which would have been impossible to keep quiet while my backpack shifted). I had to take out a couple of textbooks to fit them in, and on my desk I've left the plain gray chunk of *Mathematical Puzzles* and the thick volume *Adventures in Reading*, which bears a picture of teddy bears dressed like Renaissance scribes waving red ribbons on its front. I had to struggle to fit in my recorder and *Warriner's English Grammar*.

I start to sense that something is amiss during math class. Since I left my book at home, I don't look at the diagrams in the book as instructed but spend more time looking at the people around me. I notice that Cody and Donny keep looking at each other, giggling, and Sarah and Melissa, sitting in back of me, laugh more than usual. Twice, Mrs. Nevins has to ask the girls to quiet down. It becomes clear to me that Cody, Donny, Sarah, and Melissa have all connected on something, and I assume that what they've connected on is little ole me.

Perhaps it is better to be really, really different from people instead of being simply different. This way, you don't need to worry about conforming or trying to act normal. With my new skin, I don't have to worry about being like everyone else because it is virtually impossible now. I don't have to be part of Sarah and Melissa's clique, nor do I have to try to get in with Cody and Donny's good graces. Even if they form a supergroup now, it is of no consequence to me. Now that I don't have any hope of being ordinary ever again, I don't need to worry about my looks or my opinions or how to fit in. It's the most liberating feeling I've ever had.

I show up at my session with Mrs. Goldberg the least prepared that I've ever been. I haven't done any practice exercises. Mrs. Goldberg is understandably confused by this, but I make up for my delinquency by suggesting alternative exercises that we might try—as if I'm the one who is supposed to create the curriculum—then work on them avidly. Mrs. Goldberg softens a bit and soon enough is offering her usual encouragement. By the end, she gives me a whole sheet of stickers as a reward. They are "Stickers of the World" and show cartoon people in different countries. A girl with a headdress resembling a gravy boat stands in front of an oversize windmill: Holland. A copper-skinned woman turned sideways, her arms forming a Z, stands in front of a lopsided pyramid: Egypt. A man in a black suit and red kerchief, a bull about to rear-end him, stands in front of a Spanish-style church; the sticker reads "New Mexico," but I'm pretty sure that's wrong. These stickers were not made by the sharpest tool in the shed.

After my session with Mrs. Goldberg, I go outside to wait for my mother. There are a couple of girls waiting for their parents, too. They are younger than I am and have tiny pom-poms in their hands. Cheerleaders. Or future cheerleaders. They are chewing gum and laughing together. Both of them have their hair in ponytails, and they are wrapped in nylon jackets. Their faces are red from the chill. At their age, I had no idea what would become of me or what I would have seen by now. I wonder if they'll grow up to know what I know.

Our Mercedes appears outside the building, but it's not my mom. I make out the serious figure of my dad, who pulls up with a slight halt. My heart mimics this movement. I open the door and get in.

"Hi, *beta*," he says, and we don't talk for the next couple of minutes, as he drives down the residential road that I myself walked down a couple of weeks before on my way to the park. When we get to Yates Avenue, I expect us to turn and head to our own subdivision, but my father gets into the lane that heads to the park. The light is red, and for a moment, I think he's made a mistake.

"I know, Kiran. I am taking you to the park."

"But I have to go to the library tonight. I have a book report due on Monday and I need to use three—"

"Not tonight, Kiran. If it's due on Monday, you vill go this weekend. Ve need to talk."

The backpack on my lap seems to exhale depressingly when he says this.

I'm so upset about not being able to construct my costume at the library that I don't realize how bizarre it is that I am going to the park with my father. It is not bright outside as it was during my first scandalous visit, nor is it dark like the nighttime discovery of Rodney. It is orange outside, the trees and blades of grass glazed in sunset. In all the debauchery, I'd forgotten what a beautiful place this is, a peaceful, restful place. All the same, I am with my dad, and as we drive up the roadway and stop near a large willow tree, I feel the usual nervous pangs.

When my father turns off the car, I reach for the door handle, thinking that we are going to take a walk, perhaps sit under the tree. Its long, leafy tresses sway gently in the breeze, a thick carpet of shed branches at its trunk, and it looks like the sort of calm conversational spot in *Winnie the Pooh* or *The Wind in the Willows*. My father doesn't reach for his handle, though, so I retract my gesture and look at the keys dangling from the ignition.

We sit there for a minute not talking at all. My heart is pounding in my ears again, and for a second I think that I might have a migraine. The usual cosmic cruelty continues, however, and I remain possessed of my senses.

"I vork very hard for you and your mom, Kiran," he says. "I always have. When your mom and I immigrated here in 1975, I knew that I vould have to vork hard to make it in this country. Your mom and I passed by the Statue of Liberty vith forty dollars in our pockets. And look at everything ve have today. Look at everything you have. You have alvays gotten vhat you vanted, vhen you vanted it. When you vanted to take ballet, ve let you take ballet. When you vanted a new backpack or a new book, ve let you buy those things. Ve've made sacrifices—so many sacrifices—so that you can be happy and do vell in school and make something of yourself here.

"Vhen I grew up in Delhi, I lived in a bungalow vith my parents and Gita Massi."

Gita Auntie, my father's sister, lives in Houston with her husband and my cousin Jaideep.

"I never got to do anything besides my schoolvork. I alvays vanted to learn how to play the *tabla*, but I never even asked my parents if I could because I knew that ve did not have enough money. And because I vorked all the time at my uncle's bicycle shop. I alvays hoped that one day I vould have enough money to let my own kids do vhat they vanted to do, and I have seen that happen."

He pauses here and swallows. His voice is still hoarse from the other night, and I can hear the saliva catching in his throat. He reaches into his back pocket and pulls out a handkerchief into which he dispenses a loud burst of air and snot. It sounds like a rubber nose that a clown might pinch. I want to laugh, but while my father is bending over to blow his horn, I happen to glance over at him and notice what I noticed about my mother the other day: he looks tired. Not only that, but he has aged. I've always thought of my father as the same way he's always looked; in fact, when I picture him, I imagine him as he is in the Olan Mills portrait that we had taken three years ago—he in a gray, '70s-style suit and red tie, my mother in a subdued black *salwaar kameez*, and I, age nine, in my own miniature gray blazer and clip-on red tie. In that picture, my father is thirty-seven, his smile rather white, his eyes, behind oversized plastic glasses, not necessarily happy or jolly but full of purpose. Up until this moment, my mental default has always imagined his teeth just as starkly white, his eyes just as active, but I see in the car, under this shedding willow, how much wear and tear his features have taken. His teeth, which are bared as he blows his nose, have turned off-white, even yellow around the edges, and his skin is somewhat patchy, darker just under the cheekbone, at his temples, and under his bottom lip.

"Vhen your mom and I first came to this country, ve both had to vork to put ourselves through college at the University of Cincinnati. I vould vork as a security guard at a bank, and she vould vork as a part-time nanny. Ve lived in a small apartment in a dangerous part of town, and ve vould have to valk straight to vork and back because the neighbors vould give us dirty looks. Men vould say bad things to your mom, and once some men almost attacked her."

Neither my father nor my mother has ever told me this, and I imagine the fear on my mother's face. I envision her running away from a band of hoodlums, and I crumple slightly in my seat as I see that darling woman's face, contorted in terror as she runs to a tiny house with a crumbling porch roof and a spare light gleaming from its front window. In my mind, the house looks very much like the front of our temple—the pundit's Upanishad-furnished residence—and then I remember my mother telling me years ago over a spontaneous batch of *idli* and *sambar* that she and my dad used to live close to the temple.

"Your mom and I put ourselves through college. Ve did not have a TV. Ve did not even have a phone for the first year that ve lived here. Ve knew nobody at first, but then ve met all of the uncles and aunties you know. Rashmi Auntie and Sanjay Uncle vere our first friends, and they really made the effort to introduce us to others." Then he adds, "Probably because Rashmi Auntie loves to make food for people." He chuckles, and suddenly I realize that this might just be a real bonding session instead of a showdown. I laugh, too.

My father pauses. If we were in our kitchen right now, this would be the moment when he would pull his teacup close to his lips, holding it in both hands, extracting warmth from it while staring pensively at the refrigerator. Instead, we are in this car, which is starting to become cold as the heat slinks away and the chill from outside starts to set in. As if echoing this transformation, my father's sudden cheerfulness disappears.

"Your mom and I tried to have a baby for a few years. A few times," he pauses again, "she did get pregnant, but..." This time, he stops. I am totally baffled. I do not understand how someone can be pregnant and not have a baby, but I don't say anything.

"Then ve had you, Kiran. Do you know vhat the name 'Kiran' means?"

I don't. How have I not thought to ask before? "No, I don't," I say. My voice sounds so small.

"It means 'light.' 'Ray of light.' Your mom thought it vas the perfect name. I vasn't totally sure because 'Kiran' is sometimes a girl's name." His voice catches here. "But you veren't a girl."

He pauses.

"You aren't a girl."

I feel a buildup in my bladder, as if I'm going to wet the car seat. I wish the willow would erupt in flames, that the whole world would explode so that this moment would end.

"Your mom and I did not vork so hard for so many years so that ve could raise a son who vould act the vay you do. Ve have given you everything, and you are ruining vhat ve have done for you. So you need to think about vhat you vant to do vith all our hard vork. You have to think about how every time you play vith your mom's things, you are hurting us. You are making our lives difficult."

I burst into tears right as I hear this last sentence. My crying does not resemble the way people cry in movies. There is no full wail or graceful trickling of tears. My crying is choppy, broken up by unseemly heaves. My voice sounds like a goose squawking.

I have never felt so ineffective as a boy. My crying proves right everything that my father is accusing me of.

He continues, unfazed. "I do not vant to have this conversation again, Kiran. I am tired. Your mom is tired. Don't make us tired anymore."

With this, he starts the car and backs out of the lot. He switches gears and coasts back toward the entrance. Or exit. Dusk has fallen fast, and the sky is navy blue. The trees and the grass, the wind and the chill, the autumn—they are all still doing their thing, oblivious to the passing by of this father and son. As Krishna, did I not sit in a field and bend them to my will? How, then, can they ignore me?

When we get home, my mother is sitting at the kitchen table reading the newspaper. The TV is on—more news. She looks up as we enter, and I expect her face to be hardened. Instead, she smiles sweetly and asks how my day was. Her eyes are compassionate. Maybe she realizes that she had something to do with the way I turned out. The photo album of her in *khatak* garb and the way she made me adore it—does she remember that?

My father goes into the hall to hang up his coat, then goes to his study and starts working. I can hear the usual rhythmic sounds of his work—the turning of pages, the quick clack of his fingers on the calculator, his throat-clearing. My mother serves me *pakora* with tangy coconut chutney. I am finishing them when my father appears with his camcorder.

"Vhat are you eating, Kiran?" he asks happily. It is as if the park moment happened months ago. He has expected me to take it in as a piece of information, the way his calculator takes in figures. He does not seem to remember my tears, but all I can hear is that squawking. Looking into the small screen that he turns to me as usual, I swear that *I* look older, too.

We will never be like each other. I will never respond emotionally the way he does. We will never be more than two containers, full of the same blood but different in size, shape, owners. His belongs to the mind, and mine belongs to the heart.

Turkey and Stuffing

Some mornings you just wake up feeling a little evil.

Not that I slept for very long. I decided last night that instead of trying to sew my costume together in the library, where a prim librarian might find me out and banish me from the premises forever, I would do it at night when my parents were snoring and fast asleep. They are a loud pair, a couple of sleepy tigers in the jungle of their master bedroom, and I have a theory that you could blow up my end of the house and they would sleep through it. The thing that baffles me is how each of them is even capable of sleeping with the other snoring so loud alongside. I guess their sounds cancel each other out.

While my parents' noses rumbled, I turned on my bedside lamp, which has a shade with stars and moons all over it. I didn't turn on the main light in the room, lest the snore balance in my parents' room shift and send one to find the crack of light under my door. (A kiran giving away a Kiran, as it were.) I spread my mother's old magenta sari on the floor of my room and sized it up. I had torn up my sketch that day when my mother told me that I was not going to participate in the talent show, but recreating the design was easy, and I found that something guided me last night and made me a more capable seamstress than usual.

"Tailor," I heard a ghost of my father say, in the same stern tone he had used with me that evening in the park. Not that he would want me to be a tailor, either. The only needle it would have been acceptable for me to hold was a syringe while administering a vaccine to some patient—every Indian parent's dream.

It wasn't until I had my pink-handled scissors in my hands that I realized I was cutting up the sari. It might have made more sense for me to just wear it the way it was, or perhaps as a different sort of wrap, crisscrossing it through my legs. But as I tried to envision my drawing in my head again, I noticed that the sweep of the costume was much grander than a simple wrap around my body. The costume I had fashioned in that drawing was made of many different parts—a cinched top with gold trim, a pant-skirt combination edged with gold, a headdress of ribbons. In order to make those different things, I would have to divvy up this swath of fabric and make each component separately. So I cut the fabric up and sewed in a frenzy. It all happened more easily than I could have imagined. By the time the sun was beginning to creep back into the sky, I had finished the basic parts of the outfit.

So I am headed to school with my backpack full of cloth again, telling my mother that I have a last-minute ballet rehearsal after school and asking if she can pick me up at seven. She gives me a suspicious look, as well she should, but for some miraculous reason lets me go on my merry way all the same.

The costume still needs some smoothing out and some extra adornment. And I know exactly where I am going to get those things. I just have to wait until the end of the school day. Then I will make my move.

*

Nothing else would have brought Cody, Donny, Sarah, and Melissa together but me. The four of them have taken to greeting each other whenever they see each other, and at recess, they actually spend time playing together instead of staying on opposite ends of the playground. The four of them chat at the border of the blacktop, before it meets the grass. They giggle and look my way from time to time. I have made the mistake of staying within their line of sight and not taking my recorder to The

Clearing. The thing is, I can't help but observe the four of them. How did Sarah and Melissa, otherwise "cool" girls, end up with a hunchback like Cody and an ostrich like Donny?

Then again, Donny isn't *that* miscast as their friend. He is showing signs of becoming a true man, and given that he can pass for an actual basketball player, it is only a matter of time before Sarah and Melissa become basketball cheerleaders and start vying for his affections. For these girls, a boy's early-onset acne is nothing compared to the promise of sports stardom.

But Cody. How did Cody make it past the social barrier? He is scrawny, and sometimes I think that Donny only entertains his desire to play basketball so that he can look large next to his opponent. All the same, Cody, in his extra-baggy hooded sweatshirts and oversize jeans—billowy monstrosities of fabric with the sole aim of concealing his deformity—gets to laugh with Sarah and Melissa and be part of their clique.

But why am I dwelling on such trifles in the first place? I have a plan in motion that I should be focusing on, and a giddiness comes over me as I get closer to its execution. There is only a week until the talent show, and the next few days are going to be crucial to giving my predecessor His due on stage.

The last bell of the day finally rings, and students pour outside to the blacktop again, this time to pile onto their respective buses, which pull up alongside the building like whinnying horses at Churchill Downs. Most of the teachers are outside ushering children while the rest are scurrying around the building, gathering their things as quickly as possible so they can get out of this hellhole for the weekend. Principal Taylor herself, in a crisp black power suit with shoulder pads the size of Portobello mushrooms, paces between the main entrance to the school, where the parents of afternoon kindergarten students pick them up, and the back entrance, where the buses are ready to leave.

I stand in a small nook of drinking fountains between the entrances. People rarely use these fountains because there is another pair right beside the back entrance, and so I am able to stall here while most people push past. A couple of times, someone gives me a baffled expression, wondering why I've stuffed myself back here, but in those cases, I simply lean over as if I'm having a sip of water. Some kids give me a smirk, assuming that I ended up back here because I'm too defenseless to make it down the hall without getting pushed to the side. I respond with the weak expression they want to see.

Soon the school begins to quiet down, and the last of the buses pulls away, a whimpering cloud of exhaust left in its wake. Principal Taylor's massive figure darkens the doorway as she comes back inside, and I duck into the nook, hiding myself from her view. I hear her high heels clop down the hallway back to her office, and soon there is nothing left but the chugging sound of the school's shoddy heating system and the swish of an errant piece of paper here and there.

I walk down the hall, passing a few doorways where teachers are still packing up their things. I tiptoe past, trying not to make any noise. Usually there are children walking about like this on weekdays because there is some sort of class or event going on— like my dance class, or the latchkey program. But Fridays are different. On Fridays, our latchkey program is virtually empty. I've heard that sometimes Camille Huff, a doe-faced black girl with wispy hair and a wardrobe that includes about twenty different striped sweaters, is the only person there. But aside from her and Principal Taylor, who must eventually trot down to her pink Mary Kay Cadillac in the parking lot and speed home, there are very few people left here. In fact, I am pretty certain that the one person whom I want gone is gone by now.

I approach the art room carefully. It dawns on me that perhaps I've waited too long to come down here. Mrs. Buchanan might have already locked up for the weekend, preventing me from entering her room. I tiptoe closer and tuck myself into a small crack behind an art display case, which has a collection of Thanksgiving dioramas. Or at least that's what it seems the assignment was. There are very few Indians in the proceedings from what I can see. There are plenty of deranged pilgrims— some of them are colored green and purple and gray. Then I realize that those are the Indians. I swear I can see a tiny dot of red crayon on one of their foreheads, but I avert my eyes, trying not to think about this garbled cultural interpretation.

Someone is moving around inside the art room. Not just someone—Mrs. Buchanan. I can hear her massive shoes stomping around. At one point, I hear a bunch of keys jingling, and I identify the sound as Mrs. Buchanan's enormous mitt scooping them up and putting them in her cardigan. I should have thought this plan through a little better. How am I supposed to get into the classroom before Mrs. Buchanan locks the door? Then I hear her shoes coming to the door and realize that she's coming out. She'll lock the door and I'll have missed my chance.

A miracle happens, though. Mrs. Buchanan leaves the room wearing a fir green cardigan and a driftwood-rough skirt and heads down the hallway to the ladies' room. The door to her room is wide open. I scurry into it the way I used to scurry to the basement to get my Country Crock. I try not to think of the way that ended up, although I *have* been eating Butterfingers and other buttery things to tide me over, so anything's solvable.

The art room is sort of scary at the end of the day. It might have been bustling before, but now it's ghostly. Nothing is more terrifying than a bunch of half-finished turkeys made out of two-liter Coke bottles, and that is exactly what sits on one of the large workman tables. They are faceless at this point, only their torsos painted brown and their tails sprouting primary-colored feathers. I crawl behind their table and wait on all fours. Part of me wants to watch the doorway so that I can see Mrs. Buchanan return, but it's better to stay entirely hidden until she has left. Not looking at her ugly mug is clearly the better option.

Soon enough, Mrs. Buchanan comes into the room. She makes strange noises to herself. She grumbles a lot, and I can't tell if she's actually saying words or if it's gibberish that comes forth of its own accord. Her legs make a scratchy, swishy sound due to her stockings. Every time her feet hit the ground, it sounds like she's dropped something. She moves around a lot, and at one point I think she's headed for the turkey table I'm under. Thankfully, she swerves and goes to the marker wall, an intricate patchwork of cubby holes that have all the different kinds of markers we use in class. She spends more time than is sane organizing the markers, making sure they're all in their right places. I can tell every time she finds a marker out of place because she makes yet another grumbling noise—a gurgle, really. I get so tired of waiting on my hands and knees that I end up sprawling myself on the ground, eventually resting my chin on my hands like an angel in the Raphael painting that women in this town wear silkscreened on white T-shirts.

Finally, she walks over to her desk and hoists up what I can only assume to be an elephant. In other words, her bag. There is a quiet click as she turns out the lights, and then there is the turning of her key in the door. She departs down the hallway, the sound of her shoes like a stampede passing in the distance.

For the first few minutes, I stay under the desk. Not because I think that Mrs. Buchanan might return—although the thought does cross my mind—but because I am temporarily paralyzed at how exciting a feeling it is to be in this room after hours. No sentinel Buchanan, no castigating Sarah and Melissa, Cody and Donny. It dawns on me that this school is not such an awful place when the awful people are taken out of it. It's a place where I come to learn, where I've built my intelligence—especially with Mrs. Goldberg, who is one of the only nonawful people.

Still, I have a feeling that Saraswati Herself, goddess of education and learning, would not appreciate how I eventually wriggle myself out from under the desk and look around the room with a wicked grin.

I spread my costume out on one of the tables not covered with pop poultry. Although my sewing—*tailoring*—is not too shabby, the fabric still looks a little bare. So I set out to find what I came here for: ostentatious ornamentation. Mrs. Buchanan's room is full of viable materials: rainbow-colored beads (fat ones, thin ones, bright ones, dark ones), glitter (which comes in long plastic bottles with white twist-on tops), colored glue (either fluorescent or dark like chocolate and caramel), yarn (some of it braided with silver or gold threads to give it extra shimmer), paint (some in tiny little jars with black caps, some in little tubes that have been squeezed and twisted by reckless little hands, some in large plastic bottles that show how thick and brightly colored the liquid they bear actually is), construction paper (regular-sized or legal-sized, every pile composed of different-colored sheets so that from the side they look like a rainbow that's been ironed). These materials are scattered all over the room, as if in stations, since Mrs. Buchanan doesn't have a proper supply closet. So I have to take a handful of each type of material and bring it to the table where I've spread my garment, as if I'm the sole doctor performing a complex surgical procedure on a patient.

By the time I've finished gluing and weaving everything together, I hold an assortment of shining armor in my hands. I realize that I haven't just crafted something that Krishna would wear. I've fashioned a conglomerate of all the garments that I've seen the gods and goddesses wear in those paintings. There is something of Lakshmi and Saraswati's saris in the way that the "shirt" falls, but there is also something of the puffy pants that Krishna and his warrior friends wear in their pursuits through hills, fields, jungles, battlefields. I even have the idea to thread together a large number of beads that I can wear like long chains around my neck. They look like the large carnation garland that the elephant-headed Ganesh wears in His portraits or like a bejeweled version of the cobra around Shiva's neck. They also resemble the necklaces that Madonna used to wear in her early videos. As I start putting away all of the materials and wait for the glue to dry, I start humming "Dress You Up in My Love."

Once I have my arms over my head and am swinging my hips in a circle—"dress you up in my looooooove"—I throw my head back and happen to look at the clock. I gasp. It's already ten till 7:00, ten minutes until I'm supposed to meet my mom. Ten till 7:00 on a Friday afternoon. Not a time for anyone to be at this school, except the janitors. I perk my ears up and try to see if I can hear them moving around. Sure enough, I hear the faint sound of small wheels rolling along the hallway.

I'm used to seeing the janitors at work when I stay later with Mrs. Goldberg. It seems like a lonely job, moving slowly down paper-littered corridors with nothing but a yellow bucket of suds and a large mop that looks like the impaled head of a sheepdog. I think about that display case in the hallway and how the janitors must look forward to its contents changing; at least then they have something new to look at. Other than that, they have the same stretch of sneaker-burned, sticky floor to wipe clean every day. And no matter how clean they make the floors, no matter how many times they drag their mops across that surface, the same gaggle of kids—or their younger siblings, another generation of floor-scuffers and litterbugs—will be back to dirty it up again.

The janitors have a reason to be here, though. I, on the other hand, don't know what I am going to tell my mom if I'm late. I still have all the supplies to put back and clean up, but that will take me at least fifteen minutes. How could I be so foolish? None of this plan was thought through. I simply had the idea and ran with it. My new skin has made me assume invincibility. I've been moving around for the past few days as if I have no one to answer to.

Isn't that the way things should be? Clearly, if I've been deemed worthy enough to succeed Krishnaji, I can find a way to magically clean this room like Mary Poppins. Maybe if I just sit on the ground and meditate about it hard enough, or play the recorder that is smushed in with my fabric, I might just find myself back home. But even I know that won't happen. I am the divine made mortal, not the divine made divine, and there are certain limits to being reincarnated as Kiran Sharma. I chuckle for a second thinking what Krishna would have made of Mrs. Buchanan if she had been in his forest. One minute spent with that clog-hooved nightmare and he would have run out of the trees screaming about yogis and fogeys.

Once I think my costume is dried, I fold the various pieces carefully and put them back in my bookbag. Giving a last glance around to make sure that everything looks the way it did when I snuck in here, I head toward the door and peer cautiously out of the small square window that is in its top right corner. I have to do a *relevé* on the balls of my feet to see out of it, but no one seems to be in the hallway. I don't even see the long cord of a janitor's vacuum snaking across the tile. I open the door, still moving cautiously, and am just about to shut it behind me when I hear laughing. It's not innocent laughter. It's laughter with a purpose—mischievous laughter. It's not coming from the hallway, however. It takes me a second to realize that it's coming from outside.

I turn around and look out one of the long windows running alongside Mrs. Buchanan's room. Outside in the dark, I can make out a few kids horsing around on the lawn that borders this side of the school. When I see the murky outline of a kid throwing back his head and laughing with some difficulty, his curved shoulders jutting out grotesquely, I realize that I am watching Cody. He is with Donny and the girls.

I go back into the room and shut the door, transfixed by the sight before me. It's too dark in this room for them to see me—indeed, I finished my project under relative dark given the early autumn night—but I can make them out more clearly the closer I get to the window. The buttery lights that are perched on the rim of the school's roof have come on, and between my squinting and their glow, I can make out quite clearly the jolly looks on the kids' faces.

HOW IN THE HELL DID THEY BECOME FRIENDS? I yell to myself in my head, yet again. I just don't get it. And not only are they hanging out together, but now they're sticking around *after school* to hang out? It just doesn't make any sense. Where in the hell do Sarah and Melissa's parents think they are right now? The football game? Of course—they probably go to the football games in that large patch of light next to the high school every Friday, apprenticing themselves to the older girls who discuss loftier things than Lip Smackers chapstick. But still, that begs the question: why would these girls forgo that cesspool of popularity for Donny and . . . Cody?

Soon enough, pinpoints of cigarette light give me my answer.

The four of them are smoking up a storm out there. And they remind me of those kids in the park. Part of me wants to break through the window and yell at them, warn them that they are headed for a wayward, destructive existence, but at the same time, I know that my fascination with what those kids were doing has not diminished in the least. If I placed one of those burning sticks to my lips, would I be cool like these four? Would I be headed toward a life of waywardness or achievement?

That devilish feeling I felt this morning returns, except it's multiplied by a hundred, transforming my blood into fire. Every humiliating, intense experience I've had recently has instilled anger in me, but the anger is compounding, and now I feel like it's reached the height of its powers. Without thinking, I turn around, walk to the table bearing the pop bottle turkeys, and start pulverizing them. I grab one and rip its feathers off. I take another and chuck it across the room. It hits the pencil sharpener attached to the wall. I take three at a time, throw them on the floor, and start smashing them under my feet. I see one of those plastic jars of Crayola paint—red—unscrew its cap, and scatter paint all over the rest of them. I hit them with my hands— my arms, really—and send them flying through the air. Real turkeys don't fly, but boy, do these turkeys lift off. I keep pounding them with my fists, and the red paint has gotten all over my hands. I am hitting the faux poultry so hard that I could be bleeding but wouldn't know it for the paint.

I don't stop at the turkeys. In the spare seconds I have between throws and poundings and punches, I can still hear the four of those kids laughing, can still hear the garbles of their speech through the glass. I proceed to ruin the marker wall, unleash the rest of the Crayola paint, lob fistfuls of beads across Mrs. Buchanan's desk, then push everything off her desk onto the floor with both hands. The mug that holds pencils and pens breaks against the floor, and pieces I can't even see scatter across the room and under tables. The last thing I do is to jump up and swat at the papier mâché heads on the wall. A pig, a California Raisin, a Paula Abdul in a tilted checkered hat—I make them all fall to the floor and wreak my footstorm havoc on them.

The only thing that stops me is realizing that in my frenzy I may have jostled the bag on my back and ruined my costume. I slink off the bag and open it. The costume is fine, but Mrs. Buchanan's room . . . her room is streaked with ruined art. Donny and Cody, Sarah and Melissa, however, are still living it up outside.

If they can smoke, so can I. I pick up two of the disemboweled turkeys and some of the papier mâché mess from the floor and walk over to the kiln. I open it up, stuff the bunch of crumpled paper into it, slam the lid closed, and flick the switch on. I wipe my hands together as if I've loaded a dishwasher, then turn on my heel and leave quietly.

*

"How was rehearsal?" my mother asks as I get into her car.
"Good. Sorry we went late," I say, so coolly that I shudder.

*

I am so steeled by the revenge that I've exacted on Mrs. Buchanan and SCAMMED (a sort of acronym I fashion from the names of that quartet of traitors on the ride home) that I don't think of the real ramifications of what I've done. It's not until I lie down for bed—not even until my parents have retired for the evening and their snore overture begins—that I sit bolt upright and think of the janitors in that building. I think of the building itself—flames licking at bulletin boards all over, Mrs. Goldberg's mug charred black with smoke—but I also think of actual people being injured or killed. I wish I were not just a god but Superman, capable of flying to the school and breathing a frigid wind that would frost the people in it to safety. I wrap my arms around myself, caressing my skin as if I can unlock its godly power. But nothing happens, nothing *keeps* happening, and I start scratching my skin, cursing it, crouching down on the floor as if in physical pain. I always thought that revenge was supposed to feel victorious. Krishna Himself danced a happy jig every time He bested demons, but I find no such joy in what I've done.

Cody, Donny, Sarah, and Melissa must have run away from the inferno in complete wonderment, laughing at how they would probably miss a ton of school for what had happened. Maybe they went to the football game anyway, a part of the acceptance and chicness of that event after all.

The night proceeds in spurts of crying and total exhaustion. A few times I wake up on a pillow damp with tears. I cannot decide if the fact that it's now Saturday and there is no school is comforting. This way, I will have no knowledge of the extent of the damage I've caused. I will have only this agony.

*

God bless those janitors.

As my parents and I see on a noon broadcast of the local news—the local newscasters look downtrodden on Saturday, clearly wanting to be at home lounging like everyone else—one of the janitors, Bob Randolph, a wan thirtysomething with the eyes of an eighty-year-old, smelled smoke in the building and got to Mrs. Buchanan's room just as the flames were burning through her door. He ran to the nearest red belt buckle of an alarm and pulled it. Unfortunately, the sprinkler system had already had twenty years to invite dust and decay, so it didn't exactly quell the fire. It did, however, stall it in time for the firefighters to arrive and put it out.

What's left after their efforts is not as awful as it may have been, but it's not exactly a pretty sight, either. As we see on the TV, a hole like a cigarette smoker's dirty mouth has been burned into the side of the building. Mrs. Buchanan's room is obliterated, the roof caved in. The steel frames of the windows from which I watched SCAMMED have twisted and look like tartar-coated teeth. A couple of streaks of black climb out of the hole like mutant tongues. The full shot of the school makes the damage look relatively minimal, a black splotch on a picture, but the close-up shot is ghastly, fierce, gnarly.

An equally repugnant sight comes on the screen soon enough. It's Melinda Maines, all corporate Joan Collins in a garish hot pink suit and earrings so big they look like gold meteors that fell onto her face. She stands in front of the wreck as boisterously as any other event she would be attending, like this is an exciting thing to behold instead of a mysterious fiasco. Indeed, if her microphone were a corndog, she'd practically be at the Ohio State Fair.

"The blaze was discovered at approximately seven fifteen p.m. by Mr. Randolph, who says he saw four young students near the blaze around the time of his discovery. Those children, whose names cannot be released at this time, are being questioned thoroughly. Mr. Randolph believes that the mishap may have been the result of improperly disposed-of cigarettes."

It's too perfect. It's just too perfect. Sarah and Melissa wanted to be friends with Cody and Donny? Cody and Donny wanted to be friends with Sarah and Melissa? Well, they got what they wanted, and now the police are grilling them. Maybe they'll be executed—burned at the stake! No, no, that won't happen, but it's just . . . too perfect.

I guess I should learn a moral from this: that it shouldn't matter what actually happened to the school or what part I actually played in the disaster, but that I did such a terrible thing so recklessly and that I have caused four otherwise uninvolved children to be blamed for it. And I do, faintly. But more than anything, I thank my lucky stars. For once, I feel like I've actually come out on top. For this, I am truly thankful.

Dress Rehearsal/Sari Séance

The gymnacafetorium looks like a chiffon dragon vomited all over it.

It's Wednesday, the day before the talent show. Every year, Mrs. Nevins runs a dress rehearsal, which is supposed to be an assuring run-through of the acts but more often than not turns into a battle of egos. Put a few dozen girls in bright pink, red, blue, gold, and silver sequined costumes, then put them in the same room and see what happens. Many of the girls are wearing tap shoes, the sounds of which, when compounded like this, sound like a storm against the floor. Some of the more down-home girls are wearing clogging shoes, and their sound is heavier, like throwing a rock into a well. The girls who are not wrapped in sequined bodices or decorated with faux feathers are wearing sleek leotards and leg warmers. One group has decided that it is going to perform a routine dressed as the Smurfs, and a couple of them have done themselves up in full costume to give Mrs. Nevins a full picture of what they will look like. They are wearing white thermal underwear, have stuffed their long hair into collapsed-pillowcase hats, and have smeared their faces with blue face paint. Whereas my attempts at making myself blue have heightened my mystique appearance-wise, these girls look totally freakish. The blue is way too fake, and in addition to their worker-elf air, they are holding batons, as if the first thing that comes to mind when one thinks of the Smurfs is their incredible acrobatic flair. With their batons clutched in their hands like tridents as they march about and laugh, they are demonic—hypothermic Oompa Loompas who have escaped from Willy Wonka's chocolate factory to murder us all.

I have not worn my real costume today. I can't let people know my true performance intentions due to the religious character I am portraying. True, Mrs. Buchanan hasn't been to school at all this week due to the utter destruction of her classroom—and, it would seem, her entire purpose of existing—but I am too wise to risk Mrs. Nevins scrapping my act. Instead, I have dressed myself in my white sweatsuit, which I wear very rarely, and red sneakers. I am wearing a Cincinnati Reds hat, as well, to at least feign normality.

The people who are not practicing on stage have to line up along the right wall of the gymnacafetorium. The front of the line is next to a door that leads to stage left. Most people sit down, their backs against the painted brick, but they don't seem to notice that all the dust—from outside, from this musty school, from the food lint of Cheetos and Chips Ahoy—is tainting their costumes. I stand, knowing that my sweatsuit in particular would be ruined by that muck.

Sarah and Melissa are obviously absent from the proceedings, which makes this rehearsal all the sweeter. The two of them were supposed to be part of that five-girl routine to "Rhythm Nation," but the act has been reduced to three in light of their out-of-school suspension. The trio of remaining dancers, dressed in their black baseball caps, black T-shirts with the sleeves rolled up, white jean shorts, black socks, and Keds, are visibly addled in trying to redo their act. The purpose of having a larger group of girls was to engage in a series of canon sequences that would make them look like a hip drill team. Instead, their attempts end prematurely, making it look like they are simply out of step with each other. At one point, Tessa Fuller, the girl on the far left, starts crying and halts the practice. Everyone in the room looks on as she starts trash-talking Sarah and Melissa. While most others sympathize with them, I have to try my hardest not to burst out laughing. Part of me wants to suggest that they do a routine to "Like a Prayer" instead; the image of burning crosses from that music video would be relevant to Sarah and Melissa's recent problem.

When it's my turn to go onstage, I get a reproachful look from Mrs. Nevins, who is still distrustful of my taste in art since the accident at the mall. She sits near the stage at a folded-out cafeteria table that has a messy collection of sound equipment on it. The main sound panel, with all its buttons, looks like a large Lite-Brite, as if Mrs. Nevins herself hasn't progressed past an elementary school mind-set. Thank God she seems to have left behind the headphones she wore last year. It was way too self-important, let alone unnecessary, for having a job that involves operating a tape deck, and I had the sneaking suspicion the whole time that she was imagining herself in another music video—"We Are the World," in which Quincy Jones and a hundred other celebrity cohorts donned puffy black headsets and belted their hearts out for starving African children. Mrs. Nevins, as you might imagine, is about the farthest thing from a musical celebrity, let alone a starving child from Kenya.

The other kids are already snickering by the time I position myself in front of the microphone. They are still thinking of my past performances, but I smile inside knowing that they have no idea who I am now. I see the duo of wannabe Smurfs and wonder if they can see any of the blue on my face. No one has noticed it yet, which still surprises me—although I still swear that it comes and goes. I'll look at myself in the mirror and see nothing, and then all of a sudden I will see that blue sheen and run my hands incredulously over my cheeks. Last night, I started to have another migraine just from seeing my skin change color.

I open my mouth once the music begins and start singing Whitney's words. Regardless of what the kids in this gymnacafetorium think of my personality, they know that I have a good singing voice, and they all have impressed expressions on their faces when I begin. Soon enough, though, they remember that they are supposed to be finding fault with me and start commenting on how only a sissy would sing this song. Once my singing finally ends, they are talking out loud about how weird I am, and although Mrs. Nevins tries to shush them several times, I can hear the complete lack of earnestness in her voice and know that she would just as soon smash my cassette tape with a hammer than support my presence on this stage.

I shrug all this off and finish the dress rehearsal as coolly as I can. As a group, all of the cast members are supposed to sing a unison version of "That's What Friends Are For," and we oblige as best as we can from the lyrics that Mrs. Nevins hands out to us. Most of the people on stage giggle madly while we sing it, not taking the dress rehearsal seriously and yelling throughout. This show is supposed to be fun—it's supposed to be fun to do it together—and a lot of people are taking the time to enjoy the preparation and kick back. I, meanwhile, cannot fall into so easy a trap. This year, the show is not about joking around and simply enjoying myself. It's about joining my talent and my spirituality.

But then another member of the Rhythm Nation starts crying and practically tears her costume off in frustration. It's then that I remind myself to have *some* fun.

*

At night, which I have come to see as my witching hour, I hold a tiny séance to prepare myself for the show.

Part of me is extremely sad that my parents don't know I'm performing tomorrow night, especially since they've come every past year, but in the midst of all their frustration with me, they seem to have forgotten that it is now almost Thanksgiving, when the show usually occurs, and that Dad should be packing up the camcorder while Mom takes the still camera. Instead, they retired early tonight after watching *Primetime Live*, my mother, then my father, paying me hardly any attention as I pretended to do math homework at the kitchen table. I listened to my father's feet thud up the staircase in the foyer, reminded as I often am of the difference between the way he ascends heavily and the way my tiny feet whisper up the stairs. I waited a reasonable amount of time before I ascended, too—just after taking a couple of sticks of butter out of the refrigerator, of course.

I turn on my beside lamp, sit on the floor of my room, and lay the instruments of my séance before me: the sticks of butter, already softened in their wax paper; the recorder, which I have wrapped in Reynolds Wrap to make it look silver; my costume, folded into a glistening pile of magenta and gold, along with a peacock feather I've plucked from our living room decorations; a page from *Penthouse* that shows a man from the waist up, his bare torso and strong shoulders and chiseled face; and a picture of Krishna that I tore out of a library book. It shows Krishna broad-shouldered and blue, holding a flute in one hand and a bow and arrow in the other. It shows Him as strong and handsome as I want Him and me to be, and I place it in the middle of all of the objects to stress its importance.

I light a little Strawberry Shortcake candle that I won at a school fair a few years ago. I never planned on lighting it and wanted to keep it in pristine condition forever, but I figure that this séance is an important enough occasion to open its candy-striped box and pull the mini replica of SS's head out, a cowlick wick sprouting from its top. Once it is lit, I turn the lamp off, relishing the way the candle bumps warm light all over my room.

While looking at that flame, I remember the time that Mrs. Nolan had us make hot chocolate during our fourth grade holiday party. She brought in a little burner that fit between the blackboard and a filing cabinet at the front of the room. She put a pan on top of the burner and mixed a delicious brew of Swiss Miss, milk, water, and miniature marshmallows. While we sat at our desks and ate the red- and green-sprinkled sugar cookies that Hannah Skinner's mom made for us, Mrs. Nolan stirred the hot chocolate and tried to turn it into a science lesson.

"Class," she said, pointing toward the flame under the pan, "see the flame underneath this pan?"

We nodded dismissively, focusing most of our attention on the chewy delectability of the cookies.

"Most people think that the hottest part of a fire is the orange part of it," she continued. "But that's not true, class. The hottest part of a flame is actually this blue part right here." She pointed lower, the tip of her finger almost touching the fire. In her demure black sweater and red skirt, she seemed like an unlikely pyromaniac. "The hottest part of the fire happens here. See—you learn something new every day."

I didn't think much of her observation then, but as I look at the SS candle in my room, I focus on the blue of its flame and make a connection to my own life: I am like that flame. I may not be as normal or confident as the other kids I know, but I feel things much more intensely than they do. I *burn* more intensely than they do. Haven't John Griffin and his goons called me a "flamer" before? I know what they mean by that—a boy who is so sissy that he is "flaming gay." Perhaps I am, just not in the way that they think. They have no idea what sort of emotional flood rages in me every day, how alternately high and subtle my sexuality can be. Like a fire that works and rages to provide a glow but whose efforts are invisible to us, I struggle secretly but powerfully.

For the first time in my life, I wonder if there might be people just like me in my school, other "flamers" who have the same sexual desires I do, just not overtly. I am the figurehead of a secret, sacred brotherhood of blue flame souls—the first blue boy. Accompanied by the instruments of my return to this blue Earth, I close my eyes and hum "Om" to myself while feeling genuinely happy for the first time in a very long time. All of my worries about the show and my parents and my (lack of) friends melt away like this mock-SS's wax head. It is only when a thick stream of pink wax curls up on the carpet, oozes against my foot, and stings me back into reality that I pack up my gypsy sideshow and go to bed. The sky will soon lighten as it always does, and there is no more hopeful moment than that: when time is tomorrow but still carries a strain of today, when we're wiser and reborn all at once.

Another Op'nin',
Another Showdown

The night of the show.

This morning, I told my mother that I had another impromptu rehearsal after school. To further solidify the lie, I told her that we're working on a holiday ballet for my dance class and that I'm playing the Little Drummer Boy. My mother's eyebrows rose excitedly, and I think somewhere deep inside of her she interpreted that as meaning I was undertaking *tabla* lessons at last! But then she recognized the words as a holiday song and nodded once. Had my story not been so interesting, she might have told me the ballet was as forbidden as the talent show. But I've gotten too good at lying.

I stuffed my costume in my bag again, not taking any books with me this time. Yesterday, I had to skip my study session with Mrs. Goldberg in order to go to the dress rehearsal, and I feel as detached from my schoolwork as I've ever been. Normally, I would find this upsetting, but I find it liberating today. Everything is in service of this performance, and if my schoolwork has to suffer, so be it.

How did I get here? I ask myself again. How did everything come down to this one measly performance in a measly little wannabe-gym in a measly little brick edifice in a measly little Ohio town? How, of all places, did Krishna decide to set his circus down here? I guess for the same reason that my parents decided to set their circus down in Ohio. Some migrations have no logical explanation.

Mrs. Nevins and her crew have transformed the gymnacafetorium into a veritable auditorium. The special red velvet curtain that they save for special occasions like this has been installed. The lights in the room, normally gold with fluorescence, have been turned off entirely, and instead, there are two full moons of spotlight projected onto the red curtain, as if we're at a movie premiere. Instead of the usual cafeteria tables that fill the space, there are several rows of black folding chairs arranged so neatly that they resemble metal ears of corn.

This year, there's a disco ball hanging from the ceiling. Mrs. Nevins is a lunatic.

When I get to the theater—rather early, considering that I did not go home between the end of school and the 7 p.m. cast call time—Mrs. Nevins is already in a turquoise sequined dress, her hair very big and unmoving due to hairspray. (Now I know why she didn't attempt the earphones; they would never have fit over her hair volcano.) She is wearing a ton of makeup, and her nails look like shiny red beetles eating her fingers. She is visibly nervous. Part of me warms to her, thinking how noble it is of her to give up so much of her time for one night of talent. She gets no incentive for doing this show aside from seeing us students have our fifteen minutes—or, rather, five minutes—of fame, and she is so excited for us that she has dressed herself up nicely. She even tries to be polite when she sees me saunter in. She looks up at me and smiles briefly before bending back down over her soundboard and making sure everything is in place.

The other acts gradually come in. Some of them move with cool anticipation, some of them are crazed. The Rhythm Nation still hasn't quelled its civil unrest, and the girls are still trying to figure out how to fill up their routine with cheerleading-style moves. Without pom-poms in their hands, however, their "rah rahs" are basically Hitler salutes. The Smurfs are all here, too, even scarier now that all of them are in full costume.

Then I see Mrs. Buchanan make her way into the dimness of the room.

She is so obviously saddened by what has happened to her room that it freezes me in my tracks. She is dressed in even more layers than usual, wearing a puffy winter coat that looks like someone donated it to her via Goodwill. She is wearing galoshes that track in dirty trails of water, and even in this relative darkness, the pallor of her face is even lighter than usual. The art room wasn't just a classroom but her place of work for over two decades, a place where she had supervised the beloved, if often demented, art projects of countless little children. Perhaps before she became such a smarmy schoolmarm she was a buoyant and loveable figure.

Then I hear her growl hello to Mrs. Nevins and my feelings of pity instantly disappear. She's Gargamel to these rambunctious Smurf-demons.

I am very nervous, but not in the way that I have been in the past. Right before my other talent show performances, regardless of whatever humiliation the previous year's act might have brought, I have normally felt a productive anxiety that turns my jitters into magic. This year, I feel no such heartening force.

As Mrs. Nevins herds us into the nearby classroom that acts as our dressing room, I can see tons of students and their parents arriving and seating themselves in the black folding chairs. Unbelievably enough, Sarah and Melissa both show up with their parents—the Turners and Jenkinses, respectively—and I see that their parents are just as ostentatious as they are. Their mothers look like the grande dames from *Designing Women*, and their fathers—with their long, brushed hair and sport coats—look like a cross between the cops on *Miami Vice* and suave car salesmen. Maybe that's because they *are* car salesmen, although Mr. Turner sells new Pontiacs and Mr. Jenkins sells used Hondas. Sarah and Melissa look downtrodden in the same way that Mrs. Buchanan does, and when I notice my fellow performers pointing at them and making fun of their punishment, I instantly feel a little better.

I also see Cody and Donny show up, although neither of them is with his parents. It would take Cody breaking the world cigarette-smoking record to pull Beverly away from her TV set,

I'd wager. They steer clear of Sarah and Melissa, which is a shame because I'm sure Sarah's and Melissa's fathers would love to toss them in a used car's trunk before pushing it into the Ohio River.

Next I see Mrs. Goldberg. She appears with a man at her side, and for the first few seconds, I don't register who he is. It's her husband. He is very large, the type of man who must shop at "big and tall" stores, and his hair is dark and curly. He is wearing a teal sweater with a white shirt underneath, and his feet are so big that I can't tell if he's wearing boots or just large black shoes. When they seat themselves—in the front row near the middle— he puts his hand around her waist protectively. Somewhat surprisingly to me, she follows his hand's lead, moving down into the chair as if guided by it.

What will Mrs. Goldberg think when she sees me in my costume, a real-life depiction of the drawings she so thoroughly enjoyed? What will she—and Mrs. Buchanan—think when they see me defying them and putting that art on stage instead of tacked up on a bulletin board? I am manipulating Mrs. Goldberg in my head the way I would any other expectation or idea. I focus on the act of her watching me. I wonder what it would be like to shock her with my act, to make her thrilled with fright. It might feel so amazing to scare her into seeing why I am even more brilliant than she thinks. Regardless of the pivotal and pleasant role she has played in my life until this point, Mrs. Goldberg's function this evening is to bear witness to my bizarre uniqueness just like everyone else. Tonight, the people out there are not so much an *audience*—something that hears—than they are an *experience*—something that senses and feels.

I'm still not in my real costume. I can't put it on yet because if Mrs. Nevins sees me in it, she will immediately recognize it as too religious—or as too Indian, which amounts to the same thing— and will become suspicious of my act. So I am still dressed in my bright "street clothes." The kids around me are starting to become suspicious of my getup, especially because they know I've dressed in a blazer and clip-on tie in past years (with the exception of Sebastian, of course). They all look at me as I look at the audience, and I cannot help but wonder why they should pay any attention to me when they have their own acts to tend to. I guess it's because they know that usually I sit in a corner and concentrate on what I'm going to be performing instead of walking around all antsy. Nothing gets past them when it could possibly lead to my degradation.

My mind-set is not so uneasy, though. I don't even care anymore if this act is graceful. I want it to be fierce in its message. I want it to be as warlike and in-your-face as Krishna's daredevil stunts. I want it to show these closed-minded people what true Indian panache is. Perhaps Hanuman the Guinness Book Wonder was onto something: perhaps we do have to dance the hell out of time and space to make a mark on the world. Perhaps true beauty is not prim and reverent but messy and a little bit ugly. Look at all these addled amateurs around me—the Rhythm Nation, the Smurfs, the cheerleaders and lip synchers and *dear God, is that a hopscotch act*? Let them have their innocent wandering. I, meanwhile, will get tangled in my sari-suit and do something that has never been done before. Or that hasn't been done in thousands of years.

Mrs. Nevins eventually rushes into the classroom and commands us to line up in order of stage appearance. I am stuck between Tiffany Myers—the girl, as you might recall, whose father works in "produce" at the local grocery store—and Stevie Olson, a tow-headed box of a boy who smells like a mixture of onions and cologne. Tiffany is dressed in a purple leotard and is holding a purple hula hoop that she plans to swing around herself while bopping to "Jimmy Jimmy" by Madonna (for a change). Stevie is dressed like a cowboy and holds a cardboard guitar for his Garth Brooks lip-synch number. Mrs. Nevins is a veritable shepherd as she waves us into the gymnacafetorium. We line up along the wall as we practiced during the dress rehearsal, each of us trying to act oblivious to the crowd but not able to help ourselves as the people in the audience point at or whisper about us. I walk delicately, nervously, thinking not about the people as much as I do about my act.

All of my frantic preparation has come down to this. Somewhere above me, through the concrete ceiling of this room, through the thin smog that hangs over this suburb, through the deep blue darkness of the sky and perhaps through the watery sheet of a firmament, Krishna is looking down and grinning.

*

The show starts with the usual speech by Principal Taylor, who is wearing the same sort of power suit she would wear during the school day. She seems to be playing a version of herself, and her speech is as stiff as her collar. The audience claps timidly after her curt welcome, unsure whether it deserves applause while restless to see us children strut our stuff. Mrs. Nevins gets behind her table, and the sound of her pressing "Play" on the tape deck for the first song makes a loud click. It is the gunshot at the beginning of the race.

The temporary curtain pulls back—the result of heavy pulling by Wilford, a hefty guy with a black baseball cap and ponytail who helps us out every year but never utters a single word. Onstage is last year's toast of the town, Kevin Bartlett, with the same cardboard guitar he used then strapped to his hip. The music gears up, and it's "Pour Some Sugar on Me" by Def Leppard. The audience loses its mind. Half of them are on their feet before ten seconds are up. The kids in line with me, along with the audience, start clapping in time to the music—something they do with almost every act regardless of its tempo. An appearance by "Eternal Flame" a couple of years ago was so laced with clapping that it sounded like the Bangles were being spanked into oblivion. The crowd, kids and adults alike, is never able to maintain the same level of enthusiasm throughout an act—especially when it's a boring lip-synch deal like Kevin's—so the clapping tapers off midway, leaving the performer in a worried state. The sonic fireworks of Def Leppard's screeching sound almost cruel as he strums silently and finishes with a half smile.

The shitstorms keep on coming, one right after the other. The Rhythm Nation finally takes the stage, with two of the girls colliding at one point and the other trying to tend to them. One of the girls—I can't even tell them apart at this point—ends up breaking down in tears again and gives the audience a fierce grimace.

They are followed by Tommy Wilkins doing a few "magic" tricks in a cape and top hat. From what I can tell, he basically plays a game of solitaire with himself and takes a bow. He does this to a soundtrack of "The Entertainer" by Scott Joplin; the audience claps, of course, and somewhere Scott Joplin turns in his grave and wishes he were capable of dying again. When Frank Martin follows up this act by playing the very same song on the out-of-tune upright piano by the stage, I start to wonder if Mrs. Nevins has an actual brain, let alone any idea how to plan an artistic event.

When I see that there are five acts ahead of me, I make my stealthy exit. While Holly Tyler is lip-synching to "End of the Road" by Boyz II Men, I stand up and walk briskly out of the gymnacafetorium. I get a few quizzical looks from the kids on the wall but am unnoticed by Mrs. Nevins and her nonbrain. I walk to the classroom and pick up my bookbag, then head down a hall to the farthest bathroom I can find. An air of intense concentration surrounds my bathroom visit, not just because it is the night of the talent show but because I need to make sure no one comes into this bathroom while I'm in it. I lock the door.

I open my bookbag, ever aware that this is to be the most important makeup job I have ever done. Making myself up may have been play in the past, but this time my beauty must be worthy of a god. I pull out my mother's eyeshadow and rouge compacts, along with some *kajol* and Magenta.

I made sure to steal a brand-new eyeshadow compact for tonight. My mother keeps many of her unopened compacts in a separate drawer in the bathroom, and until now I have avoided opening them. But seeing as this was such an important night, I took one of them and am now opening its shrink wrap to get to the untouched blue powder inside.

I stop just before my powdered finger touches my cheek. There, in the mirror, I see that ghostly blue glow around my face. Its intensity, as it tends to do, shifts as I look at it. My cheek flashes bluer, then my forehead, then my nose. I start to cover this disco ball face with eyeshadow, but my skin still seems to glow in and out of focus. By the time I am putting on my eyeliner, I realize that I'm having another migraine. The splotches are coming in and out, and my body feels like it's on fire. I push through, finishing my eyes perfectly, but I smudge lipstick across my face as a head cramp overtakes me. Of all the times . . . and yet I should have expected it to strike me here, when I am at my most stressed.

I cannot surrender now. It is as if God Himself is giving me direction to continue and is making my skin flash in anticipation of this grand coming-out. It is no longer a hobby but my *duty* to seal my lips in brightness, to sheathe my body in my costume creation, to slide the bangles on my wrists, to wrap bead necklaces around my neck, to fasten the ankle bells to both of my feet and, at last, to crown myself with the black wig. For the last step, I stick the peacock feather into the curls and step back from the mirror.

I look absolutely perfect. As opposed to the past, this time I do not mistake the image in the mirror for someone other than myself. I do not think of that reflection as separate from me, some *Twilight Zone* Kiran staring through shiny glass. It is clearly I, through the silvery, fiery splotches that turn this bathroom into a battlefield of ceramic and stars. I am no longer playing make-believe, trying to mold myself into something I am not. I am no longer a precocious child dressed in shiny rags and synthetic, colored dust, bewigged and bedazzled in pursuit of a more exotic self. What I have forgotten during my various struggles these past few weeks is that *Kiran* would have striven for such grandeur anyway, just as *Krishna* never saw it any other way than to conquer the world with his individuality. Kiran is just as great, just as godly, just as genius as Krishna because he never settles for the mundane. Kiran fights battles and has his own snakeheads to dance on. Kiran settles for nothing but a Krishna-worthy Kiran.

I pick up my silver recorder and place it by my lips. The visual it makes is a snapshot I will never be able to erase from my memory, more indelible an image than any I have ever seen printed on Kodak paper or in the tiny window of my father's camcorder.

I return to the "greenroom" cautiously. Everyone is in the gymnacafetorium enjoying another lip-synch performance, this one by Crystal Hicks, a rambunctious young girl who moved to our town this summer from Indianapolis. She decided to break down the walls of being the "new girl" by being a kiss-slut, and I think she has smooched everyone from John Griffin to Kevin Bartlett (to Sarah Turner, for all I know). Her mother, a pretty-faced woman with big bangs, is already rumored to be the best room mother in the school because she makes killer M&M cookies with peanut butter cookie dough. As if paying homage to her mother's tongue for sweets, Crystal's song of choice is "Sugar Shack." She is wearing a pink shirt with matching pink shorts, the ends of both garments rolled up. One fat ponytail, tied with a pink ribbon, loops around her head. Crystal is holding a broken-off broomstick with a Styrofoam disc shoved onto it; the disc is covered in pink Mylar paper to make it look candy-like—an instant lollipop prop. Say what you will about the Hickses, they certainly know how to have some sugary-sweet fun.

After Crystal has done her last sashay up and down the stage, it is Tiffany Myers's turn, and the moment the speakers pump out "Jimmy Jimmy," I am more nervous than ever. It's such a different nervousness from the one I feel around my father, which takes my breath hostage; from the one I feel around my classmates, which makes me hang my head and pass them as quickly and quietly as I can; from the one I feel around Ashish and Ajay and Ashok and Neha and all the other Indian kids, which takes my speech and makes it awkward and misunderstood; even from the one I feel from myself, when I feel my lust overtaking my senses and better judgment at the same time. This nervousness is a culmination. All of the components of my life have been in chaos, and all the various forms of panic I've experienced have curled together to make my whole body pulse.

My vision is still going in and out, and now it feels like I might have a fever. Except when you have a fever, you feel chills. The world around you feels cold because you are so hot. I feel hot but the world feels hot, too. Every time the splotches come into view, I stare through them, focusing on Tiffany to steady myself. Except Tiffany is doing a hula hoop act, so the movement of her swiveling hips isn't exactly helping things.

I realize that there is some hubbub among the performers and that, lo and behold, it's because I've gone missing and I'm up next. From here, I can see Mrs. Nevins's crazed silhouette motioning at the kids, and I know that now is the time to step forward and leave caution to the wind. Tiffany is hand-bopping downstage, really getting the crowd into her act, and neither the audience members nor the kids lined up against the wall will be able to say anything as I rush up to the stage. As I'm thinking about what it would feel like to scurry into that throng of people amidst a swish of multicolored cloth, I find that I am doing it. I am gliding toward Mrs. Nevins and seeing her face scrunch up as she tries to examine my costume in the darkness. I see her jaw fall open as she reaches for the tape deck, and for a second I step outside myself and see what I look like as I smile at her, motion for her to push Play, and continue up the small staircase that leads to the backstage area. Tiffany is bowing and waving to the audience with her free hand while her other hand clutches the hula hoop.

The moment I hit centerstage and poise my flute to my lips—the lights bright in my vision and making the splotches even bigger—the moment I hear the collective hush come over the audience, the moment I hear the cheery synthesizers of the music begin, I understand what an absolutely luxurious moment it truly is. How many times do you get to stand in front of an audience that has no other responsibility than to see you unveiled in your full glory?

The moment Whitney hits her first wailing notes—"There's a *boy* I know . . . !"—I heave my body into dancing like I've never done before. Both Marcy and Hema-the-nappy-carnation-lady would be mortified to see the part-ballet, part-*khatak*, part-bananas technique that I employ, but I have never felt so free and easy with my body. It is as if I am channeling all of the intense devastation of this migraine into my art, and I truly feel like an artist who is sacrificing himself for his aesthetic. My costume feels like a sensuous mist around me. When I kick up my leg in an arabesque tinged with jazz, the magenta silk surrounds it, and I can feel it drop with me as I pull away and scurry to the other end of the stage. Every once in a while, I hear myself emitting a low rumble that modulates into a high-pitched note. I am not so much singing as I am growling. I can't be sure whether the audience is even hearing these noises, but it is as if my mind keeps shifting between that mirror Kiran and the unified Kiran who is both in and *in front of* the mirror at the same time. I am onstage and watching the stage. I am surrounding me, and it as if I am very self-conscious and free at once. At one point, I do a move that I've never even practiced: I tumble on the stage and do a head roll, then stand up and jump, my costume swishing around me; from deep down somewhere, a part of me is telling my body to do something completely outrageous—grotesque, even—so that my mind can be shocked and then marvel in the audaciousness. It's like hearing someone you love talk in a voice that you never knew they could make, like the time my father got a gold watch from my mother at Holi and instead of his usual lecture about why she shouldn't spend money on gifts of any kind, he lovingly cooed, "I *looooove* it": you feel like you know something for certain, and then it changes its colors and smacks you upside the head with its daring. At first, the change surprises and unsettles you, but then you take in the surprise and embrace it and wish life could always be so gloriously unpredictable. When I first thought of the talent show this fall— what seems like ages ago, while scratching Barbie smiles off my desk—who knew that I would be onstage doing this? Wearing this costume, this skin, choosing this song, having gleaned a life's worth of debauchery in a few short weeks? Everything in my world, everything in *the* world, can be as capricious as this act—the way I am spinning in as fast a circle as I can, the lights, the visual muck of the crowd, the hem of my own golden-magenta creation, the strands of black hair flung across my powdered face, the entrance of a blue-flame boy into the world. What is a more beautiful thought than the one that questions everything you take for granted?

I am so caught up in my dancing that I do not realize I have stopped spinning but my vision has not. The swirls of the audience and stage in my eyes have overtaken the splotches, and now I cannot tell which way is up and which way is down. By instinct, I lay myself on the floor, knowing that if I stay standing I will lose my equilibrium and fall to the floor anyway. I am now rolling around onstage like Jennifer Beals, except I have an enormous fabric garment on me that tangles up and makes one big magenta and gold swishy mess. The wig is almost falling off now because of the sweat pouring out of me, and Whitney's voice pierces higher as if in response to the chaos I am feeling: "Oh, how will I knooooooooooow?!" To me, her voice sounds like the point just before music becomes microphone feedback—it is caterwauling and scratchy, a glorious screech. And just when her glorious screech resounds for the last time, I feel all of the swirls come crashing down on me—not solely at my eyes but all around me and on top of me. Then it all goes black.

It takes me a second to realize that I have not fainted but have simply lost my sight. I know this because after the music stops, I can hear the audience's silence. Which is not really silence. They still make noises: the crinkling of the paper programs in their hands as they fan themselves, the scuffing of their sneakers as they teeter from foot to foot, the many errant coughs that you always hear in public places, the quiet sobbing of a baby. All the while, I cannot tell if I am imagining a wind passing through the gymnacafetorium or if it's the large metal fans that Mrs. Nevins has had the janitors put in the back of it to cool people. I lie here for a moment and take in both the silence and the perpetual noise of this ambushed crowd.

Then the clapping begins, and before unconsciousness joins my blindness, I know—somewhere deep down I just know, regardless of what has happened these past few weeks, regardless of the fact that I didn't think they were there—that it's my parents who've begun it.

*

Sitting in my hospital bed feels like being in my parents' bathroom all over again. I'm in another white room, although the brightness in here comes not from a skylight but from the humming peppermint sticks of fluorescent bulbs that line the ceiling. Although it is nighttime, a good hour since a collection of hands lifted me offstage and into an ambulance, the lights seem to act like nocturnal sunlight, tricking me into being wide-awake when I should be asleep. Or *trying* to be asleep in my bed at home.

It all happened so fast, through the veil of blackness. I kept mixing up the whispering of the fabric around me with the whisper of people's voices. The voices of my parents—urgent but measured—soon morphed into the baritone of a doctor whose hands are cold and refreshing in their touch.

I smell him before I see him. He smells like Listerine and sweet soap, and he breathes through his nose, swatting my skin in soft, warm breaths.

My vision is still dodgy as he places his stethoscope against my chest. The touch of the cool metal, when experienced with the sensation of having his breath and hands and voice around me, makes my body temperature go into overdrive all over again. After so many days of alternating my body's makeup—hotblooded, cold-blooded—I can't decide what my normal setting is.

I want so desperately to keep this man separate from those men in the magazine and from the men in the woods, but I can't. I can see him only on a canvas of lust, not a doctor but a specimen. I can only identify the moments as he examines me as sexual, and a profound sadness comes over me because of this.

Then I hear my parents come into the room and immediately zap out of that haze, like when someone walks in on you peeing.

"It's a classic case of fatigue, most likely from lack of sleep and dehydration," the doctor says to my parents briefly but sympathetically. I avoid looking directly at them, mainly because I am so tired of seeing varying expressions on their faces. Will they greet me with anger, disappointment, frustration? Concern? Dare I say it—joy?

I am so busy thinking about my parents that I almost miss the next part of the conversation.

"We noticed in your son's paperwork that you give him a rather large dosage of daily medication."

"Vell, he is not often vell," my mother says quietly. Without looking at her, I know that she has her hands deep in the pockets of her white cardigan.

"I don't normally advise such a large dosage, and I am particularly concerned over the administration of a silver supplement, which can have some horrible side effects."

"Such as?" my mother asks.

"Such as turning people's skin blue."

The doctor goes on to explain that the silver, if deposited into the bloodstream for a prolonged period of time, can become embedded in the skin. He underscores its rarity, and I, my jaw wide open, expect him to end this explanation with a dramatic hand flourish at me, proclaiming me the NEWEST MEMBER OF THE BLUE-SKIN GANG—TA-DA! His behavior never gets that intense, though. He merely walks over to me and tilts my washed, makeup-free face toward the light.

"See," he says, his voice still calm. "It's hard to make it out, but you can see it if you look hard enough." I feel my parents' faces near mine. My mother says she can't see it. My father admits failure, too. But the doctor reiterates his warning and receives an acknowledgment from both my parents that they'll never give me that medicine again.

Once the doctor has left—after prescribing that I drink at least eight glasses of water a day and take a nightly sedative—my parents stare at me. The doctor has left the door open, and I can hear the busy sounds of the hospital—rolling gurneys, the occasional moan, the plop of the nurses' white shoes against the floor, the pressing of buttons and opening of filing cabinets, ringing phones, and beeping intercoms. I try to focus on those sounds instead of on my parents.

In this moment, having been told that my skin is not the result of some divine ordinance but rather the result of a faulty drug, I feel like the doctor has cruelly plucked out the feathers of my peacock crown and thrown them at the foot of my bed. I imagine leaping up from these sheets and tearing my pillowcases up to find a dirty mess of more peacock feathers inside. But then I understand that just as I never had Krishna-ordained skin, I never had peacock feathers, either. The only reason I ever felt heartened by these things was because I imagined them into being. My creativity urged them into life like a magician shoving a dove from his empty hands.

But that can be beautiful. I've been creating my own whimsy— or at least my heart has—and that whimsy has led me to exhibit my artistic self in its most unfettered state. The world can be as uncommonly beautiful as you want it to be as long as you give yourself over to that whimsy, however melancholy and lonely it may be sometimes.

As if coming to the same thought, my mother falls to the bed, clutches my right hand, and begins to cry. It sounds like a dog's whimper, and for some reason, even though it's not like she is bawling, it affects me more than any crying I've ever heard. Hers are tears of exhaustion; she's tired of worrying, tired of judging, tired of walking through life on edge. It dawns on me that the last time my mother clutched my hand like this was when she discovered me covered in Estée weeks ago. It is this revelation that pushes me to look at her. Her eyes, those eyes locked in wrinkles, look as wide and impressionable as mine when she opens them, more tears sliding out and down her cheeks. She has worn *kajol*—a sign that she didn't just attend the talent show but got dressed up, too—and its blackness has run down her face and onto the bedsheet. Under her white cardigan, the pearly fabric of her salmon-colored *salwaar kameez* shines brilliantly against the floor. My mother, the crumpled lotus.

I expect her to say something—to thank God that I am all right, to tell me how beautiful my performance was. Instead, she stands up and walks over to the tiny table in the corner of the room and pulls a tissue from a small Kleenex box, the kind decorated with blurry sea swirls. She dabs at her face and blows her nose.

All the while, my father remains standing, dressed in his tan jacket. No tears, no words, just looking at the floor where my mother was. He has combed his hair, and his forehead shines in the light. He looks handsome and put together, however solemn his mood. Then, as if penitently, he takes a step forward, places a hand on my forehead, and smoothes back my hair, which is still sweaty and matted down from the wig.

No great conversation ensues. I eventually slink away from the hospital wrapped in my mother's winter coat, with a white paper bag of sleeping pills clutched in one hand. Our drive home almost mirrors our usual drive home from temple.

Except for a palpable feeling of tenderness. It's not what people usually think of as tenderness—kindness mixed with affection—but a literal feeling of fragility, a tendency to bruise easily. It is as if by having one of us tumble weakly to the ground, we now understand that in our own unique ways, we are each the person in the hospital bed, alone if not for the loyal soul clutching our hand.

Epilogue:
Cymbalism

It's been a whole month since my parents and I last came to the temple. Not that a month is really all that long. It's really just four visits, one per week, and the proceedings are generally the same. The pundit is still curled up at the front of the room, speaking in his singsong voice. The men and women are still divided as they always are, and they still have those reverent smiles on their faces. In the kitchen, a few women—Rashmi Govind among them—are preparing the *prasad*. The faint aroma of fruit wafts from the counter to our noses due to the sweet but slimy cocktail of bananas, apples, mandarin oranges, and grapes that is the centerpiece of their preparation. I hear a laugh escape from the women before they realize how loud they're being and go back to whispering. Those whispers give away the thing that is different about their otherwise ordinary procedure: my family has returned, especially the problematic Kiran, and the game of who will welcome my parents back into the fold openly—versus who will do so cautiously—begins.

My mother and father have seated themselves toward the front of the room, probably so that they don't have to see all the people looking at them. Or perhaps they are simply pious. Indeed, my mother seems to have the same solemnity about her that she usually has when burning incense: she has her orange *dupatta* wrapped around her head and sits even more rigidly than my father does. Ever since that night just over a week ago when we came home from the hospital, my mother has been moving with a sort of peaceful grace. She has accepted some new truth, however small, and it is quietly strengthening her.

A similar aura has taken over my father, except that there is still a hard edge to him. After the hospital incident, he returned to being aloof toward me, and the tension that I thought was gone has returned a little bit. Things are obviously smoother between us, but that doesn't mean that they are without rough edges. I did my ballet exercises in the basement on Thursday because I didn't want him to see me. I feared that one look at me prancing about might make him regret the quiet evasion he's been trying out. His behavior remains the way it was in the hospital room: it is as if he thinks that, by emotional telepathy, his affection will wend its way from his body to mine across a room or through a wall.

Yet, the other night while I was falling asleep—the blue, diamond-shaped pills the doctor gave me casting their sandman spell—he came into my bedroom and hovered in the doorway. He stood there for a few moments, just watching me, then quietly came over to my bed and leaned very close to me. His breath was so heavy that it would have woken me up had I been asleep. Perhaps he knew that I was only pretending to be asleep. But I got the feeling that he was staring not to find me out but to *figure* me out. For him, I was no longer a shameful thing but a ship in a bottle, something to be examined and appreciated and solved. Then, almost inaudibly, he whispered, "I love—" and then faltered, fading slowly into the house again.

At school, Mrs. Goldberg acts the same way, although I can sense an extra dose of pride coming from her. After all, due to my sudden fainting spell, neither Mrs. Nevins nor Mrs. Buchanann nor Principal Taylor could bust me for my religious display on-stage, and when Mrs. Goldberg places a different kind of star sticker on my next spelling test—a blue one made of two triangles on top of each other—I understand that she is acknowledging my achievement with a religious display of her own.

The kids at school are more aloof than that. Sarah's and Me-

lissa's parents famously decided last week to pull the girls out of
the school and send them to Immaculate Souls, the conservative
Catholic school fifteen miles from here. I remember Cody telling
me a while back that it's a terrifying school and that there's a
myth that all the nuns there are completely bald and wear necklaces made of baby skulls under their robes. The kids there also
wear uniforms, stiff plaid and white garments that are probably
itchy. I love the idea of Sarah and Melissa, once adorned in myriad accessories and colors, reduced to clothing as fashionable as
a neck brace. Their faces are probably as grave and frowning as
Mrs. Buchanan's. I've taught them all what happens when you
cross my path.

There are still all the other kids at my school, though, and
they treat me with a new fascination when I walk down the halls
and sit at my desk. I'm the kid who would have been laughed at
had I not survived a little death onstage. Now there is a little bit
of immortality added to my public persona, an ability to defy
pain, and I giggle inside thinking that, in at least this respect, I
have made myself a god.

I don't exactly have any friends, and there will always be the
John Griffins of the world who twirl around and then pretend
to faint in front of me as I walk down the halls, but I have realized just how much more I know than they do. What do these
bullies know of lust, of sex, of the fine line between divinity and
depravity? It would be one thing if they knew what I felt and
could understand it and then made fun of it. But they do not
have the ability to empathize with what I feel, and that makes
them completely meaningless. I live in a kingdom of one.

Cody and Donny are long gone from my life, but you would
never guess that anything had changed from the way they keep
at their basketball games. Whereas the time they spend on the
playground bothered me so much in the past, I now look at it
with a good-riddance type of relief. I know that I will never be
like them, and now I don't even want to be. I am not meant for
basketball, just as they are not meant to dance and dress up. My
imagination is for creating my own private world, and I'm wasting it if I try to be a part of theirs.

Why have I felt it so necessary for us to be the same? What is it about that confining, brick fortress of a school that has made me believe it is the only place that exists? I only go to this school because my parents happened to come to America, to move to Ohio, just happened to build a particular house in a particular area of this town and send me to the closest school. If any one of those steps had not happened, I would be somewhere else. I could be living in a smoky, fragrant, lush area of India if it weren't for one decision. Why should I let one decision prevent me from living the lush life I might otherwise have had?

I sit in this temple and look around at the paintings of the deities on the walls. Lakshmi and Saraswati and Sita, Their eyes surrounded by *khajol*, Their cheeks and lipstick so red that they could be covered in Estée: They're the pretty girls, the ones with good fashion sense and grace. They have their loyal servants and friends, the Hanumans and Ganeshes and so forth. But They also have their male equivalent, who makes music for Them and the other women, who mimics their beauty by painting His brilliantly blue face and clothing Himself in fabric as glimmering and glorious as Theirs. He was born different, but instead of lamenting his fate, He embraced it. He saw his peculiarities as unique treasures, and He saw love and admiration and luxurious, delicious grandeur come His way as a result.

From where I stand at the back of the temple, I don't expect anyone to approach me. But I feel a tap on my shoulder and turn around. It's the pundit. Our sweet, loving pundit. Regardless of everything that has happened with the Singhs, he gives me a smile and offers me that pair of gold hand cymbals. I take them from him gently. An enormous sense of compassion comes over me, and there in the back of the temple, I drop down and touch his feet the way you are supposed to touch the feet of your elders when you want to be especially reverent. When I pull back up, I am already crying, the tears like silver chains from my eyes.

He goes to the front of the room and finishes the service, inviting everyone to join in *aarti*. Everyone stands up as the music begins. Mrs. Jindal rushes—or waddles briskly—to her harmonium to join the melee, and soon everyone is singing. All of the other kids are at the front of the room, pushed forward by their parents, as usual—and led by Ashok and Neha—but I am back here, out of sight and out of mind for a moment. I am alone with my cymbals, which I push together again and again. I experiment with rhythms, make the peals fast and then slow, play them over my head, under my legs, spinning in a circle. I make fiery music and dedicate it to the Lord, to the strength He gives us when we think we are becoming weaker. Sometimes we are so consumed by the flame, burning so painfully in its heat, that we can't see the utter gorgeousness of the fire.

Acknowledgments

I would like to thank

my parents, Vinay and Lalita, for being as surprising as they are supportive. You have taught me how to love along with how to laugh throughout every hardship. Your hard work and the sacrifices that you have made go far beyond any accomplishment of mine;

my incredible brothers, Rajiv and Vikas, for always having my back and for giving me a childhood full of happy sibling moments;

my extended family—especially my aunt Usha, for recognizing and fostering my artistic inclinations early on in my life;

my incredible friends, without whom I would not survive;

my phenomenal writing teachers—Edmund White, Joyce Carol Oates, A. J. Verdelle, Paul Muldoon, Lynne Tillman, and David Ebershoff—for being so encouraging. Also, the entire staff of the Creative Writing Program at Princeton for running the best writing program in the world;

my agent, Maria Massie; my editor, John Scognamiglio; and point person, Peter Senftleben, for their strong faith in little Kiran—as well as everyone at Kensington;

Mary Davison, my first music teacher, for her strong faith in little me. You are missed.

Kim Dasher gave me the incredible gift of finishing my first draft within the comfy confines of her apartment. Ursula Cary,

Kendra Harpster, Beth Haymaker, and Alex Lane all read early drafts of this novel and gave me helpful feedback.

Last but never least, a million thanks go to Chris Henry, BFF extraordinaire, for finding the humor in everything. It's so easy.

BLUE BOY

Rakesh Satyal

ABOUT THIS GUIDE

The suggested questions are included
to enhance your group's reading of
Rakesh Satyal's *Blue Boy*.

DISCUSSION QUESTIONS

1. Kiran spends a large part of the novel being very studious. What role do his studies play in his general behavior? Why does he focus his attention on such things?

2. Kiran uses specific words often and also highlights others that he likes particularly. How does language figure into Kiran's intellectual life? His emotional life?

3. Kiran's relationships with his parents differ greatly. How would you describe his relationship with his mother? With his father? Does one parent love him more than the other, or are their manners of loving just different?

4. The town in which Kiran lives, Crestview, is described in detail. What sort of town is it? What is the demographic of the inhabitants? And how does that demographic differ from Kiran's family? From the other Indian families?

5. Kiran has very strong reactions to both female figures and male figures. How are his reactions different? With women, in particular, how does their treatment of him affect his self-perception? For example, how are the teachers in his school and the other Indian mothers similar and different?

6. How knowledgeable is Kiran about Hinduism? About other religions? Does he fully understand them, or does he view them differently depending on his mood?

7. Kiran asserts that American life has more of an impact on him than Indian life, but is that really true? Which culture informs Kiran's behavior more—American culture or Indian culture?

8. How would you describe Kiran's sexuality? Is he hypersexual, or does he simply feel that way because of his confining surroundings? Is he fully gay?

9. What role do names play in this book? And furthermore, what role does name *calling* play in this book?

10. Is Kiran a happy child? A sad child? How about at the beginning of the novel versus at the end of the novel?

Please turn the page for a special
Q&A with Rakesh Satyal!

Why do you feel that your work is particularly relevant and timely?

Indian American literature has remained relatively serious until now. There is plenty of wonderful, very moving work in the genre, but I do not feel that the genre has a fair share of *playful* literature, along the lines of what has happened with Hispanic American literature or even East Asian American literature. This book is a little more humorous and playful with the genre, and that is why I believe that it has something new to offer.

How much of the main character, Kiran, is based on you?

I would say that more of the events closer to the beginning of the novel resemble my own childhood. (The Abraham Lincoln story, for example, is one widely known by my friends.) Certainly, I share Kiran's imagination and his urge to be creative and, like him, I engaged in many rather flamboyant activities as a child, including (but not limited to) singing, dancing, doing visual art, etc. But as a writer and especially as an editor familiar with the world of publishing and the specifics of real life-translated-to-fiction, I was very careful to make Kiran very much Kiran and to distance him from my own life. For example, I have two brothers, whereas Kiran is an only child; my parents are quite different from the parents in the book. That said, I wanted to make sure that the reader could see quite clearly how Kiran could be a product of those two parents but not necessarily be *like* them.

Do you feel that you are "making fun" of Hinduism?

Not at all. I believe in many of Hinduism's rather wondrous elements. One of those elements, directly and indirectly, is a real sense of spectacle, and my aim in the novel is to show how a young child already prone to hyperbole and extravagance would interpret that magic in his own life. At no point in the novel could one say that Kiran approaches Hinduism with bad intentions or doubts Krishna's power; he approaches the religion with the utmost reverence, as did I while writing the story, and at the end, we see him comforted by the religion because it is really his only true friend.

How do you fit your writing life into your job as an editor?

People ask me this a lot because they assume that I never sleep and that I am a total workaholic. This is definitely not the case. (I spend way too much time watching *Lost* and marathons of *America's Next Top Model* that I've already seen a million times for that to be true.) I work hard at my job but try to get my work done at the office and somewhat at home during the weekdays. I try to be creative every day in some way, and I generally work in spurts, so I'll do a lot of writing one weekend and then do a cabaret show another week and then pleasure read a lot another week; it's all a give-and-take. I am either too scattered or too lazy to write every day (as 99 percent of writing instructors would suggest), so I have to figure out how to fit it in on my own creative time.

What do you want people to take away from your book after having read it?

Most importantly, I want them to have laughed good-heartedly. And I want them to have seen the world somewhat differently—to understand how hard childhood can be for the culturally and sexually marginalized but also how such isolation affords a child a very strong sense of self.

Connect with Us

Visit us online at
KensingtonBooks.com
to read more from your favorite authors, see books
by series, view reading group guides, and more.

for sneak peeks, chances to win books and prize packs,
and to share your thoughts with other readers.

facebook.com/kensingtonpublishing
twitter.com/kensingtonbooks

Tell us what you think!

To share your thoughts, submit a review,
or sign up for our eNewsletters, please visit:
KensingtonBooks.com/TellUs.